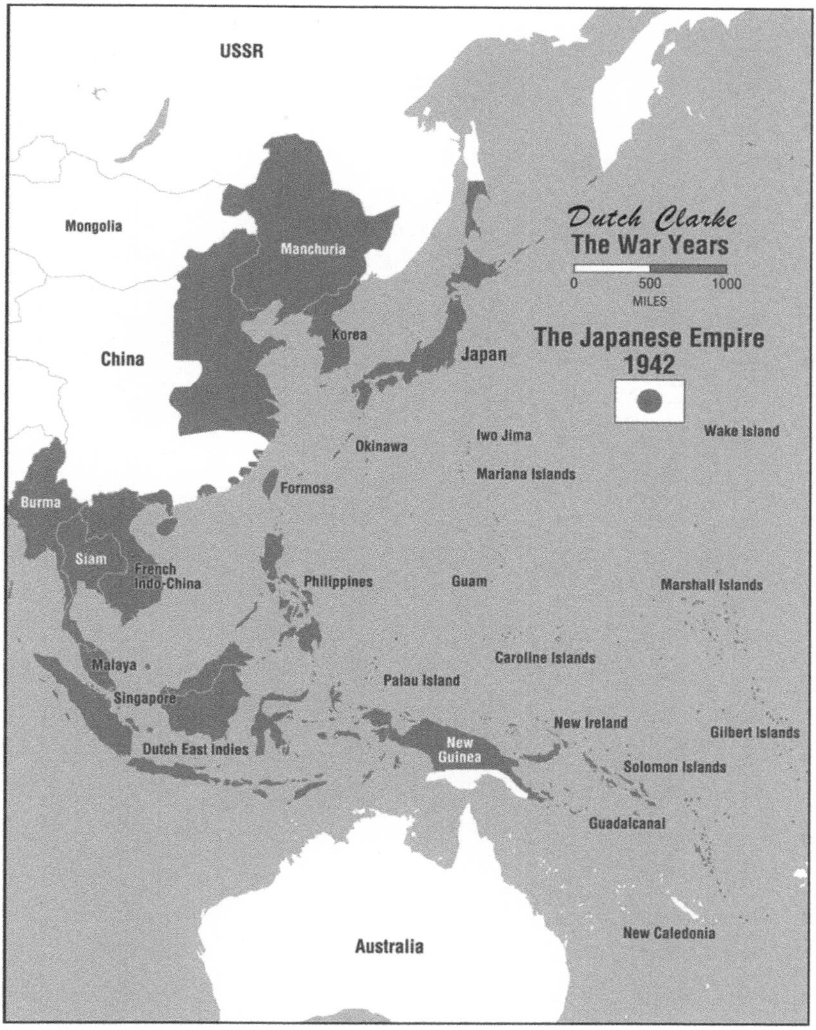
USSR
Mongolia
Manchuria
China
Korea
Japan
Dutch Clarke
The War Years
0
500
1000
MILES
The Japanese Empire
1942
Okinawa
Iwo Jima
Wake Island
Mariana Islands
Formosa
Burma
Siam
French Indo-China
Philippines
Guam
Marshall Islands
Caroline Islands
Malaya
Palau Island
Singapore
New Ireland
Gilbert Islands
Dutch East Indies
New Guinea
Solomon Islands
Guadalcanal
New Caledonia
Australia

THE WAR YEARS

Brian D. Ratty

Sunset Lake
Publishing

Brian D. Ratty

Sunset Lake Publishing
89637 Lakeside Ct.
Warrenton, OR 97146
503.717.1125
#93-1015196

First Edition published in June 2008
Second Edition published in July 2014

ISBN-13: 978-0615987286
ISBN-10: 0615987281

Create Space Title ID: 4673102
Printed in the USA

My story is dedicated to all the men and women who lived their lives, gave their sweat, and spilled their blood during the turmoil and struggle of World War II. No greater generation ever walked the face of this Earth.

Author's Note

Dutch Clarke-The War Years is my second installment in a series of four books on the life and times of Dutch Clarke. The first book, The Early Years, was first published in 2002. More information on my books: www.DutchClarke.com.

Writing this series is a great adventure for me. I don't write for profit or praise; I just enjoy telling a good story. If others find Dutch's chronicles interesting, informative and entertaining, my rewards will have been realized. The War Years was especially challenging; the gold standard for war stories is quite high, with the likes of 'Saving Private Ryan,' 'Band of Brothers' and many more. When I approached the writing of this book, I decided that historical events and places would help shape my characters while hopefully giving the reader a true feel for these tragic times. While wars are won with guns and bullets, they are also fought by men and women doing thousands of different jobs. Dutch becoming a combat photographer is but one such example.

Over sixteen million American plowboys and cowboys answered their country's call by donning uniforms, with tens of thousands of American women also joining the ranks. Of this number, some 291,557 did not return home, and another 670,846 came back with scars and wounds that would haunt many of them for years to come. This war was a devastating disaster brought on by the Axis Powers of: Japan, Germany and Italy, exacerbated by peace-loving Americans who, early on, didn't want to get involved. After December 7th of 1941, however, our country stood as one, determined to defeat this evil. The costs were horrible and the journey long, but in the end peace prevailed, and today America is free because of this greatest generation.

When many of these American soldiers returned home, with war still raging inside of them, they found a homeland at peace and prospering. Some, thinking it was as if the war years had just been forgotten drank too much, had failed marriages, or suffered cold sweats and nightmares. Back then, we had no six-bit, politically correct terms for their condition; society offered them just one two-bit word: work. And work they did, building America into the economic powerhouse and free-world leader that it is today. We share our tomorrows because of their yesterdays.

CONTENTS

CHAPTER ONE

We were a tiny speck floating in no particular direction across the vast Pacific. The cold ocean spray across my face jarred me awake. Groggy at first, I tried to regain my reality. Before my raft mates had fallen asleep, I had promised to be on watch, but then dozed off. The ocean was rolling with long swells, with a breeze out of the south. In my exhausted state, this pitching motion and fresh air had been just too much for me.

In the east, I could make out the first signs of the coming morning. The sky just above the horizon had a pink and amber glow. Sunrise would happen fast, as it always did in the South Pacific. Looking around the raft, I saw that my four Aussie mates were still sleeping. No need to wake them now, I thought. God knows they can use the rest, after last night. They looked peaceful yet pathetic in their dirty, tattered and torn clothes. The sun, sea and thirst would be our enemy for the day. They would need all their strength, and then some, to face what lay ahead.

Repositioning my body against the side of the raft, I realized how wet my butt and legs were. But then, all of us had the same problem, as the bottom of the float had only woven canvas straps that were open to the sea. The Japanese raft was made out of light-weight balsa wood and wrapped with gray cloth strips. The soggy craft was about fourteen feet long and six feet wide. There was no survival kit, no oars, no nothing. It was seaworthy, but that was about all.

Turning my head, I began watching the light show in the east. My mind was racing, my thoughts not really clear. I knew the month was March...the year 1945...but I had no idea what day,

7

and I had no idea where we were or where the tides might take us. I had no idea about anything to do with the future. I did know that we had escaped, last evening, from a rusty old Jap POW freighter that had come under attack from the air or from a submarine. Something had blown a hole in the side of the Hell Ship we were imprisoned in. The breach in the hull was big enough for some prisoners to jump into the ocean to escape.

Luck had smiled on me in many ways, last evening. First, I was fewer than twenty feet from the blast when the shell hit. Second, any shrapnel from the explosion had missed me. Third, when I jumped into the water, no rifle fire pursued me as I swam away from the mired boat. The guards topside of the freighter still had their heads down and lights out. And, finally, I was lucky that I had only been in a Jap POW camp for the past twelve months and still had most of my wits and strength. The other poor devils on that doomed ship had been in captivity for years and had little of either remaining. Yes, I was lucky…but then I have always been lucky when it comes to surviving.

Reflections

A water drop ran down the fogged window. The outside lights of a passing town shone through its clear path. My mind was lulled, not so much by the reflecting lights as by the rhythm and movement of the train. The sound of its wheels racing over the ribbons of steel made a melancholy melody. The noise was muted, yet loud. Focusing on the window of my small compartment I could almost make out my reflection. My body was tall and trim, just over six feet and 168 pounds. Clean-shaven, with a full head of brown hair, I had a square jaw with a small cleft in my chin and dark-blue eyes. Some might say I was good-looking but the reflection I saw was just ordinary. Born in May of 1920, I was twenty-two years old and, after a year of surviving in the rain forest of British Columbia, strong and healthy. But something else glared back that was less encouraging. My fate was in doubt; I had no idea of where I would sleep or where my next meal might come from. Still, I comforted myself with the thought that thousands of young men were feeling the same emotions, this very night. Why not? It was June of 1942. The whole damn world was at war, and millions of men would be making this same journey in the coming years.

Laura and her parents had said their good-byes to me almost three days ago, in Ketchikan, Alaska. When the wheels of the plane lifted off the tarmac for Seattle, I began missing her, and the long, lonely train trip to California had not helped. Missing her was an understatement; loving, longing and craving would be more real. We had shared a true adventure during the last year in British Columbia, an adventure full of sadness, splendor and love. While we had not yet consummated that love, I knew that someday, God be willing, we would. She was my soul mate, my future, and my love...

I had to let go of these thoughts and get her out of my mind! Where I was going, I could not afford the luxury of a personal life, and for me to dwell on her and her family would only make my immediate future seem bleaker.

A knock on the compartment door jolted my mind back to reality. A black face beneath a black cap soon appeared in the half-opened doorway.

"Mr. Clarke, we will be arriving at the station in an hour. Anything else I can get you, sir?"

Looking at my watch, which read 9:30, I replied to the porter, "Yes, if the club car is still open, I would like one last beer for the road. Is that possible?"

"Sure is, sir. It would be my pleasure. Even if the car is dark, I'll get you that beer. What kind you want?"

"Falstaff, if they have it...or any other. It really doesn't matter." Getting up, I reached into my pants pocket and retrieved a five-dollar bill. Handing it to the porter, I said "You keep the change. Where I'm going, I won't have much use for it!"

"Yes, sir! I'll be right back. Don't you worry none. I'll get you that beer."

Stretching my legs, I looked around the small drab drawing room. It was dark and musty-smelling. I was sure that I was not the first -- nor would I be the last -- recruit to make the thirty-hour train trip riding in this room. When I'd boarded in Seattle, I had expected Uncle Roy to be at the station. Instead, I received a telegram with his apologies. It seemed like the petroleum business and war both made for good excuses. Still, I really didn't blame him; it was three thousand miles from New Jersey to Seattle, and plane tickets were hard to get, even for a person with priority standing. What he did send me was the upgraded train ticket to my Pullman compartment and a short note about keeping my head down and my eyes open. His closing words still rang in my brain: "Don't be first, don't be last, don't volunteer and, most of all, don't lose your life in Mr. Roosevelt's war!" A grin crossed my face as I thought, *Good old Uncle Roy, one last dig about the war and Mr. Roosevelt.* He just doesn't understand why I enlisted in the Marines when he could have gotten me deferred and working at some safe desk job at one of our gas plants.

"Shit, he'll never understand," I said out loud. But then, he was doing his part for the war effort. America needed petroleum products, and one thing that Uncle Roy and my late grandfather had built were the refineries to provide those very products.

After Grandfather passed away, I inherited half the business but couldn't envision myself parked behind some desk, counting up columns of numbers and lunching at faceless country clubs. Even if the world hadn't been at war, I couldn't have envisioned that. I had other things to do, other ways of proving my worth. No, Uncle Roy could take care of the business and the money while I searched. But searched for what? Maybe a way to avenge Pearl Harbor and Laura's dead husband entombed aboard the Battleship Arizona. Maybe for some answers to a world gone mad, and a way for me to contribute to my country. What I searched for was as elusive as the black gold my grandfather had sought.

The porter reappeared at the door carrying two beers on a small tray, each with a glass inverted over the top of the bottle. "Thought you might like two for the road, sir. One is compliments of the Southern Pacific Railroad, with our best wishes."

With a smile on my face, I remarked, "Two beers! How nice. Thank you, and thanks to the SP railroad!"

Taking the tray, I slid back down on the seat behind the small compartment table and reached for my Bull Durham.

The porter, still in the half-opened door, said, "You take care, sir, and God bless you and all the young men on this train." As he closed the door, he ended, "I'll call ya just before we get to the San Diego station."

While taking swigs from the first bottle of beer, I rolled and lit a cigarette. The beer was cold and smooth, the tobacco strong and harsh. "All the young men on this train," the porter had said, and yes, I had seen them when I boarded. There were four day-coaches filled with young recruits who looked no older then seventeen or eighteen, or maybe younger. Young men and war: what a deadly mixture of human misery.

Soon the smoke from my cigarette filled the little room, adding to its stench. As I reached for the second bottle of beer, my thoughts raced back to Alaska, to Laura and her family, and there I remained until we arrived.

Reality

Stepping onto the platform just after 10:30 PM changed my life forever. The next few years would mold my personality and plant the seeds of my life-long convictions. Before me was the United States Marine Corps at Camp Pendleton, California. Here I was to spend the next ten weeks at boot camp, and from there…God only knew.

Looking down the dimly lit platform, I saw a large group of recruits from the train standing in line. Grabbing my small valise from the porter, with a nod and smile, I started to walk towards the men, some six or seven cars down.

The night was warm, and the fresh air felt good to both my lungs and face. From behind the group of recruits, a man appeared, wearing an olive-drab uniform with a funny-looking hat. "Hey, bozo, are you with this group?" he yelled out.

Looking around, I found that he was yelling at me. "Yes," I shouted back.

"Then get your ass up here, boy. You're holding up my parade!"

Hurrying my walk, I joined the line of recruits.

Standing with the group, the Marine turned to the recruits and said, "Welcome to the United States Marine Corps. My name is Sergeant Brice. I will be escorting you to a reception facility at Camp Pendleton tonight. All of you have a brown envelope that contains your orders and your personnel file. When we arrive at the reception hall, you will deposit your envelopes with me, after which you will be given a meal and then bedded down for the night. There will be no talking and no playing 'grab ass' during this time. You will speak only if spoken to by a uniformed Marine. I repeat, there will be no talking and no 'grab ass!' Corporal Johnson, take the men."

From out of the shadows appeared another Marine, who began barking out instructions to the group.

It took four buses and forty-five minutes to transport the hundred and fifty recruits to the reception facility at Camp Pendleton. During this time, the only noise heard was that of the wheels singing across the asphalt. Sitting back on my half of a hard bus bench, I watched the city lights slowly fade to the darkness of the sand drums of Camp Pendleton. A reception center sounded pretty good to me and a meal even better. Maybe being a Marine Boot wouldn't be as bad as I had been told.

Upon arrival, we were led single-file from the buses to a large building, and through its open doors. Above this doorway was a lit sign that simply read 'Always Faithful.' Inside, we were given a form to fill out, asking for our name, address, age, blood type and which city we had departed from. During this time, I recognized a couple of faces from my flight from Ketchikan. One of the fellows must have recognized me, as well, because he nodded to me from across the room.

After finishing the form I stood up, as instructed, and walked to the table where Sergeant Brice was. Here I deposited my form and brown envelope on the table. Without looking up, the Sergeant bellowed instructions for those of us done to stand along the wall in the back of the room.

Soon, one of the young recruits from Ketchikan was standing by me. Leaning towards me, he whispered, "Are you Dutch Clarke?"

Taken a back that he knew my name, I answered, "Yes. How the hell do you know?"

"I read about your survival in British Columbia in the local newspaper. I thought that was you when you got on the plane in Ketchikan. My name's Kurt Benson, and I know Laura's father."

Just then, I felt something on the other side of my head, and turned to see Sergeant Brice's face six inches from mine.

"Get off my ear," he yelled. "I said no talking! Do you two jackasses understand those words?"

"It was my fault, Sergeant. I recognized this man from back home. He's sort of a celebrity there, and I wanted to say hello."

"Celebrity?" the Sergeant shouted. "So we have a celebrity here, do we? Well, there ain't no room for any celebrities in this man's Marines, so keep your mouths shut, Girls, or I'll put my boot down your throat. Do you read me, Idiots?" roared back the Sergeant.

The look on the Sergeant's face told me he meant business.

Thanks, Kurt, I thought glumly. *This isn't what I needed.*

"Yes, sir," I finally said.

"I can't hear you, Boot. Say it again, louder," he shouted.

This time, both of us sang out together, in one loud voice, "Yes, sir!"

After the Sergeant backed off, I could feel the eyes of all the other recruits looking our way. They all knew that what they had just witnessed was a sign of things to come. We were nothing more than Girls, Boots, Rainbows, Idiots, or whatever else they called recruits. We were in the Marines now, and there was no going back.

A few minutes later, we were lead into a large cafeteria, or what the cooks behind the serving line called the 'Mess Hall.' Here we were given stale sandwiches and cold coffee. The hall itself was half-dark and large enough to feed a thousand people. Our group sat quietly around the tables in one corner of the massive room. Fifteen minutes later, Sergeant Brice had us on our feet and grouped into four columns to march to our barracks.

The march took about twenty minutes down dimly lit streets that had white two-story buildings on each side. Each building looked freshly painted and had walkways framed with little white stones. None had any lights on. Finally we turned a corner to see one building with lights on and doors open. Here we stopped.

From the building, Sergeant Brice was joined by two other uniformed soldiers wearing the same funny hat he had. They talked for a moment and then the Sergeant started calling roll in alphabetical order.

"When you hear your name, fall out and follow each of the corporals to your assigned barracks. There will be no talking. Lights will go out in ten minutes. If you have to use the head -- that's the toilet to you Girls -- do it quickly. We want your asshole in your bunk at lights out. Do not let us find any of you Boots talking or walking after lights out. Do you understand?"

The group shouted back, "Yes, sir!"

Being at the front of the alphabet, I was in the first group of recruits. We were lead inside the front of the building and up some wooden stairs, then down a short corridor. At the end of this hall was a doorway with the doors propped open, revealing a large, long room that had rows of bunk beds on each side.

The corporal stood in the middle of the room, shouting, "Find yourself a bunk fast. The head is at the other end of the barracks, don't screw around. Lights out in ten minutes."

Hurling my valise on a top bunk halfway down the row, I ran for the head. By the time I reached the urinals, I was second in line behind my friend from Ketchikan. He seemed to take forever. Finally, I relieved myself and made it back to my bunk just as the lights went out.

Laying there in the dark, I was confused and disoriented. Feeling around, I could tell the bed was made up. Was I supposed to sleep in my clothes? No, hell no, I thought. Slipping off my shoes, pants and shirt, I wrapped them together and laid them at the foot of the small bunk, next to my valise. Crawling under the single blanket, I could hear whispering from all around the barracks. Finally, the guy below me poked the underside of my bunk and whispered, "Are you sleeping in your clothes?"

The voice was that of Kurt; all I needed to do was get caught talking again! Finally I replied quietly, "No...hell no."

It had been quite a day, and I was tired. Glancing at my watch, I saw that it was 12:15 AM. Within a few moments, the whispering stopped and the snoring began.

Sergeant Crane

For some reason, I was awake before the lights were turned on. I must have heard the bay doors open and the corporal walking down the long row of bunks. Then he turned on the lights and started beating a metal trash can with his riding crop. After a few seconds of loud banging, he yelled, "When the lights come on in this squad bay, you are supposed to be at attention!" As I was fumbling to get dressed, he walked around the bay, still shouting. "Assholes and elbows, fall in at the front of the barracks in three minutes. There will be no second wake-up call! Assholes and elbows, fall in at the front of the barracks in two minutes. Move it! Move it!"

Ninety seconds later, there was a long line of recruits running down the front stairway to the open front doors of the barracks. Looking down at my watch, I saw that it was just 5:30 AM.

As I stumbled outside, the corporal was forming our floor into four rows. Standing in the second row, I realized that it was still dark out, with no light in the eastern sky. The only illumination came from a street light in front of our barracks, which cast long, dark, dancing shadows of the men forming ranks.

Suddenly, our corporal shouted, "Attention!" Then the corporal who was forming the first floor of recruits also shouted, "Attention!" So here we were, one hundred and fifty Idiots standing in line, at attention, listening to the sounds of the wind and morning crickets. We must have stood there for a good three or four minutes before, out of the inky shadows, a tall, slender man appeared, wearing a pressed Marine utility uniform. He was holding a swagger stick with both hands in front of his body. He stood there for a moment, some fifty feet in front of both groups, just looking up and down our ranks. His funny little hat kept his face in shadow from the street light above.

Finally he spoke, in a loud, firm voice. "I'm Gunnery Sergeant Crane, the lead Drill Instructor for Dog Company. I'm in charge of what the Marines loosely call recruits. You will notice I didn't call you Marines because, from what I have seen here this morning, I'm not sure any of you will make it through the next ten weeks of training. You are the sorriest bunch of people I have seen in my eighteen years in the Corps. Our country must be in bigger trouble than I thought, because they are scraping the bottom of the barrel to send me Rainbows like you! I ask for men and they send me plow boys. I ask for tigers and they send me Soda Jerks. I ask for sixteen weeks of training and they cut it to ten. Well, Rainbows, you will have sixteen weeks crammed into ten. This will be the longest and hardest ten weeks of your young lives. You had your last laugh when you met me." Pounding his riding crop into the palm of his right hand, he started walking up and down the line of recruits. Pausing every now and then, he continued, "This is not a vacation, this is not camp, and I'm not the camp master. Mommy will not be bringing you breakfast in bed, and you are not going to be playing grab ass with your girlfriend or driving dad's car to the malt shop. For the next ten weeks, your ass is grass and I'm the lawnmower."

When he walked in front of my row, I could finally see part of his face from under his hat, and I discovered that he was wearing sunglasses in the dark! Stopping and turning to our group he said in a belittling tone, "When I or any other real Marine on this post tells you to do something, your reply will always be. 'Aye, aye, sir!' Do you understand?"

The group replied, "Aye, aye, sir!"

"I can't hear you clowns," he shouted back.

Louder came our response, "'Aye, aye, sir!"

Walking back to where he'd started, he turned once again and yelled, "Sergeant Nelson will be leading you clowns to chow. After that, you will be given what all of you need, a Marine haircut, after which you will be called Mop Heads. You will then be taken to supply, where you will be issued Marine clothing to replace the Rainbow uniforms you are wearing. Sergeant Nelson, Sergeant Brice take the men." Turning his back on us, he briskly walked back into the shadows from which he came.

There was total silence for a moment. His appearance and mannerisms reminded me immediately of a character from a childhood book, Ichabod Crane from The Legend of Sleepy Hollow. Somehow, I knew already that he was the headless horseman we would all come to fear.

Always Faithful

The sergeants stepped forward and shouted in unison, "Right face! Forward march."

By the time Sergeant Nelson started us marching, I could see a red dawn brightening the eastern sky. He led us down a few blocks and then turned the group right at a large athletic field. As we marched along, the only sound was that of our shoe leather beating against the blacktop, and the occasional cadence count from Sergeant Nelson.

"Hup, two, three, four...hup, two, three four."

The first floor group with Sergeant Brice, from last night, followed us. Then, suddenly, the still air was cut by the loud sounds of multiple bugles blaring out their morning song. It was 6:00 AM, and air rang with the sounds of Reveille.

A few moments later, we reached a large, single-story building. Stopping the group, the Sergeant had us turn towards the building, "This is the Mess Hall for Dog Company. You will be taking all of your meals here. You will march single file into the hall and there will be no talking. Once inside, you will take a tray and go down the chow line. You will take and eat what's given to you. When you are finished with your meal, you will take your empty tray, I repeat your empty tray, to the KP area for cleaning, and any paper trash will be stowed into the appropriate trash cans. You will not take any food with you. You will eat all the food on your tray. Marines do not waste food. Do you understand?"

"Aye, aye, sir!" was our loud reply.

"After your meal, you will form your ranks on me here again. You will not wander off or go to the head or talk to anyone. Do you understand?"

"Aye, aye, sir!"

"Fall out in rows," barked Sergeant Nelson.

Standing on the stairs, waiting to enter the hall, I felt the first rays of the morning sunlight brush my face. Turning, I could see the bright red ball just rising over some buildings in the distance.

A new day...a new adventure, I thought.

Inside the door on the right was a stainless-steel table stacked with steel trays. Next to them were piles of utensils, napkins and plastic glasses. Next to the table was a long row of stainless-steel serving tables with steam rolling off the covered food. On the other side of the room were rows and rows of bench-type tables, enough to feed hundreds of men, but not half the size of the chow hall we had used the night before. At the far end were large open bays and trash cans. The room was clean and humid but smelled stale from the lack of fresh air.

We were the first group in the hall, and I was about the twentieth person in line. Grabbing my tray and utensils, I followed along the column. Behind the serving tables were two men, dressed in white cooks' clothing. The first cook was having fun by shouting out, "Well, lookie here! We have new Rainbows. They're not even Mop Heads yet. Come on, boys. I made you the 'house specialty' for breakfast, SOS. You'll just love it! Take all you want, but eat all you take."

Approaching him, I held out my tray. On it he placed a piece of toast in the large compartment, then poured some kind of white gravy over it. The gooey mixture looked and smelled awful. The next cook slopped a large spoonful of peaches into one of the two smaller compartments. At the end of the line were cartons of milk and large pots of coffee. Taking two cartons of milk, I moved to an empty table, a few yards away. Moments later, Kurt from Ketchikan sat down across from me. At first, I didn't even look up. I was more interested in the white slosh on my tray. Taking my fork, I scraped the gray off the toast and cut into it. The soggy toast tasted like grease and moldy milk. It was awful!

From across the table, Kurt whispered, "Do you know what SOS stands for?"

His whisper caught me off-guard. Slowly looking up I shook my head no.

"Shit On a Shingle…that's what it stands for. I've had this before. It's not so bad after you get by the grease," he whispered again, with a big smile.

Returning to my food, I started to wash it down with my milk, and finally I got a good look at Kurt. He couldn't be much older than eighteen and still had freckles on his light-brown face. His hair was blonde, his eyes green, and when he smiled, his young face lit up like a candle. His body looked firm but seemed to fit loosely in his civilian clothes. He didn't look like much of a Marine, but I liked him, even though he talked too much.

From the Mess Hall, both groups were marched back to the barracks, where we used the head and made our beds. Then we marched off to the post barber shop, this time following the first-floor group. Upon arrival, we were again placed in single file, standing at attention while we waited for our turn with a barber.

The line moved surprisingly quickly. The recruits entered the shop looking like normal people and left, a few moments later, looking like bowling balls. This was not surprising to me, as my recruiters in Ketchikan had warned me about the first Marine butch haircut.

Sergeant Brice was directing traffic at the front door. Giving me a hand signal, he shouted, "You're next, Boot…move-it, move-it. Take the chair in the back."

When I entered the room, a recruit in the last chair was just standing up. The well-lit room was long and narrow, with five barbers and chairs. Behind the chairs were the barber stations with sinks and, above that, each station had a mirror. On the floor were piles and piles of cut hair. It looked dirty, it felt dirty. As I slid into the still-warm chair, the barber snapped his cloth around me and turned the chair towards his mirror. Grabbing his electric shears, he turned to me with a smile. "How would you like it, Mac?"

Not thinking, I smiled back at him and answered, "Give me a trim, just enough to keep the hair out of my eyes."

At that instant, from the other end of the room, Sergeant Brice screamed out, "There will be no talking in this goddamn room. All I want to hear is hair hitting the floor! Do you read me, Boot?"

"Aye, aye, sir!" was my loud reply.

Smiling ear to ear, the barber winked at me and proceeded to shave my head in just under sixty seconds. As he removed the dirty apron, I rubbed my head and stared at myself in the mirror. Damn, that was fast!

Getting to my feet, the barber turned his back to the front of the room and whispered, "It will grow back…trust me."

From the barber shop, we marched some dozen blocks or so to the quartermaster's warehouse. Along the way, we saw many other units marching up and down the side streets between long rows of barracks. We could hear the cadence of their DI's shouting out, "Hup two, hup two, hup two three four." The morning air was still cool and, on my now-bald head, almost cold. At one point, we passed a group at parade rest, with their Sergeant nowhere in sight. The group must have been close to graduation because, below their caps, I could see hair almost a half inch long. As we passed one of them yelled out, "Ha, look at these 'Mop Heads,' just back from the barber. Sorry, boys! It's going to be a long ten weeks!"

Another chimed in, "Rainbows…a whole group of Rainbows."

He then changed to a cadence call, "Rainbow, Rainbow don't feel blue. My grandfather's Four-F, too."

With our haircuts and civilian clothes, everyone on base knew who we were and where we were going. That was everyone, except us.

At the quartermasters, we were all issued clothing and gear, the standard 1041 outfit for all new recruits. The standard issue had ninety-six items, from shirts to socks, from belt buckles to boots, from a sewing kit to a shaving kit. There were fifteen or more supply stations, with stacks of clothing and gear. Marines working in front of the stacks were passing out all the different items to our long Rainbow line. God help any man that didn't know his size, for the men passing out the items only asked once. If there was silence, you got what you got. There was no measuring, no fitting, no trying it on, just screaming out your size and hoping the guy behind the counter grabbed from the right stack. Later, we found out that one poor sap got boots two sizes too big, and another got his dress uniform two sizes too small. As we received each item, it was packed into our Marine green duffle bag, which had been the first item issued. Slowly moving down the line, I watched the haphazard way the thousands of items were passed out to recruits who had no idea of what they were getting. At the end of the line, the last station, we were issued two pair of black boots, one pair of black dress shoes, one pair of canvas shoes and one pair of rubber shower clogs. Sitting at a desk next to the station was the quartermaster. Each recruit was shown a list of the items just issued and instructed to sign a form regarding items received. Looking down the list, I wasn't at all sure I had all the items, but I said nothing. No one said a word; we just signed and trusted that our green duffle bags had all the right items.

We were back at our barracks by 11:00 AM -- or, in military time, 1100. After we stowed our duffle bags next to our bunks, Sergeant Nelson blew his whistle and called the group to attention.

"I'm Sergeant Nelson." He turned to the Corporal standing next to him. "And this is Corporal Johnson."

The sergeant was tall and lean, with a body built like a Marine recruiting poster. His features were square and clean, with a bronze complexion from the hot sun.

"We will be your daily DI's for the next ten weeks. You Mop Heads are the 4th Platoon of Dog Company. The floor below is the 3rd Platoon, and in the barracks next to us are the 1st and 2nd Platoons, who are halfway through their basic training. As you learned this morning, Gunny Sergeant Crane is the lead Drill Instructor for this Company. Lieutenant Cunningham is your platoon leader. Captain Roberts is the commanding officer of Dog Company, and his boss is Colonel Jacob, the CO of the 2nd Battalion 3rd Marine Training Regiment. I tell you this so you know the chain of command. You do not, I repeat, do not want to be called in front of any officers in this chain of command. If there is a problem, either Corporal Johnson or I will take care of it, or, God forbid, if we can't, Sergeant Crane will. Do you understand?"

"Aye, aye, sir!"

Holding one hand to his ear, he barked, "I can't hear you!"

This time, with gusto, the barracks floor replied, "Aye, aye, sir!"

He continued, "We will march to noon chow in one hour. In the meantime, you Mop Heads will shit, shower and shave. But because we have only ten showers, you will do this in groups of ten, and take no longer then five minutes to complete your business. Do you understand?"

"Aye, aye, sir!"

"Also during this time, each of you will empty out the contents of your duffle bag and neatly place all items on your bunk for inspection by myself or Corporal Johnson. Do you understand?"

"Aye, aye, sir!"

Stripping at my bunk, I was in the second group of ten. We each carried in a towel and the shaving kit we had just been issued. The shower room was long and skinny and filled with steam from the first group. Wet Marine soap was in the racks, so we all got busy washing off the dirt and loose hair. Exiting the shower, I made my way to a sink, wiped the fog off the mirror, and began shaving. Using my towel, I rinsed my face off. When I looked up into the mirror, I saw half a dozen guys staring at my nude body.

Turning, I wrapped the towel around my waist and angrily asked, "What the hell are you guys staring at?"

Finally, one of the guys answered, "What's that on your shoulder, some type of tattoo?"

Looking down on my left shoulder, the reason for their attention dawned on me. What they were glaring at was the scar from a bear clawing some five inches across and eight inches long. It had taken many stitches to sew it up. The scar was still quite red and protruded out from my skin. The recruiters in Ketchikan had, in fact, called it my 'Bear Tattoo.'

Before I could say a thing, Kurt standing two sinks down said, "He got that fighting off a grizzly bear, up British Columbia."

Once again, Kurt had opened his big mouth. These guys didn't need to know that story. Damn, I wish I hadn't done that newspaper interview, I thought.

One of the guys standing next to me exclaimed, "No shit...a grizzly bear?"

Then, from the open latrine door, Sergeant Crane's voice roared, "What the hell is going on in here, ladies? You Mop Heads are not at a tea party. Make a hole."

In an instant, the guys between me and Sergeant Crane were gone, leaving the Sergeant staring at me. With his sunglasses gone, I could see his face under his campaign hat. His steel-gray eyes glared at me like lightning bolts. His face was weathered, with a dark, rough complexion and age lines from years in the sun. His uniform was so starched and pressed that I was sure it could stand in a corner on its own. Walking towards me, he moved his stare from my face to my scar.

"What the hell is that?" he asked sarcastically, "A drunken tattoo artist get to you, Boot?"

"No, sir," I replied.

"Then what the hell is it?"

"It's a scar from a bear-clawing...sir."

With his voice still roaring, he replied, "I know who you are, Clarke. You think you're something special, some kind of celebrity. Sergeant Brice told me all about you. What the hell would a Boot like you know about bears...I think you're a bold-faced liar. Some drunken Indian gave you that lousy tattoo to impress us dumb Marines. Well, it won't work. I've seen recruits like you before, trying to get a leg up in the Corps, and they're all the same, bold-faced liars. I'll be watching you, you can count on it!"

Just then, Sergeant Nelson appeared at the door behind Crane. After a few more moments of glaring, Crane turned and walked towards Nelson. He stopped at the doorway and yelled, "Watch Clarke. He thinks he is some kind of celebrity. There's no room for prima donnas in my outfit!"

Nelson nodded as Crane left the room.

The latrine was dead quiet for the longest time, with not even the sounds of dripping water. Finally Nelson ordered, "You Mop Heads are done. Move it, move it, for the next group."

"Aye, aye, sir!"

Returning to my bunk, I quickly changed into one of my new utility uniforms. By the time I had the uniform on, I was sure that both floors knew all about my 'dressing down' from Sergeant Crane, but there was nothing I could do about that. Continuing to lay out my gear from the duffle bag, I must have looked visibly shaken, because Sergeant Nelson appeared.

At first, he just stood at the foot of my bunk, watching me neatly arrange the items. Finally, he said in a low tone, almost a whisper, "Don't worry about Sergeant Crane. He's a China Marine and he likes his recruits in the old Marine mold. Keep your nose clean, do what you're told, and you'll be okay." Then, with a small grin on his face, he turned and walked away.

Continuing to work with my gear, I thought, w*hat the hell is a China Marine?*

At noon sharp, Corporal Johnson blew his whistle and marched the group off for chow. After eating, we returned to the barracks to dress down into our physical training clothes, then spent the next two hours sweating in the hot Southern California sun.

Corporal Johnson was the PT instructor and faced us with a lengthy program of exercise. Being in top physical condition, I had no problems with the calisthenics and was usually the only Boot to finish each set. It dawned on me halfway through that maybe I should be dogging it, like the other Boots, so as not to bring attention to myself. But I didn't.

After PT, we returned to the barracks, hot and sweaty, only to be told to dress again in our utilities. What followed next was two hours on the parade grounds. This was the first of many lessons in close-order drill, instructed by Sergeant Nelson. It started simple: how to stand at attention, right face, left face, about face, cadence counts, etc. In the weeks to follow, Sergeant Nelson would create a cohesive drill unit that would rival all other platoons on the base.

After evening chow, we returned to the barracks for a two-hour lecture and demonstration on how to make a Marine bed, complete with white collar and hospital corners. It was hot and stuffy on the second floor and, during the demonstration, two of the men fell asleep, standing on their feet. Corporal Johnson, who was giving the lecture, used the shaft of his swagger stick to poke each man hard in the gut. Then they were each dressed down, verbally.

"You do not sleep during my instructions, Idiots! You do not sleep until I tell you to sleep. Because you have insulted me, both of you will be in charge of the latrine for one week. That means that each of you will clean and scrub the latrine each morning and evening, during your free time."

Free time! I thought. *When does that come?*

Just then, Sergeant Nelson entered the room and blew his whistle. The squad came to attention as he strolled to the center of the room and said, "It's 2000 hours. Lights will go out at 2100. Reveille will be at 0530, and you will fall in, out on the street, at 0540, dressed in your PT clothes. Do you understand?"

"Aye, aye, sir!" was the loud reply.

"Between now and 2100, you will have your free time. I have opened the day room at the top of the stairs. Here you can write home to Mommy or read the Marine Manual, which I have provided. Or you can take care of business by polishing your boots or organizing your foot locker. You will not, I repeat, will not play grab ass during this time. The smoking lamp will be lit for the next hour. If you smoke, you will use the butt cans on each window sill. Beginning tomorrow night, we will have a fire watch posted all night on each floor. I will cover these duties in tomorrow's lecture."

Slowly, he turned and walked towards and then through the open bay doors, blew his whistle, and shouted back, "Dismissed."

We all stood there like dummies for a moment, not knowing what to do next. Finally, someone shouted "Yes!" and we all broke ranks with a gasp of relief.

Turning, I walked to my bunk, where Kurt was standing.

"Which one are you going to do, Dutch?" he asked.

"Which one what?"

"You know...write a letter, read the manual, polish your boots, or what?"

"None of the above," I said with a smile.

Standing next to my bunk, I stripped down to my skivvies and t-shirt. Grabbing a butt can and reaching into my kit for my Bull Durham, I climbed the top bunk and sat Indian style while rolling a cigarette. As I lit it, I noticed Kurt still watching. He shook his head with a grin and said, "You know, you can buy those already made now."

"Yeah, I know. It's just a habit I have. There's something soothing about rolling your own smoke." Truth to tell, I was proud that I could roll my tobacco as firm and round as any store-bought. A few moments later, I noticed four or five guys standing at the foot of my bunk, talking to Kurt, who was sitting on his bunk below.

Finally, one Boot looked up at me and said, "Show us your tattoo. We didn't get a chance to see it."

"Yeah, Dutch, how about it?" another asked.

Looking down at them, I replied, "Come on, guys. It's no big thing."

"Please?" said another.

Their faces were now all turned to me, and others started joining them at the foot of the bed. As their group started to crowd down the aisle, I answered, "Okay, but it's no big deal. It's just something that happened."

I rolled up my left t-shirt sleeve, which normally covered most of the scar. The guys crowded around for a good, close look.

"Damn, that must have hurt," one guy remarked.

"What happened to the bear?" another asked.

"Maybe I'll tell you, some time. For now, let's enjoy this free time."

The guy sitting on the top bunk next to me reached out for a handshake, saying, "I agree. I'm James Wilson from Seattle."

Taking his hand, I shook it. "I'm Dutch Clarke from Ketchikan."

That started it. Within minutes, the whole barracks was shaking hands and introducing themselves to each other. There were guys from all up and down the West Coast. Kurt, Hank Marks and I were from the furthest north, while others were from Seattle, Portland, San Francisco, and Los Angeles, as well as two

Boots from nearby San Diego. Seventy-six young men, short and tall, skinny and plump, ranged in age from seventeen to me, the old man at twenty-two. I liked them all instantly.

At 2100, the whistle blew and the lights went out. Butting my second cigarette into the can, I reached down and placed it back on the window sill.

From the bunk below, Kurt whispered, "Good night, Dutch."

"Night."

Lying back on my bunk, I heard the sounds of rustling and whispers soon turn to snoring. I thought about getting under the covers but it was just too hot. Staring up at the ceiling, I heard the gable fan at the end of the barracks making its swishing noise as it tried to move the stale hot air out.

Soon, I realized just how tired I was. It had been a long day… my first day in the United States Marines Corps. If this is the worst, then I can take whatever lies ahead, I reflected, and fell asleep before another thought could pass.

Routine

The next weeks blended together like the sea and the sand. We had a routine: Reveille at 0530, an hour and a half of PT, and then marching to the morning meal. After chow, we would have three hours of classroom lectures with the 3rd Platoon. The instructors were either Sergeant Nelson or Sergeant Rice. The information they taught was everything about standing fire watch, guard duty, military organization and the code of conduct. On two occasions, Sergeant Crane gave lectures on Marine tactics and military protocol. Both times, he wore his Class A dress uniform, which was quite impressive. Being a Gunnery Sergeant, he had not only Sergeant Stripes on the sleeve but also two lower half-round rockers below. In addition, the lower part of the sleeve had six hash marks, one for every three years of service. On his dress blouse on the left side were four rows of colorful and distinguished ribbons. Just above these medals he proudly wore his Expert Rifleman Badge. His presence and presentations were always a bit arrogant but commanding and captivating.

For some reason, his lecture on protocol resonated in my mind. "The salute given to all officers is a salute to the rank, not the man. You might not respect the man wearing the rank, but you will always respect the rank," he told us.

After noon chow, we would spend another ninety minutes doing PT. After that, it was two or more hours of close-order drill instruction, all of which was done outside, with the weather well over ninety degrees and the humidity the same. Once every hour, our platoon would take a break for a swig -- and only a swig -- of water and a salt pill, to help control our water loss due to sweating. And sweat we did, with many of us losing three or more pounds of body weight in an afternoon.

After evening chow, it was back to the barracks for another hour or two of lectures and demonstrations from Corporal Johnson or Sergeant Nelson. Most of what they taught was basic military survival: how to prepare for inspections, how to mark and identify your gear, hygiene, and so on. I found Johnson and Nelson to both be firm but fair when dealing with us. They were professionals doing a job. Nelson was about twenty-five years old and roughly my size. Underneath his campaign cap were blue eyes with short cropped-brown hair. He walked and talked with confidence but had a bright smile when needed. Johnson was my junior in age, around twenty or twenty-one. He had a sandy complexion with a personality to match; the Corporal was all business, with a fire in his belly that seemed to be about proving something to the Marines, or perhaps just to himself.

There were a couple of screw-ups in the platoon, and they were ridden hard by our DI's, but not vindictively, like I was sure Sergeant Crane would have done. For the most part, those who messed up were given latrine duty or required to march on the parade grounds during our free time.

One of our first assignments was to memorize the eleven General Orders that all Marine sentries are required to know. This assignment was to be completed during our free time. Sergeant Nelson's instructions were quite clear: "Woe to any unfortunate Mop Head who cannot shout out, verbatim, all eleven orders. Such a recruit will incur a firestorm of wrath from all of his Drill Instructors." With this in mind, our platoon set out to memorize the eleven orders on our second night of free time. Each recruit was given a printed list of the orders, which contained about a hundred and thirty-five simple words, such as: '*1. TO TAKE CHARGE OF THIS POST AND ALL GOVERNMENT PROPERTY IN VIEW*' or '*5. TO QUIT MY POST ONLY WHEN PROPERLY RELIEVED.*' For some reason, I had very little trouble committing those orders to memory. But that was not the case for about half the bay. Soon I began coaching other recruits, and continued to do so, long after Lights Out. This tutoring was a good opportunity to better get to know my fellow Mop Heads. Lying back in my bunk, that night, I was confident that all of us 'clowns' would sleep better, having memorized the eleven General Orders.

Saturday mornings were spent scrubbing the barracks -- or, as it was called, 'Having a GI Party.' Everything, every nook and cranny, was cleaned, polished or painted. This activity was but Act One of weekend inspection. After noon chow, it was Act Two, personal preparation like organizing your footlocker and clothing, and making sure a quarter would bounce six inches off your made-up bed. Then, at 1500 hours, came the third and final act. The platoon would be called to attention and we'd wait for a senior NCO or junior officer to strut down the bay and inspect our day-long efforts. Sometimes we waited for over an hour to hear the footsteps of our approaching inspector. This waiting time was the worst, as it allowed all of us to worry about what we had missed or forgotten. The penalty for failing an inspection would be two or three hours of extra drill, the next day.

Sundays were the best. Each recruit was required to dress in their Class 'A' uniform and attend the church of their choice. There were many chapels on the post, so I decided to try a few before making my choice. In the end, I selected the Catholics; their church was air-conditioned and the sermons were short. After church, we would return to the barracks for a light drill in our dress uniforms. After the noon meal and 'mail call' came free time until Lights Out. This was the opportunity to do your laundry, write home or read, if you could find any reading material other than the Marine Manual -- or, as it was called, the 'Guide Book.' It was also a time for playing cards, talking, and making friends. Soon I found myself hanging out with both Kurt and Hank from

Ketchikan. They were both fisherman, like me; we had a lot in common. Also, for some reason, I took to Jim Wilson, the skinny kid from Seattle. He couldn't have been much more than a hundred and ten pounds, dripping wet, and he wore funny-looking reading glasses and wasn't very Marine-looking, even in uniform. But he could tell stories and jokes that would make you belly laugh for hours. And he had a way with his voice. He could sound just like Sergeant Crain or Nelson, if he put his mind to it. He loved to sneak into the latrine and grab one of the toilet brushes to use as a riding crop. Then, dressed only in his skivvies and t-shirt, he would march down the row of bunks, barking out orders in Crain's voice: "You clowns have had your last laugh when you met me." Other times, in Nelsons voice, he would shout, "You Mop Heads are idiots! Move it, move it," all the while beating the toilet brush across his hands. The whole bay would burst out laughing. He was so funny that I gave him the nickname of 'Comedian,' which stuck with him throughout his time in the Pacific. He was a good guy, and fun to be around.

At the end of the second week, a few changes were made. Our reveille was moved from 0530 to 0600, half an hour more sleep and half an hour less of morning PT. Another big change was that our heads were now sprouting fur. We had gone from Mop Heads to 'fur balls'. Also, Sergeant Nelson split our platoon into four permanent squads, with four recruits as squad leaders. I was named leader of the 2nd Squad, a position I wasn't sure I wanted. Then again, he didn't ask.

The Fifth General Order

On the third Saturday, after inspection, I was told to report to Sergeant Nelson's office. This office was really a small private billet across from the Day Room where he and Corporal Johnson slept. It was never a good thing to be called to his 'office;' most of the time it meant trouble. Wondering what the hell I had done wrong, I hurried to report.

As always, the hatch (door) was closed, so I gave it three very firm knocks and brought myself to attention. From the other side of the door, Sergeants Nelson's voice rang out. "Who is the idiot pounding on my palace door?"

"Recruit Clarke, sir."

Nelson shouted back, "Show yourself."

Opening the door, I entered the room and braced myself in front of Sergeant Nelson. He was seated behind a small desk, with a brown file folder open. The room had two bunks on each side, with footlockers and chairs at the foot of each bed. Above each bed, tacked to the walls, were Marine recruiting posters. The desk was in the middle of the room, and behind it was a window with a small table under it. On the table were a hot plate, coffee pot and two white coffee mugs. The room was Marine clean.

Looking up from the desk, Nelson said, "Do you like my palace?"

"No, sir…I mean, yes, sir," I said with frustration.

Sergeant Nelson looked back down at the file and continued, "The platoon has drawn guard duty this week. I have assigned your squad the first duty, starting at midnight. Your name is at the top of the roster. You will relieve Carter from the 3rd Platoon at 2400. You will be relieved at 0400 by Recruit Benson from your squad." Reaching down, he picked up the typewritten roster and handed it to me. His gaze now squarely on mine, he continued, "You will wear utilities, and I want you and your squad to look and be sharp. Carter will relinquish his training weapon to you, and you will relinquish that same weapon when relieved. The weapon is not loaded, but I want you to treat it as loaded. Do you understand? Do you have questions?"

"Yes, sir. What is the password for tomorrow?"

"The challenge is 'York.' The reply is 'Sergeant.' I do not expect you will see a soul, at that hour on a Sunday morning, but if you do, use the challenge. Understood?"

"Aye, aye, sir! One more question. What are we guarding, and where do I report?"

"Your mission is to guard the drinking fountains directly across the parade grounds from this barracks."

I paused a moment. "Aye, aye, sir!"

That afternoon, I briefed my squad about the 'mission' and passed out the schedule for each man. Stressing the importance of sharpness, I reminded them of Sergeant Nelson's orders. Before chow, I went to the laundry and picked up two freshly starched and pressed utilities. After chow, I spit-shined my boots and belt buckle to such a high gloss that I could see my reflection. Just before Lights Out, I dressed in my uniform and retired to the latrine, where I would wait. Passing the time, sitting on a commode, I reread the half dozen letters Laura had sent me during the past few weeks. Her words were full of home, love and happiness, and her envelopes were full of the scent of her perfume. While I had long ago memorized each letter's contents, it was a joy just to see and smell them again.

At 2345, I exited the barracks and walked across the parade grounds towards the fountains. The night was dark, cool and silent. Approaching the other side, I could easily make out Carter, standing at parade rest under a nearby street light. Next to him were ten drinking fountains, raised on a small wooden platform. The raised area was about thirty feet long and four feet wide.

As I moved into the light, Carter jumped to attention, bringing his weapon to port arms as he shouted, "Halt! Who goes there? Leather"

Damn, I thought. I know tomorrow's challenge and password but not today's! 'Leather' must be the challenge. I'll have to guess the password.

Searching for what might be the right password, I finally shouted back, "Neck."

There was a moment of silence, and then he replied, "Approach."

"I'm Clarke from the 4th Platoon, here to relieve you."

Handing me his weapon, he remarked irritably, "Good. You can have this silly duty. Standing guard on drinking fountains is just too dangerous for me."

As he was about to leave, I asked, "What's the procedure? Do we march or stand?"

"I was told to stand, but then who the hell knows for sure? Good night!"

Nodding, I opened the bolt of the weapon to double-check that it was unloaded. Then I took my place, standing at parade rest next to the first fountain. Within seconds, I became aware of just how dark the night looked, and how quiet it was. The only sound I could hear was that of the street light lamp making a low humming noise. That one lamp seemed to be the only light on my side of the field. After a few minutes, my eyes adjusted, and I could see stars in the sky. Soon, I could even make out the shadowed outline of the row of barracks across the way. It was too quiet and too dark, and a little bit spooky.

Just then, I heard footsteps approaching at the end of the platform. I sprang to attention, raising the weapon and shouting, "Halt! Who goes there? York."

"Neck," came the reply.

"No, sir. That is not the right password. Halt. You may not approach!"

Far down the platform, the figure walked out of the shadows and into the light.

"The hell you say. That is the right password, Idiot."

Oh God, it was Sergeant Crane.

He staggered as he approached. "Clarke! I might have known it would be a shit-head like you. You don't even know the goddamn password. You are one sorry SOB."

By now, he was standing in front of me, and he reeked of booze and was slurring his words.

"Boy, you come to attention when I talk to you."

Jumping to attention, I replied, "Aye, aye, sir!"

Placing the brim of his hat under the brim of mine, he yelled, "Who told you to guard this post standing at parade rest, and why don't you know the password?"

I hesitated, and then replied, "The sentry I relieved told me the guarding procedure, and the password changed at 2400...sir."

He glared at me from under his campaign hat, his face flushed with anger, and for the first time since my run in with that grizzly, I tasted fear. His eyes were bloodshot, and his uniform spoiled and wrinkled.

"Give me that goddamn weapon. I will show you how to guard this post."

"No, sir. I will not relinquish my weapon."

"The hell you say," he growled as he reached down and jerked the gun out of my hands. "You watch me, Idiot, or I'll use this weapon to thump your head!" Throwing the gun over his shoulder, he marched -- or, I should say, staggered -- down to the end of the platform. Making a wobbly about-face, he started stumbling back towards me. Just a few steps from me, he lost his balance and fell to one knee on the platform. He was stunned for a second. Then, using the gun as a crutch, he regained his stance. Marching over to me, he shouted, "Go get Sergeant Nelson. I want his asshole out here now!"

"No, sir. I cannot leave my post."

There was a long moment of silence. Then he yelled, "Clarke, that is an order. I want you to move your ass now!"

His face was twisted with anger. I didn't know what to say or do. His whole body was twitching and I was full of fear. Finally I shouted back, "General Order Number Five: To quit my post only when properly relieved."

He fell silent for the longest time, his face changing from anger to puzzlement. Then he reached down and threw the weapon back at me. I caught it in midair. Suddenly, he turned and walked away into the night, mumbling, "Saved by the order. We Marines are always saved by orders." Turning his head to look back at me, he shouted, "I'll take care of you later, Clarke. You can count on it."

Abruptly, he was gone into the darkness and it was quiet again. I was so shaken by the experience that my hands trembled, but I knew it could have been worse. Then again, I was sure it still would be, after he talked to Sergeant Nelson.

Benson relieved me at 0400 sharp. As I made my way across the field, I thought, Well, at least the drinking fountains are in safe hands. I wish I was.

But I was wrong. I never heard about the incident again. Either Sergeant Crane was embarrassed the next morning or the episode got lost in the fog of all that booze.

Ready on the Firing Line

Rapidly, the morning classroom gave way to field exercises and demonstrations. Corporal Johnson taught all the physical assignments, such as hand-to-hand combat, bayonet training and

Judo. He was an expert at Japanese Judo and enjoyed selecting the largest Boots, myself included, and throwing us to the ground in an effortless style. He taught us that it was all about balance and leverage. Once I mastered those concepts I became modestly efficient in throwing my fellow Boots to the mat.

Sergeant Nelson was the weapons expert. He had a working knowledge and expertise with every small arm a rifle platoon might use. From handguns to hand grenades, from submachine guns to our primary Springfield 1903 rifle, we were taught how to use, strip and maintain each weapon. The training was so intense that I found myself dreaming about how to disassemble and assemble each weapon.

Every recruit was required to qualify on the rifle range. Once qualified, the Boots were issued a badge to be worn on their Class A uniforms. There were three designs of badges: Rifleman-bronze bar, Sharpshooter-bronze bar with hanging cross and Expert Rifleman-gold bar with hanging crossed rifles. From what I could see, there were few Expert Badges on the base. Sergeant Crane and Nelson had them, while most others didn't, so I knew this award was hard to achieve. It became my goal to shoot for the gold.

Before the three rounds of qualification, we were given two sessions of practice. The rifle range was tucked into a small valley surrounded by scrub grass and sand dunes. At one end of the basin were sand-filled cement ramparts with a long, deep dugout behind. Here Marines would connect 5'x 5' paper targets to racks that would move up and down behind the rampart. Each Boot then fired five rounds of live ammunition from the standing position, five from the sitting position and five from the prone position. Before each exercise, fresh targets would be raised above the wall and, after five rounds, lowered below the wall. Here the range Marines would examine the target for accuracy. After the examination, the target was raised again. A red flag, called Maggie's Drawers, would be waved in front of the target for each shot that had missed. For each shot that hit the target, a long stick with a large white dot on top would point to where the target was hit. The bull's eye of the target was only about ten inches across, and black. The next circle was about thirty inches across, and dark gray. The final circle was sixty inches across, and light gray. The recruits would fire from down-range, some hundred yards (the length of a football field). There were twenty lines of targets.

The range was a grueling seven-mile march from our barracks and, on our first afternoon of practice, the temperature was close to a hundred degrees. By now, we had all been issued training rifles, but they were of WWI vintage. When we arrived at the range, the ordnance Sergeant issued newer rifles for the live fire. Along with the rifle came three clips, with five rounds each of live ammunition.

Sergeant Nelson had the first squad on the firing line. He gave one last demonstration on the correct use and firing of the weapon from the standing position, then stressed range safety. Stepping back, he shouted, "Load and lock...ready on the left, ready on the right, ready on the firing line. Commence firing!" With that, the squad opened fire.

The noise and smell was both exciting and frightening. After the first five rounds, the line fell silent and the targets were pulled down. Moments later came the results. A few Maggie's Drawers were lofted, but most of the bullets had found their way into light gray. Next, the squad would shoot from two more positions.

The second squad went next. Standing in Lane 7, the order came: "Load and lock, ready on the left, ready on the right, ready on the firing line. Commence firing!" With that, I begin squeezing off my five rounds. There was sweat running down my face and I had to blink my eyes a couple times. The rifle recoiled sharply against my shoulder. The feeling was familiar, after all that hunting in British Columbia, and I was confident of my score. After the range fell silent again, the targets went down and, moments later, up again.

In front of Lane 7 came not one or two but five passes of the red flag! All Maggie's Drawers! I could not believe it.

Just then, Sergeant Nelson approached and remarked, "Clarke, I'm surprised. I thought you would do better."

Turning my head towards him, I replied, "I know I'm better, Sergeant. There has got to be something wrong with this weapon."

"Give it to me. Let me take a look."

Opening the bolt, I turned and handed the rifle to the Sergeant.

Just then, from behind the third squad, came Sergeant Crane. Approaching us he shouted, "What the hell is going on here? What's the hold up?"

Sergeant Nelson replied, "Recruit Clarke thinks there might be a problem with his weapon."

"Did Clarke get Maggie's Drawers? Well, the problem is not with the weapon. It's with Clarke!"

Turning to me, he continued, "You have one excuse after another. You're one sorry, burr-headed idiot to blame your weapon because you can't hit the broad side of a barn."

"Actually, he might be right, Sergeant Crane. The rear sight looks a little bent," Nelson replied.

"Bull shit. That's just an excuse," answered Crane. Turning he grabbed a weapon out of the hands of the recruit standing in Lane Six and tossed it to me.

"Here, Clarke. Try this one. Maybe it's broken, too. Or are you afraid to admit it's all your sorry-ass problem?"

Crane was staring at me, just like the night at the drinking fountains, but this time I didn't taste fear. I turned to Sergeant Nelson. He looked at me and nodded his approval. Approaching the firing line, I slid the bolt open and squeezed five rounds into the rifle's magazine. Unlocking the safety, I shouted, "Ready on the left, ready on the right, ready on the firing line."

"Commence firing," Sergeant Nelson called out.

The sweat was gone; my eyes were clear. Within fifteen seconds, the magazine was empty. The target moved down and within seconds up again. This time, no red flag, just five beautiful white dots, all pointing inside the black bull's eye!

Letting out a sigh of relief, I turned to see Sergeant Nelson grinning and Sergeant Crane marching off, carrying the bad weapon.

Finally, Nelson commented, with a smile, "You wouldn't want to be the ordnance Sergeant this afternoon. Good shooting, Clarke. Carry on."

"Aye, aye, sir!"

After qualifications, I was one of only two recruits in our platoon to be awarded the gold Expert Rifleman badge, an emblem I would wear proudly on my dress uniform.

Hurry and Wait

Our first pay call came at the end of our sixth week. That Saturday afternoon, Sergeant Nelson lined us up in the barracks bay and shouted out instructions. "The pay officer is here. Each of you will smartly go to the Day Room when your name is called. You will stand at attention in front of the pay officer and sing out your name and serial number. You will receive your pay in cash, and you will sign a voucher that you have received your pay. Do you understand?"

"Aye, aye, sir!"

Each man received forty-six dollars. We were told that, upon completion of boot camp, that amount would be raised to fifty-two dollars. Marines would never get rich; then again, no man in the barracks had joined for the money.

'Mail Call.' What great words for any solider! Ours came twice a week and it was always a big event for all Boots. Laura had been great, with one or more letters every week. I even got a letter from her father, Skip, which was a pleasant surprise.

My letters to Laura had been slow and few, but I was sure she understood. It was Uncle Roy that I had not heard from, and I was getting concerned. Then, in the seventh week, I received a letter on Hotel El Cortez stationery from Roy. Opening it, I found five new one-hundred-dollar bills folded inside his note. These bills I quickly stuffed into my trousers' pocket, as no one needed to know about my finances. His letter read:

August 3, 1942
Dear Dutch,

Sorry for the delay in sending you this letter. This war has made for strange bedfellows as I'm now working with the Roosevelt Administration for the Navy's need of petroleum products. This has kept me on the road for the last few months. As you can tell from the stationery, I have been here in San Diego for the

last week. I have been meeting with an Admiral
King about specialty lubricants for his
submarines. Maybe you have run into him. He said
he's up at Camp Pendleton a lot. Well, just a
thought. He's a hell of a nice guy, so if you
ever need anything look him up.

A grin crossed my face. *Yeah, sure, I get to meet lots of admirals here*, I thought.

I tried twice to give you a phone call but
each time they told me that recruits can't take
telephone calls. Admiral King got me your
commanding officer's name, Colonel Jacob, but
when I called him, he transferred me to a
Sergeant Crane. This guy sounded like a real jerk
and I told him so! But he said he knew you, and
that he would pass on the message that I called.
I hope he did!

Sorry we couldn't have gotten together for
dinner or something. This hotel is the best, and
their food is outstanding. We would have had a
grand time! I still don't understand why you
joined the Marines, when you could have been home
helping with the war effort. Oh well, what's done
is done…

PS. I have put some pocket money in here
for you. Let me know if you need more. Business
is going just great!

Putting the letter back in the envelope, I shook my head in disbelief that he had phoned the Colonel and then talked with Sergeant Crane. Uncle Roy just didn't get it. This military life was a mystery to him, and I would most likely pay the price. And that part about 'business is just great' -- being a war profiteer was something I didn't like!

At the end of our eighth week, there was a feeling in the air that we were all going to make it. We had changed, our heads had hair, our bodies were firmer, and our minds were sharper. We walked with a swagger and we could curse like any good mud

Marine. These weeks brought other changes, and I marveled, watching young boys becoming young tigers. We had worked hard and it was beginning to pay off. Our platoon could out-march, out-shoot and out-swim any other unit on the post.

Liberty

As a reward for the platoon's hard work, Sergeant Nelson announced that on the coming Saturday we would get a twelve-hour pass to San Diego. Two buses would depart at 1000 and return at 2200 sharp. God help any recruit not back from liberty at 2200, as they would be listed AWOL (absent without leave) and court-marshaled. The 3rd Platoon was not as lucky, and was spending that day practicing close-order drills again. Sergeant Nelson enjoyed telling us that bit of news.

The day of our liberty dawned clear and hot. Dressed in our Class A uniforms, we loaded the buses for the fifty-minute drive to downtown San Diego. The Marines had printed up a little tourist guide about the city that was passed out to all. The booklet listed all the places of interest and all the rules of liberty. Much of the city was 'off limits,' but the brochure did suggest places to go and things to see, although they were things most Marines had little interest in: museums, libraries and tourist venues. What our bus talked and laughed about was broads, beer and boogie.

Kurt, Hank, Jim, and I were going to stick together, to enjoy this fragrance of freedom. Our liberty started by us walking around the area of the bus station. Here we found restaurants, cafés and many bars. The guys wanted beer, cold beer, so into a bar we went...and minutes later, out we came, since my friends were all underage. We tried two more saloons with the same results.

By now, the Comedian wasn't laughing, "Damn, it's just not fair. I can give my life for my country but I can't vote or drink a cold beer? It makes no sense!"

Kurt piped up. "Dutch, you can go buy some at a store and we can drink them in some park."

My response was not a welcome one when I said, "If the MP's catch us, we'll all spend the night in the brig. I don't think that's a good idea."

Finally Hank came to my defense. "Hey, guys, leave him alone and don't make him do what he doesn't want to do."

"I have no problems doing it. Just not here and not now."

"You're right, Hank. Come on. Let's get some chow," Kurt added.

We had a fair meal at a sidewalk café on a busy street in the hot sun, but the boys groused about the cost of the food and were sure that the owner was 'sticking it' to the GI's. After lunch, we did some girl-watching and then grabbed a cab and decided to try the Art Museum, since it was air conditioned. It was nice and it was cool, but after eight weeks at boot camp, it was boring.

When we walked out of the museum into the blazing hot sun, I looked across the street…and stopped. There, in its entire splendor, stood the old Hotel El Cortez!

It was a grand tall building with a large blue canopy above the front entrance. Beneath the awning, a doorman dressed in a red-braided uniform was helping people come and go. The sign above the canopy read "Air-Conditioned Rooms."

My mind began to race. Why not? I thought. Turning to my pals, I pointed to a bench beside the museum. "Why don't you guys take a load off, over there in the shade? I'll be back in minute."

"What's going on? Where are you going, Dutch?" Kurt asked. Starting across the busy street, I turned my head and answered, "Trust me!"

Walking past the doorman, I nodded with a smile and pushed at the brass revolving door. While the door was moving, I straightened my tie and brushed off my uniform.

The lobby was massive, replete with stone columns, marble floors, overstuffed furniture and the smell of money. My footsteps echoed as I walked towards the front desk. My mind kept saying, Strut, Dutch, strut. Act like you belong here.

Behind the desk were two gentlemen. The one facing my way was reading a book, while an older gentleman behind him sorted out mail. The bookworm was a skinny fellow with a dark suit and dress shirt with one of those old-fashioned starched collars. His face was narrow and, below his bony nose, he had a pencil mustache. Above his nose, he wore a pair of pince-nez glasses. As I approached the desk, he didn't look up.

After a few seconds of standing there, I cleared my throat.

Looking up at me, he said in a superior tone, "May I help you?"

"Yes. I would like a room, please."

He stared at me and my uniform with contempt. "I'm sorry, sir. That won't be possible. We are booked solid."

Smiling at him and raising one of my hands, I commented, "You mean in this tall, grand, old hotel there is not one room available for a weary traveler like myself?"

He did not smile back but replied, "There is the Governor's Suite, but I'm confident that it would be out of a soldier's price range. You might want to try the YMCA."

Looking him straight in the eye, I asked, "How much is it?"

He glared, "It really doesn't matter, sir. We do not accommodate soldiers."

My face turned red with anger, and I could have punched him right across the counter, but I didn't.

"That's too bad," I remarked. "My Uncle Roy -- that's Roy Clarke -- was just a guest in your hotel, and he highly recommended your establishment. I will have to tell him of my treatment. Do you know who he is?"

"I'm sorry, sir, but I don't know the gentleman. As I said, you can try the Y."

Just then, the older man behind the clerk stepped forward. With one fluid body bump, the surly clerk was no longer in front of me.

With a pleasant smile on his face, the older man said, "I'm Mr. Hudson, the manager. And yes, Mr. Clarke of Gold Coast Petroleum was a guest here, last week. You are his nephew?"

"Yes, and his business partner."

Nodding and smiling at my response, he continued, "I'm sure we can accommodate you, sir, but unfortunately the Governor's

Suite is the only room available, and its rate is ninety-eight dollars a night."

"Mr. Hudson, I have no problem with the rate, but I want to make sure that the suite is air-conditioned, and that there is a radio in the room. And, oh yes, that you offer room service to your guests."

Reaching for a registration card, he answered, "Yes, on all accounts. And If I might add, our room service menu is the finest in all of San Diego. And how long will you be staying with us, Mr. Clarke?"

Reaching into my wallet, I removed my military ID and two crisp one hundred-dollar bills. Placing the ID and one bill on the desk, I said, "This will cover the room." I placed the second bill on the desk. "And this will cover my room service needs. I will be staying until nine, this evening."

He gave me an astonished look. "Yes, sir. I understand. Let me fill out this registration card and you can sign it. Would you like the bellboy to show you to your room?"

"No, thank you. I can find my way. But you can have Room Service send up...hmm...a dozen bottles of iced Falstaff beer, a large bowl of potato chips and...oh yes, some nuts. Salted nuts, if you have them."

Sliding the card and room key across the desk, he answered, "Yes, sir. Right away!"

After signing, I took the key and started to walk away, but stopped and turned back to Mr. Hudson. "And newspapers. Please send up the New York Times and your local paper. I haven't heard the news for a long time. And tell Room Service that I'll be in the room in ten minutes."

"Yes, sir."

Crossing the lobby, I exited briskly through the revolving front door. With the doorman watching, I whistled to my pals across the street and made hand signals for them to join me. Within seconds, they were standing by me.

"What's up, Dutch?" Kurt asked.

Looking them in the eye, I said in my most commanding voice, "We are all going to walk into this grand hotel together. Then we are going to stroll across the lobby to the elevators. I want you Marines to be absolute gentlemen -- no cursing, no laughing, and no grab ass, just like you're on the parade grounds for a Saturday inspection. Act like you belong here. Do you understand?"

"What the hell is going on, Dutch?" Hank asked.

"Just trust me a little longer and you'll see."

They did just as I asked. We walked casually across the lobby to the elevators, in all our uniformed pomp and splendor. And all the while, I could see Mr. Hudson, out of the corner of my eye, smiling as he watched.

Getting into the elevator, I said to the lady operator, "Governor's Suite, please."

"Yes, Mr. Clarke."

There was snickering and smiles from my guys, but no one said a word all the way to the twenty-first floor.

When the car stopped and the doors opened, the operator remarked, "Just to your left, Mr. Clarke. Room 2102."

We exited the car and in a flash she was gone. As we walked down the hall, the Comedian started to imitate the elevator lady. "Mr. Clarke, the Governor's Suite is Room 2102, don't you know, Mr. Clarke?"

With this, we all started laughing and pushing each other along.

Putting the key into the door of Room 2102, I stopped and turned to the guys. "I have a little surprise for you, boys -- we're going to have those cold beers, after all!" Opening the door, I let the guys go in first, and then added, "This is all ours until 2100."

The boys were quiet for the longest moment as they entered the room. Then Jim shouted, "Woo! Look! The room has its own bar..." And then, from Kurt standing by the windows, "And look at this view! It looks like we're in Heaven!" And finally Hank piped up, as he sank into a chair, "Feel that air conditioning? Here is where I want to stay!"

Walking into the room, I found myself in a space half the size of our barracks. On the left was a long dining table behind which stood a bar with four stools and a mirror that ran the length of the area. On the right, a row of windows was flanked by overstuffed chairs, sofas and small tables. At the far corner was a large upright

Philco radio, with a game table and chairs in front. The main salon was impressive beyond my grandest expectations.

By now, Kurt was opening the double doors at the rear of the room. He shouted, "Guys! Come look at this damn bedroom. You won't believe it!"

We all walked to where he was standing, and found ourselves looking at a room that contained the biggest canopy bed I have ever seen. On one side, a window overlooked the city, complete with a seating area with plush leather chairs.

Just then, Hank's voice echoed from the bathroom that connected. "Check this out! It's bigger than our whole latrine -- and there's a bath tub!"

Walking into the tiled room, I saw a large sunken tub at one end of the room, along with double sinks in the middle and a private toilet room at the other end. The tiles on the floor and walls were hospital-white and Marine-clean.

The Comedian started running the water in the tub, then turned to me and asked, "I wanna be first in the tub. Is that okay, Dutch?"

"Sure, why not?" I answered.

Walking back into the living room, Kurt grabbed me. With an ear-to-ear grin on his face, he asked, "Dutch, did you rob a bank this morning, when we weren't looking? How can you afford this?"

"I can't. My uncle sent me some money. Where we're going, I'm sure we won't have much use for it, so why not enjoy it now?"

Just then, there was a knock on the door. The room fell quiet, as if the guys feared that the cops were outside. Grinning, I walked to the door and opened it.

"Room Service," the bellhop said as he pushed a table-clothed cart into the room. On top was a large bowl full of ice and twelve bottles of beer, a bowl full of potato chips, and a smaller bowl filled with nuts. Folded between the bowls were two newspapers.

"Where would you like this, sir?"

Pointing to the bar area, I answered, "Let's set it up over there."

By the time the bellhop was done, all three of my friends had a cold bottle in their hands and were fighting over the church key.

As I walked back to the front door with the bellhop, he stopped and whispered, with a serious look on his face, "Are your friends old enough to drink, sir?"

Smiling back at him, I reached into my pocket and slid a five dollar bill into his hands as I answered, "They are today."

He smiled and nodded his approval.

That's how it started, six glorious hours of living like royalty. We drank, we nibbled, we bathed, and we listened to the radio and read the papers. The news from overseas was not good. All of us were confident that we would soon be on some distant battlefield and in some future headlines. We tried to shake off such thoughts, but we all knew what was coming.

I was the last to bathe. When I returned to the living room, I found Jim standing at an open window, dressed only in his skivvies. Kurt and Hank had their heads sticking out of the open window next to him.

"What the hell are you guys doing?" I demanded.

Kurt poked his laughing face back into the room and answered, "The Comedian is pissing out the window, and the doorman and a cab driver down there think it's raining! Damndest thing I've ever seen!"

Shaking my head, I told the guys to get back inside. The last thing we needed was for the cops to be called, or one of the guys to fall out of the window. Their stunt reminded me that, inside these new men's bodies, they were really just boys…

It was time for food, before we got into trouble. They were still laughing and giggling about the golden shower when I passed around the menu.

Finally Kurt burst out, "Woo! Get a load of these prices. And here I thought the café screwed us, today. These guys are crazy. A buck for a hamburger and two bits for a coke!"

Then Hank added, "Four bits for French fries and six bits for a piece of pie!"

Finally, I broke in. "Look, guys, the meal is on my uncle, so order whatever you want. Forget the prices. Let's enjoy the food and the company."

Jim turned to me. "Okay, then, how about a bottle of champagne to go with this fine food?"

Kurt looked up from the menu. "Why not two bottles?"

"Okay, why not two? But, come 2100, we are out of here. Agreed?"

They all nodded.

We ate our food sitting at the long dining room table, with Tommy Dorsey playing on the radio in the background. The meal started out rowdy and noisy, but once we had a taste of the prime beefsteaks and potatoes, the room grew quiet. We all agreed it was, without a doubt, the best meal we had ever eaten. Good food, good music, good company and good wine. We couldn't have asked for anything more.

After dinner, we sat around, drinking our wine and talking about home and family. The guys were happy, homesick, and a little tipsy. We had just about polished off the final bottle of champagne when there came a knock at the door.

Kurt jumped to his feet. "I'll get it."

From behind me, the door opened, and I heard a female voice say, "Housekeeping. Do you need anything?"

Kurt quickly ushered the young lady into our room. "You can keep my house anytime, honey."

By now, we were all standing and looking at the girl. Hank gave out a low wolf whistle, and Jim's eyes were popping out of his head. She was a Mexican girl; petite, young and pretty even in her drab maid's uniform. Over one arm, she carried fresh towels. Her eyes were dark brown, and they sparkled as a smile lit her face. She stood there for a moment, looking back at all of us, and then asked, "Are you boys Marines?"

"You're damn right we are, honey," replied Hank.

Still smiling, she moved further into the room and laid the towels over the back of a chair. Our eyes were fixated on this shapely young lady.

Looking around at us again, she continued, "I know what all Marines want...and I am going to give it to you boys!"

The room fell silent for a second. Then Kurt cried out, "All right, doll. We're here to have some fun!"

My mind started racing. We could be in real trouble here.

"I know," she said, "because my brother is a Marine, just like you, and he's fighting on Guadalcanal."

The smiles on our faces melted away instantly. Her brother was a fellow Marine, and he was where we might soon be. Guadalcanal had been all over the news. We had lost many good Marines on that island in the Pacific. Her words jarred us out of our champagne fantasies and back to reality.

Moving towards Kurt, she continued, "He tells me that all that Marines want to do is kiss girls. Okay!"

With this said, she placed her two hands on Kurt's face and stood on her tiptoes to give him a kiss on the cheek. Next she moved to Jim, then Hank, and then me, doing the same for each of us. Finally, she walked towards the front door and concluded, "Now I've given you all what you wanted. I hope you'll always be safe Marines. God bless you and America…good night, boys."

In the blink of an eye, she was gone.

We were speechless. She had been sexy, yet innocent, so tender, so loving.

Finally, Kurt remarked, "Did you smell that perfume?"

Jim sighed. "Did you feel how soft her lips were?"

Hank added, "And that body! What a beautiful body."

The last to comment, I said, "Let's finish off the wine before we head back."

At 2045, we departed the hotel…but not before we took one last long look at the room that had brought us so much joy. Before leaving, I asked the guys to keep our activities a secret. The last thing I needed was trouble over buying booze for my under-aged friends. They agreed.

On the bus ride back to base, there was a lot of bellyaching from the other guys about the heat, the cost of food, and the fact that there had been no broads, no beer and no boogie. Kurt, Hank, Jim and I sat quietly, with smiles on our faces. It was a liberty none of us would ever forget.

The Gauntlet

The next week was final qualifications on the obstacle course. All recruits had to finish the course in fifteen minutes or less. If they failed to qualify, they could be held back for further training. Each platoon would be given two chances to complete the course within the allotted time. The course itself was two miles long, going mostly uphill on loose sand. Along the way, there were a large number of different hurdles that had to be traversed, obstacles like high walls that had to be scaled, cliffs that had to be climbed by using ropes, and swinging bridges over muddy ponds. The base record for the course was ten minutes, twenty seconds. The platoon would have to run the hurdles while wearing full battle gear, which meant an extra seventy pounds of weight.

On the first day of the qualifications, we were paired by squads, with two men leaving every sixty seconds. My running companion was Kurt. He was strong, with long, muscular legs. He could run like a cougar, so I knew I had competition. Sergeant Nelson started each pair, using his whistle and a watch to record the start times. As his shrilling filled the air, we were off.

The first hurdle was a long row of old tires lying on the ground. High-stepping through twenty wheel openings takes balance and coordination.

Kurt took the early lead, but by the third obstacle, scaling a twenty-foot wall, I had caught up. The day was hot and the humidity high. By now, we were both nothing more than sweat-balls running along a sandy trail. At the half way point, I took the lead and never looked back. Stumbling across the finish line, I gasped for breath as Corporal Johnson recorded my finish time. A few seconds later, Kurt joined me as I was pouring water over my head. He was out of breath and panting like a new puppy. "I almost beat you, Dutch. Boy, can you run!"

That evening, the results were posted in the Day Room. My time was ten minutes, thirty-four seconds; Kurt's was ten minutes, thirty-nine seconds. We had the best times in the platoon. Sergeant Nelson made a big deal about our times, and challenged us to beat the base record, the next day. Kurt and I shook hands and accepted the challenge, knowing it could be done.

Before leaving the Day Room, I noted that five guys, including the Comedian, had times over fifteen minutes. When I talked to Jim about his time, he put a good face on it and told me that he had fallen down twice and was confident that he would be okay, the next day. His words were positive...but his expression was doubtful.

We were fortunate to be the first platoon on the course the next morning. The morning was cool and the air still crisp. It was a good omen for our attempt to break the base record. My squad was the last to start, and Sergeant Nelson held Kurt and me for the last. We stood like Olympic athletes, waiting for his whistle. Then we were off.

I took the early lead and was determined to hold it. My rifle and backpack seemed lighter today, and my legs felt stronger. By the halfway point, I still had a good ten or fifteen seconds on Kurt. The breeze on my face felt cool and refreshing.

Finally I came to the last obstacle, a muddy pond that had to be crossed by a swinging rope line attached to a log A-frame. As I reached for the rope, I saw the Comedian lying on the ground, on the other side of the water.

"What the hell are you doing, Jim?" I screamed as I swung across.

"I twisted my damn ankle. You keep going. I'll be all right."

With beads of sweat rolling down my face, I stopped and looked down at him. He was holding his right ankle and there was a look of pain in his eyes.

"You've got to finish this. You have to get going!" I blurted out.

"I can't. It hurts too much. Please, you keep going," he answered in agony.

Reaching down, I grabbed him under his shoulder blades and pulled him up. "The hell you say."

With effort, I got him standing; then, in one fluid motion, I put him across my back like a fireman. His extra weight made me stumble a few times as I started moving down the trail.

He protested from my back, "Dutch, you can't do this…"

My run was now down to a stagger, but I was moving forward. Coming around a bend, I could see the finish line, some fifty yards ahead.

Just then, Kurt arrived at my side. "You need help, Dutch?" he panted.

"No, you keep going," I mumbled back. And he did.

A few moments later, we stumbled across the finish line, and I slid Jim off my back into the waiting hands of Corporal Johnson. Out of breath and exhausted, I fell to the ground, joining Kurt. We just breathed for a few moments, gasping the cool morning air into our lungs.

Looking up, I could see Sergeant Nelson hovering over us. "Do you guys want to know your times?"

We nodded, still unable to speak. "Benson: ten minutes, twelve seconds. Clarke: ten minutes, twenty-eight seconds. Good show!"

Panting, I asked, "And Wilson, sir?"

Looking down at his clipboard he replied, "Wilson: 14 minutes, 52 seconds."

Smiles beamed across our faces. I looked over to where Jim sat, rubbing his ankle; he glanced my way, with a nod and a tear. There is a special reward for doing the right thing, a reward more valuable than all others. God, what a great feeling!

The Brotherhood

A few days before graduation, I was ordered to report to Sergeant Nelson's office. Standing before his hatch, I knocked three times.

From the other side of the door, I heard, "Who's tapping on my timber?"

"Recruit Clarke, sir."

"Show your face."

Reaching down, I opened the door and brought myself to attention in the doorway.

Sergeant Nelson was at his desk. He looked up. "Come on in, Dutch, and stand at ease."

He'd called me by my first name, which had never happen before. Marching to the front of his desk, I stood at rest. He had a brown file open on his desk and was making notes on some forms inside.

After a moment, he looked up again. "First, I want to tell you that what you did on the obstacle course the other day was outstanding. A Marine never leaves another wounded Marine on the field. Good job." He continued, "I've been reading your personnel file and I'm impressed, not so much with the file but with you, the man that has been here for the past nine weeks. You're a born leader, a crack rifle shot and, from what this file says, an expert at survival. In other words, you're just what the Marines are looking for, but maybe better placed than in a rifle platoon." Nelson had a serious look on his face, an all-business look, as he continued. "I talked to Lieutenant Cunningham, and he talked to the Company CO, and we all agree that you should be offered a position at Officers Candidate School."

The room fell silent with his last words. My mind was trying to absorb what he had said about OCS, and I remained speechless.

"Well, Dutch, what do you think?"

"Is this an order, sir? Do I have to go to OCS?"

"No, Dutch. The Marines recommend candidates. They don't order candidates."

"I noticed you didn't confer with Sergeant Crane. I'm sure he won't agree with your recommendation."

"That might be so," Nelson replied.

"I thank you and the brass for your consideration, but I would prefer to stay with the platoon, sir."

Looking down, he closed the file and stood up from his desk, then walked around to the front. "You know where you're going -- advanced weapons training for the next six weeks, and then, more than likely, off to the Pacific. You'll end up on some hell hole of an island, getting your ass shot off by some Jap. I would think OCS would be a better option. More than likely, you'd end up a platoon leader, with a better chance of survival."

"That might all be so, sir, but I don't have a college education and I would rather stay with this platoon and these men."

"Very well", he replied. "Any questions?"

I thought for a moment, and then answered. "Yes, sir. You once told me that Sergeant Crane was a China Marine. I have never heard that expression, and I don't know what it means."

By now, Nelson was sitting on the corner of his desk, "They are old-time professional soldiers. They served time in China, fought in Central America and Haiti, and have written half the history of the Marine Corps. They are the old breed, salty noncoms and twenty-year officers. They don't necessarily like the ninety-day lieutenants and ten-week Boots." He stopped for a second and then, with a large grin on his face, concluded, "But they're okay. You just steer clear of them."

Graduation came on Saturday, August 8, at 0930. Twelve platoons, over nine hundred men, formed on the main parade field and marched to the music from the base band. It was an impressive sight. There was a color guard in front, and columns of men marching around the field, led by their platoon leaders and the noncoms that trained them. Being a squad leader, I was in the front row as we marched by the reviewing stand, with all the officers standing and saluting. With the flags flying and the men marching, the band played the 'Marine Hymn,' God Bless America' and 'The Stars & Stripes Forever.' For some reason, my uniform seemed to fit better, I felt taller, my mind was right, and I was on the beam. But then, no Marine ever forgets the day they became a member of the brotherhood.

After the ceremonies, Lieutenant Cunningham and Sergeant Nelson personally handed out the 'Eagle, Globe & Anchor' insignia for our uniforms. We were now Privates in the United States Marines Corps, and proud of it.

Back at the barracks, Sergeant Nelson made a few announcements. He would post the list of reassignment orders on the bulletin board by 1600. There would be company liberty the rest of the day, and base liberty for Sunday. We should all be packed and ready to move out to our reassignments by 1000 on Monday. He and Corporal Johnson were getting a new group of Rainbows on Monday night. So the barracks was to be left Marine-clean for the next group of Mop Heads. With that, he shouted "Dismissed!"

At 1600, we all filtered into the Day Room. Looking over the shoulders of the men in front, I read the list. As we had all guessed, the entire platoon, except two, was reassigned to an advanced weapons-training company not a half mile from our barracks.

The two exceptions were Private Neil, a police cadet before enlisting, who was assigned for MP training, and Private Larson, who was assigned to the Motor Pool for training. Larson found this puzzling. He couldn't change a flat tire, let alone repair an engine, so he attributed this assignment to Marine revenge against him for criticizing all of the marching.

The list was complete…with the exception of my name. Look as I might, my name was nowhere to be found.

Walking out of the Day Room, I crossed the hall to the open door of Sergeant Nelson's room. When I knocked on the jamb, he looked up from his desk and motioned me in. Corporal Johnson was lying on his bed reading a magazine. The room looked brighter, larger and friendlier than the other times I had been in it.

Coming to attention in front of the desk, I said, "I just read the reassignment list in the Day Room, and my name isn't on it."

Looking up, Nelson replied, "I noticed that. The company office was closed when I picked up the list, so I couldn't inquire. We'll have to wait until Monday morning to see what's up. I'm sure it's just some snafu. You get packed and ready to go with the other guys. I'll get your orders, first thing Monday."

Then Johnson chimed in. "Trust me, this won't be your last Marine snafu. It happens all the time. One time, I waited two weeks in Hawaii for orders sending me to Hawaii! Get used to it, Dutch. Just another snafu."

Nodding my understanding, I departed thinking about the word 'snafu,' a popular acronym for 'Situation Normal: All Fucked Up.'

CHAPTER TWO

T*umbling into a hole with the world spinning around me, my body was pulled ever deeper into the abyss. The light of the sun with its warm rays on my face was my shroud, and the only sounds were that of the wind and a single white dove above. Falling into the next life, I looked forward to the peace. Scared but resigned I prayed, Oh Lord, let me go. But how could I let go? Not now. Not before the murky image of Colonel Hisachi's ghastly deeds came into focus. My hatred for his memory was stronger than my fear of death....*

"Dutch...Dutch, wake up."

My eyes opened slowly as I was pulled back to reality, with all its ugly consequences. The sun was still low in the sky, and that white dove was a screaming seagull flying above the raft. The boat was rocking with the ocean swells, and it took me a moment to realize where and who I was.

"What's up?" I finally stammered.

The Padre was in my face, or I should say Chaplain Captain Jasper Young of the 14th Royal Australian Engineering Regiment. He outranked us all...but had no delusions about his role. He was our spiritual leader and looked to me for more practical leadership. And why not? He and the other men on the float had been in

Japanese prison camps since early 1942. They were nothing more than skin and bones, and totally exhausted. The Padre had long ago realized that survival and hope made the best sermon for his flock.

"It's Corporal Bates. I think he's dying. Can you take a look at him?"

Nodding yes, I dragged my limp legs across the short, sea-swamped raft to where Bates was. Sergeant York and Private Patterson had Bates propped up between them, resting him against the side of the raft. Our little boat was like a cork, rolling and pitching with each ocean swell, causing sea spray to wash across all our faces.

Patterson was first to speak. "He took a bullet, last night, and didn't tell us. He moaned all night and then this morning, when we found the wound, he stopped groaning and started shaking. If you look at his face, it looks like he's dying. What do you think, Dutch?"

"Where did he get it?' I asked.

"In the upper back, on the left side," York replied.

As I looked down at Bates, he slowly opened his sunken eyes. His face was racked with pain, but there was still life in those eyes. He watched me as I moved closer.

"Can I take a look at that hole in your back?" I asked.

He blinked his eyes 'yes' and slowly moved his upper body over the lap of York. The back of his shabby shirt was stained with dried blood and salt water. Just a few inches below his shoulder, I could see the entry hole of the bullet. Taking my fingers, I probed around the wound and then tried to slide my little finger into the center, to see if the hole was open.

Bates wrenched with pain and let out a cry.

I stopped. From what I could tell, the bullet was deep, and close to his heart or lung. Reaching down, I helped Bates sit up again, with his right side resting against the raft.

All the Aussies were looking at me. Finally, the Padre asked, "What do you think, Dutch? Can you remove the bullet with the knife you got off that dead Nip last night?"

The knife I'd taken the previous night was a rifle bayonet, which was a far cry from a surgical scalpel. It was big and clumsy, and who knew how clean it was?

Turning to the guys, I answered, "I'm no doctor. The wound looks deep, and I think the bullet is close to his heart. The bayonet's too big and awkward. He will die if I try."

"He'll bloody well die if we don't try," Patterson said, clearly anguished.

Turning from the guys, I looked again into Bates's face. The sunlight was harsh, and drops of sea spray ran down his pale, hollow cheeks. There was wind in his matted brown hair but his eyes seemed brighter now, with more life than just a few minutes ago. He reached up and grabbed one of my hands, pulling me close to whisper, "Please try."

About Face

Transportation for the Third and Fourth Platoons arrived at 1000 on Monday. My pals and I really didn't say good-by, as we were confident I would soon be joining them after the snafu was resolved. That morning after chow, we had even laughed about my orders being held up, and the Comedian offered that our next liberty would be on him, if we liked the YMCA -- at which Kurt joked that he probably meant the YWCA.

I watched the buses pull out from the dayroom window, wondering why Sergeant Nelson hadn't been on hand to say farewell. Turning from the window, I sat down at the desk to write a letter to Uncle Roy. The room was warm and the barracks uncommonly quiet, with the only noise coming from the gable fan that had serenaded me to sleep so many times.

The blank piece of stationary was still vacuous five minutes later. Finding the right words for Uncle Roy was difficult. How could I tell him that Semper Fi -- the Corps motto: Always Faithful -- was more than just words? How could I tell him about the pride and glory I was feeling at being an ordinary mud Marine? Knowing how he felt about the war and my enlistment, I would have to choose my words carefully.

Just then, from the front stairway, I heard footsteps running up. Turning I found Sergeant Nelson in the doorway.

He walked into the room with a puzzled look on his face. "All morning, I've been over at company headquarters, trying to find out what happened to your orders. They had no idea. They called the assignment officer at battalion, and he had no paperwork about your reassignment. In fact, for some reason, he didn't even have your DD214 file. Finally, he called Regiment, and they referred him to the CO of the Second Battalion, Colonel Jacob's office. They have all your paperwork and files. Don't ask why, they just do. Now I'm told to have you report to Colonel Jacob's office ASAP. Do you even know where Battalion Headquarters is?"

Stunned by his information, I finally answered, "No, Sergeant, I don't."

He gave me detailed directions to Headquarters, some fifteen blocks away, and off I went.

As I quickly walked towards Battalion Headquarters, my mind was reeling. As far as I knew, no recruit had ever set foot in Company Headquarters, let alone Battalion. These places were for officers and NCOs, and were off limits to privates like me. I kept thinking, *what the hell is going on*?

Battalion Headquarters was a large, two-story brick building, complete with flag pole and old cannons out front. Three large steps led up to the door, above which a shining brass sign read '2nd Battalion – 3rd Marine Regiment.' The building, sparkling in the early morning sun, was rather intimidating. I must have saluted a dozen times before entering the front double doors. Wearing my utilities, I felt out of place; all of the other personnel were dressed in Class A uniforms.

There was a Corporal just inside the doors at a reception desk. As I approached, he said in a commanding voice, "State your business, Private."

Bracing myself, I replied, "Sergeant Nelson of Dog Company ordered me to report to Colonel Jacob's office, sir."

Picking up the telephone, he gave me the once-over and asked, "Your name, Private?"

Within seconds of the Corporal's phone call, I was given instructions on how to find the Colonel's office. On the second floor, I found a long corridor that ended in front of a wooden door with a frosted-glass window. On the window, painted in black and gold, was 'Commanding Officer, 2nd Battalion 3rd Marine Regiment.'

Bringing myself to attention, I knocked on the hatch three times.

There was no reply.

After a long moment, I reached down and turned the knob, slowly opening the door. Inside, I found myself looking into a large office where five men were working. Four of the men, two on each side of the room, had stacks of papers on their desk. The room was filled with the sounds of the pecking typewriters. No one looked up as I entered and walked down the row of desks. At the far end of the room, the fifth man was reading from an open brown file. Approaching him I noticed a small name plate on his desk: 'SGT MacDonald.'

Bracing myself again at the front of his desk, I said, "Private Clarke reporting to Colonel Jacob's office as ordered, sir."

He looked up from his paperwork and took a good, long look at me. "At ease. So, you're Clarke. I'll see if the Colonel will see you now." Taking the brown file folder, he got up from his desk and moved to the door behind him.

My mind was reeling again. I'd had no idea that I would actually see the Colonel. It had been my impression that I was only going to pick up my paperwork at his office.

A few moments later, the Sergeant returned and ushered me into the CO's office.

The office was spacious and bright. On one side stood a round table, flanked by overstuffed leather chairs. On the other side was a wall full of maps. At the very end was the Colonel's mahogany desk, with a credenza behind it, and above the table was a large wall emblem for the Battalion. Sitting behind the massive desk was Colonel Jacobs, framed by an American flag on one side and the

Battalion flag on the other. It was an impressive and daunting sight.

Smartly marching up to the front of the desk, I brought myself to attention, saluted and stated, "Private Clarke reporting as ordered, sir."

The Colonel had his head down, reading from a file. He had an unlit cigar in his mouth, which he was chewing. I stood there at attention, with my right hand still in the air, saluting for the longest moment before he returned the salute without looking up.

Finally, he raised his gaze and took a long, hard look at me before saying, "At ease, Private." Repositioning his body in his chair, he continued, "I've been in the Marines for over twenty years and I've seen a lot of strange things happen over those years, but this tops them all."

The full bird Colonel was a distinguished-looking man with jet-black hair and graying temples. While his face showed some aging, his green eyes were bright, and his gaze was still strong and lively. Picking up a piece of paper from the file, he read its contents: "Effective on 8 August, 1942 at 1200 hours, Private Dutch R. Clarke, Serial Number 23344323, is promoted to the rank of Second Lieutenant United States Marine Corps Reserve." Putting the paper down, the Colonel looked over at me and continued, "I've seen field commissions before, they're not so unusual. I've even seen battlefield commissions where a Private is promoted to a Second Lieutenant in the middle of a fire fight. Those aren't so unusual either. What makes this promotion so strange is that, on the morning of 8 August, you were just a recruit. By midmorning, you were a Private, and by noon a Second Lieutenant. Now that is unusual! But what makes it even more interesting is who issued and signed your orders." Reaching down, he picked up the paper again and read, "As ordered by the Secretary of the Navy, Frank Knox." While still holding the orders, the Colonel looked up at me and, chewing his cigar, went on, "Your orders go on to relieve you from Camp Pendleton and reassign you to the OWI command in Hollywood, California. Lieutenant, you know some powerful people in high places!"

Standing in front of the Colonel, I was stunned and speechless. One thing was for sure: Uncle Roy's fingerprints were all over these orders. Confused by my situation, I was mad as hell at him.

The Colonel broke the silence, "Well, Lieutenant?"

Clearing my throat, I regained my voice, "Let me assure the Colonel that I don't know any of these 'powerful people.' This is not something of my doing. Can I turn the commission down, sir?"

A broad smile crossed the Colonel's face as he answered. "The Secretary of the Navy does not make suggestions, he gives orders! Do you understand that, Lieutenant?"

"Aye, aye, sir. But I don't understand. What is the OWI command?"

Leaning back in his chair scowling, he answered, "It's a sweet little job working for the Office of War Information. They are the propaganda arm for the military." He turned away from me and shouted towards the door, "Mac, come in here please." Returning his attention to me, he added, "Cocktail parties, celebrities and politicians. What a way to run a war. God help the United States of America!"

Just then, Sergeant MacDonald reappeared. The Colonel asked him, "Do you have the Lieutenant's paperwork done?"

"No sir. It will take a few more hours to get his travel orders, transportation and meal vouchers ready. But the rest of his 214 file is done and ready."

Turning back to me, the Colonel remarked, "Sergeant MacDonald will help you get squared away. While you're waiting for your paperwork, the first order of business should be for you to get the correct uniforms over at the main Post Exchange. And good luck, Lieutenant, with OWI."

He saluted me while I came to attention and saluted back.

I followed Sergeant MacDonald out to his desk, where he handed me a copy of my promotion orders and rattled off instructions. "You'll need these to buy officer's uniforms, Lieutenant, and you should go back over to your old barracks and pick up your duffle bag. The Marines usually want officers who've been promoted from the ranks to turn in their 1041 outfit but I know they just burn the used clothing, so go ahead and keep yours. I should have your paperwork done no later than 1500. Then you can get transportation to the Union Station from here. Is that okay with you, sir?"

He'd called me sir! It caught me off guard. Finally, I replied, "No problem, Sergeant. But could you direct me to the main PX?"

As I walked towards the PX, my emotions went from low to empty. Something the Colonel had said kept racing in my mind: Cocktail parties, celebrities and politicians... what a way to run a war. This was not why I had joined the Marines. And then there were my pals in the Fourth Platoon. Would I ever see them again? And what would they think of me being a Lieutenant? For the most part, we didn't even like officers.

My emotions turned to anger at Uncle Roy, who had butted into my life once again. But in the end there was nothing I could do about it. I was a Lieutenant, and I was going to work for OWI. Life has many strange turns and I had to make the best of this detour.

Although there were a half dozen Post Exchanges on the base, only the main PX sold goods for officers. But one thing was certain: when I walked into the Exchange, I didn't look much like an officer.

At first, the civilian clerk in the uniform department was dubious about my carbon-copy orders. It was only after he made a telephone call to Sergeant MacDonald that his caution turned to salesmanship. All military officers are required to purchase their uniforms and other personal items. I'm sure that, once he knew I was a real officer, he viewed me as a big ticket. Therefore, he was quite disappointed when I only bought two khaki dress uniforms and some extra bars and insignias. He couldn't understand why I didn't purchase a couple of woolen and formal white dress uniforms, complete with swords. And the thought of me buying only one hat and no shoes at all frustrated him even more. The fact was, my clothes in the duffle bag could do double duty, with some minor changes. For that, I could thank Sergeant MacDonald.

While some slight tailoring was done on my new uniforms, I had lunch and did some more shopping. The last item I bought was the 'Officers Handbook,' a manual I was sure to need.

That afternoon, walking out of the PX in one of my new uniforms with gold bars glistening in the sun, I looked like a Marine Lieutenant, but I didn't feel like one. It took a few minutes for me to realize that the enlisted men saluting me wanted a salute back. Damn, what a strange feeling it was to be an officer!

Back at the barracks, I attached my Rifleman's Badge on the left side of my new blouse. It was the only symbol I had that, at one time, I had been an enlisted Marine. Taking my garrison cap from my duffel bag, I pinned a gold bar on it. Laying out my remaining new uniform on my old bunk, I folded it neatly and stowed it in my bag. Placing my cap on, I was turning to leave when I found Sergeants Crane and Nelson entering the barracks bay. When their gazes reached mine, a puzzled look ran across their faces.

Walking towards me, Crane shouted, "Clarke, what the hell are you doing in that goddamn uniform? You are one sorry SOB to be impersonating at officer!"

He was still on me. I felt my face flush with anger, but not with fear. Not anymore. Glaring back at Crane, I let him move to the foot of my bunk before I replied. "It's Lieutenant Clarke now, Sergeant Crane, and when I talk to you, you will be at attention."

He didn't brace. "I don't believe your sorry ass is an officer any more than I believed that 'bear tattoo' bullshit. You're one sad Marine to cross me, boy," he screamed back.

Reaching into my blouse pocket, I pulled out my promotion orders. Bypassing Sergeant Crane I handed them to Sergeant Nelson. He looked down at the orders and then, with the biggest smile I had ever seen on his face, said, "He's right, Sergeant Crane. And his orders are signed by the Secretary of the Navy!"

Grabbing the orders out of Nelson's hands, Sergeant Crane yelled, "I don't believe it." But when he read what was written, his expression turned from anger to compliance in the blink of an eye.

With grit, I remarked, "Saved by orders. We Marines are always saved by orders. Remember those words, Sergeant Crane? I do. Now I'll ask you again to come to attention when I talk to you."

This time, both he and Sergeant Nelson instantly came to attention.

There was so much I wanted to say and I wanted to say it loudly…but I didn't.

Bringing my face within inches of Crane's, just like he had done to me so many times before, I calmly remarked, "For some reason, you have been riding my ass ever since I got here. They tell me you're a China Marine and have helped to write most of the USMC history. You're the old Corps and I'm the new, but we're still both Marines. That Nip sniper out in the Pacific can't tell the difference between the old and the new because we both bleed Marine red. Your job is to train young boys into fighting men, and for the most part it's done well, but it can be done a hell of a lot better when you finally realize that the new breed is going to be writing our future history. So don't piss on the men and tell them it's raining, they know better. Do you understand what I'm saying, Sergeant?"

He paused for a moment before replying, "Aye, aye, sir. I'm sorry."

With the low rumblings of the gable fan sounding in the background, I watched a drop of sweat roll down Crane's twitching face as I prepared to give my first official command. "A Marine is never sorry. A sorry Marine is a dead Marine. Sergeant Crane, you are dismissed."

He fumed under his campaign hat for a moment and then, in tribute to my rank alone, gave me a crisp salute, which I returned. Turning on his boot heel, he marched out of the bay.

As the doors swung shut, I told Sergeant Nelson to stand at ease. With Crane gone, I extended my hand towards him and said, "Before I leave, I want to shake your hand and thank you for my training."

He was caught off-guard for a moment, but then shook my extended hand with a firm grip, and a grin.

I continued, "I have a favor to ask you, Dick. That is your first name, isn't it?"

"Yes, sir."

"When you get a chance, will you tell the guys in the platoon what happened to me? That snafu was bigger than expected. They are sending me to the OWI Command, up in Hollywood. If you or any of the guys get up that way, please look me up."

"I knew you'd make a good officer. I just didn't know how fast it could happen! Don't worry, I'll tell the guys. I have no idea what the OWI is, but I'm sure Hollywood is a hell of a lot better place to be than some flea-infested foxhole in the Pacific."

Sadly I replied, "Maybe so."

Tinsel City

The trip north was delayed by almost three hours. Our train was twice moved onto rail sidings as long freight trains carrying war materials passed us by. Even in the dark, I could make out the silhouettes of flatbed cars loaded with tanks, trucks and artillery, all heading south. Their destination was San Diego and then on to the Pacific...the direction I should have been heading. Instead, my destination was north and, as Colonel Jacob had said, to 'Cocktail parties, celebrities and politicians.' My prospects looked bleak.

Arriving at the Hollywood station at 2300, I asked a cabbie about hotels on Melrose Avenue. He told me that rooms were hard to find in Hollywood, but that I could try the YMCA in downtown LA or sack out in the train station, which is what I did. The night on the hard wooden bench was long and uncomfortable, so when Reveille rolled around, I was ready to take a shower and hit the road.

At 0800, a cab dropped me off at the address on my orders, 5555 Melrose Avenue, but a large sign across the entrance read 'Paramount Studios.' Could this be another snafu?

There was a small guardhouse, alongside massive iron gates, which controlled the entrance, so I went there and inquired. An older gentleman, in a guard's uniform, was sipping coffee just inside the open sliding door.

Dropping my duffle bag and removing my orders from my pocket, I said, "Pardon me, sir. I have orders to report to OWI offices at this address. Can that be right?"

Setting his coffee down, he joined me in the open doorway and read my orders. Shaking his head, he answered, "I've never heard of any OWI outfit on this lot, but let me make a phone call."

Stepping back into the guardhouse, he dialed a few numbers and was soon talking to someone on the other end.

Turning back to me, he asked, "Do you know what OWI stands for? Is it a production company or a union office or what?"

"I was told it's the Office of War Information."

Returning to the phone, he passed on the information and then, smiling and nodding he hung up the phone.

Just as he returned to the doorway, a long, red convertible pulled up to the gate.

Looking over and waving to the driver, the old guard pressed a button and said, "Good morning, Mr. Gable." With this the gate rolled open and the car entered the lot. Turning to me, he continued, "You're with the Navy boys, over in the old garden cottages. Around here, we know them as the 'Party Army.' They have their own gate behind Stage Five, but you can walk there from here. Let me give you some directions."

Throwing my duffle bag over my shoulder, I started the long walk to the garden cottages. Along the way, I passed many sound stages and marveled at the size of these buildings; they were bigger than airplane hangars. The whole area was a beehive of activity, with people coming and going, dressed in all types of costumes. Weaving between them were other people, pushing carts that had painted props and backdrops, while still others pushed large lights and manhandled piles of electrical cable. It reminded me that Hollywood was still dealing with fantasy, while the rest of the world was dealing with war. Was that good or bad? I had no idea.

Just across the street from Stage Five was a long row of white stucco cottages with red tile roofs. Behind this row was another, separated by a parking lot. Each little house had a patch of green grass and a small walkway lined with flowers, leading to a front door. It was a pleasant setting, worthy of a Hollywood set designer.

The first bungalow had a small sign in front that simply read '#1 OWI HQ.' Placing my kit next to the front door, I straightened my uniform and entered the cottage.

Inside, I found a small room barely large enough for the desk that filled it. Behind this desk, a mature woman was talking on the telephone. Seeing me standing in the doorway, she waved me in with a smile, said goodbye to the caller, and hung up. "Good morning, Lieutenant. How may I help you?"

"I'm Lieutenant Dutch Clarke, reporting for duty, ma'am."

"Oh, you're here to see Commander Knox. He's the boss in our little community. He should be in the office anytime now. He usually rolls in about nine. Take a seat in our one lonely chair. It shouldn't be long. How about some coffee?"

"No thank you, ma'am."

This lady could talk, and talk she did, nonstop. Luckily, Commander Knox joined us a few minutes later. I jumped to attention as he entered the office, and he smiled and told me to stand at ease. He was wearing his summer white uniform with a blouse that had three rows of ribbons and the insignia of a submariner.

As instructed, I followed him into his office and deposited my personnel file and orders on his desk.

Sliding behind his desk, he started to review my paperwork. He was short, older and heavy-shouldered. Judging by his graying temples, gray eyes and weathered face, I placed his age in the late forties.

Finally, he looked up at me. "Your paperwork says you're a born leader, an expert rifleman, with a background in survival. Those are all excellent skills for a mud Marine, but not necessarily the traits OWI is looking for. But then I looked down and saw who signed your orders, and far be it from me to argue with the Secretary of the Navy." Putting down my file, he continued, "This show is mostly Navy, but we do have a small contingent of Marines, commanded by Lt. Colonel Ford. That's where you'll be assigned. I'll let Ford find your hidden skills. Our mission here is simple -- we're to promote and provide military information to the Hollywood community. We are the face of the United States Navy to millions of theatergoers across this nation and around the world, and it's a job worth doing well. In the last war, I was a submarine commander, and after that I was a film producer for MGM. When this war broke out, the Navy needed publicity more than they needed fat old submariners like myself, so I now command OWI. Most of my people are retreads from WW1 or have entered OWI direct from civilian life with special talents or skills. They are writers, editors, publicists, and photographers. The hundred-plus people that work for me take their mission seriously and do a damn good job. Do you understand, Lieutenant?"

"Yes, sir."

"Leave your DD214 file here, but take a copy of your orders and report to Colonel Ford over in Bungalow Seven, and good luck, Lieutenant."

Bracing myself, I gave the commander a sharp salute. "Aye, aye, sir."

My action caught him off guard. Finally, with a puzzled look on his face, he half-heartily returned my salute and mumbled, "Dismissed…Marine."

Cottage Seven was across the parking lot and down two. In front of the bungalow was a small sign that read '#7 USMC Publicity.' Once again, I deposited my duffle bag next to the front door and entered. The first thing I noticed was the smell of flowers…or was that perfume? This room seemed larger and had two chairs in front of a small empty desk, with wooden filing cabinets behind. On top of the desk was a typewriter, some small, framed pictures and an assortment of files and papers.

Just then, from a hallway at one side of the desk, a woman appeared. She was carrying a coffee cup and looked startled to see me standing in the office. "Sorry, I didn't hear you come in. I was in the back, getting some coffee. What can I do for you, Lieutenant?" she said in a low voice that was almost a whisper.

It wasn't the flowers I had smelled, it was this stunning lady.

"I'm Dutch Clarke, reporting for duty. Commander Knox sent me over from HQ to report to Colonel Ford."

"I see." She smiled as she slipped behind her desk. "The Colonel is here but he's a little indisposed right now," she continued softly. "We only heard yesterday that you were being assigned to us, and I'm afraid we are a little disorganized."

Smiling back at her, I said, "I understand, ma'am. I only heard yesterday that I was being assigned here, too."

"Don't get me wrong. The Colonel needs the help. We were just surprised how quickly this happened, since we only made the request last week."

She had a very special look, more handsome than beautiful. Her figure was trim and full, and the clothes she wore looked expensive. There was a streak of gray or blonde mixed in with her auburn hair, and after a closer look at her face, I placed her age in the late thirties. Her warm smile and twinkling hazel eyes lit up her face.

Just then, from behind the closed door at the rear of her desk, came the muffled but loud voice of a man. "What the hell is going on out there? I can't get any goddamn sleep with all that noise..."

Just then, the door opened, revealing an older man dressed only in old-fashioned riding pants and a dirty white tank top. He was startled clearly to see me standing there, staring at him.

The lady looked his way. "This is Lieutenant Clarke, Colonel. Commander Knox sent him over."

This was Lt. Colonel Ford? Bringing myself to attention, I said, "Reporting for duty, sir."

He looked me over for a moment, and then answered while turning back into his office. "Come in, Lieutenant, and bring your orders."

At first his office was dark, but soon the Colonel had all three of the window shutters open, flooding the little room with light. Under the window stood a long, red-leather couch, with pillows and a blanket at one end. Across from the couch was a large wooden desk, with rows of book shelves behind it. The room smelled of stale smoke and brandy, just like my grandfather's office, back in New Jersey. Bracing myself in front of the desk, I handed the Colonel my orders.

"Stand at ease. We weren't expecting you today." Looking down and reading my orders, he reached into his desk and brought out a cigarette and a white ivory holder. Wetting one end of the cigarette with his lips, he fitted it into the holder and lit it.

In the warm morning light, I could see that he was older than Commander Knox, somewhere in his fifties. His hair was mostly gray, with the exception of his eye brows, which were jet black and made him look distinguished. The Colonel was a short fireplug of a man neither fat nor slender. His face was round, with a large nose, but his eyes were clear and as dark as a barrel of crude. I liked him immediately.

Finally, with his gaze still trained on the page, and white smoke rising around his head, he said, "You run with some powerful folks, Lieutenant. I have never seen a set of orders signed by the big boss himself. I'm impressed!" Putting the papers down, he looked up at me and continued, "We only put in for some help last week, and now you show up. How do you suppose the Secretary of the Navy heard about my request?"

"I don't know, sir. I have never met the gentleman. Last week at this time, I was just a Marine boot awaiting advance weapons training. Now, for some reason, I'm here."

"Nothing moves this fast in the Navy...nothing but trouble. But, according to the Secretary of the Navy, here you are and here you will stay." Chewing and puffing on the cigarette holder, the Colonel went on, "I run a laid-back outfit here, so I'll call you Dutch and you can call me Colonel. We have an important job to do, and I want us to work as a team. Did Commander Knox give you that bullshit speech about being the 'face of the Navy' to millions of people?"

"Yes, sir."

"Well, that's just fine for him and his people, but from now on, you and I are the face of the Marines for these Hollywood types. If I have my way, we won't be playing second fiddle to the Navy anymore. It's going to be our own show, a Marine show. Do you understand, Dutch?"

"Yes, sir."

"Good. I'll go over your duties in more detail later. I've got a shitty schedule for today, so we'll have to do it tomorrow." Turning towards the door, he shouted, "Maggie, come in here, please."

Within seconds, the front office lady was standing in the doorway.

"Dutch, this is Margaret Meede -- or, as I call her, Maggie. She's my secret weapon and Girl Friday, and has been so for years. She'll help you get squared away."

Turning to Maggie he continued, "I'm going to try to get some sleep again. I have a luncheon at noon, so don't let me sleep past eleven-thirty. And, Maggie, get a table at the Derby for Dutch and me for tomorrow, and see if you can help the Lieutenant find some living quarters." Turning back to me, he concluded, "You're in good hands. I'll see you tomorrow for lunch."

Snapping to attention and saluting, I answered, "Aye, aye, sir," and smartly turned on my heels to leave.

Getting up from his desk, he walked to the door with me and put a hand on my shoulder. "Dutch, that military stuff is just fine when the brass is around, but not for everyday...okay?"

"Yes...sir."

Back in Margaret's office, she remarked, "I'm afraid you didn't catch the Colonel at his best. He had a late night at a film premier and then played polo with Jack Warner at six this morning. He works very hard for the Marines and I'm pleased you're here to help him. Did you just get in, this morning?"

"No, ma'am, last night. Would that be Jack Warner of Warner Brothers Studio?"

"Yes...but please don't keep calling me ma'am. You call me Maggie and I'll call you Dutch, if that's okay."

"Okay."

Maggie kept asking questions until she found out that I had slept at the train station, the night before, and had made my way to the studio without breakfast. She said her first mission was to find me a place to stay, which might take some doing, as apartments were hard to come by. She suggested that, while she made a few phone calls, I might want to step out for some breakfast. She went on to explain that there was a small Navy canteen at the end of the row of garden cottages, in the basement of the old photo studio building. "The food is good and the prices are right for OWI employees. Just tell them you're attached to us now."

As I made my way towards the photo building, my brain was on overload with information. Neither Commander Knox nor Colonel Ford had any idea why I was here. I had nothing to offer in the way of special talents they needed, and what they offered, I didn't want. And that part that Colonel Ford had said, about 'here you are and here you will stay,' scared the hell out of me. There had to be a way that I could get back into the war.

71

The Photo Studio was a two-story white stucco building with the same red roof tiles as the cottages. Just inside the main entrance was a stairwell with a sign and little arrow pointing down that read 'Navy Personnel Only'. Downstairs, I found a short hallway with open double doors at the end. Inside the doors was a small cafeteria with fifteen or twenty round tables and chairs on one side and a serving line on the other. There were only a few people sitting at the tables.

At the front of the line was a stack of metal trays, utensils, napkins and plastic glasses, just like the chow hall back at Camp Pendleton. The only difference was the sign above, which read: 'Breakfast 0700-1000 .35 cents - Lunch 1100-1400 .50 cents. Navy Personnel Only'.

Paying for a military meal would be a new experience for me. Taking what I needed, I moved down the short, empty chow line. Behind the line was a Second Class Petty Officer and one seaman dressed in cook's clothing.

Approaching the Petty Officer I smiled at him. He was an extraordinary looking man, with olive skin, a square jaw and jet-black eyes. He was tall and had a muscular body with near-perfect bone-white teeth. "Welcome, Lieutenant. You're a new face here. What can we do for you?"

"I just reported for duty with Colonel Ford in Cottage Seven. Is it too late to get some eggs?"

"Not at all, Lieutenant," he said, and slid a yellow paper across the line. "Here's the menu. Take a look and I'll get my roster to log you in."

When he returned, he took my name and my order, which he then handed off to the seaman by the grill. The PO explained that the cost of meals would be deducted from my pay on payday. With a grin, he added, "That way, my patrons don't have to fumble for change or worry about the tip." Extending his hand, he continued, "I'm Petty Officer Jack Malone. Welcome to my canteen."

I took his hand and shook it. "Thanks."

Looking more closely, I noticed his curly black hair and decided he might be Negro...but I wasn't sure, because he didn't have the strong facial features of most colored people. In any event, he had a special way about him, a personality that was both confident and straightforward.

He returned a second time, and set a glass of orange juice on my tray. "Can I ask you a question, Lieutenant?"

I nodded.

"Did you come up from the ranks, sir?"

The question caught me off guard. "Yes, I guess you could say that…but how did you know?"

"That gold rifleman's badge. You don't see many officers wearing that. It's impressive. Take a seat, sir, and I'll holler out when your breakfast is ready…And, Lieutenant, the coffee pot is always on. It's free, and you're always welcome to it."

I nodded my thanks, liking Petty Officer Malone right away.

After breakfast, I returned to the office, where Maggie was pleased to announce that she had found me an apartment only a mile from the studio. The landlord had told her it was a one-bedroom with a southern exposure, and that it rented for only forty dollars a month. Of this amount, the Marines would pay twenty-five dollars a month. She typed out the directions and told me to take the rest of the day off and be back at nine the next morning. Thanking her I said goodbye. Then I grabbed my duffle bag, swung it over my shoulder, and began walking towards the address.

The walk was refreshing on such a warm sunny morning, with the streets crowded with people doing their business. Many who passed me tipped their hats and gave me a smile, and I felt proud to be wearing my country's uniform. But also I felt guilty about being on this busy thoroughfare on such a bright, beautiful day while other Marines were fighting in distant lands. There had to be a way for me to join them.

When I met the landlord at the address, he showed me the furnished, second-story apartment. It was bigger, brighter and better than I had expected. The main room contained the living and dining areas, as well as a small kitchen. Off this room was an oversized bedroom with a bath. The apartment was even equipped with an electric refrigerator, stove and radio. After my living conditions of the past year, and then the barracks, these quarters were heaven. I signed the rental agreement and gave the landlord two months' rent in advance.

After unpacking and a quick trip to the corner market for some light grocery shopping, I sat down at the kitchen table to write letters to Laura and Uncle Roy. My letter to Laura was full of positive news and hope for the future. I even speculated that we might be able to see each other, with my new station in Hollywood. But deep down I knew how hard it would be for her to get air transportation from Alaska without military priority, and then what about the baby? Still, it was a good dream.

My letter to Roy had a much different tone. He had used his influence with the Navy to intervene in my life. I knew that, in his heart, he had done what he felt was best, but what was best for him was not best for me, and I let him know it. I closed the letter with a simple statement: 'It's my life, so let me find my own way, whatever way that might be.' Knowing Uncle Roy, I wasn't sure the letter would do any good, but I had to try.

After posting the letters, I came back, turned on the radio and opened a beer. As I stretched out on the couch, soft music flooded the room. Shadows of twilight danced across the walls, making strange patterns, and they were the last thing I remembered as I drifted off to sleep.

Fantasy Land

Returning to the cottage at nine, the next morning, I found Maggie busy working in a small room off her office. Thanking her for her help, I told her eagerly about my apartment.

She seemed pleased to hear how much I liked my quarters, and she explained that the little room she was working on would be my new office. It was tiny, about eight feet across and ten feet deep, with one small window that looked out onto the parking lot. Someone had supplied a gray metal desk and filing cabinet, and those two objects filled most of the little room. In front of the desk, there was just enough room for a single chair.

Maggie had been busy cleaning and stocking the office with supplies. Standing there, looking at the little office, I was saddened. The last thing in the world I wanted was a desk and an office.

She seemed to pick up on my mood. With an inquiring look, she remarked, "I know it's not much now, Dutch, but with some flowers and the desk lamp I have in the back, it'll be okay."

Smiling at her, I replied, "It's just fine Maggie. You've done a splendid job. I just can't see myself fighting this war from behind that damn gray flat top. Still, as the Colonel said, 'Here I am and here I'll stay.'

Maggie stared at me for a moment, then excused herself.

Sliding myself behind the desk, I ran my hands over its cool metal top, then opened and closed some of the drawers. Maggie soon reappeared with coffee and a beautiful colored-glass desk lamp. After fussing around for a few more minutes she sat down in the chair and commented, "Sometimes, Dutch, wars are fought with more than just guns and bullets. That's what we do here. We fight for the hearts and souls of the American people, so they know just what young men like you are doing to win this war. It's a big job worth doing right. I hope you'll come to understand this."

As she was speaking, I found myself thinking how beautiful and straightforward she was. Her words sounded genuine, as if they truly came from her heart as much as her head. My remarks about the war and the desk had disappointed her, and for this I apologized.

For the next two hours and three cups of coffee, Maggie and I got to know each other better. She answered many of my questions about Commander Knox, the OWI organization, and how our little Marine detachment fit in. When she talked about Colonel Ford, it was always with deep respect and admiration. He had been one of the true heroes of the first war, going to Europe as a Marine Second Lieutenant and returning two years later as a Major and Company Commander. After the war, he became one of the most powerful public relations people in Hollywood. To hear her tell it, he was individually responsible for the careers of such Hollywood film stars as Errol Flynn, Katharine Hepburn and Jimmy Stewart, to name just a few. He knew the town's players and how to make those players work for our mission -- a mission, she emphasized, as important as guns and butter. Later in our conversation, she told me that the little white cottages that were the OWI offices had been used as bungalows by movie stars back in the days of silent films. Our building had, at one time, been the cottage used by Mary Pickford. Maggie's office had been the parlor, the Colonel's office had been her bedroom, and my little office had been the maids' quarters. The bigger the star, the bigger the cottage, and we were lucky to have one of the biggest.

Maggie also gave me a tour of the kitchen, laundry facilities and large dressing room/bathroom behind the offices. In the late 1930's, the studio constructed new cottages on the other side of the lot and had planned to demolish these to make way for another sound stage, but then the war broke out. Uncle Sam now leased the buildings for a dollar per year for the duration. The whole story brought a new perspective to my surroundings, and I found myself thinking, If only these walls could talk.

Time seemed to slip away, but then it always does when you're enjoying good company. At one point, in mid-sentence, Maggie jumped to her feet, saying, "Gosh, Dutch, its eleven-thirty and you have to be at the Derby by noon." She paused for a moment, looking at me, and then continued, "Do you have any idea what the Brown Derby is?"

Looking up at her, I smiled. "I'm guessing it's a restaurant, since I'm meeting the Colonel for lunch."

"It's more than just a restaurant, Dutch, It's where the '*who's who*' of this town meet and eat. You can't be late."

"Can you give me directions? Can I walk there in a half hour? If not, please call a taxi for me."

Now she was smiling at me. "Walk? Taxi? No one walks in Hollywood, and cabs are harder to find than apartments. Come on. I'll drive you there while we talk about getting you a car."

She drove a 1940 black Buick two-door. It was a luxurious car and still smelled new. On the way, she asked if I could afford a car and, if so, what my budget might be. With the war on, only used cars were available, and even they could be hard to find, but she had a friend who might be able to help me out.

I told her that I had no idea what cars cost, but that I could afford whatever she thought was reasonable.

She turned to me with a puzzled smile. "Really? How refreshing. I didn't realize Second Lieutenants made that kind of money."

Looking back at her with a grin, I said, "You might call it an enlistment bonus my family gave me. Whatever you think is fair, will be okay with me."

When we pulled up in front of the Brown Derby restaurant, I started to get out of the car, but Maggie reached over and touched my arm, stopping me. When I turned back to look at her, she remarked, "Break a leg, Dutch. You're going to be great at this job. I'll see you later."

I returned her smile, slid out of the car, and watched her pull away. Maggie was one amazing and resourceful lady, and I could see why she was Colonel Ford's secret weapon. The only thing I didn't understand was the 'break a leg' part.

The Brown Derby could only have fit into the fantasy world of Hollywood. Part of the building was shaped like an upright derby hat some three stories tall, fashioned out of brown-painted concrete. It was a bizarre-looking structure, with a blinking neon sign on top. Walking through the main door I thought, if this is where the celebrities and politicians hang out, my country is in trouble! A stuffy-looking man, dressed in a tux, guarded the dining room entrance and looked down his nose at me as I approached.

"May I help you, Lieutenant?"

"Yes. I'm here to meet Colonel Ford for lunch."

"Colonel Ford?" He paused, looking uncertain, then said, "Oh, yes. Mr. Lennie Ford. He's at his table." He snapped his fingers.

A waiter appeared and was told to take me to Mr. Ford's table in the California Room. This particular dining room was located under the concrete derby. The room was massive, with tables on the main level arranged around a small dance floor and bandstand. The second level was three or four steps up, and had rows of tables with white linens and silverware. All of them were taken by people drinking and talking.

The last level up had a long row of leather booths, all facing out into the room. Here I found Colonel Ford sitting alone, in uniform, sipping a martini. As I slid into the booth, the waiter handed me a menu, which I placed on the table.

"I hope I'm not late, Colonel."

"No, you're fine. I got here a little early, to go over your 214 file. Did you have any trouble finding the Derby?"

"No, sir. Miss Meede drove me...or is it Mrs. Meede?"

"It's Miss. That was nice of her. I was afraid you might get lost in such a big city, after your year in the wilderness. Someday you will have to tell me why any young man would waste a year of his life living in a rainforest, like Tarzan." He nodded at the menu on the table. "You better take a look. It takes forever to get chow here."

"Yes, sir."

Looking at the items offered on the menu, I couldn't help thinking that the boys back at Camp Pendleton would have loved this place. The Derbyburger was two bucks, and you could order it cooked or raw! I had never seen food or prices so outrageous.

As I was perusing the list of options, a distinguished-looking gentleman approached our booth. "Lennie? Is that you? I've never seen you in uniform. You look grand. You should do it more often. Are you coming to the premiere tonight? If so, let's have a drink afterwards. I have a project you might find interesting."

"I'll be there, Harry. See you after the show, at Carmen's."

Nodding approval, Harry continued on to the next booth, to talk to the people at that table.

The Colonel turned to me. "That's Harry Watt of RKO. He always has a project he thinks I might like, but all the scripts so far have been about the Navy or the Army. He just doesn't understand that a film about Marines is the only project I'm interested in."

The Colonel did look good in his uniform, with his silver oak leaves and four rows of colorful battle ribbons on his chest. But these awards weren't just colorful; they told me the measure of the man. I could make out the Navy Cross, Bronze Star and Purple Heart, to name just three of the twelve. Those ribbons were only given to men who had performed with courage in battle. He and they were impressive.

Just then, the waiter appeared to take our order. The Colonel ordered his 'usual' and another martini, while I ordered the Cobb Salad, with an iced tea.

The Colonel glared across the table at me. "I don't like to drink alone. Have something stronger."

"Yes, sir." Turning back to the waiter, I amended, "I'll have a Falstaff beer."

The waiter disappeared as quickly as he had come.

Looking back at the Colonel, I commented, "They all seem to know you here, sir."

"They should. I have lunch here two or three times a week. Hell, I was here the first day it opened, back in '26. I even helped convince Jack Warner to put up the money to expand the place, a few years back."

"They seem surprised to see you in uniform, sir."

"Yeah, the clowns around this town think a uniform is something you get from the wardrobe department. But enough about me. Let's talk about our mission, and how you'll fit it."

Thus began my briefing about our mission and what the Colonel expected of me. The bottom line was that roughly twenty million people went to the movies, each week. The four major studios -- MGM, Paramount, Warner Brothers and RKO -- produced over two hundred feature films a year, to satisfy this audience's appetite. In 1941, only a handful of those films had been produced with a military storyline. This year, 1942, over thirty-five productions would deal with the war, and the Colonel speculated that in 1943 that number would double or triple.

It was our job to make as many of these films as possible have a Marine theme and, when they did, to make sure the depiction was accurate. To accomplish this mission we would wine and dine the studio big shots. The Colonel would do the actual wining and dining, while I did the leg work and follow-up.

Another part of our mission was to stage public relations events with a variety of celebrities and Marines. Those events would be covered by the press and could help with recruitment. As a case in point, a week from Saturday, the USO Hollywood

Canteen would have an 'All-Marine Night.' The Canteen had already had All-Navy, All-Army and All-Air Corps nights, so this would be the first for the USMC. The party would be hosted by a movie-star-turned-Marine by the name of Glenn Ford, along with any other top celebrities we could enlist. The hosts would entertain and serve the men, while cameras documented the party. Pictures of the event would end up in newsreels, newspapers and magazines throughout America.

As the Colonel remarked, "Mix Hollywood celebrities with Marines and we'll stampede the boys to the recruiting stations."

The final part of our mission was to help sell war bonds. Working again with the celebrities and some selected politicians, we would stage different events to promote and sell the bonds. A few weeks earlier, OWI had staged a parade of a dozen movie stars down Hollywood Boulevard and had sold over two million dollars' worth of bonds. We would conduct this same sort of event, on a smaller scale, at department stores, restaurants, factories, and movie premieres. Our job was to enlist the celebrities, select the venues and stage the events.

During this ninety-minute briefing, I consumed three beers while the Colonel belted down four martinis, two of which were paid for by different people who stopped by the table to chat. The Colonel seemed to know everyone, and everyone seemed to like him.

As he finished the briefing, he looked across the table at me. "Well, there you have it, Dutch. It's a hell of an opportunity for a young man like you. You'll be going places, seeing things and working with movies stars that most people only dream of meeting. But I have to warn you, this town is full of people who lie, cheat and steal. I call them the 'land mines,' and unfortunately most of these land mines are the celebrities themselves. Keep your eyes and ears open, and only believe half of what you see or hear. Got it?"

"Aye, aye, sir."

"Oh…and one more thing. When you get back to the office, you will find a new camera outfit on your desk. I ordered it last month and it came in yesterday, just like you. Must be destiny.

From now on, you'll be doing all the photography for our events. Before you and the camera arrived, I had to go to Commander Knox to get a photographer. He'd send me a Navy Signalman, which was fine, but the pictures that came back were always full of Navy personnel. I want our pictures full of Marine personnel so, from now on, you'll be doing the photography."

With a sinking feeling in my gut, I looked across at the Colonel, trying to absorb what he had just said. Finally, I broke the silence. "Colonel, I know nothing about photography! The only camera I ever used was a Kodak Brownie, and most of those pictures were blurry. I'm sure you can do a lot better than me, in this town full of photographers."

Frowning back at me, he said, "Well, Dutch, you better learn and learn fast. Consider it on-the-job training. And I expect all my pictures to be in focus. Do you understand, Lieutenant?"

"Yes, sir."

"Talk to Maggie. Maybe she can help you find a photography instructor. Do you have any questions?"

Trying to change the subject to something lighter, I said, "Yes sir. I was wondering how you met Maggie, and what she did before going to work for you."

An enormous smile raced across his face, "She's quite a gal. I met her in 1928, over at MGM. She was twenty-six then, doing some dancing and walk-on roles. I used her in a couple projects and thought she was a hell of a lot more intelligent than most dancers. One day, I told her I needed help staging an event, and she volunteered. That was the last time I needed to look for help. She's been with me ever since. As I said, she's my secret weapon." He paused a moment, and his smile turned serious as he continued, "She's too old for you, Dutch. And anyway, I don't think she likes men in the amorous way. Well, we have to get out of here. I have an appointment at two-thirty."

His reply caught me off-guard, since I hadn't been asking about her for personal reasons. And that remark about not liking men 'in the amorous way...' What the hell was that all about? I felt my face go flush with embarrassment, and didn't know what to say, other than, "Aye, aye, sir."

As I looked up to slide out of the booth, a lady approached our table, shouting, "Lennie, darling, is that you? God, you are one good-looking soldier!"

She was a vivacious woman wearing a tight, revealing, yellow sundress with more cleavage than I had ever seen. From the layers of makeup on her attractive face, I knew she had to be a celebrity.

The Colonel stood up and threw his arms around her in a big hug. "Carole! How nice to see you. Don't you look spectacular in that dress!"

Carole turned her face my way and asked, "Lennie, who is this fine-looking young soldier with you?"

"This is Lieutenant Dutch Clarke. He just came to work for me. Lieutenant, this, of course, is Ms. Carole Lane. I'm sure you know her from all of her films."

Getting on my feet, I fumbled for an answer, since I had never seen or heard of her before. Finally, I lied, "Yes, I certainly do. It's very nice meeting you, Miss. Lane."

When she extended her hand to me, I didn't know whether to kiss it or shake it, so I did the latter.

"Sweetie," she said, "you can call me Carole." She smiled and winked at me.

I could feel the eyes of people around our table staring, and it made me feel uncomfortable.

Finally, the Colonel asked, "So, Carole, are you coming to our party at the Hollywood Canteen, a week from Saturday? We really need a sexy star like you to entertain all the Marines that'll be there. What do you say?"

Reaching out again, she recaptured my hand and asked, "Will you be there, Dutch?"

"He'll be there," the Colonel stated before I could speak. "He's our official photographer."

"Oh, I love photographers. You can count on me, Lennie." Turning to leave, she stopped and turned back to me. "See you there, Dutch. Maybe you can take some new publicity photos for me. God knows, I need them!"

"Yes, Miss Lane. I'll look forward to seeing you again."

As she walked away, most of the eyes in the restaurant watched her jiggle across room.

Looking back at the Colonel, I remarked, "That's quite a woman..."

He whispered, "Remember those 'land mines' I talked about? Well, she's one of them. When she reached thirty, her career started rolling downhill like a snowball, so be careful. The older actresses, like Carole, love young bucks like you. They'll wear you like a trophy and throw you out with the trash."

It took almost a half hour to hail a cab on Wilshire Boulevard. Maggie was right: depending on cabs was a fool's errand. Leaning back in the seat, I rolled down the window and let the warm air wash over my face. My head was still spinning with information and details that I didn't fully understand. What kind of shit hole had I fallen into? I worked for a command that believed propaganda was more powerful than bullets, my commanding officer had martinis running through his veins, and I was working in a town full of liars and cheats. And, to top it all off, I was supposed to be thrilled about the whole thing, and show my appreciation by taking pictures!

I hadn't joined the Marines to meet movie stars, drink booze or become a photographer. I had joined to defend my country and kill Japs! Colonel Jacobs had been right when he described this duty: 'Cocktail parties, celebrities and politicians, a hell of a way to run a war. God help the United States of America.'

CHAPTER THREE

66 "Try, Dutch. Please try," he whispered again.
I nodded, and his face mirrored his relief, but my
decision didn't relieve my doubts. York, Patterson, and the Padre
were all staring at me. Hope was all we had, and I hoped I'd made
the right decision.

Looking at them, I finally said, "I'll try...but let's give it some
time. Maybe the sea will flatten down a little. There is no way I
can go digging for the bullet with this raft bobbing around."

They nodded their agreement.

Crawling to the other end of the raft, I rummaged through the
dead Jap's belongings. The night before, I had stripped his dead
body of all his worldly possessions before rolling his naked
remains back into the sea. There was a pair of trousers, a shirt, an
undershirt, boots and a cartridge belt. He must have lost his rifle to
the sea, but hanging from the belt was his scabbard bayonet and, a
cartridge pouch with two clips of ammunition. Most importantly,
his canteen was still half-full of water. We'd each had a mouthful
of it, the night before, and I figured if we were careful that we had
enough for a couple more days. After that, God only knew what we
would do for drinking water.

Reaching down, I removed the bayonet and examined it
closely. The knife was fairly sharp, and pointed at the end. Using
the backside of the cartridge belt like a razor strop, I began
sharpening the blade even further. While my hands worked, my
mind planned the procedure. If the bullet wasn't too deep, maybe I
could dislodge it with the point of the bayonet, though I had no
way to suture up the wound if I removed it. Well, I could pack the

hole with strips of cloth from the undershirt and then tie it down with other bandages made from the trousers. But what if the wound was deep? What if the raft moved while I had the knife deep inside his shoulder? I had no antiseptics, so what if he got an infection? I supposed I could use sea water to clean the knife, the wound and the bandages.

And what if we didn't do anything? Would he die?

There were just too many 'what ifs' for comfort.

By mid-morning, the sea had calmed a little. With the sun getting hot, I decided it was time to try. Looking across to my mates, I gave instructions for York, Patterson, and the Padre to sit with their backs against the long side of the raft, and to lay Corporal Bates face-down across their laps. Before we started, I gave the Corporal a swig of sweet water and asked if he still wanted me to try. With a forced half-smile on his face, he nodded again.

"When you get him over your laps, hold on tight. I don't want him flinching around when I have the knife in him."

It took a few moments to get him laid out. He groaned with pain at the slightest movement of his upper body. Kneeling down in front of the men, I cut away the blood- and salt-stained rag the Corporal was using as a shirt. Using part of the Jap's undershirt, I used sea water to wash away the dried blood so that I could get a better look at the entry hole.

The Padre started reciting Psalm Twenty-Three: "Though I walk through the valley of the shadow of death...I will fear no evil..."

Looking up at Jasper, I smiled and nodded. Using my finger, I probed around the wound again, and this time I thought I felt the bullet, close to the entry hole. Taking some rags, I wrapped the bayonet's upper blade so that I could hold it. Using the pointed end, I slowly probed the opening.

The Corporal let out a groan, but his body did not move.

About an inch in, I found the bullet, lodged in what remained of his back muscle. Taking the knife, I cut small slits in the skin and muscle around the hole. With each slice, I heard him cry out with pain, but again his body didn't move. With little or no blood coming from the wound, I probed with the knife at a small angle.

Soon, I found the bullet's pointed tip. Sliding my little finger down into the hole, I used it and the point of the knife to pull and drag the slug out.

Bates let out a loud scream, and then his whole body went limp.

Jesus, did I kill this kid?

"Does he have a pulse?" I shouted.

The Padre answered, "Dutch, he's fine. I think he just passed out."

Working fast, I packed the wound tightly with a slender twelve-inch strip of cloth to act as a wick, with one end hanging outside of the wound. Using other pieces of clothing, I bandaged the wound as best I could and tied the whole area off with the trousers. It wasn't neat or pretty, but it was as good a job as I could do with the tools I had.

Letting my body fall back against the opposite rail of the raft, I asked, "How's his pulse?"

"Strong and constant, thank the Lord," replied the Padre.

The sight of these four pathetic souls reminded me of the blessings of life. It is so precious that we fight until death not to lose it. With my hands shaking with relief, all I could think was, *Thank you, dear Lord, for guiding my hands and mind....*

New Horizons

The office was quiet and deserted when I returned. As promised, on top of my desk was a large case that held the new camera outfit. On top of the case was a note from Maggie, saying she had some errands to run for the Colonel and would see me the next morning. She ended the note with an interesting comment: 'Here's the opportunity the Colonel talked about. Maybe you can find your future with this camera.'

Sitting down at the desk, I pondered her remarks, as I had no idea how opportunities, futures and cameras might work together. Opening the case, I found an olive-drab folded box-camera, a large tube with a polished reflector, and many other assorted accessories. The instruction manual was neatly folded in the case lid. Taking the hundred-and-twenty-page manual out, I read the cover: 4x5 Speed Graphic Camera Model 1940. Shaking my head in disbelief, I returned the manual to the case, closed the lid and snapped it shut. Sitting in the quiet office, I felt lost. How could I possibility learn photography in a week? Still, I knew the manual was the starting point, so I decided to walk to the cafeteria for some coffee and a little reading.

Lugging the heavy camera case into the canteen, I found an Oriental cook behind the line, cleaning the stove.

"Hello Lieutenant. Sorry, we're closed."

"I just came in for some coffee. Is the pot still on?"

"Sure. It might not be fresh but it's hot and black."

Walking over to the pot, I poured a cup and asked, "Is the boss still here?"

"Black Jack? Yeah, he's still here. Do you want me to get him for you, sir?"

"Are we talking about Petty Officer Malone? I don't know him as Black Jack."

"Sorry, sir. That's his nickname. I shouldn't be using it with officers. I just thought everyone knew. Do you want me to get him, sir?"

"No. I just wanted to say hello and thank him for the coffee. Don't bother him."

Taking my coffee I moved to a table and placed the camera outfit on it. Opening the case, I removed the manual and started reading while drinking the stale brew.

Some moments later, I heard, "Hi, Lieutenant. I thought that was your voice."

Looking up, I found the PO coming my way, with a large smile on his face.

As he got to the table, he concluded, "What do you have there? Looks like a new camera."

I smiled back. "From what the manual says, it's a 4x5 Speed Graphic Camera, Model 1940…but it's still a mystery to me."

Looking down at the outfit, he remarked, "Wow! I've never seen a C6 in olive drab before."

"C6? What's a C6?"

"It's what the military calls this type of camera. Can I take a look, sir?"

"Sure. Sounds like you know a lot more about it than me."

Within moments, he had the camera out of the case. Opening it, he examined how it worked, holding the camera up to his eye. "First time I've held this model. There are lots of improvements. Better lens…better focusing system…and its got that new focal plane shutter that goes to 1/1000 of a second. This is quite a camera, Lieutenant! Did you just get it, sir?"

"Yeah. It appeared on my desk, this afternoon. Colonel Ford has given me the duty of unit photographer, but the only camera I've ever used was a Kodak Brownie. I've never seen such a camera like this. How do you know so much about photography?"

Putting the camera down on the table, he said, with a look of pride, "Photography is what I did before the Navy got hold of me. In 1937, I was a photographer for TIME Magazine. Then, in '38 and '39, I worked as a cameraman for a film production company in Chicago. But that was a long time ago, sir."

His answer made no sense to me. Why would such an experienced photographer be slinging hash in a chow hall like this? I searched for the correct words, as I didn't want to embarrass him. "So…how did you end up as a cook in the Navy?"

His expression turned from pride to resolve. "In 1940, when I joined the Navy, the recruiters told me that I'd be made a Signalman. But after basic training I was sent off to cook's school instead. Guess the Admirals don't want colored folks as photographers. My two-year hitch was up this year, but because of the war they won't let me out. And to pour salt in the wound, they put me in charge of this cafeteria in the middle of the industry I wanted to work for. So I'm stuck here…but it's okay. Light hours and light duty." He shrugged. "Sorry, Lieutenant. I didn't mean to bend your ear. Guess I'm just letting off some steam."

"Don't worry about it. Can you join me for a minute? I'd like to pick your brain about photography."

Sliding a chair out next to me, he sat down and we talked for almost an hour, mostly about the assignments he had done for TIME Magazine. He talked about the different cameras he had used over the years, and how he'd experimented with smaller-format cameras that used 35MM film. These small cameras were much better for what he called 'photojournalism.' He seemed to know all the camera brands and models, which ones worked and which ones didn't. He was a fountain of information.

At one point, the conversation turned back to his duties as a cook, and why the Navy did what they did.

"It's not just me, Lieutenant. Take Seaman Riku, over there cleaning the stove. He's Nisei, a Japanese American, born right here in L.A. in '21. Can read and write both English and Japanese fluently. Went to Hollywood High School and then on to UCLA to study film production. In early 1941, he saw the war clouds coming, dropped out of college and joined the Navy to be a translator. But he ended up in cook school, too. But it's worse for him. They won't even give him sea duty, because he's Japanese."

"It must be rough to be Japanese American in these times," I agreed. "Seaman Riku told me your nickname. Do they call you Black Jack because you're a Negro?"

With a broad smile on his face, he said, "No. When I was working in the South for the magazine, I did a lot of assignments in the slums. The poor folks there could roll ya for a stick or a stone, so I started carrying a blackjack for protection. People soon were calling me the 'blackjack photographer.' I never lost a camera or the nickname."

"Do you still carry one?"

"A sap? Yes, sir, I do, but it's out of habit, not fear. Don't think anyone in the canteen would mug me for my apple pies!"

With his big-shouldered physique, I respected Black Jack Malone right away. He was intelligent and resourceful, with a good sense of humor. From the look of him, I was convinced that he was able to take care of himself, too.

Finally, I got up the nerve to ask him if he would be willing to give me a few photography lessons.

He hesitated for a moment and then, with a big grin, answered, "Sure. Why not?"

He went on to explain that we would need to buy some supplies and yet more camera accessories for the lessons. We agreed to meet at Cameron's Camera Shop on Wilshire Boulevard on Saturday morning.

As I was getting ready to leave, a serious look crossed Jack's face. "Can I ask you a question, Lieutenant?"

"Sure…but please call me Dutch."

With a surprised look on his face, he said, "Okay, Dutch. If you say so. When did you get your commission?"

Getting to my feet, I admitted, "Last Saturday morning, I was just a recruit going off to advance weapons training. By that afternoon, they'd promoted me to Lieutenant and sent me here. The whole thing was just one big Marine snafu! So I'm stuck here, just like you." Rolling the camera manual into my pocket, I reached out and shook his hand. "See you Saturday morning at Cameron's. And thanks for helping me out."

With a twinkle in his eyes, he nodded. "You bring the camera, I'll bring the knowledge, and we'll have you shooting like a pro in no time."

Dropping off the camera outfit at the office, I started the walk home. My thoughts kept going back to the Black Jack and Seaman Riku. All day, I had pissed and moaned to myself about my lot…and then I met them. Prejudice had raised its ugly head and really shafted these two guys. Maybe it was time for me to change my attitude and start having some fun with this snafu. And maybe, just maybe, along the way I could help these guys, as well. If the Marines wanted me as a photographer, then I was determined to become the Leonardo da Vinci of photography.

The next morning, when I arrived at the office, I found Maggie on the phone. Looking up from her note pad, she smiled and nodded at me. Walking into my office I unrolled the manual from my pocket, and laid it on my desk. It was starting to look 'dog-eared,' as I had read it from cover to cover twice during the previous night. Sliding behind the desk, I removed the camera from its case and opened it. It was time to put the words to practice.

There were dozens of little metal stops, gears, levers, knobs and tracks that made the camera work. In the course of the next few minutes, I surprised myself with my basic understanding of how it all worked. It was really just a light-tight box with a lens at one end. All those metal parts simply controlled the box and the lens.

My mind was deep into the levers and gears when Maggie broke the silence from my doorway. "That was the Colonel on the phone. He's in San Diego today, making travel arrangements for the soldiers coming up to next weekend's party. He wants to know if you have any friends down there you would like to invite. If you do, please give me their names and units. When he calls back, this afternoon, I'll pass it on to him."

I smiled to myself at the thought of Kurt, Hank, and the Comedian. I knew they loved to party. Maybe I'd even include Sergeant Nelson, if he could get away.

"Sure," I said, "I have three or four. I'll write them down for you...and good morning, Maggie."

"And good morning to you, Dutch," she said with a sheepish look. "I'm sorry about that. I'm just not used to having someone in the office with me...but I like it. Let me get you some coffee."

When she returned, I had the list written out, and handed it to her. Sitting on the corner of my desk, she had other news for me. The friend that had helped her buy her Buick was going to help me find a car. He would be calling her back later in the day.

As she sat there, talking about cars, I realized again how beautiful she was. Her makeup looked natural and, while her figure was full, she tastefully disguised it. She was just the opposite of Carole Lane, for Maggie was elegant in both dress and manner. That remark the Colonel had made about men and the 'amorous way' kept racing through my mind. I just couldn't understand it.

"Oh," she remarked, "the Colonel said you would need some help with the photography. How's it going?"

Holding the camera in my hands, I told her about Chief Malone and the lessons he'd agreed to give me. She was surprised to hear of his talents, and pleased that he would help. That, in turn, brought up the subject of the supplies and accessories I would need, and how I could get them.

"Simple" she said. "You give me a list of what you need. I'll type out a requisition form and send it to Headquarters. They'll send it to Supply, and Supply will send back what you need, or a voucher so you can purchase it locally."

"And how long will that take?"

"Usually two or three weeks."

"That won't do. The Colonel wants me shooting by next weekend. Guess I'll just buy what I need, for the next few weeks. I'll wait on giving you that list until I see what Chief Malone suggests."

"That's what most of us do. When the Colonel and I first started here, it took four weeks to get three typewriter ribbons. Now I order them in case lots and have over fifty ribbons in my desk. If you need some cash, I can help out."

"No, I think I'll be all right…but thanks for offering. But I will need to open a bank account. Any suggestions?"

Right after lunch, Maggie's car guy called and told her he'd found two possibilities. One was a 1940 Ford four-door sedan with 23,000 miles, for $1,250. The other was a 1939 Chrysler Royal two-door coupe with just 9,000 miles, for $1,300.

He said the Chrysler had been stored in a garage since 1940 and still smelled new. Seems the owner had been a pilot with the Air Corps but had been killed at Hickam Field on December 7th. His parents had kept the car in storage and only agreed to sell it when they found out that another solider needed it.

I was definitely interested in that coupe.

After lunch, Maggie and I both talked to Colonel Ford on the phone. She passed on the information I had written out, and I asked him if there were any further instructions for me. He just kept going on about my photography and how important it was for me to be ready for the USO event. I assured him I would be prepared.

After talking to the Colonel, Maggie drove me to a local bank, where I opened a new account. Using the last of my Ketchikan fishing money, I transferred just over three thousand dollars from my savings account in New Jersey to my new checking account. The next stop was Western Union, where I wired Uncle Roy, asking for another three thousand and giving him the banking information. I closed the telegram with a smart ass comment:

'Being an officer is getting expensive. Look at the money we could have saved!'

Our last stop was my apartment, where I asked Maggie if she would like to come up, see it, and have a beer.

With a funny look on her face, she said, "I don't think so, Dutch. Maybe some other time."

I had the urge to reach out to her and ask again, but I didn't.

The next morning, when I arrived at the office, I found a very large man sipping coffee and talking to Maggie.

"Good morning, Dutch. I would like you to meet John Craft, my friend that helps me out with cars. John, this is Lieutenant Dutch Clarke, your customer."

When he got up from his chair, I was astounded by his size. He was enormous, standing well over six foot ten, and he looked to weigh well over three hundred pounds. He had no neck and his face was round, with a rough complexion and a dark beard that hid his chin.

He extended his hand. "Hello, Lieutenant. Nice meeting you."

Taking his hairy hand, I was amazed by the sheer size of it. He was dressed in a business suit that had seen better days and, when he talked, the whole room filled with his low, gravelly voice.

"Good morning, Maggie. And hello, Mr. Craft. Did you bring the car?"

"Sure did, Lieutenant. It's out in the parking lot. Would you like to see it?'

"Sure."

My first impression of it wasn't the best. The car's color was Marine green, or maybe Army brown, or somewhere in-between. It had black-wall tires and black rubber running boards on both sides. Its shape was small, with a pointed front end and tapered back. In short, it was a funny looking car.

But when he opened the door and I slid behind the driver's seat, my impression changed. It did smell new, and the soft cloth upholstery was as clean and fresh as it must have been on the showroom floor. The front bench seat was big enough for three, and there were two small jump seats behind the front bench.

John handed me the keys and told me to start it up. It started on the first crank, and the motor ran as smoothly as warm butter on hot toast.

He launched into his best car pitch. "She's a real honey. Power assisted steering, power windows -- hell, even the dash lights turn colors. From zero to thirty, they're green, from thirty to fifty, yellow, and after fifty, red. It's a stick shift with what they call 'overdrive' for highway performance. That's good, with gas rationing. It's as straight as an arrow, Lieutenant."

Turning off the engine, I walked to the back of the car and opened the trunk. It was big enough to carry not only the spare tire but also any camera equipment and duffle bags I might have. Moving to the front, I opened the hood to find a flat head six engine so clean that the spark plug wires still had a factory sheen.

The car salesman in Mr. Craft just couldn't stop. "With the war on, you just don't find cars like this. Chrysler only made four thousand of this model. It might be a 1939, but '39 was the best year Chrysler ever had, and with these low miles you should get years out of this baby. What do you think, Lieutenant?"

There was no point in being coy. "I'll take it."

We went back into the office, where we did the paper work and I paid Mr. Craft.

After he left, I said to Maggie, "Thanks again for your help. I love the car. That Mr. Craft is an unusual guy, a real giant of a man. I wouldn't want to meet him in a dark alley."

"He's not what you think. Truly, he's the gentlest, kindest man I've ever met. Our first perceptions of people aren't always correct."

Looking into to her, pleasant face, I thought, Isn't that the truth!

Having a car might have been a luxury that I needed for my job, but taking care of all the paperwork was a pain in the butt. The rest of the day was spent registering it with the state, getting insurance, securing a parking permit from the studio, and then accruing gas ration coupons at OWI Headquarters. Nevertheless, driving my new coupe from place to place was a real joy, and by day's end I had bonded with the car and couldn't understand how I'd ever lived without it.

In Focus

On Saturday morning, I met Black Jack at Cameron's Camera Shop. When I entered the store, I saw that Jack was already there and talking to a man at the front counter. As I approached, Back Jack introduced me to Ed Cameron, the proprietor. He was a funny-looking little man with a skinny body and a neatly trimmed reddish-blond beard. His nose was large and straight, dominating his face. On this nose, he wore pince-nez glasses over his pale green eyes. He reminded me of the little guy on the beach, in the cartoons, the one that always had sand kicked in his face.

His store, however, was big, and it clearly catered to professional photographers and film makers. Jack had given him a written list of what we needed, so we followed him around as he filled our order. We purchased what was called a 'changing bag,' a wooden tripod, a dozen 4X5 film holders, two fifty-sheet boxes of 4x5 film, a case of flash bulbs, and an instrument called a light meter. This last item must have been important, because Ed showed Black Jack three different models before he decided on one. During this shopping, Ed and Jack talked photography, so their conversation was mostly Greek to me.

Finally, with all our items on the front counter, Ed totaled up the sales ticket and slid it across the counter to me.

"If you're using a voucher, Lieutenant, I'll need to copy down all the information."

The total cost of our few items astounded me: $133.50.

"Wow. That's a lot of money! I'm not using a voucher. I'll be paying with a personal check."

Ed looked up at me, and for the first time a smile crossed his face. "Okay, Lieutenant, then I can give you a discount of twenty percent for cash."

Reaching for my checkbook, I asked, "Why such a generous discount?"

"Simple. It takes hours to do the paper work for purchases made with a government voucher, and then we wait three or four months for payment. Cash is king, in my store."

Sliding a check across the counter, I remarked, "I'll remember that."

Black Jack asked, "Do you have a 35mm Leica in?"

"No. They're European-made. We can't get any new ones, with the war on. We do get a few used ones in, from time to time, but I don't have any now," Ed replied.

"Well, keep me in mind if a good Model III comes in. I sold my model II in '39, and now I wish I'd kept it."

Opening the trunk of my car, I placed the new items next to the camera case. "Where do we go now, Jack?"

"Wow, I like your car, Dutch. Is this from the motor pool?"

Looking down at it, I knew the color would make people think it was a military vehicle, but I didn't care. "No, I bought it yesterday. It may look Marine green, but it's all mine."

With a large smile on his face, Black Jack replied, "Well, Dutch, at least it matches the color of your camera. How about driving us over to the Zoo, and I'll give you your first photography lesson."

"Why the Zoo?"

"Because that's where the penguins are."

"Penguins? Why penguins?"

"You'll find out soon enough."

Sitting at a picnic table, under the shade of a large ash tree, Black Jack Malone gave me my very first photography lesson. He started by telling me that the word photography came from the ancient Greek language, that it meant 'to write with light,' and that light was the essence of all photography. He had brought along a general book on photography and used it to illustrate the concepts of light, film types, exposure control, focusing, flash, and more. Next, he mounted the open olive-drab camera on the tripod and explained in great detail all the workings of the Speed Graphic. While his instructions were precise, they were given with a great deal of patience, and he answered all of my questions, making complicated concepts easy to understand. Jack was a born teacher, and he made learning fun. Time just flew by.

After a lunch of hot dogs and Cokes, we went to the penguins' cage. Here he explained that the secret of working with black-and-white film was correct exposure control.

"The Penguins have three colors -- black, white, and a golden stripe on their nose. If we expose them correctly, our negatives will have three opposite shades: white, black and gray. This exercise will teach you to look at your negatives for whites, blacks and then the one-hundred-eighty-six shades of gray in-between. Do you understand, Dutch?"

"I think so."

Using the light meter we had just purchased, Jack helped me select the correct exposure. Then I shot four pictures, two using just daylight and two using flash bulbs as what Jack called a 'fill light'.

Next, we went to the peacock cage, where we performed the same setup.

"The negatives of the peacocks should have small amounts of black and white, with lots of shades of gray. When you put the negatives of the penguins side by side with the peacocks, you should see a big difference."

I was feeling a bit lost, but I didn't want to admit it.

It was late afternoon when we started the drive back to Hollywood. The ride was quiet, with my mind swimming with thoughts of photography. This assignment was more complicated than I had expected, with too much to learn and too little time.

Black Jack must have been reading my mind, for he broke the silence. "Photography will come to you, Dutch. Don't let the concepts bog you down. Once you've mastered the mechanics, you can concentrate on your subjects and the pictures you're taking. That's the fun part."

"I know you're right, Jack, but the Colonel hasn't given me much time."

The car fell silent again.

As we approached the city, my thoughts turned to appreciation for Black Jack, who was so willingly giving me his time and expertise. The thought of offering him money crossed my mind, but I wasn't sure how he would react to it.

Finally, I said, "Thanks, Jack, for all your help today. I'd like to buy you a drink and a good meal. What do you say?"

"You don't have to do that, Lieutenant. Today was an awakening for me. I hadn't realized how much I missed photography."

"Please, just call me Dutch. And I want to. How about if we stop off at the Brown Derby?"

It was the only restaurant I knew.

With a shocked look on his face, he answered, "The Derby...they don't serve colored folks there, Dutch. But I know a little Mexican place where the drinks are good, the food's better, and people of all colors can sit down together."

His comment caught me off-guard. Prejudice had raised its ugly head again.

"Okay," I assured him, "you're on."

Our conversation, over Mexican beers and margaritas, was warm and interesting. Jack told fascinating stories about his assignments in the Deep South at the height of the Depression. He talked about pictures he had taken that were sad, heartwarming and sometimes uplifting. He was proud of his work. When I asked questions about his family or personal life, he always found a way to turn it back to me. That part of Black Jack Malone seemed to be a closed book.

With all of his questions about my life, he seemed genuinely interested and so, for the first time since joining the Marines, I told him a little of my story of survival. He loved the part about Laura giving birth in the wilderness, and about my dog, Gus, and my horse, Blaze. But one thing was unusual. He never asked me why I spent that year in British Columbia. I guess he thought that would be prying into my private business.

He had been right about the restaurant: its patrons were of all races, and the food was even better than the drinks. The Mexican meal I had was the best ever.

As we were getting ready to leave, I remembered a question I had forgotten.

"Where should I take the film to be developed?"

Leaning back in his chair, he sipped the last of his margarita and replied, "You have three choices. The Navy has a small lab in Cottage Four, but I wouldn't trust the Signal Corps with my film.

You can drive it over to Ed Cameron's. He has a good lab in the back, but he'll charge you an arm and a leg. Or you can try Paul Barnett, who runs the still lab for the studio. He really knows his stuff. If you decide to ask him, tell him we're friends and take a bottle of Chivas Regal. He loves that Scotch."

As usual, Black Jack Malone was a fountain of knowledge.

First thing Monday morning, I took four film holders containing eight sheets of exposed film to Paramount's Still Photo Lab. The front office was small and had a bittersweet smell of photographic chemicals. Here I met Paul Barnett. While dropping Petty Officer Malone's name, I asked him if he'd consider developing my film.

"The Signal Corps has a tank over in Cottage Four. Why don't you ask them?"

"Jack tells me you're the best," was my reply.

"You just don't trust the swabbies, do you, Lieutenant? Don't blame you. Okay, I'll soup 'em for you and make the proofs." He took down my name and phone number and told me they would be ready the next day.

Just before leaving, I slid a brown paper bag across the counter top.

"What's this," he asked.

"Jack tells me you like Scotch whisky, and I had an extra bottle of Chivas Regal."

With a large smile on his face, he replied, "That PO is always right."

Colonel Ford was in the office all week, making final preparations for the big event on Saturday night. Maggie and I were kept busy, making phones calls and running errands for him. Monday afternoon, I was sent to a print shop in downtown LA, where I picked up the final program for what the cover called 'The Marines Invade the Hollywood Canteen.' It was a small, four-page booklet that outlined the evening's rules: no booze, no broads, no fighting and no swearing. Menu: donuts, hot dogs, Cokes and coffee. Entertainment: A half-dozen Hollywood stars were listed. And, on the back cover, a list of thirty volunteer hostesses who would be serving the troops.

The Colonel had a thousand copies printed, but only expected about five hundred Marines to show up at the event. The USO used the old Madonna Dance Hall each Saturday night as the 'Hollywood Canteen;' on the other six nights, it was a dime-a-dance joint.

The next morning, Maggie gave me six hand-addressed envelopes that I was to deliver to the invited celebrities. Taking out a city map, she marked each star's address with a red pen.

"More than likely, they won't be home, or you won't get by their 'gate keepers,' but try. It's very important that they show up for the event. Each envelope has a program and a personal note from the Colonel, thanking them in advance for their appearance. If you get a chance to meet any of them, please stress the event and our thanks."

The stack of envelopes read like a Who's Who of Hollywood: Bing Crosby, Bob Hope, Red Skelton, Greta Garbo, Marlene Dietrich and Carole Lane. It took me almost three hours to find the addresses and deliver the envelopes, and in the end Maggie was right. I didn't personally meet any of them.

Late that afternoon, Paul Barnett called to tell me that my film and proofs were ready. After picking up the pictures at the lab, I rushed over to the cafeteria to show them to Black Jack.

He was on the phone, so I grabbed a cup of coffee and sat down at a table to look at the proofs. Laying the pictures of the penguins beside the photos of the peacocks, I did see the difference the Chief had talked about. Looking down at my first professional pictures, I felt a sense of excitement and pride.

Just then, Jack approached my table. "Hi, Dutch. Hey, you got the proofs! Let me take a look at the negatives."

Holding each negative up to the overhead light, he examined them without comment. Then, putting them back into their clear little sleeves, he said, "Not too bad, for a first timer. Did you notice that only the negatives where you used flash are in focus? The others are out of focus because of camera shake. We'll work on that problem in our next lesson."

Looking down at my proofs, I could see that he was right. "Gosh I didn't spot that, at first. Should have I used the tripod?"

"Yeah…but you can't always use one. You have to learn to keep your arms tight to your body. It's just like the way you were taught on the rifle range, only now you're shooting with a camera."

I felt some of the wind leak out of my sails, but I knew I would improve with time. "Thanks Jack…I'll remember that."

The next morning, the Colonel called me into his office to talk about my photo assignment. There would be a reception line, just inside the front of the hall. He wanted four or five pictures of General Small, the area commander, Glenn Ford, our movie-star-turned-Marine, and the Hollywood Mayor as they greeted the arriving troops. Then a few pictures of the troops, eating, drinking and having a good time. Next, seven or eight pictures of the celebrities entertaining the men. And, most importantly, he wanted twenty-five to thirty group shots of the celebrities with four or five different Marines. After taking each picture, I was to use a little book he gave me to write down the names and hometowns of each Marine. After the event, we would send out press releases, along with pictures, to each of the Marine's hometown newspapers. Or, as he put it, "Here's local Marine hero Joe Blow hobnobbing with Marlene Dietrich at the Hollywood Canteen. Now, what red-blooded American boy wouldn't want to be in that picture? This will be just great for recruiting!"

Maggie had typed out the instructions for my assignment, which she handed to me. It sounded simple enough, but it wasn't. The idea of taking twenty-five to thirty group shots, with four or five different Marines in each shot, would require keeping track of over a hundred names, hometowns and faces. And how could I identify the negatives to make sure that the right face went with the right name? It was a daunting task, and I wasn't even sure I could take the pictures, let alone handle the logistics.

"You look lost, Lieutenant. Is there a problem?"

"No, sir. I was just thinking about how I could best do this assignment. That's a lot of names, hometowns and faces to keep track of, besides all of the other pictures you want."

"Improvise, Lieutenant. Improvise. When a Marine is given an impossible task, he improvises."

"Aye, aye, sir."

Back in my office, I pondered the problem and had to admit that I had no idea how I could accomplish this assignment. Finally, picking up the phone, I called Black Jack and asked him to meet me for a drink after work. After some hesitation, and my insistence that it was 'important,' he agreed. Petty Officer Malone was the only person I knew who could give me the right advice.

We decided to meet at a local bar where many of the studio workers went. I got there first, and ordered a scotch on the rocks. I hadn't drunk any hard liquor since last winter in the wilderness, but I needed one, today. As I sat there, nursing the cocktail, my mind painted the bleak prospect of my first failed assignment.

"You look like you lost your best friend, Dutch."

It was Black Jack, with that easy-going way and confident smile. Relieved, I stood up to greet him.

"Thanks for agreeing to meet me, Jack. Sit down and I'll buy you a drink."

Nodding his approval, he sat down. "So, what's so important?"

Reaching into my pocket, I pulled out the assignment sheet and passed it across the table.

He took a few moments to read it.

"The Colonel went over this list with me, this afternoon," I said glumly. "I'm at a loss over how I can complete this assignment."

"Wow! He expects a lot from one photographer. Even a seasoned shooter couldn't fulfill this job. The organization of the shots alone would be a tall order."

Just then, the barmaid appeared. Jack gave her his order, and then turned his attention back to me.

I looked for courage to ask my next question. "How about you shooting the event and I'll direct and do the logistics? We might make a great team. Maybe your talent and my gold bars could help us both out. I'll even pay you for your time. What do you say, Jack?"

Uneasiness crept over the table as he thought about my question. Finally, he said, "I don't want your money, Lieutenant. And I don't want to be the only Nigger Sailor in a room full of mud Marines. It's not healthy."

His choice of words caught me off-guard. I tried to reassure him. "You don't look very colored to me, and the Marines are part of the Navy, so a sailor at the USO won't stand out. And anyway I'll be there."

"What the hell could you do, sir? Beat the bigots off with your gold bars?"

My face got hot with anger. "Yeah, and my bare knuckles, if I have to. You're my friend, and anybody that crosses my friend crosses me."

The table went quiet again, and the Chief looked me straight in the eye, with a deeply puzzled expression on his face.

"The last white man I trusted was my father...and in the end, he ran out on me. But there's something about you, Dutch. Something I like. There's just one condition," he said as his drink arrived. "I don't want any money for helping you."

"Well then...how about me loaning you my car for a weekend?"

Jack grinned from ear to ear. "The Staff Car? Now, don't get me wrong, it's a great car on the inside...but I don't think I'd be able to pick up many ladies with that Army-brown color. No, Dutch, I don't want your car. BUT...I would like to borrow your camera, to take a few pictures of my girlfriend."

"Consider it done!' I said, and we raised our drinks and clinked our glasses together.

With that toast, a special bond was formed, a bond based on trust and friendship. Silently, I vowed not to be the next white man to let Black Jack Malone down.

"But how in the hell do we shoot a job like this one?" I asked.

"I started out doing press photography," he said, "so that's no problem. We'll need more film, another case of flash bulbs, and a half-dozen more film holders."

"I'll pick those supplies up tomorrow," I assured him. "Anything else?"

"Yes. Get a black grease pen. When you use that little pad to write down the names and hometowns, make sure you write them from camera left to camera right. Then write a big bold number, using the grease pen, on the back of the page. Pin that number on the bottom part of one of the uniforms. I'll make sure to keep the number in the lower frame of the picture. That way, we can identify who's who in any given negative. Then, when we make the prints, we'll crop out the slip of paper with the number. I've done this before, with big groups, and it works just fine."

With a grin on my face, I leaned back in my chair and finished my scotch.

"Now, why the hell didn't I think of that? Black Jack, you're a photographic genius."

We spent the next hour -- and another round of drinks -- going over the other details of the assignment. Jack was full of confidence, and that confidence rubbed off on me. For the first time, I started to look forward to the USO event.

We also agreed to meet on Saturday morning at my office, where Black Jack would give me my second lesson. This time it would be about 'steady shooting' and depth of field. After the session, he would borrow the camera, and then meet up with me again at Madonna Dance Hall at 1900 hours. The party was from eight to eleven, so that would give us an hour to get set up.

Lights, Camera, Action

The Colonel had hired Hollywood Lights to provide two of their big search lights outside the Canteen. They were being set up when I arrived. Finding some off-street parking, I removed the supplies from the truck and made my way to the front of the Hall. It was a warm evening, with little or no breeze, and I was sure it would be hot and stuffy inside.

Making my way through the open front doors, I found Petty Officer Malone dress in his summer white uniform, waiting for me. With a big smile on his face, he told me, "Tonight, I'll call you 'Lieutenant.'"

Grinning back at him, I nodded my head in approval.

One of the volunteer hostesses showed us to a small anteroom in the back where we could layout and arrange our equipment. Using the black changing bag, we loaded eighteen film holders with thirty-six sheets of film. At some point during the evening, we would have to reload all these holders again.

By seven-thirty, we were ready to go. Taking the camera and case, loaded with film holders and flash bulbs, we stepped out onto the dance floor. The Marine band from Camp Pendleton had already arrived and was on the bandstand. The sounds of the practicing instruments filled the hall with disjointed music that sounded like an accident waiting to happen. Standing in a corner, we watched the beehive of preparations.

A few minutes later, the Colonel arrived, dressed in his Class A uniform, with all those impressive battle ribbons pinned on his blouse. He was talking to a few people in the front when he spotted me. Looking over, he gave me a wave, signaling for me to join him.

When I got to his side of the room, he stepped away from the other people so that he could talk to me privately.

"What the hell is that Navy guy doing here? I told you I didn't want to use any more Navy photographers."

He looked angry. Maggie had told me that he had a fiery temper.

"He's not a Signalman, sir. That's Petty Officer Malone. He was a photographer for TIME Magazine before joining the Navy."

Reaching into his blouse pocket, he pulled out a pair of glasses. Putting them on, he peered across the room to where Jack was standing. Looking back at me, he said, "Malone from the cafeteria? He was a photographer for TIME?"

"Yes, sir."

"Who told you that you could use him?"

"You did, sir. You told me to improvise and I improvised."

Just then, Maggie tapped the Colonel on the shoulder and said, "The General is here, Colonel. I thought you should know."

He nodded while still glaring at me. Turning to leave, he stopped and said, "Well, I sure as hell hope his pictures are as good as his pies...for your sake, Lieutenant."

Smiling back at him, I replied, "They are, sir. They are."

Just before the opening of the doors, Jack and I took our first set-up. It was a picture of the reception line, with General Small, Colonel Ford, Private Glenn Ford, Mrs. Ann Davis, the USO representative, and Johnny Grant, the mayor of Hollywood. At eight sharp, the band started playing and the front doors swung open. We shot three additional pictures of Marines, all tagged with little numbers, shaking hands and filing through the line. After each shot, I carefully recorded each person's name and hometown, from camera left to right, in my little book. As we were finishing, someone shouted, from outside of the open doors, "Move the line! There's a lot of Marines out here."

Grabbing our equipment, Jack and I elbowed our way outside, where we were greeted by the sight of a two-abreast khaki line that snaked its way for over a block. There was still some daylight, so we shot a few pictures of the line and the search lights, now spilling their beams into the gradually darkening sky.

As we headed back towards the front door, I heard my name being called out from the line. "Lieutenant Clarke! Lieutenant Dutch Clarke!"

Turning and looking down the line, about halfway, I saw Hank Marks waving and jumping up and down.

"Jack," I said, "you go on in. I want to say hello to some pals. I'll be right there."

As I walked down the line, nearly all of the soldiers saluted me. This made me increasingly uncomfortable as I approached my friends.

It was the Comedian who first shouted, "Attention! Officer on deck!"

My three pals all braced themselves and, with the biggest smiles on their faces, gave me a sharp leatherneck salute, which I proudly returned. After that, it was handshakes and slapping each other on the back. The other Marines standing around us were dumfounded. They had never seen an officer so friendly with lowly Privates.

"Come on, you guys. Follow me. You don't have to stand here, unless you want to shake hands with a General."

They all laughed and started after me.

Finding a table close to the dance floor for the guys, I motioned for Black Jack to join us.

As he was making his way across the room, Kurt whispered, "I saw you working with that swabbie. Isn't he a Nigger? How did you hook up with him?"

Over the sounds of the band playing, I angrily whispered back, "He's a Petty Officer in the Navy, and he's a Negro. Never use that 'Nigger' word when you talk about him to me. Got it?"

Kurt looked bewildered. "Sorry, Dutch. I thought that's what they were called. We don't have any...Negroes...in Ketchikan."

And he was right. I could not recall having seen one single colored person in all the years I had lived up there.

When Jack arrived beside me, I said, "Fellows, I'd like you to meet Black Jack Malone. He's the best damn photographer in the Navy and, more importantly, a very good friend of mine."

They all shook hands and introduced themselves to Jack. Then Jack took a picture of all four of us. Getting ready to leave, I explained to the guys that I had to work the party, but that I would sneak over to talk to them whenever possible.

At nine, the floor show started. First out was Red Skelton. He did ten minutes of gags and jokes, with the whole room doubled over with laughter. Next up was Marlene Dietrich. She came out in a revealing dress and, in her deep, sexy voice, sang some love songs. While she was on, I asked Red Skelton if he would allow me to take a few pictures of him with some soldiers. He was pleased to do so. I did the same with Miss Dietrich while Bing Crosby and Bob Hope did gags, a few soft-shoe dances and some songs.

The last act was Carole Lane. She sang a few numbers but for the most part just talked to the guys about home and country. Carole's act surprised me. She wasn't wearing all that much make-up, and her dress, while sexy, had style. When she talked to the audience, she seemed to be talking from her heart. Her closing story was about how her brother joined the RAF in 1940 and was killed the next year in the skies over London. The way she told it, amplified by her stage presence, brought tears to the eyes of many in the audience. Then, with the rest of the cast joining her, she sang the closing number, 'God Bless America.'

It brought the house down, with whistles and applause. The performances were outstanding, especially with the stars acting so friendly and down-to-earth. They provided much more than just entertainment -- they provided a way to forget the war, and then to remind us what we were fighting for. An audience full of soldiers always loves a good show, as they're so pleased the entertainers cared enough just to show up.

After the performances, the volunteer hostesses danced with the men while the stars worked the room, signing autographs. Jack and I were like one-armed paper hangers, taking down information and shooting pictures as fast as we could. At one point, Jack had to reload our film holders, so I snuck over to my pals' table.

"What did you guys think of the show?"

With smiles on their faces, they all agreed that it was the best damn show they had ever seen.

"When do you guys have to go back?" I asked.

"We have to be on the bus at 23:30," the Comedian answered.

"Gosh, I wish there was a way I could get you to stay the night."

Just then, I felt a tap on my shoulder. Turning, I found Carole Lane standing there. Reaching out, she gave me a big hug and kissed me on the cheek, saying, "Dutch, darling, you haven't said hello to me all night, and you promised to take some pictures."

The look on my friends' faces was priceless. That's when the idea flashed to me.

"Carole, I'd like to introduce you to some friends of mine. I was wondering if I might bring them up to your home tomorrow and take a few publicity pictures of you giving them your autograph, out by your pool."

"How do you know I have a pool, Dutch?"

"When I delivered the program to your house, I saw it, and it occurred to me that it would make a great backdrop for PR shots."

"Why didn't you come in and see me, sweetie?"

"Your gate keeper wouldn't let me pass. I think she said you were out."

"Mrs. Jackson's my housekeeper, not my gate keeper. Next time, call first. I'll always see you. And okay, let's take some pictures around the pool. How about eleven, tomorrow morning?"

My friend's sat speechless, their faces frozen in expressions of disbelief, as I talked to Carole Lane, who was some kind of sex goddess in their minds. Just then, Jack returned with fresh film and suggested we take a picture of Carole with my pals. After the picture, I told them that I would try to get approval for them to stay over -- a plan to which they whole-heartedly agreed.

As we were leaving to catch some more shots with Carole, she turned to them and said, "Good night, boys. See you tomorrow morning…and don't forget your bathing suits."

As we moved to the next setup, Jack whispered, "What's happening tomorrow morning with Miss Lane and your friends?"

I told him about my idea and her agreement.

"Well, I'm sorry, Dutch, but you'll be on your own, tomorrow. I have other plans."

Trying not to panic, I assured him that I understood. This time, in my enthusiasm, I'd outsmarted myself, and I'd have to improvise again.

Just before the party ended, I found Colonel Ford and told him that Miss Lane had offered to let us shoot some more photographs the next day with my Marine friends. I asked him if he could make the arrangements for them to stay over.

"Where will the guys sleep? And who's doing the shooting, you or Malone?"

"I have room at my apartment, and I'll be doing the photography."

He hesitated for a moment. "After her performance tonight, how could anyone say no? I'll square it with their CO by saying it's a personal favor to Miss Lane. But they have to be on the afternoon train back to Camp Pendleton tomorrow, and you'll buy their train tickets. Do you understand, Lieutenant?"

"Aye, aye, sir."

By the end of the evening, over a thousand Marines had passed through the turnstiles, and Jack and I had shot eighty-four images of the event. Our supplies had dwindled to a few sheets of film and only four remaining flash bulbs, just enough for the next day.

My friends were delighted to be staying over, and they helped Jack and me as we carried the camera equipment and exposed film to my car. As the guys piled in, I took Black Jack aside and thanked him again for his support and friendship.

His parting comment was classic: "Never thank a photographer until the proofs are back."

On the way home, between being teased about being an officer and the color of my car, I stopped and bought two six packs of beer. When we got inside my apartment, I had the guys get out of their uniforms so they could iron them for the next morning. Here we were, four guys drinking beer, smoking and laughing, dressed only in our skivvies. Our conversation, for the most part, was about their advanced weapons training, my job at OWI, Sergeant Nelson, and other friends in my old platoon.

We talked until the last drop of the last beer had been shared by all. By then, it was late, very late. Jim finally fell asleep on the floor and Hank in the easy chair.

As I got up to leave Kurt on the couch, he asked, "You okay, Dutch?"

"Yeah, I think so. Why? What are you worried about?"

"You're the most gung-ho Marine I have ever met. All the way through boot camp, you talked about killing Japs…and now they've got you armed with a camera. It just doesn't make much sense to me."

"Me neither, but don't worry about it. All things change, and this, too, will pass. Somehow, someway, someday, I'll get back into the fight. Good night Kurt."

The Picture

The next morning, Mrs. Jackson, Carole's housekeeper, greeted us with a smile and showed us around to the pool. As the boys were marveling at the grandeur of the home and grounds, she reappeared with ice tea for all. It was a warm, sunny day, and I was busy trying to find good spots to take our pictures when Carole walked out from the house. She was wearing a red one-piece swimsuit that fit so tightly to her shapely body that I thought my pals' eyes would pop out.

Watching them stare at her, she said, "Good morning, boys. Don't you all look handsome in those uniforms!" Turning to me with a smile, she teased, "And good morning to you, Dutch. Did Mrs. Jackson let the gate down for you?"

"Good morning, Carole. You look just beautiful in that bathing suit."

And she did, with her long blonde hair, fair complexion and the striking red suit. She looked as sexy as any woman I had ever seen, and she knew it. She loved the attention and compliments.

"Where would you like me, Dutch?"

The boys still hadn't said a word. Her appearance had again rendered them speechless.

The first two shots I took were at a pool-side table. Using the shade of its umbrella, I shot the pictures with available light. The guys stood around her while she sat, signing her autograph on a publicity picture. They loved it, and I loved it, but something in the back of my mind said that the Marines wouldn't.

Next, we moved to the cabana, where I shot Carole in a lounge chair, signing her photo, with the guys kneeling around her. For this shot, I used flash as a fill light. But again, there was something in the back of my mind saying that the Marines wouldn't like it. Then it dawned on me -- we were seeing just a bit too much of Carole falling out of that bathing suit.

"Carole, do you have a wrap to go with that suit? I don't want to be too racy."

She frowned at me as if I had just insulted her, but said, "Yes, I have a top in the cabana. I'll get it."

While she was gone, I moved the lounge closer to the pool. When she came back, wearing the floral top, it did just what I had wanted it to. For the first time, I started giving detailed directions. Having her sit again in the lounge chair with her feet off to one side, I asked the Comedian to lay face down across the foot of the lounge and in front of her, so she could use his back as a writing table. Next, I positioned Kurt and Hank on their knees, on either side of her lounge. Directing the guys, I told them to look at her signing the photo, while she watched the boys watching her. Looking through the viewfinder, I sensed something special. Using my last three flash bulbs, I took the pictures. The expressions I saw in the camera were wonderful. I only prayed that my focus and exposure would be correct.

When we were done, she asked if we wanted to stay for lunch. Begging off with genuine regret, I explained that I had to get the guys to the train station on time or the Colonel would have my hide. Before we left, she signed personal notes on her PR photo for all three of my friends. They were in heaven.

As we all walked to the car, Carole reached out again and kissed me on the cheek, then remarked, "I want to see those proofs, Dutch...and I want you to personally bring them by, so we can go over them together, okay?"

With my pals watching and my face red, I replied, "Sure. Why not? And thank you."

All the way back, in the car, the guys kept ribbing me about Carole. It didn't stop even as I walked them to their train. Finally, it was time for them to go.

With the sound of the last 'all aboard' hanging in the air, Kurt grabbed my hand and shook it. "Being your friend has been amazing, Dutch. We always have such a good time. Promise that you'll tell us, in detail, what happens when you deliver those pictures to Carole!"

"Yes, promise," both Hank and Jim hollered.

Feeling my face getting red again, I awkwardly answered, "Aye, aye."

CHAPTER FOUR

Six days had passed since our escape. The enemy remained the same, hunger and thirst only its face had changed from the Japs to Mother Nature. If we didn't find some immediate relief, the results would be the same. Two nights ago, we had drunk the last of the fresh water from the dead Nip's canteen. Seven days had passed since our last meager bowl of rice. My raft-mates and I were slowly dying.

It was hot, beastly hot. There was no shade on the raft, so we all sat with our backs to the sun. When it was cooler in the mornings and evenings, we would sit around and talk. But in the heat of the day, the float was silent, with only the sounds of the sea lapping against the boat. The ocean kept us moving northwest; we had no way of controlling this direction. Like a leaf falling from a tree, we floated at the mercy of the currents.

The only good news was that Corporal Bates's wounds were slowly healing. Each morning, I drew out another inch of the wick I had placed inside his wound. It was a miracle he hadn't developed an infection from my surgery. Although his arm was still in a sling, he was now beginning to move it without as much pain. I wished I could say he was stronger every day, but he wasn't. None of us were.

As I sat there thinking, my fingers were wrapped around the little vial hanging on my chest. This small bottle was wrapped inside a condom tied on my dog-tag chain. Had the Japanese ever found such a personal possession, it would have meant my instant execution. But the contents of this bottle were worth the gamble. It had become my habit to touch this talisman and think about its contents many times a day. It helped remind me that I had to survive so that its contents could survive. Death was not an option. It was this daydream that kept me going.

The silence was broken by the loud squeals of birds over the raft. We hadn't seen birds since the first day after our escape. Looking up, shading my eyes, I watched them fly above us, moving in our general direction. Then, just above the horizon, I noticed it for the first time: low-hanging clouds that looked to be only a few miles north of our position. Those low clouds could mean land...

No. I wouldn't get my hopes up, at least not yet.

Turning away, I went back to my daydream...but a few minutes later I was drawn back to the horizon.

It was still there and looked even closer.

Could this be just a mirage, a figment of my half-dying imagination? Shaking my head clear, I looked closer and strained my eyes.

It was there. Now, I even could make out a speck of green, in front of the clouds.

"Land!" I shouted. "I see land!"

My shout startled my mates. Their heads bobbed up, and their bodies moved to find the direction I was pointing.

Then the Padre screamed, "Thank the Lord! I see it, too."

Corporal Bates was next, and then all of them saw it. There was hope again, and excitement on their faces.

"Are we going in the right direction?" Sergeant York yelled.

"I think so," I replied, "but it looks like it's miles ahead of us."

Judging distances over the open water could be tricky. What I had thought was just a few miles must have been over ten. It took us almost three hours to get close enough to clearly see the land. It was just a small atoll, and it appeared to be a few hundred yards long and forty or fifty yards wide. It was surrounded by a sandy beach, white as tooth powder, above which grew a plateau of brown sea grass. In the center of the little island stood a small grove of weather-beaten palm trees. In reality, it didn't look to be much, but it was land, and to us it looked like paradise.

We were still over a mile off-shore from the atoll when I noticed that the current was now moving us more west than north. If we didn't change direction quickly, we might float right by the little island.

"We have to go more north or we won't make it." I moved to the rear of the raft. "I'm going to jump in and try to push us in that direction. I won't be able to see the island from behind the raft so, Bates, you keep pointing in its direction so I know which way to swim."

"There might be sharks in the water," the Padre warned.

"Yeah...so you guys keep an eye out for me."

The water was cool and actually felt refreshing. I only hoped that I still had enough strength to move the raft in the strong current. Placing my hands on the side of the boat, I started kicking.

I couldn't tell if our course was changing or not. I just kept looking over the side of the raft to see which way the Corporal was pointing.

After a few minutes, I shouted, "Am I doing any good?"

No one replied...and then came two splashes next to me. The Padre and Sergeant York had joined me in the water.

Smiling at me, York remarked, "You need more horsepower, mate!"

"I told Patterson to remain topside to watch for sharks," the Padre added, grinning.

With good spirits, we went on swimming and pushing. Soon the Padre and York sang out a couple verses of an old sea shanty:

"Once I had an Irish girl and she was fat and lazy, Away, haul away, Oh, haul away together..."

Three sets of legs were better than one, but I didn't know how much strength these guys would have. But as we kicked and pushed, adrenalin pumped through our veins, surprising us all with our energy levels. Bates shouted out a few times that we were moving in the right direction, while Patterson kept watching the water around us. We gave it all we had, but at the end of an hour, we were spent. I could tell by the looks on their faces there just wasn't any more left in them. My own energy would do for a few minutes more, but they were hanging on more than pushing. I didn't blame them; they had done more than I could ever have expected.

"We're almost there," Bates shouted. "Don't give up now, mates."

Then Patterson jumped in. "The hell with sharks. You need a fresh pair of legs."

His zeal was contagious. For the next few minutes, we were moving again.

Finally, the Padre looked over to me, gasping for breath. "I'm done for, Dutch. I can't go on," he said, and stopped kicking. Then York stopped, too. I was next. I let my legs go limp, and they sank low into the water.

As I cursed myself for giving up…I felt it. The bottom of the ocean was under foot. It was still deep, but I could stand with my head just above water.

"I feel the bottom," I hollered, out of breath.

We were too exhausted to say anything more. Getting my legs going again, I started walking, pushing at the raft. A few moments later, all the guys were stumbling across the sandy bottom.

Minutes later we were pushing the raft up onto the beach. Collapsing in the shallow surf, we caught our breath and looked out across the sweeping Pacific Ocean from whence we had just come. We were on solid ground, and we could scarcely believe it. Thank the Lord!

Respect

Bright and early on Monday morning, I took our exposed film and another bottle of Chivas to Paul at the studio lab. He seemed surprised to see me -- and another gift -- so soon.

"There should be about ninety sheets of film in these two boxes. They're really important shots, Paul."

"Wow, that's a lot. Do you want individual proofs or four-up contact sheets?"

"I think contact sheets will be easier to handle. And thanks again for helping us out."

"No problem, Lieutenant. They should be ready tomorrow. I'll call you. And thanks for the Chivas," he said, with a pleased smile.

When I got to the office, Maggie and the Colonel were going over a list of the VIPs who had attended the USO bash. They both seemed very happy with the event and were astounded by the total number of Marines that came. All in all, the party had been a big success.

"How about your photography, Dutch? How much film did you shoot?" the Colonel asked.

"I took about ninety sheets to the lab, this morning. They should have the proofs back tomorrow, sir."

"I still don't like Chief Malone being there. Guess I just don't trust the Navy when it comes to Marine events. But the proof will be in your proofs," the Colonel said with a smile.

The office was a pleasant, upbeat place that day. Working with my notes of the names and hometowns, Maggie and I made out a sheet of all the local newspapers. She had a book that listed all the papers in America, complete with their mailing addresses. Our final typewritten list ranged from Maine to Alaska, from Florida to Hawaii, with many points in between. The final count was one hundred and five hometown papers. While we worked on the newspapers, the Colonel wrote the press release. His final draft was a recruiter's dream. He dropped all the right names, from celebrities to politicians, generals to volunteer hostesses. He painted the event as a gala Hollywood party thrown to honor America's heroes, the United States Marines. Reading it made me feel proud to wear the uniform. My CO was one hell of a promoter.

That evening, the Colonel stopped me on my way out the door. "I sure hope your pictures do justice to all the work we've done. Without the pictures of the hometown heroes, the papers either won't run the story or they'll bury it. You're on the hot seat, Lieutenant."

Forcing a confident smile, I replied, "Aye, aye, sir."

But that night, I prayed to the photography gods.

Early the next afternoon, Paul called to say that the proofs were ready. When I arrived at the lab, he had all the contact sheets and negatives on the counter, waiting for me.

"That was fast, Lieutenant. Your order is right here and ready to go. There were ninety-six sheets of film, so we have twenty-four eight-by-ten contact sheets. I numbered the negatives in the same order we removed them from the film boxes."

Looking down at the stack of prints I saw that my pictures of Carole Lane were on top. At a glance, they looked just fine, and I breathed a sigh of relief.

"Looks like you guys had quite a party," Paul remarked with a grin. "I know now why the OWI is called the 'party army.' It's got to be great duty. And you had some nice shots of good-looking ladies. The lab boys liked the darkie the best. She's one hot gal."

Hurriedly taking proofs and negatives in hand, I thanked Paul for his work. But as I drove back to the office, his comment about the OWI, and about the 'darkie,' kept racing through my head. Miss Dietrich did have a sun tan, and I was sure it must have photographed even darker. That had to be it. But the OWI comment wasn't true. The party had served a very serious reason. Maybe I should have tried to explain to Paul....

No. I wasn't going to defend the OWI because, deep down in my heart, I knew Paul was right.

When I walked into the office, Maggie told me that Sergeant Nelson was on the phone. Placing the proofs and negatives on her desk, I went into my office to talk to Dick. He had called to apologize for not coming to the USO party. It was his weekend with the new 'mop heads' and he couldn't get away.

I told him about the party and what he had missed. In turn, he told me that the event was all the buzz around Camp Pendleton. I gave Dick my new address, and he promised to look me up the next time he was in LA.

Our conversation was short, only a few minutes. As soon as I hung up the phone, I returned to Maggie's office for the proofs, but she and they were gone.

The Colonel's door was ajar, so I looked in. There they both were, with magnifying glasses, looking at the contact sheets.

"Come in, Lieutenant," the Colonel boomed. And he didn't look happy. "Did you look at these proofs before you brought them in?" he demanded.

"No, sir. Just the top sheet. Is there something wrong with them?"

Colonel Ford was red-faced and angry, "You might say that. I didn't give you that god-damn camera so you could go around shooting cheesecake. You're a member of the United States Marine Corps, Lieutenant, and I expect you to act like it. Do you understand me?"

"Yes, sir. I thought the pictures of Miss Lane might be too racy, so I had her put on a top over the swimsuit. But I didn't think it was 'cheesecake."

"I'm not talking about those god damn pictures. It's this Negro girl. Who the hell told you to take pictures of her?" he growled, and slid two contact sheets across his desk.

Looking down, I about fainted. There were six images of a half-dressed colored gal wearing only a white towel. In some shots, she was laying on a bed; in others, she was standing by a shower. You really couldn't see anything, but they were provocative. They were, indeed, 'cheesecake.'

I knew immediately that they were Black Jack's pictures, but I didn't want to tell the Colonel so. The last thing I needed was for Petty Officer Malone to be on his shit list.

Looking up from the proofs, I stared at the Colonel and answered, "I didn't shoot these pictures, sir. I give you my word, as an officer and gentlemen. I'm sure it's just some lab snafu."

The room fell silent for a moment. Maggie had a strange expression on her face, as if she was holding her breath, waiting to see which way the wind would blow.

Standing there, I just looked the Colonel in the eye.

"Okay," he said at last, "I'll buy that. But you tell those lab clowns I don't want any more snafus. Understand, Lieutenant?"

"Aye, aye, sir." Drawing a steadying breath, I asked, "Other than the snafu, how are the pictures?"

Reaching down, he slid a few contact sheets to me. "Take a look. I think they're just great. There isn't one bad picture in the bunch. When the Navy was doing my work, we sometimes lost a third of the shots because of bad exposures." He gestured at the contact sheets. "But what the hell are those little numbers doing in each of the group shots?"

"It's how we kept track of who's who in each shot. When we make the prints, we just crop out the numbers."

The Colonel looked at me as if a light bulb had just come on in his head. "I never considered the logistics. Good thinking, Lieutenant."

"It wasn't me, sir. It was Petty Officer Malone. He's done this kind of photography before, and he knew just how it should be organized. All I did was improvise."

"Okay, okay, you both did a good job," he replied with a grin.

"Colonel," Maggie interrupted, "take a look at this image of Carole and Dutch's friends. I think there is something special here." She handed a contact sheet to him. "It's Negative Two. I think it would make a great recruiting poster."

Moving around the desk, I peered at the proof over the Colonel's shoulder. It was one of the shots by the pool, the one with Carole using the Comedian's back as a table. It did look pretty good. I had been very lucky with both the setup and the exposure.

"I like it," said the Colonel. "Let me see the negative. If it's sharp, we'll get some prints made."

The negative was razor sharp, and the Colonel instructed me to get half dozen prints made, right away. He would then send the picture up the chain of command.

"I'll bet my pension that this picture will be in every Marine recruiting station by the end of next month," the Colonel remarked with a grin.

And he was right -- it was.

Back in my office, I telephoned Black Jack at the cafeteria to tell him that the proofs were in. He was out, so I left a message for him with Seaman Riku. By late afternoon, I had all the proofs and negatives back in my office. As I was writing who was who, on the back side of the contact sheets, the Colonel stuck his head in.

"I'm on my way out. Good job, Dutch. And tell Petty Officer Malone he has good taste in ladies." He grinned. "A lab snafu, eh? Come on, Lieutenant, I didn't just fall off a turnip truck. Good night."

Some moments later as I was getting ready to leave, Black Jack came in the front door.

"Is everybody gone, Lieutenant?"

"Yeah. You must have gotten my message. Come into my office and I'll show you the proofs."

As he followed me in, he said, "Sorry to be so late, but I do want to see the proofs. If they're any good, maybe I can get a good night's sleep, tonight."

"Oh, you'll get a good night's sleep, alright! Do you want to see the Colonel's favorite shots?"

"Sure."

I slid the two contact sheets of his lady friend across the desk and watched his expression. It went from happy to panic in a single heartbeat.

"Oh NO! Dutch, didn't you remove my shots before you gave them to the Colonel?"

"I didn't even know your shots were there. Why didn't you tell me about them?" I pulled a long face. "You can't imagine what happened here, this afternoon."

"What happened?"

Pausing for a long moment, I said soberly, "I leave for cook school, tomorrow."

The room fell silent, so silent that I thought I heard Black Jack's heart beating. His face was frozen, deadpan with disbelief.

Not able to let him hang there any longer, I started to laugh.

"You son of a bitch. Is this a joke?" he demanded.

I shook my head yes and we both had a good laugh.

Finally, I told him exactly what had happen that afternoon, including the Colonel's comment about 'falling off a turnip truck.' We both agreed that we had dodged a bullet and would need better communication, in the future. Then we sat down and reviewed all the proofs.

Black Jack was happy, the Colonel was happy and, by god, I was happy.

Virtue

Most of the rest of the week, the Colonel was out of the office. It seemed that Harry Watt of RKO had finally found a project about Marines, so the Colonel had volunteered to work with the studio writers. That meant that Maggie and I would handle the leg work of getting PR out to the local newspapers. She was such a joy to work with that the time just flew by.

Late on Friday afternoon, I was in my office, filing away copies of the releases when I heard the phone ring. Maggie answered it, and I could overhear her muffled conversation from the next room. I thought it must have been a personal call because she talked a good while before appearing in my doorway.

"The telephone is for you, Dutch, and I'm leaving. See you Monday," she said with a smile as she turned to leave.

"Good night, Maggie." I reached for my phone. "Hello?"

The line was quiet for a moment. Then a woman's angry voice declared, "I'm mad as hell at you, Lieutenant."

Her tone caught me off-guard. "I beg your pardon. Who is this?"

"This is the woman who just today found out that one of my pictures might become a Marine poster. This is the woman you promised to bring the proofs to. This is Carole!"

Finally, her voice and face matched up in my mind. Taking the proofs to her had completely slipped my mind.

"How did you hear about the pictures?"

"I was having lunch at the Derby today when Lennie stopped by my table and told me. Why didn't you bring the proofs up, Dutch?"

"Gosh, Miss Lane, I just don't know what to say. We've just been so busy here."

"That's what Maggie said." Sounding slightly mollified, "Okay, how about tomorrow night? We can have dinner and look over the shots."

For some reason, I was hesitant about spending an evening with Carole Lane. Maybe it was the Colonel's comments about 'land mines.' I hated to lie, but lie I did. "Gosh, Miss Lane, that would be nice, but I have to go to Camp Pendleton this weekend. How about if I bring them up sometime next week?"

There was a long pause. Then she sighed, "Okay, sweetie. I guess I can forgive you, this time...but gals like me don't like to be ignored. See you next week. And have a good time with all those solider boys at Camp Pendleton."

As usual, I spent Saturday morning on cleanup detail and preparing my uniforms for the coming week. In the afternoon, Black Jack gave me another photography lesson. He had a date for that evening, so I was back at my apartment by five-thirty. Uncapping a beer, I raised the blinds and slid open the windows for some fresh air. The Southern California weather was almost getting boring, always sunny, warm and bright. As I was just about to sit down on the couch, there was a knock at the front door. Moving across the room, I opened it…to encounter Miss Lane in the corridor. Speechless for a moment, I stood there, stunned by her presence.

"Well, aren't you going to ask me in, sweetie?"

Fumbling for words, I said, "Hello, Miss Lane, Sure. Come on in. How did you know where I lived?"

As she moved past me, her perfume lingered on the air. Walking to the center of my living room, she looked around and then back to me. "How quaint. If you must know, I called Maggie and she gave me your address. She didn't know anything about the Camp Pendleton trip, so I thought I'd just stop by, to see if you'd gone yet."

That's the problem with lying…one lie always leads to another, I thought.

"I had some transportation problems. Maggie just gave you my address?"

"No, I told her you had some proofs for me to pick up. Are you sorry to see me?"

"No! Just…surprised. I don't have the proofs here."

"I know that, sweetie. I just thought I'd come by to see you."

She was wearing black shorts with a yellow halter top that showed off her attractive body.

"Do you have any champagne?"

"No, sorry, I don't. I have beer. Would you like one?"

"How basic! No, not right now." She came a step closer. "There's no trip to Camp Pendleton, is there, Dutch?" Another step. "Are you afraid of me? You must know I've been coming on to you, ever since we met."

Fumbling for words again, I asked, "Why me?"

"Why not you? You're young, and handsome, and new to Hollywood. You need someone to show you the ropes...and I'm good at that."

Standing there, with the window backlighting her hair, she looked like she had a halo. Her blue eyes were staring right at me, and she had an odd look on her face.

"Maybe I'm not your type of girl...or maybe you don't like girls. Or just maybe you still have your virtue. Now, wouldn't that be sweet? Or maybe you haven't been motivated enough."

With both arms, she reached behind herself, unsnapped the yellow halter top, and let it fall to the floor. In the warm evening light, her firm breasts looked golden melons. She placed her hands under them to raise them even higher.

I just stood there, flatfooted and astonished. I didn't know what to say or do.

Moving across the room to me, she asked softly, "Do you like what you see? Why don't you touch them? They won't break."

Then she was standing right in front of me. As the blood rushed to my groin, my caution waned, and my rational thinking somehow vanished altogether. The only emotion I felt was lust...and that was new to me.

Reaching out, I placed one of my hands on her breasts. She watched me for a moment, with a smile on her face, then pressed her warm body against mine and kissed me.

Her lips were sweet. Finally, when she broke away, I went back for more. This time, her lips were warm and wet. Soon I felt her hand on my manhood.

As our lips parted again, she whispered, "It's so much better when we both do it."

"I don't have any experience," I whispered back. "That's my little secret."

With that strange, sexy smile on her face, she murmured, "I'll be gentle. It's been a long time since I've had a virgin."

The word virgin made me instantly embarrassed and sorry I had said anything.

Just then, there was a knock at the door. Like two kids stealing candy, she and I both about jumped out of our skins. We abruptly parted.

"Are you expecting somebody?" Carole asked as she hurried to retrieve her top from the floor.

Standing there, I shrugged in answer to her question.

There was a second knock. Moving towards the door, I watched Carole put her top on as quickly as she had taken it off. By the time I reached the door, all my caution and reason had come back. Swinging it open, I found Sergeant Nelson standing in the hallway.

Gathering my thoughts, I winked at him before he could say a word. "Come in, Sergeant. Did you get that transportation snafu fixed? Are we ready to go? You know the General's going to be mad as hell that I'm so late."

As he walked by me, I saw a puzzled look on his face, but he answered, "Yes, sir." When he saw Carole standing by the couch, his puzzled look changed to a startled look.

"Sergeant this is Carole. She came over to see me off." Turning to her I continued, "I'll see you next week, Miss Lane, when I get back from Camp Pendleton."

She stood there for a moment, looking at me thinking. Then she walked towards the door, smiled at Sergeant Nelson, paused and turned back to me. "I'll look forward to next week, Dutch. We'll talk more about virtue...or should I call you Lieutenant? Good night, boys."

As the door closed, Sergeant Nelson's jaw almost dropped to the floor. He stood there for a long moment, shaking his head in disbelief. "What the hell was that all about? And wasn't that Carole Lane, the movie star...sir?"

Over a cold beer, I told him the expurgated version of Carole's visit and how the Colonel had warned me about 'land-mines' like her. The Sergeant wanted as many details as possible. While I was answering all of his questions, his expression was so intent that it made me feel like Walter Winchell, the Hollywood gossip commentator. In the end, I managed to satisfy his curiosity, and we both had a good laugh.

Over our second beer, he explained that one of his new mop-heads had gone AWOL, and that the recruit had been picked up by the LAPD. The Sergeant had traveled to LA to bring him back, but the paperwork wouldn't be done until the next morning, so he had decided to look me up.

Thanking him for his timely appearance, I invited him to bunk on my couch. We had a magnificent evening.

Changes

First thing Monday morning, I took Carole's negatives over to the lab and had a duplicate set of proofs made. When I returned to the office, Maggie was there, all in a twit. She wasn't sure she had done the right thing by giving Carole my home address.

"When she called me on Saturday, I didn't know what to say. I've known her for years. I guess you could say we're friends, so when she said that you had proofs for her to pick up, I gave out your address. Was that okay, Dutch?'

"Don't worry about it. It was just a mix-up. I'll get the proofs off to her today."

"Did she tell you about her engagement? I couldn't believe it when she told me, on Friday. I didn't think that girl would ever get married again."

Shaking my head in shock, I replied, "No...she didn't say a word."

Confused, I sipped at my first cup of coffee. How could Carole come on to me when she was newly engaged to be married? It looked as if she really was one of those 'land-mines,' and also a snake in the grass.

When I picked up the proofs, I slid them into a small brown envelope and wrote a short note to accompany them.

```
Miss Lane, here are the proofs. I marked the one
the Colonel sent to Headquarters. I hope you like
them. Sorry I couldn't bring them by personally
but we are just swamped.

Lieutenant Clarke

Ps: Congratulations on your engagement
```

Sealing up the envelope, I called a cab and sent it off to her. I had wrestled with the postscript and almost didn't include it, but I wanted her to know that I knew. Her look and scent had haunted me all weekend, so part of me was disappointed, but another part of me was relieved.

The rest of the week was consumed by three War Bond events with comedians Abbott & Costello. Maggie managed all of the leg work and logistics while I did the photography. They turned out to be good guys and real patriots, and they even volunteered to do more in the future.

The following week, the Colonel called Maggie and me into his office for what he referred to as an organizational meeting. In the past few weeks, he had been working with the writers over at RKO, and was still dressed in what I called his Hollywood uniform: brown riding pants, red polo shirt, and white silk ascot. Sitting in front of his desk, he looked more like a film director than my commanding officer.

"I heard back from Headquarters. They loved the picture of Miss Lane and they agreed it would make a great recruiting poster."

"That's great news," Maggie said. "Dutch, that's a real feather in your cap."

"Actually," the Colonel continued, "they liked it so much that they want a dozen more posters, using the same general theme. Dutch, I want you to write out your picture ideas and have them on my desk by tomorrow."

"Aye, aye, sir. What new celebrities are you thinking about using?"

A surprised look raced across his face. "Celebrities? The Marines don't want new celebrities, they want Carole Lane. We are going to make her the 'Marine Sweetheart.' A few months from now, there won't be a man in uniform who doesn't know who she is."

The thought of working with Carole on more shots sent a chill up my spine. And what the Colonel was talking about was a big project, one that would require lots of thought, travel and organization.

"Is there a problem with this, Lieutenant?" he asked sternly.

"No, sir. I'm just not sure Miss Lane will give us the time we'd need to do that many pictures."

He smiled smugly. "She'll give us whatever we need. I've already talked to her. Money can't buy this type of publicity. To be the Marine Sweetheart is a distinction worth millions."

"But what about the logistics, Colonel? We can't shoot all those setups around her pool. We'll have to travel, and there will be a lot of planning involved."

"That's right, Dutch. I want your picture ideas to be as fresh and creative as possible. Use whatever locations you think necessary. I want images that recruits can relate to, like the first one -- simple, sexy and all-Marine."

"I can help with the logistics," Maggie offered.

Shaking his head, the Colonel said, "No, as far as the logistics go, that brings us to the second part of our meeting. It seems that General Small called the office a few times, last week, and no one was here. He didn't like that. So I convinced him we need more help. Dutch, I want you to ask Petty Officer Malone to transfer into the Marine Corps. I watched you two work at the USO party, and you make a great team. Putting your ideas, direction and organization together with his photographic skills, we should have great pictures." Turning to Maggie, "We can convert the old dressing room into an office, and the laundry room into a small darkroom. That way, we can control all aspects of our work. The General will get us whatever we need."

My mind went blank for a minute. How would Black Jack react to such an idea? All I could think about was 'why?'

Finally I blurted it out. "Why would he want to transfer in, sir? And won't this take a lot of time and paperwork?"

"I've already talked to General Small. He tells me we could have all the paperwork done in a few days. And you tell Petty Officer Malone that there won't be a demotion in grade. He'll come into the Marines as an E5 Sergeant."

The offer didn't sound like much of a deal to me. It suddenly occurred to me that it was up to me, to bargain for the Black Jack.

"But, sir, why would he want to transfer in the first place? He has a soft job at the Canteen, with a Petty Officer pay, and he pretty much calls his own shots. Making him a Sergeant is no incentive. On the other hand, if I could tell him he'd be E8 Master Sergeant, that might make the difference."

"Master Sergeant? No way. I can't do that. That's an increase of three pay grades. How about Staff Sergeant?" the Colonel asked.

"Seems to me that if he's going to provide the Marines a million dollars' worth of publicity, they can offer him a promotion to E7 Gunnery Sergeant," I responded.

The Colonel slid a cigarette into his white ivory holder and lit it. With white smoke rising above his head, he sat back in his chair and thought for a moment. Finally, with a small grin on his face, he said, "You'd fit right in as a Hollywood agent. That's a promotion of two pay grades, an increase of over thirty-six bucks a month. But okay. When can you talk to him?"

After work, Black Jack and I met for drinks. Knowing that timing was everything, I only talked about the new photo assignment with Carole Lane, during the first round. He had some great ideas, which I scribbled down on a cocktail napkin. During the second round, I made my pitch. He was quiet during my proposal, watching me inquisitively.

"Well, what do you think, Jack? Do you want the promotion?"

He thought long and hard about my question, and finally responded, "If the Marines were offering me combat duty, I'd jump at it, but they're not. While I like the idea of being a photographer again, I just can't see this nigger in Marine green. Finding a black man in the Marines is like finding a preacher in a whorehouse, very unusual."

His choice of the 'n' word caught me off guard. That racial divide kept coming between us, and I didn't know how to fight it.

"You know, Black Jack, that's all changing. The Secretary of the Navy has already ordered the integration of all races into the service. And with the war on, who knows where this promotion might lead? It's better than slinging hash. It puts more money in your pocket and, best of all, we'd be working together."

He just looked at me for the longest time, swirling the ice in his drink. "I don't know, Dutch. Gunnery Sergeant...Why not Master Sergeant? Or, better yet, Lieutenant?"

Smiling back at him, I said, "I tried for Master Sergeant but the Colonel wouldn't budge. He started low and I started high, and we finally agreed at E7. But it's your life and your decision. I have no problem with telling him that you turned me down."

At my words, his face turned from serious to excited. "Are you kidding? I would have transferred as a buck private to get back in photography! I just wanted to get the best deal I could. But it sounds like you did all the negotiations for me -- and a good job you did! Bet I'll be the only colored Gunnery Sergeant in the Marines. Now, that's one hell of an accomplishment."

The next morning, I gave the Colonel a list of twelve proposed photo set-ups, and told him that Petty Officer Malone had agreed to transfer over. He seemed very pleased. Before the day was out, Maggie gave me a handful of forms for Black Jack to sign.

Walking into the deserted canteen, I found the Jack seated at one of the tables, doing paperwork. Grapping a cup of coffee I joined him. After some small talk, he looked over my forms and signed where Maggie indicated. Then, just as I was about to leave, Seaman Riku approached our table.

"Can I talk to you a minute, sir?" he asked.

"Lieutenant, this is Seaman Riku. He knows what's going on. Do you remember me telling you about him?" Jack asked.

"Sure. Sit down, Riku. What's on your mind?"

It turned out Seaman Riku had an idea: if newspapers would run pictures of Miss Lane as the Marines' sweetheart, why wouldn't MovieTone News do the same? That way, our story could reach millions of movie-goers, each week.

The idea, providing film clips of each setup sounded crazy at first, but as he explained it in more detail, I warmed to it. He went on to tell me that he had attended UCLA as a film major before enlisting, and that he could shoot and edit the film. He also knew his way around the darkroom and could be a big help with our new lab. The long and the short of it was that Seaman Riku wanted to transfer to the Marines, too.

Watching him, I knew this would be a problem. He was a small guy, about five feet four inches tall, with jet-black hair, a round face, and dark, almost-black slanted eyes. His complexion, while yellowish, was fairer than I expected for someone who was Japanese. He was a pleasant guy, but as he was talking, I kept catching myself thinking, He's the enemy. He's a Jap.

"It's a good idea," I admitted. "Do you have the equipment to do all this?"

"No, sir."

"But we can rent whatever we need from Ed Cameron," Jack piped up.

"I don't know what the Colonel would say to such an idea. Maybe this would be too much change for him," I responded reluctantly.

"Then let's not ask him, let's show him," Black Jack suggested. "You and I can shoot 16mm film of our first few set-ups and have Riku do the editing. Then we sit the Colonel down and show him the clips. He'll see the potential right away."

"No, I'm not quite convinced. Something about this is bothering me."

He looked at me soberly and then asked, "Is what's bothering you the fact that Riku's a Jap, sir?"

Instantly I realized that he was right.

"I'm only half-Japanese," Seaman Riku asserted with a sour face. "My mother's Korean."

"Lieutenant, didn't you tell me that the Secretary of the Navy has ordered the integration of all races? If you can help me conquer those racial barriers, why not Riku?"

Looking at Seaman Riku, I knew that his battle would be a hell of a lot harder than Black Jack's. We were at war with Japan…but that didn't mean that we were at war with all people of Japanese descent. Still, it was a fine line.

Finally I said, "Okay, we'll give it a try." Turning to Riku, I continued, "But no promises. It will be up to the Colonel, not to me. Do you understand?"

With a big smile on his face, Riku answered, "Yes, sir."

That weekend, Black Jack and I went to the Cameron Camera Shop to buy supplies and rent the film gear we would need.

Ed was pleased to see my wallet again. The film camera outfit was a 16mm Bell & Howell with a turret lens, a tripod and a light bar with three flood-lamps. The used outfit rented for fifteen dollars a week, or he would sell it to me for three-hundred-and-fifty. Still having my doubts, I chose the rental. The camera took hundred-foot loads of film, so we purchased eight rolls and three additional lamps for the light bar. As he was totaling up the sales ticket, I reminded him about my discount for cash.

"Oh…that's right, Lieutenant. Let me refigure this."

As he was doing so, Black Jack asked again about any used Leica cameras.

Looking up with a big smile on his face, Ed put down his pen and reached for a metal case behind the counter. Laying the camera box on the glass top, he said, "Got this in, just yesterday. The soon-to-be-ex-wife of a studio executive is selling off everything of her husband's, out of spite." Opening the case, he continued, "Seems he loved his Leica III, but he loved his secretary more. His loss could be your gain."

Inside the case was a small camera body, along with all kinds of accessories. Black Jack's eyes lit up like a pair of fireflies. "What's the price?"

"Hundred-seventy-five dollars."

"Wow! That's more than they cost new!"

Turning on his salesmanship, Ed remarked, "You can't buy them new anymore. Besides, you get everything in the case -- camera body, three lenses, three view-finders, light meter and all the accessories. The outfit's in mint condition, better than new."

As they haggled, I reached into the case and lifted out one of the lenses, in its soft leather pouch. Underneath the pouch, I found a small metal object about the size of a pack of cigarettes.

Taking it out, I asked, "What's this?"

Black Jack put down the Leica body and took the object from me, "Wow, it's a Spy Camera."

"What the hell is that?"

"It's actually a Minox camera, the smallest camera ever made. They say most of the spies in Europe use these to steal war secrets. It takes strips of 16mm film, and you get about fifty or sixty shots per roll," Black Jack answered.

Ed looked stunned by my find, and started fumbling for words. "…That shouldn't have been in there! The spy camera isn't included. I can sell it alone for a hundred dollars."

"Now, wait a minute," I objected. "You just told us that for a hundred-seventy-five bucks we got everything in the case. Isn't that right?"

"Yeah. But…"

"Ed, you didn't even know the Minox was in there. I'll bet you didn't pay one extra dime for it," Black Jack remarked.

With a sheepish grin, he said, "Yeah...you're right. I didn't even look through the case. She was so happy about screwing her ex-husband that she didn't care about the money."

Smiling back at Ed, I said, "I'll buy the outfit. You can consider it as your contribution towards the war effort."

He stared at me for a moment and then nodded his head in reluctant agreement.

My plan was to give the Leica to Black Jack as a token of my thanks for teaching me photography. He turned my offer down, but he did agree to joint ownership until we went our separate ways.

The spy camera quickly became my camera of choice. I even had small, concealed pockets sewn inside my utility uniforms so it would be available to me in the field. While its picture quality was not that of the C6 or the Leica, it was good enough for documenting events.

Little did I know, on that October day in 1942, just how important that purchase would turn out to be.

On The Road

The 'Marines' Sweetheart' assignment started with three set-ups at Camp Pendleton.

The concept of the first few pictures was simple enough: use new recruits in everyday training settings with Carole Lane. Each of our locations was designed around a different tag line that would be included in the final poster. Because of all our equipment needs, we drove the staff car down to Camp Pendleton, while Miss Lane came down to join us via the morning train.

As Black Jack set up at the first scene, I drove to the station to pick her up. On my way over, I kept reminding myself that our assignment was Job One; my personal emotions couldn't be allowed to interfere. But when I saw her standing on the platform, I had butterflies. In the early morning sunlight, she looked sensational in her black, off-the-shoulder dress.

Her reaction to my arrival was polite and professional, but as cool as the morning breeze. During our drive to the first location, we talked about the day's schedule and the different types of shots we would be doing. She had brought along a garment bag full of clothes and, although helping her with her wardrobe was not a duty I had planned on, it had to be done.

The first setup was at the induction barber shop. I used the same chair and barber that had clipped my hair months before. He didn't recognize me, but that wasn't surprising since he didn't even look my way once Carole was on the set. Nobody did; she captivated the whole room.

We used new Rainbows with lots of hair. First the barber buzz-cut half the head, and then we took pictures of Carole and the recruit reacting to the haircut. The tag line for this picture was, 'Welcome Aboard.' It was cute, sexy and all-Marine. After the still shots, we set up the film gear and shot it again, using different recruits but the same general concept.

An hour later, as we were breaking down the gear to move to the next location, I noticed that Carole was working the room. She moved to each separate barber station, talking to the guys and signing autographs. She was warm, friendly and very down-to-earth with the men. After the barbers, she moved outside and walked down the long line of Rainbows who were waiting for their haircuts. I was sure the Drill Instructors didn't like this departure from discipline, but what could they say?

For the second set-up, I had Carole change into an evening dress, complete with white high heels and gloves. Then we drove to the firing range. Here I met Sergeant Nelson and his platoon. The tag line for this picture would be: 'Ready on the Firing Line.' Our pictures were of Carole holding a rifle, standing with Sergeant Nelson, who was giving her instruction. We used some of his recruits in the background, watching the extraordinary scene.

Everyone seemed to enjoy this set-up, especially Sergeant Nelson. Our best images were of her facial reactions as she actually fired the weapon. The sun was hot, the dust high, and her outfit awkward, but she was a real trooper. While we broke down to move again, Carole mingled with the members of the platoon. She could be a real flirt, surrounded by young men in uniform, but she knew how to turn it on and off at the drop of a hat.

Our final shots were taken back at my old barracks. I used two recruits, having them sit on the lower level of a bunk while they polished their boots. Carole went into the latrine and dressed in black shorts, canvas shoes and a borrowed fatigue shirt. But when she returned, there was something wrong. The shirt was too loose, too military. Taking her back into the latrine, I tied a black belt around her waist and opened the top two buttons of her shirt. Then, moving behind her, I pulled the garment tight to her body and used clothes pins to hold it tight. Watching in the mirror, I couldn't believe the change. She filled out that fatigue shirt like no one else ever had. In the reflection, she smiled back at me, and I blushed.

Returning to the barracks bay, we shot pictures of her working a mop and bucket while watching the guys polish their boots. At first, the recruits couldn't keep their eyes off Carole, but with a little direction the image came together. The tag line for this picture: 'Ready for Inspection.' By the time we finished, Sergeant Nelson and his platoon had returned from the range, and the barracks filled up with guys staring at Carole and her uniform. Between the wolf calls and the whistles, she loved every minute of it.

As we were breaking down the setup, Sergeant Nelson pulled me aside. "Lieutenant, can I get a copy of my picture with Miss Lane...and maybe her autograph?"

I smiled back at him. "Sure. But I'm surprised, Dick. You're star-struck, just like the rest of us!"

On our way out of town, we dropped Carole off at the train station. The drive over was full of conversation about the day's activities. She liked the locations and loved the attention of the men. And, after talking about each set-up, Black Jack seemed confident we would have some great pictures.

If they were happy, I was happy.

Arriving at the station, Carole asked me to help her with the garment bag. As we walked towards the platform, she said, "Dutch, we should talk. I don't want you to have the wrong impression about what happened at your apartment."

Looking for answers in her face, I didn't reply. What could I say?

On the platform, I handed her bag over to a Red Cap and turned to walk away. Reaching out, Carole stopped me. "We're going to be working together a lot...and we should be friends. Please keep an open mind about me. Life isn't always black or white."

With the butterflies back in my stomach, I looked her right in the eye. "I really appreciate you doing these pictures for the Marine Corps, and I wouldn't do anything to screw it up. And as far as 'we' are concerned, 'we' can be friends. But friendship starts with honesty."

Smiling, she stepped towards me, gave me a kiss on the cheek, and whispered, "You're right. And your secret is safe with me. Honest."

Gazing again into her dark blue eyes, I was embarrassed. I wanted more but, instead, I nodded and turned back towards the car.

When the proofs came back the Colonel seemed pleased. A few days later, Seaman Riku finished work on the film clips and delivered a copy to me. He told me that a friend of his at the studio had recorded the sound track, using a script that I had pecked out on Maggie's typewriter. This friend knew Clark Gable, who had just enlisted in the Air Corps, so he'd asked him if he would do the narration. And Gable had agreed!

The timing couldn't have been better. One of the concerns that kept gnawing at me was Riku's Japanese ancestry. Just the week before, the LA Times had run a big story about the plight of Japanese-Americans, and how the government was overreacting. The LA Times was like the Bible around the office, so I knew the Colonel must have read the story.

Black Jack borrowed a film projector and I found a white bed sheet that I could hang on my office wall as a screen. Closing the window shutters, we invited Maggie and the Colonel into the office. As they found a place to stand in front of the bed sheet, I turned off the lights and started my simple pitch: "If hundreds of newspapers are going to carry the 'Sweetheart' story...why not movie theaters?"

Then Black Jack switched the projector on, and my little screen jumped to life. The first scene up was a title graphic that simply said, 'Official USMC Office of War Information Film.' Next came the clips of Miss Lane in the barber shop, then on the firing line, and finally the mop-and-bucket scene.

The three short segments ran just under a minute and half. The camera work and editing were excellent, but it was the voice of Mr. Gable that put it over the top, giving the film that final professional feel.

As I turned the lights back on, I continued, "Now, what would happen if MovieTone picked up these clips as part of their war news? We could reach millions of additional people each week with our 'Sweetheart' story.

Looking over at the Colonel, I noticed that he was still staring at the blank bed sheet, deep in thought.

I moved in front of him. "Well, Colonel? What do you think?"

The room was quiet for a moment. Then he said, "I like it…and I know the story editor over at MovieTone. He's always looking for human interest stuff. I think the General will like it, too. It's a whole new way to reach a whole new audience. Good idea, Dutch!'

"It's a great concept," Maggie echoed.

"Well, that's just it, sir. It's not really my idea. And while Sergeant Malone here did the filming, it was Seaman Riku who came up with the concept and did the real work."

"Who the hell is Seaman Riku?" the Colonel asked.

"He worked for me over at the canteen," answered Black Jack. "He's the oriental cook, sir."

"He's Japanese-American," I added, "and he went to UCLA and majored in film studies before enlisting. And he knows his way around a darkroom, too, sir."

After thinking for a moment, the Colonel said, "I've read in the paper about what's happening to the Nisei. They're really getting the shaft. Are you telling me he wants to transfer in?'

I nodded.

The Colonel rolled his eyes. "The Navy is going to hate me if I steal another person."

"With the Sweetheart Program, they're going to hate us anyway, sir," I remarked.

As the Colonel walked towards the door he turned and said, "Okay...I'll send the clips down to General Small and see what he says. But if Seaman Riku gets in, he stays at his present pay grade. Understood?"

Smiling back at him, I replied, "Yes sir."

The following week, Riku's transfer as E3 Lance Corporal was approved, but that turned out to be the easy part. Getting the film equipment we needed proved to be nearly impossible, so I purchased the outfit we had been renting from Ed Cameron.

In that same week, the Colonel persuaded the people over at MovieTone to use our clips. The footage started running in theaters on the first part of November and proved to be a big hit with the audiences.

Over the next five weeks, we completed the 'Sweetheart' assignment by shooting at locations all over Southern California. We took pictures of Miss Lane helping out with induction physicals, and taking the Marine oath with recruits. Next, we had her fitting recruits for uniforms at a supply depot, then working on a Jeep at a motor pool. Finally, we went to the Mojave Desert, where we got some great pictures of her riding an M5A1 tank, feeding hot chow to the men in the field, and firing a 75mm howitzer.

Our final set-ups, to be taken in San Francisco, were of departing Marines boarding a troopship. The ship was scheduled to leave at 1600 hours on the Monday before Thanksgiving. We drove up, the day before, to scout our locations and make final arrangements. Carole, in San Francisco for the weekend, had agreed to stay over for the pictures. She was to meet us on the dock of Pier 38 at 1130, as the Marines would start loading at noon.

When we arrived at the pier that morning, the weather was overcast, with a light breeze and drizzle. The picture we had envisioned was Carole checking the men in as they walked up the gangway. Its tag line: 'Off We Go.'

When we found the right position for our cameras, we realized how gray everything was. The ship they would be boarding was six stories high, one solid blob of gray paint. The weather was gray. Even the uniforms the Marines were wearing would photograph as gray. Looking at a gray black-and-white picture is like listening to a relative who talks too much and really doesn't have anything to say.

After thinking about the problem, we decided to use the movie lights for our stills. That way, we could paint more light into the scene. Also, we'd see whether Carole had something white or black to wear, to give us some contrast in the shots.

By 11:30, there was over eighteen hundred Marines waiting, two abreast, in a line that snaked its way down and around the rain-swept dock. Each solider was dressed in full battle gear, carrying their weapons and duffle bags. They stood at ease, smoking and talking in the light rain. Watching and listening to them made me wish it was me, standing there in battle gear.

By 11:45, Carole still hadn't arrived. The Loading Master, a Navy Lieutenant JG, told me he would start loading on time. I asked for a few extra minutes, but he turned to the long green line of men and asked, "You want them to stand in the rain while we wait for some dame to show up?" And he was right.

As I stood next to the gangplank, waiting, just before noon, I heard a car horn blasting and turned to see a cab making its way through the line of the Marines. It stopped at the bottom of the gangway, the rear door opened, and Carole leaped out, waving to the crowd and shouting, "Sorry I'm late, boys. The traffic was awful!"

Next came the wolf calls and whistles. The long gray line jumped to life with her appearance...but then, it always did.

Running over to the taxi, I grabbed her bags and rushed her into the warehouse where she could change.

"Sorry I'm late. I overslept."

"Don't worry about it. Do you have anything pure white or black to wear?"

"I have my tennis outfit. White shorts and sweater."

Taking off my rain coat, I handed it to her, "That will work. Wear my coat over it. But hurry."

It did work, and we got some great shots of her loading the men. As the line of soldiers passed Carole and walked up the gangway, I was surprised by how many of them called her 'Sweetheart.' Our publicity campaign was working!

Our final shot was taken aboard the ship. Carole changed into slacks and a blouse, and donned a pilot's bright-yellow Mae West life jacket. We positioned her with a half dozen Marines standing and sitting around a life boat. All of the men were wearing olive-drab life jackets or life belts on top of their battle gear. Carole was holding navy signal flags as if she were sending a message. The line for this picture: 'Be Safe.'

It was mid-afternoon by the time we were done, so we rushed to get our gear off the ship before it pulled away from the dock. As we were leaving, Carole worked the long line of Marines standing by the rails. The guys touched her, kissed her and shook hands with her. There was something in their eyes that reminded me how sad this scene really was. Many of these young tigers would never see home again. Their young faces would haunt me for months to come.

Carole was the last to leave the ship, waving and shouting to the guys as the gangway was being rolled back. With its mooring lines off, the old gray tub blew its horn, quivered and let out a few groans before starting to move. We all stood there in the drizzle, watching the lone ship leave its birth and lumber towards the sea.

At that, Carole was the first to break off and run for the warehouse to get out of the rain. We soon followed.

As she was changing and drying off, I asked, "Do you want me to call a taxi for you?"

"My train doesn't leave until 7:00. What are you guys going to do?"

"On our way out of town, we're going to stop for some Irish coffees to celebrate the last shot of the last location."

Wiping her face with a towel, she said, "That sounds good. Can I join you?"

Her question surprised me. She had not socialized with any of us during the assignment. I looked over to the guys; they smiled and nodded their approval.

"Sure," I said. "But it will be crowded in the staff car."

We arrived at the Buena Vista before the dinner crowd and found a quiet booth in the back. With our first drinks in hand, we toasted the success of the campaign and thanked Carole for her work. The coffee drink was hot and creamy, with a kick to it. Looking across the table, I noticed that she hadn't touched hers.

"Is there something wrong?" I asked.

"I feel sorry for those guys. I think the first toast should be to them."

"Here, here," we agreed.

Carole sat quietly, listening to us talk through the first round of drinks.

About halfway through the second round, she interrupted. "Lieutenant, I have a favor to ask. I'm not feeling very good. I'm sure it's just some kind of bug, but I was wondering if you would mind riding back with me."

Concerned I asked, "Do you need a doctor?"

"No, no, I'm sure I'll sleep it off on the way home. I'd just feel better if someone I knew were on the train, in case I did need help."

Looking over the top of his drink Black Jack remarked, "Lieutenant, we could drive your car back and drop it off at your apartment. I'm sure we'll beat you home, with all the stops the trains make, these days."

I glanced across the table, and saw that Carole did look exhausted. "Okay," I answered, "but we better get a move on. I'll need time to buy a ticket."

Arriving at the station, I deposited Carole's bags with a Red Cap and settled her in the coffee shop. The ticket lines were long; it was just a few days before Thanksgiving. When my turn came, I was informed that the train was sold out. All that remained were a few club-car seats.

"We can't even guarantee that there will be any seats in the club car, Lieutenant," the clerk said. "You might end up standing all the way."

"What time does the train get into Hollywood Station?" I asked.

"6:08 a.m.," he replied.

The idea of standing for eleven hours wasn't appealing, but I took what he had.

By the time I returned to the coffee shop, they were calling our train.

Carole's drawing room was towards the front of the train, while the club car was at the very rear. After getting her situated in her compartment, I found the porter and asked him to make up her bed. Tipping him five dollars, I explained that I would be in the club car if she needed anything more.

Just as I returned to the open door of her compartment, the train started moving. Sticking my head in, I told her, "I found the porter. He'll make up your bed in a few minutes. I sure hope you feel better."

Looking at me with tired eyes, she replied, "Please don't worry. If I can get a little sleep, I should feel better. You know, Dutch, you could stay in here with me...although I'm afraid I won't be very good company."

"No, that's alright. I'll be in the club car, if you need anything."

"Thanks. I feel better just knowing you're on the train. Good night."

The moving train made for a wobbly walk down the long line of cars. As I moved through the dining car, I spotted an open chair and stopped for a sandwich. It was half past eight when I walked into the club car. At the front end of the carriage was a small bar with a few stools, and next to it some stand-up round tables.

The smoky, noisy car was packed with people having a good time. As I made my way through the crowd, I noticed a Marine Captain sitting at the far end of the bar. He nodded at me as I squeezed by some people, and I nodded back.

The car was open in the center but had small cocktail tables and chairs on each side. Towards the end of the carriage, I found a small, empty table. Just across from me was an upright piano. Behind it sat a Negro gentleman, working the keyboard, filling the car with background music. This will be a hard place to fall asleep, I thought.

When the waiter came by, I ordered a brandy and a cup of coffee. Looking around the car, I guessed that over half of its occupants were soldiers or sailors. Just as the waiter returned with my drink, a young couple approached my table and asked if they could sit in the two empty chairs. Smiling, I said, 'Sure,' and then returned to watching the piano player.

Nursing my drink for almost an hour and half, I was debating whether to order another when I heard a commotion coming from the front end of the car. First there were some whistles, and then some applause.

Looking up, I saw Carole walking through the crowd towards me. She was wearing a revealing black cocktail dress and had a yellow flower in her hair. Her beauty transformed the smoky little room.

The girl sitting next to me whispered to her boyfriend, "Isn't that Carole Lane, the movie star?"

Getting to my feet, I said aloud, "Yes, it is." As Carole approached, I asked, "Are you okay?"

Smiling but looking surprised, she asked, "Don't I look okay?"

She explained that, after a couple hours of sleep and a hot meal brought in by the porter, she felt 100% better -- so good, in fact, that she wanted to join me.

As we stood there, talking, the piano player stopped and shouted, "How about a song, Miss Lane?"

The crowd clapped, and people shouted, "Please, Miss Lane," and "How about it, sweetheart?"

Winking at me, she turned towards the crowd and threw her arms up. "Okay, folks. But one of you guys has to buy me a champagne cocktail."

The car filled with applause as she walked to the piano and whispered in the player's ear. He smiled and started stroking the keys. Carole's selection was 'Don't Sit under the Apple Tree,' and it was a hit with the audience.

Sliding back into my chair, I watched her perform. By the time she completed the song, there were two glasses of champagne on the piano.

"More! More!" the listeners shouted.

Reaching for her first cocktail, she said, "Okay, but let me have some of this bubbly first."

The car fell quiet. While she drank, she continued, "Some of you might know me as Carole Lane, while others think of me as the Marine Sweetheart. I'm very proud to be that Sweetheart, and the man who conceived that idea and did all of that outstanding photography is with us tonight." She extended one arm theatrically in my direction. "Lieutenant Dutch Clarke, please stand up! He is the greatest photographer I've ever worked with."

The car filled with applause. I stood up for a second, red faced and embarrassed, then ducked back down into my seat.

Finishing her drink and holding the empty glass up to the audience, Carole called, "Okay...for my next song, how about 'Moonlight Cocktails?'"

As she sang, the waiter returned to my table with another brandy. Leaning towards me, he whispered, "This is with the compliments of the Captain at the bar."

Looking through the crowd to the far end of the car, I spotted the Captain holding his glass up to me. With a nod, I retuned the toast.

One song lead to another, and then another. Between each number, Carole would talk to the audience, just as she had done at the USO show. She even told the story of her dead brother and the RAF again. There wasn't a dry eye in the room.

Around eleven, I got up to use the head. As I was leaving, I winked at Carole, who was still performing, and pushed my way through the audience. The closest toilet was at the end of the dining car, so I had to cross the platform between cars.

When I returned, I found the Marine Captain smoking on the platform. Walking past him, I stopped and said, "Thank you for the drink, sir."

"My pleasure, Lieutenant. So, you're a photographer?"

"Yes, sir. I'm attached with OWI in Hollywood."

The Captain extended his hand. "I'm Thayer Soule. Funny thing is that's what I do, too. And, judging by your uniform, I'll bet you came up through the ranks."

"Yes, you're right, sir. I'm Dutch Clarke. Are you a combat photographer?'

"Yes. Photo Officer, First Marine Division. Just got back from Guadalcanal. I'm on my way to Quantico, in Virginia, to set up a training program for other photographers."

My heart skipped a beat. I couldn't believe how fortunate I was to be talking to a real combat photographer. He was a little older than me, with jet-black hair and dark complexion. His uniform was impeccable, and his body filled it out. We stood there and talked for the longest time. I fired questions at him like a machine gun in battle, with his answers ricocheting around my brain. He gave me details of what it was like to be a combat photographer. It sounded dangerous, but exciting and rewarding. Finally, I asked if he could get my crew and me into his program. He wrote down my contact information but his answer was not encouraging.

"Sounds like you have a 'Rabbi' in high places."

"What's a 'Rabbi'?" I asked.

"A 'Rabbi' looks out for people they like. An editor I once worked for was made a Marine Colonel, and when the war broke out, he became my 'Rabbi.' Because of him, I got my direct commission, without any military experience or training."

"I don't have a 'Rabbi.'"

"From what you've told me, I think the Secretary of the Navy is yours. If that's so, my advice is 'if you can't fight 'em, join 'em.'"

Just then, Carole came through the door from the club car, and she didn't look happy.

"Dutch, where the hell have you been? I came down to have a drink with you, not to entertain this goddam car all night."

Looking down at my watch, I realized how long the Captain and I had talked.

"I'm sorry. This is Captain Soule. He's a combat photographer, just back from Guadalcanal. We were talking shop."

The Captain extended his hand toward her.

Carole walked right by it, clearly angry. "How nice. Solider boys talking war. When I get back from the little girl's room, I'd really like to have a talk with you, Lieutenant."

As she disappeared into the next car, I apologized for her rudeness.

"That's okay. The Nips treated me a lot worse. I've got to get some shut-eye, anyway. I'll do what I can for you and your crew, but don't get your hopes up."

Shaking hands, we said goodbye.

When Carole returned to the table, the anger was gone in her face, replaced by regret. Her moods could change like the wind.

"I'm sorry I talked to you and your friend that way. I just felt so alone when you didn't return."

"I don't think you could ever be alone in a room full of fans."

Leaning over, she kissed me on the cheek, "How sweet. Let's have another drink."

Over the next couple of hours, we drank and danced. She even sang a few more songs. Around two in the morning, the waiter called for last round, but we didn't need any more. She was tight and I wasn't feeling any pain.

Grabbing my arm, she slurred, "Sweetie, walk me back to my compartment. I think I've had too much bubbly."

Helping her walk down the line of moving cars was an adventure. She laughed and giggled as she bounced through the aisles. When we got to her compartment, she fumbled for the key and then handed it to me. As I opened the door, she slipped right by me, grabbed my neck tie, and pulled me into her room. Once inside she kicked the open door closed.

The only light in the drawing room was from a small reading lamp above the open bed. Still holding my tie, she pulled me close and gave me a wet kiss. With the little room swaying and only the sounds of the rails beneath our feet, she broke away and started removing my tie.

"We shouldn't do this. You're engaged to be married," I whispered.

With the moving window light reflecting in her hair, she pulled my tie off and answered, "You're right...we shouldn't."

Next she unbuttoned my coat. It fell to the floor.

"We really shouldn't do this," I said again. "I have a girlfriend back home."

She had my shirt open and her hands on my chest. As the train rattled through a crossing, she murmured, "Yes...I know...you told me about her... we shouldn't."

We kissed again, and I felt her hand on me. I was aroused. "I haven't done this before," I confessed.

"I have."

As we moved to the bed, I remember the train rolling by Paso Robles. Our fervor didn't stop until the train did, at the Hollywood station. And it wouldn't have stopped then if it hadn't been for the third knock on the door by the porter. In between Paso Robles and Hollywood, there had been passion, cigarettes, pillow talk, and more passion. Carole had a sexual appetite I could not have imagined. While she was demanding, she was also patient and found ways to deal with my inexperience. The liaison was exhausting and at times challenged my stamina.

After the third knock, we scrambled to get dressed, making small talk as Carole pulled on her clothes and threw on her makeup. When we finally opened the door to leave our love nest, I realized how stale the little room was; it smelled of passion, with cigarette smoke still hanging in the air.

Giggling, Carole whispered, "Whatever you lacked in experience you made up for with enthusiasm."

I laughed, but I felt embarrassed, and sorry for the little room's next occupant.

As I stepped down onto the station platform, the early morning sun felt good on my face. I handed Carole's bags to a Red Cap, then reached up to help her down.

As we moved towards the station, she said, "My driver should be here. Do you want a ride to your apartment?"

"I don't think so. The walk will do me good."

Her mood changed again. With a cool, distant look on her face, she replied, "Suit yourself. I'm going out of town for the holidays. Maybe we can see each other again, after the first of the year. It was fun, Lieutenant."

With that said, she walked away without even glancing back to me.

It was a five-mile hike to my apartment but I don't remember a step. My mind was working overtime. There had been no intimacy in my first sexual encounter, and I realized that I had envisioned something more. What about her abrupt departure? Had I been a disappointment? And what about Laura? Had I spoiled our love? How about combat photography training, and the Captain's comments about my 'Rabbi'? All of these disjointed thoughts and more ran through my head like water through a faucet. With Carol's scent still hanging on me, I was thoroughly perplexed.

My Rabbi

Driving to San Diego, I spent Thanksgiving with Uncle Roy, staying at El Cortez. He had the same suite I had shared with my pals, months before. He had invited Admiral James King and his wife, Ellen, to join us for Thanksgiving dinner at the hotel. The Vice Admiral was in charge of procurement and logistics for the Seventh Naval District and reported directly to the Secretary of the Navy. The Seventh District covered the Western part of the United States, including Alaska and Hawaii. Uncle Roy had written to me about the Admiral but I had never met the man before.

The dinner conversation proved to be very informative. The Admiral knew a great deal about me and my assignment with OWI. At first, I was surprised. Why would such a powerful man care about a lowly Second Lieutenant?

Using my ears instead of my mouth, I soon found out. Uncle Roy and the Admiral were old college chums. The Kings still owned their family home, back in New Jersey, which Uncle Roy watched over. Our company, Gold Coast Petroleum, was selling specialty lubricants to the Navy, so Roy and the Admiral talked frequently.

As I sat there quietly, it suddenly dawned on me…the Admiral was my 'Rabbi.'

The rest of the dinner talk was all about family and mutual friends. The Kings were nice enough people, and the conversation light and pleasant. After dinner, Mrs. King excused herself and returned to the Navy Base to care for their sick child, while we men retired to the bar for cigars and brandy. Sitting in the grand old barroom, with its overstuffed leather chairs and teak wood paneling, I was intimidated, but then I had been so all night. The Admiral was a giant of a man, with a chest full of ribbons and an armful of gold braid. His commanding voice filled the old room. This was no place for a shave-tail Second Lieutenant, so I sat quietly, watching the Admiral and Roy enjoy themselves.

At one point, their conversation paused and the Admiral turned his attention to me. Swirling a brandy snifter in one gigantic hand while puffing on his cigar, he remarked, "Secretary Knox and I liked your Sweetheart Program. It's good for morale. Good job, Lieutenant."

His statement caught me off-guard, and I fumbled for a response. "I'm surprised you and the Secretary even know about it, sir. While fighting this war with a camera was not my choice, it's an important job that has to be done."

"We also know about the make-up of your crew. Secretary Knox loves that integration stuff. If you ever have any problems, let me know."

Then Uncle Roy interrupted about some business matters before I could reply. As they talked, the Admiral's use of the word 'problems' kept racing through my mind. Should I ask him about combat photography training? Could he help me or would he hinder? What about a transfer to a combat unit as just a mud Marine? No…like Captain Soule had advised, 'If you can't fight em, join em.'

Later, as we were getting ready to leave, I shook hands with the Admiral again and said, "I've got a great crew, sir. If you ever have any photography work, please keep us in mind."

With a big grin on his face, he replied, "I'll do that, Lieutenant. And who knows what the future might hold."

Driving back to Hollywood, I kicked myself for being so timid. The Admiral and Roy had controlled the conversation through dinner and drinks, with me as quiet as a mouse. There was so much I should have said…so much I wanted to say. But then, the best speeches are always written on the drive home.

Just before Christmas, Colonel Ford called me into his office for what he called an 'early Christmas present.' On this particular day, he was dressed in his uniform and looked all military as I stood in front of his desk.

"I have some great news for you, Dutch. It seems the Marines have seen fit to promote you to First Lieutenant."

Reaching into his pocket, he pulled out two silver bars, placing them on his desk in front of me.

"These were my old bars, and I thought they might bring you luck, like they did me."

Picking them up, and wondering whether my 'Rabbi' had a hand in this, I thanked the Colonel.

Reaching into his desk drawer, he continued, "I have more news. Hollywood OWI has been awarded the Presidential Unit Citation for our efforts selling war bonds. Also, the Marine Corps has awarded, exclusively to the staff of this office, the Navy Unit Commendation for the 'Sweetheart Campaign."

Sliding two colorful ribbons across to me, he concluded, "New silver bars and some color for your blouse. Can't get much better than that."

Looking down at the ribbons, with the bars in my hand, I felt both proud yet disappointed. "Yes, sir," was all I could say.

That evening, when I returned to my apartment, I put the ribbons and silver bars on my kitchen table and opened a Coke. Sliding into a chair, I held the awards in my hand and pondered my pride and disappointment. The young Marine faces on that departing troopship had been haunting me for weeks. By now, they would have arrived at their destination and might be fighting in some big battle...and here I sat, with a promotion and medals. It just didn't seem fair. I had joined the Marines to put out Nips, not propaganda.

CHAPTER FIVE

Exhausted, I staggered to my feet. Behind the little island the sun was sinking, and I knew I had to do some exploring before it got dark. Looking down at my mates, it was clear that they were in no condition to join me.

"I'm going to have a look-see before it gets dark," I told them. "If you feel up to it, drag the raft further up the beach. I'll be right back."

Jasper nodded at me as I started up the shoreline. Brown sea grass grew on the embankment just above the white sandy beach. My legs were wobbly from days of inactivity, so climbing up the small hill was harder than I expected. In the center of the atoll was a grove of weather-beaten mangrove and palm trees about thirty feet tall. Walking towards them, I noticed how the ground around them was littered with dead and rotting leaves that gave the air a fetid scent. As I stumbled through this debris, I tripped on a large husk that was almost black in color. Picking it up, I realized it was a coconut pod.

Gazing at it for a moment I wondered if our prayers had been answered. Putting it next to my ear, I shook it.

From deep within, I heard a sloshing sound.

Excitement lifted my spirits. Looking around, I found two more, gathered them up, and ran towards the beach.

Back at the raft, I grabbed the bayonet and began hacking away at the outer layer of the pod. Inside the husk, I found a small, brown coconut shell, which I cut out.

Holding it in my hands, I moved it close to my mates. "Listen."

As I shook it again, they heard the liquid inside, and their faces lit up like a Christmas tree. Taking the knife, I managed to drill two small holes in the top of the hard shell and lifted it to my mouth. Dribbling out of the hole came the wet, bitter taste of coconut milk. After I had taken a small mouthful, I passed the coconut on to the Padre, who looked at it for a moment and then handed it to Corporal Bates. As they drank, I prepared the two remaining husks. In the end, we all savored a few mouthfuls of liquid and then, breaking apart the shells, ate the moist, sweet coconut meat.

Watching the faces of my friends, I felt like I was passing around food at a church social. The guys said nothing, but it was clear that they enjoyed every bite. By the time we'd finished, the sun was down and our little beach was lit only with starlight. After pulling the raft up to the sea grass, we all laid on the beach and quietly watched the evening sky.

Finally, the Padre broke the silence, asking me, "Are we saved?"

Looking back at him in the dark, I answered, "I don't know. But we're better off tonight than we were last night."

The next morning we had a coconut breakfast and explored the tiny island. As we walked towards the far end, we could see more atolls running in an almost straight line, due north. The closest one looked to be about a mile from our location.

Rounding the point of our island, we made our biggest discovery. Four or five miles northwest from our position was a very large, craggy island that seemed to grow out of the sea. It had been the clouds above this landmass that I had seen yesterday. On the north end of that island were high mountains that were partly hidden by clouds. The shape then flattened as the land sprawled south. Around the island were high, gray granite cliffs that ran straight down to the surf. On the southern part of the land, not covered with clouds, we could see verdant patches. With its rugged beauty, it was an ominous sight.

"What do you think, Dutch? Could we make it over to that bloody island?" the Padre asked.

"Maybe. There might be Japs on it...but it does look like heaven."

Moving to higher ground, I climbed halfway up a palm tree for a better look. Because of the high cliffs, I couldn't see any signs of a beach around the island. There were some tall rock outcroppings towards the south end, and I suspect that there might be a lagoon there. In front of the large island, the sea current in the channel flowed south and looked treacherous. The small atolls to the north of us acted as a barrier to the big island. Between each of these small islands, open water flowed and then turned into the channel. As all of this water mixed, it picked up speed and flowed south. With a powerboat, there would be no problem. With our raft, however, I was sure that if we tried to cross the channel here, we would be swept south.

Returning to my mates, I explained about the current and suggested that we move from island to island, up the line of atolls. When we were north of the big island, we could float south and use the channel's current to make landfall.

They liked the idea and agreed.

As we finished our walk, we found a grove of tall bamboo. Using the bayonet, I cut down some of the larger shoots to make poles. At the raft, I had Jasper and Sergeant York start making mats from palm leaves so we could have some shade on the boat, while Bates and Patterson set about weaving a primitive rope out of sea grass. While they worked, I crafted two crude oars, using the bayonet as a draw knife on two of the larger poles. Our final task was to gather more coconut pods and load them into the float.

By noon we were ready to go. Dragging the raft into the surf, we rowed away from our inland, heading to the northeast. About half a mile out, we felt the current start to move us back towards the west. Paddling with all our strength, we finally landed on the next atoll, late that afternoon.

Walking up the beach, we could see the next island more clearly. It looked to be the biggest of the atolls and even had some rock outcroppings on its western shore. The next day, we landed on it, just before noon. This island was much like the last two, but had a longer and deeper landmass. Cutting down some bamboo, we tried spear-fishing in the rocky area of the beach, but had no luck.

Early the next morning, as we were getting ready to leave for the next atoll, Sergeant York shouted, "What the hell is that, out there in the surf? Is that a bloody shark?"

Looking up from the raft, I caught a quick glimpse of a large object rolling out to sea. Running over to the rocky area, I jumped up on a tall rock for a better view. Just a few yards out, I could see it swimming: a large sea turtle.

Running back to the boat, I screamed, "That's our dinner -- a sea turtle. Let's push off and try to catch it. You guys row while I make a lasso to collar it."

Dragging the boat down to the surf, Jasper asked, "Have you ever caught a turtle before, Dutch?"

With a big grin on my face, I answered, "Nope...but I've caught a lot of big fish."

As my mates rowed, I took one of the long bamboo poles and made a hole in its side, near the top. Next, I threaded some grass rope through the hole, making a hangman's loop with a slipknot. This way, I could hold the long pole out from the boat while sliding the loop around the turtle's neck.

By the time I looked up, Corporal Bates was kneeling at the front of the boat, pointing with his good arm and yelling instructions about the turtle's direction.

Holding the pole over the water, I replaced him at the bow and shouted, "I can see him. He's just a few yards away. Come on, mates, pull!"

Moments later we were just behind him. Taking the pole, I reached out and tried to slip the loop around his neck, but I missed. Carefully, I made a second try...and I got him!

Pulling tight on the rope, I closed the noose around his neck and felt a tug.

Turning to my mates with a smile on my face, I hollered, "Like taking candy from a baby."

Pow! The little tug turned into a gigantic yank which pulled me headfirst into the ocean. With one hand on the pole and the other on the rope, I was being dragged down ever deeper into the water.

Regaining my composure, I realized that I had to either let go or kill the turtle in the water. The turtle was pulling me with great strength. Opening my eyes, I pulled myself along the pole to its noose. Looking below, I could see the turtle's legs moving as I floated just above his shell. Reaching down with one hand I removed the bayonet from its scabbard on my waist. With one quick, powerful slash, I drove the point of the knife between his neck and his left front leg.

Instantly the water in front of me filled with blood, and the turtle stopped swimming. With sharks around and blood in the water, this was suddenly the last place I wanted to be.

Looking up, I saw the underside of our raft in the distance. Quickly moving to the other end of the pole, I swam for the surface, dragging the dead turtle behind me. It was a long swim up, and when I broke the surface, I was gasping for air. It was still another forty or fifty yards to the raft, and by now my mates were yelling at me that there were shark fins just behind me. Putting the knife in my mouth, I started swimming for the boat.

I don't recall a single stroke. It was as if I flew across the water. Handing the pole to Sergeant York, I grabbed onto the side of the raft and, with one fast and powerful leap, pulled myself in. As my mates worked to drag the dead turtle in, others fought off the sharks with their oars.

With the carcass in the raft, we started rowing for the next island. But because of the open webbing in the bottom of our boat, the blood seeped through, and sharks followed us, all the way.

We fought them off as best we could, but these sharks were so bold that one made an attack, ripping a small chunk of balsa wood off from the float. We were relieved to finally reach shallow water and the shoreline.

Dragging the dead turtle out of the boat, I was surprised at its size. The shell was almost three feet long and two feet wide. As we pulled it up the beach, I estimated its weight at roughly a hundred pounds. We finally knelt around it and examined the strange yellow-brown creature, with its narrow head and hawk-like beak.

"So...how do we eat it?" the Padre asked.

"Just cut the legs off and eat 'em," Corporal Bates answered.

"It would taste a lot better if it was cooked," I suggested.

"Cooked! Sure, mate. We'll just throw it on the barbie."

Turning to Sergeant York, I asked, "Do you still have that lens from your broken glasses?"

York nodded, reaching into his tattered pocket for it.

Taking it, I walked over to some dead dry grass, just up from the beach. Grabbing a handful, I returned and laid the fuel on the sand. Using York's lens, I focused the sunlight on the dry grass.

With the Aussies watching my every move, in a few moments I had smoke, and then small flames.

They got the idea and soon our little fire was big enough to cook with. We cut the turtle meat into chunks and, using bamboo sticks, held it over the open fire. We had eaten all kinds of wild creatures, back at the prison camps -- snakes, rats, and birds, cooked and raw -- but this was, without a doubt, the best of all. We could now understand why some people considered turtle a delicacy.

At last, with our bellies full, we ended our meal, wrapped the leftover meat in palm leaves, and stuffed them into empty coconut shells. Using the bayonet again, I cut away the turtle's large, hard shell, then buried the remains of the carcass in the sand. Finally, using wet sand at the shoreline, we washed and cleaned the shell, as best we could, and set it out to dry. It would be useful if it rained, or if we found any fresh water on the big island.

At twilight, we sat around the open fire, drinking coconut milk and reflecting on the day. The conversation soon turned to my belly flop into the sea, and my comment about taking candy from babies. The Padre told me that I should become an Olympic swimmer after the war, because he had never seen anyone swim so fast.

"Funny what happens when sharks are after you, mate," added Private Patterson.

Something special happened that evening, something I will never forget. While I had known these poor devils for months, this was the first time I had ever seen them laugh. And while I bore the brunt of their laughter, it made me so happy, seeing them enjoy themselves that I wanted to cry.

Later, as the fire died down and the stars came out, Corporal Bates asked me, "How did you learn all this survival stuff? Were you what you Yanks call a Boy Scout?"

"Nope. Never joined," I replied.

"Then how?" the Padre inquired.

In the firelight, I could see them all looking at me, "Guess I can thank my Grandfather, he taught me the meaning of survival."

Pals

The rain felt wet and fresh on my face. As I jogged down the boulevard in shorts and a Navy t-shirt, the people along the way looked at me as if I was crazy. But, just like a kid, I still loved running through puddles and feeling the spray on my legs and body. Californians considered rain as a weather event and used little black umbrellas so they wouldn't melt, but this rain freshened my thoughts.

Christmas had come and gone. While I'd had many offers to spend the holidays with friends, I had elected to stay home alone. It had been a time to reflect, read and catch up on my writing. Sometimes, your own company is the best.

Rounding a corner and listening to the rhythm of my feet splashing in the rain, I thought about the year's events. 1942 had started in the cold wilderness of British Columbia and would end on this rainy night in Hollywood, California. Between those two dates, there had been love, life, war and a hope for a better future. And there had been friends, new friends. A man should be measured by the pals he keeps, and I felt tall.

My thoughts about Carole Lane, however, were different. She had been on my mind, all through the holidays. Thoughts about her hung over my head like a black cloud over a picnic.

Turning at the next street, I saw my apartment building ahead. As soon as I had a hot shower and some dry clothes, I would be ready to usher in 1943 with solitude and hope.

My plans for New Year's Eve were simple: a few cold beers, Tommy Dorsey on the radio, and a chance to finish a book Uncle Roy had sent to me, 'All Quiet On The Western Front.' The gift had been his not-so-subtle way of reminding me of his antiwar views. Although I found the book depressing, I was determined to finish it, just so I could tell him I had done so.

That evening, just as I was settling in with my book, there was a knock at my door. Opening it, I was serenaded with calls of "Happy New Year." There in my corridor stood Black Jack and his lady friend, the one from the pictures, and Corporal Riku with a beautiful, slender Oriental gal. Black Jack and Riku were both holding wooden fruit boxes full of party items.

Their unexpected appearance both surprised and pleased me.

Holding up his box with a big grin, Black Jack announced, "We brought the party, if you're in the mood."

Smiling, I invited them in. While Riku introduced the ladies, Black Jack emptied the boxes. One box contained champagne, beer, ice, and even a couple of bottles of good scotch. The other held food and party favors.

It turned out to be one hell of good party. We danced, drank and talked until the wee hours of the morning. The ladies were real nice gals, and treated my two friends with great love and respect. But it was my friends that I enjoyed the most.

Black Jack Malone

We had become very close, very fast. At first, it was the photography that bonded us, but with time it became our personalities. We were much alike, slow to anger, eager to please, and quick to laugh. His broad smile, with those bone-white teeth, could brighten any room, while his massive physique could ward off any trouble. There was much I liked and respected about this man…this friend. At first, because of the racial barrier, parts of his life seemed like a closed book to me, but after I gained his trust, that book slowly started to open.

His mother's side of the family had come from slave stock in the Deep South. They had been dirt-poor sharecroppers for decades. Lilly, his mother, was born with a special gift for music. At a young age, she started dreaming about being an entertainer, but her family would have none of that dream; they forced her into the fields after just three years of schooling.

There she remained until she turned sixteen. When her mother died in a farm accident, she ran away from home and her abusive father. Traveling to New Orleans, she started singing and dancing in various honkytonks and bars along Bourbon Street.

Developing her talent, with the help of other Negro performers, she soon established a following and began making her reputation as a blues singer. While performing at one of these salons, she met a red-haired Irish trumpet player/singer named Bill Malone. He was a good-looking, strapping young man with a tenor's voice and pleasing personality.

Bill was driven by a dream to become one of the first Irish soul singers. After working together with Lilly onstage, he enlisted her help in polishing his style. Practicing together, after-hours, she helped him find his voice and stage presence. Some months later, they formed the first 'salt & pepper' soul team.

The novelty of a beautiful Negro girl singing blues with a white, red-headed man soon became a hit with local audiences. But Bill's love for soul music was overshadowed by his love for booze and other women. At first, Lilly couldn't see the warts hidden in his red stubble, and she fell in love with him. But their love affair was like the New Orleans weather, mostly hot and steamy, with occasional storms brought on by booze and broads. As sure as night follows day, Lilly soon was pregnant. On one of Bill's few sober days, they were married, in 1917.

Having a salt & pepper theatrical act was one thing; having a salt & pepper marriage was quite another. Prejudice tainted all aspects of life in the South so strongly that, for safety reasons, they didn't tell their family or friends about their marriage.

Early the next year, Lilly gave birth to Jack Preston Malone, and people considered her mixed-raced son a bastard. But Lilly was a good and loving mother who did what she could to raise Jack in a normal, Christian home. This was a particularly challenging task because of the late hours and extensive travel they endured when performing.

In 1920, with the onset of prohibition, the family moved to New York City to seek bookings at speakeasies. In those early, turbulent days of temperance, finding and keeping gigs was difficult. The illegal bars were run by mobsters who had close ties to the bootleggers. They were more interested in selling booze than in entertaining their customers. When Lilly and Bill did get a booking, they would have to pay protection money to the local gangster with one hand while the other was paying bribes to the local cops. Working some of their early shows, they actually lost money. Finally, they were befriended by an Irish mobster, Lucky

Jack Cartwright, who had four clubs in Harlem at which they ended up performing for a number of years. Most evenings, Lilly and Bill played to an audience made up of a mix of criminals and the cream of society. Black Jack's earliest memories were of watching his parents' act from backstage at these speakeasies. It was an odd cultural experience for young Jack and, because of it, he learned how to survive with all kinds of people.

In 1928, Bill Malone ran off with a hatcheck girl, not to be seen again for many years. His departure devastated Lilly, even though by now she knew all about his warts. The inexplicable love she felt for this man would never be replaced or extinguished. But with Bill gone, Lucky Jack Cartwright fired Lilly, only to rehire her again, a few days later, after she'd changed her act back to a jazz-singing single.

During their entire stay in New York, Lilly and Black Jack lived in a small flat above a camera store in Harlem. After Bill ran off, Jack started hanging out with the wrong crowd and causing trouble in the neighborhood. Lilly, desperate for help with her son, turned to Herb Goldstein, the Jewish proprietor of the camera store below them. Mr. Goldstein agreed to watch out for Jack and give him some odd jobs around the store, each day after school.

Black Jack remembered old man Goldstein as a crabby, tough taskmaster who wouldn't take shit from anyone. He was as tight with a penny as he was with a smile. At first, the odd jobs were menial: deliveries, sweeping the floors, and keeping the storefront windows cleaned. But soon Mr. Goldstein had him mixing chemicals, working in the darkroom, and even helping with customers. Herb and Jack made an odd couple behind the counter but, with Jack's personality and Herb's knowledge, it worked. Through the help and encouragement he received from this strange Jewish mentor, Jack Malone found his way off the streets and learned to excel in photography. During his high school years, Jack went on to win many citywide photography contests with his images of street life in New York. Right out of school, these awards led to his first assignment with TIME Magazine.

With prohibition over and Jack out of high school, Lilly gave up her nightclub act and hooked up with a dance band. Once again reworking her music, Lilly started performing the popular songs of the day. The band had a national radio show that aired every Saturday night from Times Square.

The program proved to be a good showcase for Lilly and her music. She soon had offers from all around the country. In 1937, she moved to Hollywood where she starred in several Negro musicals being filmed at that time.

She was found dead in her apartment in January of 1940. Saddened, Jack came to Hollywood to settle her affairs…and, like a vulture following death, his father also reappeared. Bill had read about Lilly's passing in one of the trade journals, and traveled west to collect his part of her estate. At first, Jack was resentful and angry, but when he realized that Bill had become nothing more than a common street bum looking for his next drink, his ire turned to pity. He even tried to reconnect with Bill as his father. In the end, however, they split up a few thousand dollars and said good-bye. The last Jack heard, his dad was living in a flophouse on Skid Row in downtown LA.

With war looming, his mother dead, and his father a broken bum, Jack enlisted in the Navy. It was a sad tale about a sad family. Black Jack never told me how or why Lilly died, and I didn't ask. It was a difficult memory for him and I respected his privacy.

Riku Togo

If photography had helped me bond with Black Jack, it was my interest in Japanese culture that helped connect me with Riku. Early on, I started asking questions about Japan, its history, its people, and its language. Given my desire to understand my enemy better, Corporal Riku was the right person at the right time and place. He was a walking encyclopedia of all things Oriental. During our long trips to complete photographic assignments, he even started teaching me conversational Japanese. It was a hard language to grasp but, with his patience, I soon could speak and understand a few basic phrases in Japanese.

While Black Jack and I had personas that were alike, Riku and I were like night and day. He was a quiet thinker, always brooding, with a look on his face as if he had a secret. While he had a sense of humor, it was on the dry side, and he was slow to laugh.

One amazing talent he did have was his near-photographic memory. He could read anything and recite it back, almost verbatim. Another talent was his use of Judo -- or what he called Yudo, a kind of Korean Judo -- for self-protection. He could, with a few quick moves, have anyone of any size sprawled out on the ground. As he loved to say, 'It's all about leverage, not about size." I outweighed the little guy by a good fifty pounds and Jack by almost seventy, yet when we wrestled, we could never get him pinned. He was like quicksilver, while we were like bulls; the harder we charged, the faster he moved. We both came to respect his special talent for hand-to-hand combat.

During the First World War, Japan had been our ally, and Riku's father worked as a translator for the Japanese government in Washington DC. After the war, he was transferred to Korea as a cultural attaché. It was there that he met and married Riku's mother. Later, his father went to work for an American shipping company, and the family moved to Southern California. After Riku was born in 1921, his father quit that job and opened his own exporting firm, specializing in shipping fruits and vegetables back to Japan. The business flourished, and the Togo family soon settled into middle-class life.

Many Japanese-Americans were living in Southern California, at the time, so Riku never had to face any prejudice because of his race. Growing up, he was, in every sense of the word, 'All-American.' He went to Hollywood High School, drove a jalopy, lettered in wrestling, and attended UCLA.

But that all changed after Pearl Harbor. In the eyes of those around them, Riku and his family went from being neighbors and friends to being 'slant-eyed Nips' in a heartbeat. They lost their business, their home and all their worldly possessions. After the foreclosures and confiscations, the government moved the family to a temporary relocation camp in the middle of the Utah desert.

Riku could have been bitter. Who would have blamed him? But he wasn't. Instead, he joined the Navy, to prove to the world that he was still 100% American. I respected him for his special talents and, above all else, for his courage to remain loyal to America and to himself.

Yes, I stood tall with good friends…good pals. For the first time in my life, I was learning what trust and true friendship were all about. While fate determined our relatives, thank God we could choose our own friends.

Turning Points

Ring…ring.

"Hi, sweetie. Did you miss me?'

It was Carole on the phone. Her call was both welcome and dreaded.

"You're back! How were your holidays?"

"It was too hot in Mexico, but the holidays were just fine. I ran into Lennie yesterday, and he told me about your promotion and your new medals. Congratulations."

"Thank you."

She sighed. "We have to talk, Dutch. I thought about you way too much, over Christmas. So much, in fact, that I've broken off my engagement, and I want to see you again."

I felt my face go flush at the thought of being with her again. "I'm sorry to hear you broke off your engagement," I said.

"That's okay. It was my decision. Listen, I've been invited to the premier of Midnight Oil at Grauman's. You know, Grauman's Chinese Theatre. It's on Friday night and I need an escort. It's going to be a gala affair with Spencer Tracy, Kate Hepburn and all the Hollywood press. How about you taking me?"

A very public appearance with Carole was not something I had ever considered, and the thought scared me a little.

"Well…Sure, it sounds like fun. But I'm worried about all those people and the press. I guess I'm just a shy guy, at heart."

She laughed. "Honey, don't worry about it. They won't be looking at you, they'll be looking at me. Pick me up at seven and we can have a drink before we leave. The show starts at eight, so don't be late."

"Okay. I'll see you at seven."

"Oh, and Dutch…make sure you wear your uniform. I want people to see what a real Marine looks like."

Her last comment caught me off guard. I always wore my uniform, so her request didn't make much sense…not until Colonel Ford came into my office that afternoon.

"Remember the film I've been working on, over at RKO?" the Colonel asked.

"Yes, sir."

"Well, the script's done. The picture is going to be called Leathernecks. With a three-million-dollar budget, and George Cukor signed on as the director, it's all the buzz around town. Yesterday, I ran into Carole Lane, and she knew all about the project. She wants to play the female lead, Jackie. Jackie's the wife of a pilot who's shot down in the Pacific. I told Carole that she'd have to talk to Mr. Cukor about the part." He bristled. "She got real pushy with me, like the Marines owed her the role. Did you tell Miss Lane about the film?"

"No, sir. I didn't know anything about the film, and I only talked to Carole for a few minutes, this morning. When she called, she didn't say a word to me about the project."

"Can I ask why she called?"

"Sure. She asked me to take her to some premier on Friday night."

Thinking for a moment, he asked, "Is the film 'Midnight Oil?'"

"Yes, sir."

Shaking his head, he said angrily, "She's playing you like a fiddle, Lieutenant. That's George Cukor's latest film, and she wants a dressed-up Marine to help impress him. I warned you about land mines like her. Anyway, she's engaged to be married. Why would you want to go out with her?"

"She told me she broke off her engagement. When she asked me to escort her, it was hard to say no, after what she's done for our Sweetheart promotion."

"You're thinking with the wrong part of your body, Dutch. She told me that her fiancé was still in Mexico, making a picture. But what you do is up to you. Just don't bring any disgrace to that uniform."

"Aye, aye, sir."

After he left, I sat back in my chair and contemplated his words. Why hadn't Carole said anything about the new film? Why hadn't she told me the truth about her engagement? Maybe I *was* thinking with the wrong part of my body.

My inner argument was still raging as I drove up to Carole's house on that chilly Friday evening. She had a strange hold on me. I was attracted to her like a bear to a beehive, but deep down I knew her sweet taste would sting with pain.

Arriving at seven sharp, I rang the doorbell. Mrs. Jackson greeted me with a friendly smile and ushered me into the living room. She informed me that Carole would be down shortly, and then disappeared. The old Spanish-style room was large, with white stucco walls and red tile floors. On one side was a bank of picture windows with a view of downtown Hollywood in the distance. It was twilight, so not all the city lights were on, while in the west the scarlet sky was still gleaming. It was an impressive vista.

Centered in front of the windows was a black grand piano that had an enormous bouquet of flowers on it. It reminded me of the piano on the train, and the fun we had that night. Across the room, below a long dark timber mantle, a glowing fire filled a massive fireplace. Above the fireplace was a large oil painting of Carole looking up at the sky. In front of the fireplace was a conversation area, with brown leather couches and three overstuffed club chairs. As I started to walk towards the fireplace, Mrs. Jackson reappeared, with a glass of champagne on a small silver tray. Smiling, she set the drink down on a small table and, without saying a word, disappeared again.

Taking the drink, I walked the length of the fireplace mantle, looking at the pictures that crowded it. They were all large, beautifully framed images of Carole in different costumes from her movies. Behind the front row, I found three smaller, framed snap-shots of an older couple with a little girl. I guessed that they were Carole's parents. Rummaging behind their pictures, I spotted an old, framed, yellowing newspaper clipping with the headline 'Carol Goldstein Wins Talent Show.' The clipping had a fading black-and-white picture of a young girl seated at an upright piano.

"Do you like what you see?"

Looking up, I saw Carole standing there, dressed in a curvy, dark-green, strapless evening gown, with long white gloves and high heels. She had a white mink stole around her shoulders and a diamond tiara in her blond hair. She was breathtakingly beautiful as she walked towards me.

"I love all your pictures…but who is Carol Goldstein?"

"That's me, silly. Lane is just my stage name."

By now, she was standing right in front of me. She had not a hair out of place, and the warm evening light made her look like a golden goddess. I wanted to reach out and kiss her…but I didn't.

Looking at me with a sexy grin, she seemed to read my mind. "I'd give you a kiss," she said, "but I don't want to muss-up my makeup. We'll have lots of kisses later."

Just then, Mrs. Jackson returned with a glass of champagne for Carole. As she left, she told us that the chauffer had arrived and was waiting.

"I've got my car out front," I volunteered. "We can take it."

Looking up from her wine glass, Carole shook her head. "Sweetie, we can't take your car to Grauman's. If I showed up in the 'staff car,' I'd be the laughing stock of the Hollywood press."

She was right; a limo in Hollywood was a lot more impressive than my 1939 Chrysler coupe.

Standing by her pictures, Carole pointed out certain images and named the movies from which they'd been taken.

Her comments surprised me. Instead of being proud of her accomplishments, she heaped criticism on them. There was not one picture on her mantel that she seemed to like, nor did the roles she'd played seem to please her. And, to hear her tell it, it was always the fault of the writers, directors, makeup artists or costume designers. Carole felt that she had never been given the right movie role, one where she could truly showcase her talents.

Wanting to change the subject, I pointed to the snapshots of the couple with the little girl and asked, "Is this you with your parents?"

With a sober look, she answered, "Yes. Dad's gone, now, but Mom is still alive."

"I don't see any brothers or sisters."

"No, I'm an only child."

Her answer stung me like a bee. Hardly believing my own ears, I asked, "What about your brother, the RAF pilot that died in the skies over London?"

She looked blankly surprised for a moment, then seemed to understand my question. "Oh, that's just a story I tell my audiences. You know. I tell them what they want to hear, just like lines from a script."

Like a hammer to glass, something broke inside of me. I felt my face grow hot with anger. "Those aren't lines, Carole, they're lies. I can't believe you can stand up in front of a room full of soldiers and tell them such a story...a story without a shred of truth in it."

She looked at me and saw my anger. "Oh, Dutch, you're so naïve. I'm an actress, not a nun. I play-act every day, all the time. My job is to entertain, not to hold confessions."

"So I suppose that being sick in San Francisco and wanting me on the train was just play-acting, too?"

She grinned. "I wasn't sick...but I did want you, if you know what I mean. And a girl like me gets what she wants."

As I placed the wine glass on the mantel, my anger changed to disappointment as the golden goddess faded to tin. "And you're broken engagement is just another 'line,' while your fiancé is still in Mexico making a picture, right? And tonight's premier is really about George Cukor and the part you want in his new movie, Leathernecks."

She stared at me, her face now red and angry. "You must have talked to Lennie. Well, I don't have to make excuses to you."

Turning to leave, I answered, "No, you certainly don't."

"Where the hell do you think you're going?"

Stopping in the middle of the room, I turned back to her for a moment. "Home, if I can find my way out of this ego palace."

"No man walks out on me, Lieutenant," she shrieked. "If you walk through those doors, I'll tell Colonel Ford you tried to rape me, and he'll have you on the next troopship out!"

Turning again at the doorway, I saw this vindictive pretender clearly for the first time. "I only wish you had that power, lady."

As I turned to leave, I heard a whizzing sound by my head; then her wine glass hit the wall next to me. As the glass shattered, the wine made long streaks on the wall.

Walking through the entry towards the front door, I yelled over my shoulder, "Goodnight, Miss Lane -- or should I say 'Miss Goldstein?'"

Driving back to my apartment, I knew my inner argument was over and that my better half had won. Finally, I was thinking with the right part of my body. And, best of all, I had not brought disgrace to my uniform.

G-Men

"Do you know what the hell is going on?" the Colonel asked with a puzzled look as he walked into my office.

Looking up from a stack of proofs, I asked, "About what, sir?"

Sliding into the chair next to my desk, he said quietly, "About you and the FBI."

His question took a moment to sink in…and then he had my full attention. Just the thought of the FBI knowing my name sent a chill down my spine. "What do you mean, sir?"

"I just got off the phone with Agent Collins from the LA office, and he's real interested in you and your politics. He asked all kinds of questions -- how long had I known you, do you vote, do you pay your taxes, are you a good American, do you beat your wife or kick dogs? All the stuff the FBI asks when they're looking for something."

"Looking for what?" I asked helplessly, bewildered.

"Hell, I don't know. I asked what it was all about, but he wouldn't tell me a damn thing."

I knew that Carole was mad at me, but could she have enough power to get the FBI involved?

No way. G-Men wouldn't do the bidding of some Hollywood bimbo. Nevertheless, the news frightened me. There was something going on, and I didn't have a clue about what it was.

"Do you think I should call them, sir?" I asked the Colonel.

He shook his head. "No. The best thing to do, when the FBI starts snooping around, is to keep a low profile. If they want you, they'll call you."

And that's exactly what they did, early the next morning. On the phone, I was given instructions to report to the downtown Federal Building at 3:00, with my passport, for an interview with Agent Collins. When I asked what this was all about, the lady on the other end of the phone said she didn't know, but she stressed the importance of showing up on time.

As I cooled my heels in Agent Collins's sparse outer office, my mind was racing as to why I was here. Sometimes a person can feel guilty when they're not; I only hoped this was such an occasion.

Finally, I was ushered into the adjoining office, where I found a small, middle-aged, skinny guy seated behind a stack of files on a desk.

When I introduced myself and extended my hand for a shake, he didn't even look up. "Sit, Lieutenant."

He leafed through some pages in a file as I looked around his office. The only picture on the wall was of J. Edgar Hoover. The rest of the room was as cold and drab as its occupant. With his thin, bony face and thick, wire-rimmed glasses, Agent Collins looked more like a high school chemistry teacher than a G-Man.

"Okay. Lieutenant, did you bring your passport?"

"Yes, sir," I said, and handed it to him.

He leaned back in his chair, slowly examining the pages. Then, taking pen in hand, he made some notes in one of the files.

Looking down on the desk, I could see my name on the file he was working in.

"Can I ask why I'm here, sir?"

Looking up from the folder with a sour look on his face, he said, "I'll ask the questions, Lieutenant."

What a pleasant man, I thought wryly.

"You entered Canada through Vancouver, British Columbia, in May of 1941, and exited though Prince Rupert, British Columbia, in June of 1942. Is that correct?"

"Yes, sir."

Flipping a few more pages in my file, he continued, "In that same May of 1941, you were given a draft deferment for one year. How did you pull that off? You didn't want to serve your country, so you went to Canada for a year?"

"No, sir. I had family business up there, and my uncle took care of the deferment. I wasn't pulling anything off."

He searched, switching to another file. "That would be…your uncle, Roy Clarke. I have a file here on him. Let's see. Oh, yes, he was on the local draft board, and he did sign your deferment…but why? What kind of family business did you have in Canada, Lieutenant?"

This guy was starting to get on my nerves. He had no right to ask about my family business, and I almost told him so…but I didn't.

"It had to do with my Grandfather's estate. He passed away and, as part of his will, he required me to travel in Canada for a year."

Now reaching for a third, very thick file, Agent Collins remarked, "Right. That brings us to Dutch Clarke, Senior, your grandfather. It says here that he and his brother, your uncle, Roy Clarke, attended many antiwar rallies, from 1938 to his death in July of 1940, including giving money to Charles Lindbergh's Nazi-loving America First committee. Also, both men were very vocal against President Roosevelt and his administration. Were they, to your knowledge, ever members of the Communist Party?"

This guy was a joke. He didn't know what or whom he was talking about.

With a sharp edge to my tongue, I said, "My grandfather and uncle were never members of the Communist Party. They were members of the Republican Party. Is being a Republican some kind of a crime, now?"

With a surprised look, he replied, "I didn't say that, Lieutenant. You did. Is there anyone else who can vouch for the fact that you were in Canada for the full year, without traveling overseas?"

"Yes, sir. Laura Patterson, out of Ketchikan Alaska. She knows where I was and what I was doing for that full year."

"So you were traveling with a woman during that year?"

"No, sir. It's a long story, one that I'm sure you have in your files, since I told it all to the Marine recruiters when I enlisted."

"Did you attend any political events or meet with any subversives while in Canada?"

By now, I was staring at him across the desk. This man was a buffoon, asking silly questions.

"No, sir. No rallies. No radicals."

Making a few more notes in my file, he finally closed it and, with an indifferent look on his face, said, "I don't see any problems here, Lieutenant. Your clearance will be approved. We'll send the paperwork on to Admiral King's office tomorrow. Thank you for coming in."

Getting to my feet, I asked warily, "What kind of clearance?"

"You'll have to ask the Admiral that."

Exiting the Federal Building was like walking out of a gym; I felt relieved and refreshed. Strolling to my car, with the afternoon sun on my face, I knew something was in the works...maybe something good. I should have known my 'Rabbi' would have something to do with this!

The next afternoon, Colonel Ford called me into his office and asked me to shut the door. Standing in front of his desk, he said, "Sit down, Dutch. I want to talk to you before we call in your crew."

Finding my chair, I noticed the serious look on the Colonel's face.

"Well," he said, "I guess the mystery about you and the FBI is over. This morning, Admiral King was kind enough to call me personally and explain what's going on. Before I call in your crew and tell them about the re-assignment orders, I wanted to thank you for your good work. I've been given assurance that any future re-assignments for you and your crew will include options to return to this office. We have done some great promotions over the last few months and I hope someday you'll consider returning."

'Re-assignment' -- what a wonderful word, I thought.

"Yes, sir," I said, "but what about your photography needs?"

With a forced smile, he replied, "They're sending me a Marine photographer who was wounded on Guadalcanal. He caught a Nip bullet in the leg and could have gone home, but he wanted to stay in the Corps. They tell me he walks slow, but his pictures are sharp and crisp."

"You seem down, Colonel. Is everything all right?"

Taking out a cigarette, he moistened the end of it and answered, "Yeah, I'm all right. I just wish I was younger and going with you. Some days, commanding this desk is hard. The world, the war, and time march by, and I wonder if I'm doing enough."

Lighting the cigarette in his holder, he finished, "Anyhow, call in your crew and I'll explain the part of your new assignment that I know about."

As soon as Black Jack, Riku and I were seated around the Colonel's desk, he told us what he knew. We had all been given a security clearance by the FBI, and we were to report to Admiral King's office, the following Monday, at 0900. We were being re-assigned temporarily to his staff, to complete a highly sensitive photography assignment. The mission could last anywhere from a few weeks to a few months, and might require travel outside the U.S. The assignment could be dangerous as we might find ourselves in combat surroundings. Therefore, we should make all necessary preparations before reporting for duty.

When the Colonel finished, Black Jack asked, "Do you know what we'll be shooting, sir?"

"No. But I'm sure you'll learn that, next week."

The mention of possible combat duty brought smiles to all our faces, and the idea of some kind of mysterious photographic mission added to the excitement.

Corporal Riku had a question, too. "What kind of preparations, Colonel?"

With that serious look again, he answered, "Get your will written, buy the government life insurance, and store all your personal belongings."

Wow!

Farewells

"Let me make the first toast to our gallant friends as they head off on their mission. May a breeze always be at your back, and the sun upon your face, and the winds of destiny carry you safely home," Colonel Ford said, holding his glass in the air.

It was Friday night, and the Colonel had taken the office out for some drinks and to say goodbye. The five of us were sitting around a small cocktail table in one of the local bars.

"Here, here!" the table responded.

The Colonel had some advice for all of us. For Corporal Riku: Forgive your fellow citizens for what they are doing to the

Japanese-Americans. Remember that most of us know the enemy is the Japanese government, not her people. For Sergeant Malone: A photographer is always remembered by his last image, but in your case it will always be that pretty young lady in the white towel. For Lieutenant Clarke: The land mines in Hollywood only seduce, the land mines in the Pacific kill, so watch where you step. He ended his speech with his heartfelt thanks and an invitation to return to OWI whenever possible.

The guys seemed to enjoy the recognition and the advice. Riku, while quiet as usual, listened to every word with a grin on his face, and Black Jack with his pearly white teeth lit up our little table with his smile. Even Maggie, with her eyes tearing up, made a little speech about 'her boys' leaving the nest, and how they should all fly back safely. Their concerns and comments reminded me how far I had come from that first morning, standing at the studio gates at 5555 Melrose Avenue. I knew, now, that I would miss the Colonel and Maggie very much.

After the first round of drinks, Black Jack and Riku excused themselves, as they both had dates. The rest of us remained for another drink and more conversation. Lennie was as warm and friendly as I'd ever seen him. He talked about WW1 and his experiences, and how he had tried to get a combat command after Pearl Harbor. He had some fascinating stories and more good advice about winning the war. Finally, looking down at his watch, he apologized as he stood to leave for a premier.

Getting up from my chair, I extended my hand for a shake.

Looking across our small table at me, he said, "That won't do, tonight, Lieutenant." Moving a few steps towards me, he gave me a bear hug and whispered, "God, I wish I was going with you. Stay safe, Dutch."

Abruptly, he let go and walked out of the bar as I stood there, speechless for a moment.

Sliding back into my chair, I remarked, "I didn't expect that. Not from the Colonel."

Maggie turned to me with teary eyes. "Yes, but you have had that effect on all of us. We love you, and we want you to return safely. It's especially hard on the Colonel, because you remind him of the son he never had. He was so proud to see you grow."

Her comments, while warming, were a complete surprise. Colonel Ford had always been 'all business' with me.

As Maggie finished her glass of wine, she asked whether I liked Italian food, saying that, if I did, she knew of a little restaurant just up the coast where the Chianti was smooth and the pasta tasty. "That is," she said with a sheepish look, "unless you have another engagement."

Beaming, I asked, "Miss Meede, are you asking me for a date?"

She looked at me across the table for a moment, then smiled. "Yes, Lieutenant...I guess I am."

In Maggie's Buick two-door, our trip up the coast took about half an hour. The restaurant, Geno's Italian Garden, was a small eatery just off Highway 101, in a small village called Malibu. The proprietor, Geno Dono, welcomed Maggie with open arms and a big hug, then ushered us to her favorite table. The red-checked table-clothed booth offered a stunning view of the Pacific. Looking out, I could still see the surf pounding on the beach, with the last rays of the golden evening sun spilling onto our table. With Italian music playing in the background I watched Maggie give Geno our wine order.

"I hope you don't mind that I chose the wine," she said. "I've been in his cellar and I know what all his best selections are."

"No, I don't mind at all. What I know about wine you could pour into a thimble."

Just then, a waiter appeared, carrying menus and a lit candle sticking out of an old wine bottle with layers of melted colored wax.

"Why don't you order for me? You know the menu, and Italian is all Greek to me."

Smiling, she looked down at the menu. "Okay, Dutch. That's trust."

As Maggie perused the offerings, I marveled at how beautiful she looked in the soft evening light. The gray streak in her hair looked more blonde, and her hazel eyes seemed almost black. Her red lips were full, her makeup understated. Unlike Carole, Maggie was a naturally attractive woman.

I can't remember what she ordered, that evening. All I know is that it was the best Italian food I'd ever eaten. Or was it the company? Food always tastes better with good company. We made small talk through our dinner and a bottle of the smoothest Chianti I have ever tasted. She took an interest in me and my family, and asked a lot of questions. I told her the short version, leaving out any references to the Oil Company and the money.

When I asked questions about her life, she always seemed to steer the conversation back to when she was a contract dancer, working for the studios. Wistfully, she told me about her many movie roles, and how she had worked in the 'heyday' of musical films. Hollywood was in her blood, and she loved the excitement of living and working in Tinsel Town. It was a sentiment I could not understand or echo.

During the evening, I did learn that she had never been married, had no current boyfriends, and had lived with the same lady friend for the past ten years. With this knowledge, the Colonel's comments about her not liking men kept ringing in my ears. As we finished dinner with two strong espressos, she looked across at me and remarked, "I'm pleased that you and Miss Lane are no longer an item. You can do a lot better."

"An item?" I asked, shocked. "Who thought we were an item?"

"Talk about you two was all over town. This is Hollywood, and people gossip about everything."

"I admit I found her fascinating...but I certainly never considered us an 'item.' It was more of a primitive attraction."

In the flickering candlelight, I could see in her eyes that she wanted more details, but it was a closed subject as far as I was concerned.

Finally I broke the silence. "I guess, sometimes, men think with the wrong part of their bodies."

"Yes they do," she agreed, "and, at times, that's too bad. Well, it's getting late. I'll drive you back to your car."

With Harry James on the radio, our conversation on the way back to town was quiet. Watching the city lights go by, I mulled over Maggie's statement about Carole and me being an 'item.'

Maybe, I thought, the gossip about us is like the gossip about Maggie not liking men -- just so much crap.

"Do you like to dance, Dutch?"

Her question brought me back to the music. Maggie was swaying her upper body to the beat of the tune as we moved down the road.

"I guess so. The truth is, I really never learned."

"Well, when you get back, I'll teach you. There is nothing like it. You just get lost in the music, and in the person you're dancing with."

As she turned the corner to where my car was parked, I knew our wonderful evening was about to end. Pulling up behind my car, Maggie turned off the engine. In the streetlight, I watched her turn down the volume of the radio and swivel her body towards me. "I had a lot of fun tonight, Dutch. Thanks."

Gathering all my courage, I slid down the seat, placed one of my hands gently on her face, and kissed her.

As I pulled back, she looked at me with surprise in her eyes, but she didn't seem upset.

I whispered," Why don't you come up to my apartment? You never did have a chance to see the place."

She placed her hands on mine. "I'm not quite old enough to be your mother, but I am old enough to be your big sister. And I don't think that would be a good idea. If I were ten years younger, I'd come up to your apartment and stay the weekend. But I'm not."

When I leaned over to kiss her again, she put a finger on my lips to stop my advance.

"I don't care about your age," I protested.

"I do."

Being young and curious the next words out of my mouth were, "But Maggie...don't you like men?"

I regretted saying them almost instantly.

With an odd look on her face, she stared at me for a moment, then said quietly, "See how gossip works? Yes, I like men. I can love any special soul, whatever their gender. Loving comes from within, and it isn't just a physical act. I know that's a lot for you to chew on, Dutch, but that's the kind of gal I am."

With this said, she reached over and gave me a sisterly kiss.

Afterwards, squeezing my hands, she continued, "One more thing, Lieutenant. You write to me and I'll write back. And when we see each other next, we'll share another bottle of Chianti and go dancing."

With soft music playing in the background, I knew it was time to go. Sliding across the seat to exit, I replied honestly, "Okay. I'll look forward to it."

Opening the car door, I stood up just as Maggie asked, "Promise?"

Bending down to reply, looking at her in the dim light, I realized how elegant this lady was, and how lucky I was to have her as my friend…and sister.

"I promise."

Driving back to my apartment, I did chew over what she had said. One thing about Hollywood -- nothing was as it seemed, and I was thrilled to be leaving purgatory.

CHAPTER SIX

E arly the next morning, with our bellies full and our sprits refreshed, we shoved off for the fourth and final atoll. It was a typical tropical day, with the sun low in the western sky and a warm breeze blowing up from the southwest. The days had been hot, well over ninety degrees, with the humidity about the same.

As we rowed towards the next little island, I marveled at how beautiful the seascape was. Like a sparkler on the Fourth of July, the ocean around each of the sandy, green atolls had a thousand winks of light glittering in the early sun. The dark-blue canopy of the sky covered the deep, blue-green water and stretched as far as I could see.

It was just like the tropical paradise I had dreamed about as a boy. I just wished that I was enjoying it from the deck of my boat with some creature comforts. I'd be sipping an iced tea...no, a cold beer...with a ham sandwich...no, a roast beef sandwich.

Such dreams of drinks and food dominated our thoughts and conversation as we made our way across the water.

Leapfrogging to the last atoll was easier than expected, and we arrived just before noon. Exploring the tiny island, we found no surprises except that just north of our position was a fifth atoll, so small that there was only a mound of sand poking out of the sea. It looked more like a sand bar than an island.

As we rounded the point of our atoll, we could see our destination across the channel, now about a mile south of us. We had come to call this rocky island Gibraltar, as the Padre said it was shaped somewhat like the real one in the Mediterranean. It was an ominous sight and, from our angle, its craggy shoreline looked impregnable. We talked about trying for it that afternoon but realized we would need all our strength to fight the current, so we decided to wait until the next day.

Finishing our stroll, we picked up driftwood for another fire. We were concerned there might be Nips across the channel, so we made our camp on the east side of the island to insure that our fire could not be seen.

That afternoon, with Bates and York weaving another rope out of sea grass, Jasper and Private Patterson tried spear fishing again, while I set off to try to kill one of the many seabirds that inhabited the island. Using a sharpened bamboo spear, I did my best trying to sneak up on these multicolored feathered animals, but they were just too fast for me. After over a dozen attempts, my arm grew sore from throwing the spear, so I finally gave up and returned to camp.

Luckily, Jasper and Patterson had fared better. They proudly returned with a couple of small fish that looked like some type of colorful sea bass. That evening, we feasted again around the open fire and thanked the Lord for his bounty.

"You know what I'm surprised about?" Jasper asked.

"No. What?"

"I'm surprised we haven't seen any breadfruit. It's supposed to be really good for you, and it grows all over these islands."

"Maybe we'll find some on Gibraltar," Sergeant York suggested.

Yes, we all agreed...Gibraltar would have it. Gibraltar would provide for all of our needs. Clearly, we had come to think of this mystical island as our salvation.

The next morning, while loading the raft at the water's edge, I sensed that something was wrong. At first, I couldn't put my finger on it...it was just a feeling. My chums were excited to be leaving, looking forward to spending the night on Gibraltar. As they took care of personal business in the brush, I had been busy planning our trip across the channel. Looking out to sea, I tried to understand my feelings of doom, but the reasons for it refused to come into focus.

Walking up to me, Jasper asked, "Are you thinking about home, Dutch?"

"No...I just have a feeling there's something wrong, and I can't put my finger on it."

The Padre turned and looked around our little island, then out to sea. "Other than a few clouds, it looks just like every other morning to me."

Of course! A few clouds... I had seen them, but not really. The pieces of the puzzle fell neatly into place.

"That's it. There's no breeze this morning, and there are no birds this morning."

"So?" the Padre replied.

"The trade winds have been with us every day, and these islands have been full of seabirds every day, so why not today? I have a hunch those clouds in the west are building to a storm, a big storm, maybe even a typhoon."

Jasper gazed west, "Wow. If your hunch is right, we don't want to be out in the channel when it hits. What should we do?"

"Hunker down here. If I'm wrong we'll just have spent an extra day on this miserable little island."

After convincing the others about my hunch, that's exactly what we did. Looking down the line of atolls, I saw that all the palm trees grew with a bend to the west, so I knew storms came mostly from the east. In accordance, we moved our raft and supplies to the other side of the island so that we would have some protection from the winds. Up the beach, close to the grass, we turned the raft upside down and tied it to bamboo poles driven into the sand. Then we took palm leaves and wove a crude roof into the bottom webbing of the boat. Under this lean-to shelter, we would have some protection from whatever rain might accompany the storm. Our final act was to place the turtle shell, upside down, in the sand close to our shelter. If it rained, the shell would collect the fresh water we needed so desperately.

With our preparations completed, we sat on the beach, watching the sky change color and talking about rain...cool, fresh rain. It had been weeks since we last had a big mouthful of water, and months since we had bathed or shaved. Oh, how we prayed for rain.

By midmorning, the sky was completely overcast, with a fresh breeze blowing up from the southeast. It wasn't until about noon that I was sure my hunch was right. By then, the western sky had darkened to a rich gray-black, and the winds had stiffened to a strong breeze. We knew the storm was coming; we just didn't know when, or how bad it would be.

First came the thunder…far away, but loud, rolling across the sky like cannon fire. Usually rainstorms start with a drizzle or sprinkles, but not in the tropics, it pours. Like the Lord turning on the shower we all ran out into the downpour.

At first, we just stood there with our mouths open, drinking up as much water as we could catch. It tasted so wet, so cool, so refreshing. Within a few moments, the turtle shell was overflowing. Running back to the shelter, I fetched the canteen and quickly filled it with sweet water. Then I stripped. Dancing in the rain, bare-butt naked, I took a shower by throwing the fresh water all over my body, all the while laughing like a kid with his rubber ducky. Finally looking around, I saw that my mates had followed my lead and were joining my nudity.

What a sight we made! Our legs, arms and head were baked brown from the sun, while the rest of our bodies were lily white. Here we were, five grown men, looking more like some strange breed of penguins, waltzing up and down the beach, giggling and splashing water on one another. It was a sight to behold. Taking my discarded clothes I moved to the turtle shell and rinsed them in the fresh water.

When I'd finished, I turned to my mates with a big smile and yelled, "The laundry is open, boys."

Ringing out the water, I hung all my clothes except my skivvies under the roof of the raft, knowing they would soon dry. Slipping on my underwear, I pulled up a coconut pod and took a seat to watch my pals do the same with their clothes.

A half hour later, we were all crouched under our little shelter, watching the downpour and the boiling sea in front of us. Our excitement soon turned to silence with the increasing sounds of the thunder, rain and howling winds. Apprehension found its way onto my pals' faces and I knew we needed a diversion. Finding the bayonet, I sharpened it with the leather belt and offered shaves to my chums. With each of them seated on a pod I knelt down and, using fresh water, carefully removed their stubble as we talked about home and our local barber shops over the howling wind. When I finished, the Padre did the same for me.

The storm got worse before it got better. By midday, a darkness fell that made Gibraltar disappear into the murk, and the lightning and thunder rolled right over us. The gale-force winds were so strong that the rain blew horizontally, more salt than fresh. Sitting under the improvised shelter, our comfort soon turned to misery as we endured the wet winds while holding on to the raft so it wouldn't be blown out to sea. Debris filled the air and pelted down on us like shrapnel from a mortar shell. At one point, the tide swell from the storm was so strong that the surf came crashing right up to us and almost drove us out, but then it receded.

We sat clinging to the raft and watching thirty-foot walls of seawater roar through the channel like locomotives, for almost three hours. With the winds finally letting up and the rain tapering off, the Padre remarked, "Boy, am I glad we weren't out in the raft! God bless your hunch, Dutch."

Sergeant York added, "I'm hungry. Is there any more turtle?"

"Eat some coconut," I replied, "What turtle we have isn't cooked."

"I'll eat it raw."

Funny thing about eating, I thought. *You can get used to it.*

Permission to Board

"Lieutenant Clarke and crew reporting for duty with Admiral King's staff," I announced.

The sign on the desk said 'Reporting In,' and the guard at the front gate had directed us to the administration building. Here I stood orders in hand. But the frumpy WAVE behind the desk didn't even look up; she only put her hand out. Her gesture caught me off-guard. I didn't know if I should shake it or kiss it.

"Well, Lieutenant?"

"Yes, ma'am," I answered with a grin.

Now she looked up at me with a frown. "Your orders, Lieutenant. Give me your orders."

"Yes, ma'am," I said sheepishly, and placed the paper into her hand.

She looked over the single sheet of orders and then looked over the three of us standing in front of her desk. "Have a seat," she said at last. "I'll go find your paper work."

We had driven down from Hollywood very early for our 0900 reporting time. Driving onto the San Diego Naval Station had been quite an experience. It was a gigantic facility, with miles and miles of all types of buildings and a harbor full of ships of all sizes and shapes. At anchorage, we saw an aircraft carrier, battleships, cruisers and lines of destroyers moored side by side. Looking down the piers, we spotted rows of liberty ships, oil tankers and other support ships. How powerful America looked, on this bright, crisp morning. The overwhelming sight made the three of us more excited than ever about our mission and finally getting a chance to join the war.

"Here's your paperwork, Lieutenant," the WAVE said as she slipped back behind her desk.

Our single sheet of orders had now grown to ten pages for each of us. I had forgotten how the Navy loved paperwork.

As we stood there, leafing through the papers, the WAVE continued, "First thing you have to do is get your photo security badges. Check out the information on your Form NSD444 to make sure it's correct and then go upstairs to Room 214 to get the badge. After you have the badges, you can get into Point Loma, where you will be staying."

"What's Point Loma?" Black Jack asked.

Looking at us as if we'd just stepped off the moon, she replied, "The submarine base. All of the information you need can be found in your paperwork. Good luck and goodbye."

As we turned to head for the stairs, I finally found my Form NSD444 and quickly glanced at it. It was neatly typed, with all the correct personal information...and near the bottom I found a line that said 'FBI Security Clearance: Top Secret.' Stopping, I pointed this out to Jack and Riku. They quickly shuffled through their papers to find Form NSD444, and discovered that theirs were marked the same.

"Lieutenant?" the WAVE shouted, calling me back. "I almost forgot. I have a message here for you from Admiral King."

Returning to her desk, I picked up a small white envelope that had my name on it. As I walked slowly back towards my crew, I opened the envelope and read the typewritten message:

```
Lieutenant Clarke,

    Please join me for dinner tonight at 1800 in
my dining room at the South Pier O-club. Dress
class A.

Admiral James King
```

Taking the note, I folded it and placed it in my pocket just as I caught up with my crew.

"So what's going on," Black Jack asked.

"Oh, nothing," I said with a grin. "I'm just having dinner with the Admiral tonight."

Hearing this news, both Riku and Black Jack smiled, then formed their lips as if kissing the air. Their message was clear.

After getting our security badges, we drove to Point Loma, where we were told that we would have a briefing about our assignment the next morning. Then we were assigned quarters in transit barracks. Jack and Riku shared a room in one building while I had a room a few buildings down, in officer's country. After getting squared away, we met up in their drab Day Room to review our orders.

The Navy hadn't missed much. We were told about shots we needed to get at the infirmary, how to mail and receive letters, where to acquire and process our film, and even how to find the chow hall.

The last sheet in the stack of orders was arguably the most interesting: Security Notification. Simply stated, it said that if we talked about or revealed any information regarding our assignment, we would be court-martialed to the full extent of military law. Furthermore, if anyone approached us regarding our presence or duties, we were to report the incident to the Commanding Officer of Station Security.

That notification was a straight-forward order to keep our mouths shut at all times. Looking at one another, we realized the implications. The stack of papers gave us a lot of information -- information we needed to know -- but it didn't give us information about why we were here or what our assignment might be. That would have to wait.

There were a number of O-clubs on the base. The one at the South Pier was the newest and, by all accounts, was reserved for only the highest-ranking officers. Driving up to the club, I thought it looked out of place, nestled between some warehouses and machine shops on a small hill overlooking the harbor. The all-white building had tall columns and looked more like a southern-style mansion, standing out from the surrounding structures painted navy gray. Walking into the marble-floored foyer, I was intimidated by the lavishness of the club and thought, *what's a shave-tail Lieutenant doing in a place like this*?

Standing just across the entrance, behind a small podium, was a Filipino steward dressed in a white blouse with black pants. Taking a good, long look at me as I walked towards him, he said with contempt, "May I help you, Lieutenant?'

When I showed him the note, his expression turned on a dime as he snapped his fingers. Instantly, another steward appeared and ushered me down a long corridor filled with old black-and-white photos of dreadnaughts, to a door that proclaimed 'Private: Vice-Admiral James King.'

The steward swung the door open and walking through it, announcing, "Admiral King, your guest, Lieutenant Clarke, has arrived aboard."

At the end of the wood-paneled room was the Admiral, seated behind a large dining table and flanked by two naval officers standing on either side of him. Behind the Admiral was a large picture window that displayed the harbor. The gleaming steel-gray vessels looked so close that you could almost reach out and touch them.

Glancing up from some paperwork, he motioned me forward. "Welcome aboard Lieutenant. Come on in."

I walked down the long table and, stopping in front of the Admiral, brought myself to attention...but my gaze was drawn to the window.

"It's quite a view, isn't it? Stand at ease, Dutch. Tonight's more social than military." Closing the files in front of him, he stood up and turned to the view, with his hands behind his back. "You look out there and you say to yourself that we can't lose this war when we have so much power...so much might. Our killing machines are the best man has ever invented and, while our soldiers and sailors might still have stubble on their chins, there's plenty of American steel in their hearts. No, you may be thinking, we can't lose this war... But if you think that, Dutch, you're kidding yourself, because the enemy feels the same way."

Turning abruptly away from the window, he continued, "Let me do the introductions. Lieutenant Clarke, this is Commander Shapiro. He's the skipper of the *Swordfish*, the submarine you'll be working on. This other good-looking colleague is Captain Alexander, my Chief of Staff. These two gentlemen will be giving you and your crew the briefing, tomorrow morning. They know all the details of your mission, while I'm more of the big-picture guy."

Each of these officers extended their hand for a shake, which surprised me. The *Swordfish* skipper had a grip as firm as stone, while the handshake of the Chief of Staff felt like mush.

I've always believed you could measure a man by his handshake. I liked the skipper, right away.

Reaching down, the Admiral picked up the file he had been looking at and handed it to Captain Alexander. "These results are encouraging. Let's hope the sea trials are as good. That will be all, gentlemen."

Both men came to attention and, in unison, said, "Aye, aye, sir." They then quickly left the dining room.

As the door closed behind them, the Admiral pushed a little button on the wall next to the table, "Let's have a drink before chow, and a conversation about how you got here." Instantly, a sliding door opened to reveal a large pantry, and another Filipino appeared. Ramón was the Admiral's private steward and would serve us through drinks and dinner.

The Admiral talked through two rounds of drinks and the best liver and onions I'd ever eaten. For the most part, I just sat through the conversation, nodding my head, saying "Yes, sir" and "No, sir." He started by explaining how close he and my uncle really were. Seems they were more than just college chums. They had been friends since high school. Roy had even been the godfather to Earl and Helen's firstborn son.

Tragically, the boy died in a car accident just before his sixteenth birthday. Roy took the loss almost as hard as the Kings. It took years before the two of them could talk about him without weeping. Late in life, his wife Helen gave birth to another child, a girl, and Roy was again a proud godfather.

I was astounded by all of the information about Roy's personal life, as it was all news to me. Either he had never told me or I had never listened. It was a sorry statement about our relationship.

"So, Dutch, you can understand why I intervened in your military career when he asked me. We had both been through so much, with the loss of my son…and he didn't want that to happen to you. Then I met you at Thanksgiving and saw how earnest you were about getting into the war. And, from all accounts, you're smart enough to take care of yourself. So I started thinking maybe my intervention had been wrong. That's one reason why you're here."

"Thank you for getting me out of purgatory, Admiral. I promise you won't regret it."

"Thank me when the war's over and you're still standing," he commented with a frown.

"You said it was one reason, sir. Is there another?"

"Yes." He reached for his brief case. "I've given you the sugar, but there is also some vinegar."

He went on to tell me about the racial problems the services were having. Before the war, because of what he called systematic segregation, people of color who enlisted were given menial jobs such as supply, cooks, motor pool and the like. But now, with the increased manpower needs, thousands of men of all colors were lining up to enlist. He told me the Army was training an entire division of Negro soldiers, and the Marines were using American Indians as code talkers, as no Japanese knew their native tongues.

The Air Corps was about to start training Negroes as fighter pilots in Tuskegee, Alabama. There was even a brigade of Japanese-Americans being trained at Fort Blitz.

Racial policies at the highest levels of government were changing and changing fast. Unfortunately, racism in the fleet still flourished, and there had been trouble, even murders, when the high command tried to integrate the Navy.

Just as Ramón was pouring another cup of coffee for each of us, the Admiral was saying, "Racism is a cancer in the Navy that has to be removed. We must accept men of all colors as our equals."

I looked up to see a small grin on Ramón's face.

"That's the other reason why you're here -- the racial makeup of your crew. Using your own initiative, you found two talented minorities that the Navy had discarded and forgotten. Now I want you to showcase these men of color to the fleet. Once the line officers and sailors see the value of the contribution your crew is making, they'll start changing their minds. It will be a slow process, but units like yours will be the vanguard to the total integration of the Navy."

"I don't understand, sir. How do I showcase my men?"

"Just by being yourself and doing your job. But it's not going to be easy. There are plenty of rednecks hidden in the Navy. Sometimes the roots of hate run deeper than the roots of reason. Your guys were accepted in Hollywood, but the people there are a little more enlightened than the bigots in the fleet, so this could be dangerous duty."

Reaching into his briefcase, he retrieved an envelope and passed it to me. Looking down at it, I saw that it had the seal of the Secretary of the Navy printed on the outside.

"The only help I can give you, Lieutenant, is a piece of paper...but it's an extraordinary piece of paper. Please read it."

Opening the envelope I removed a typewritten note on letterhead. It read:

```
General Order 1403-XKO
14 February 1943

To whom it may concern,

Please extend to Lieutenant Dutch Clarke and
his crew all military courtesy and assistance in
the performance of their mission and duties.
Under the conditions of this general order, you
will consider these men as my personal
representatives.

Frank Knox
Secretary of the Navy
```

I placed the note back into the envelope, dumb-struck by its contents. According to this document, when we talked, we talked for the Secretary of the Navy. It was an extraordinary piece of paper, and it showed how serious the Navy was about changing racial attitudes.

"Well, Dutch, what do you think?"

I looked up, astonished, and answered, "Two things are for sure, sir-- I know we can take care of ourselves and I also know we will do a good job for you, Admiral."

Leaning back in his chair with both hands clasped behind his head and a serious look on his face, he nodded. "I knew you'd be the right man for this job."

USS Swordfish

"Come right to 270, target bearing 270. Range 3500 and closing. Stand by, Tube #2," Commander Shapiro shouted into the intercom from the sail bridge of the Swordfish. Raising a red signal flag from the lookout tower next to him, I screamed down, "Roll camera."

While Corporal Riku had our 16mm camera setup on the bow of the fast-moving submarine, the red flag was to signal Black Jack, using a second film-camera set up on the deck of our target ship. It was a funny-looking target, one of two large, old, rusty garbage scows with painted red-and-white bull's-eyes on each side. But it had what we needed: a shallow draft of only five feet.

"Fire Number Two," the Commander ordered.

The moving submarine quivered as I watched the torpedo, just under the surface of the water, leap into action.

The Executive Officer standing next to Commander Shapiro had a stopwatch, and cried out, "Twenty seconds to target."

Our assignment was to photograph field modifications and the testing of the new Mark16 torpedo. This steel dagger was16 feet long and 21 inches around and it carried enough explosives to sink most any ship. When the war first started, the US Navy was using Mark 8 torpedoes which were of British design and had served their Navy well. In the warmer waters of the Pacific, however, our guys were having trouble getting the fishes to explode on contact with enemy vessels. At one point, about half of all the Navy torpedoes were duds.

Going back to the drawing board, the naval engineers experimented with a number of new designs, trying everything from using different guidance and fuel systems to improved 'magnetic' and 'contact' detonators. Late in 1942, the Mark 16 was approved for all boats using torpedoes in tropical waters. By early 1943, ten thousand Mark 16s were seeing duty on submarines, destroyers and PT boats all over the Pacific.

But then the Japanese started changing their strategy. When fired, the Mark 16 runs towards its target at settable depths of 10-18 feet. At that depth, when it makes contact, it explodes just under the waterline, which causes the most damage to enemy ships. This scenario worked for about eighty percent of the targets our skippers viewed through their periscopes. But it didn't work for the other twenty percent, because the Japanese started using shallow-draft barges, called mules, to move their men and materials inter-island. When a skipper fired a fish at these mules, it would miss by swimming harmlessly under the target.

To counter this, our engineers came up with a field modification kit that could reprogram selected Mark16 torpedoes to run underwater at a depth of only three feet. This kit was partly electrical, for the inner workings of the onboard gyro guidance system, and partly mechanical, with the placement of specially shaped metal fins on the outside the torpedo.

The process of making these modifications to the half-ton torpedoes required hours of work by the torpedo crews, who sometimes had to work in pitching and rolling seas. These shipboard conversions required steady hands and meticulous knowledge to make the delicate step-by-step modification. It was our job to document these procedures, down to the smallest detail, using still photography for a printed manual and 16mm film for a training motion picture. These training materials would then be distributed, along with modification kits, to the fleet. At least, that was the plan if the changes worked in both sea- and battle-testing. The new Mark 16MS (Modified Shallow), was a big gamble for the Navy, and it had yet to be proven.

"Five...four...three...two...contact!" the XO shouted.

Looking across the harbor, I saw the dummy fish hit the side of the old garbage scow with a large splash and a dull thud. From my angle, it looked right on target again.

Early in the week, we had reported aboard the *Swordfish*, where Commander Shapiro and Captain Alexander had briefed us on our mission. The *USS Swordfish* was an old boat, in submarine terms. Its keel had been laid in 1931, and it lacked some of the modern equipment now being used in the fleet. This old boat had been relegated to a training mission while its skipper was as fresh as paint and had four battle cruises under his belt.

For the most part, we had been welcomed by the submarine crew and, while there had been a few head-turns on the first day because of my crew, we'd had no trouble. But then, I wasn't surprised, since Commander Shapiro knew the scoop and ran a taut ship.

The first few days, we worked in the torpedo room with the boat's engineer, Senior Chief Carson, making the modifications and taking our pictures. In the next few days, we successfully completed three test-fires, using dummy torpedoes that had different-colored dye bags as 'detonators.' Using these dyes, we knew exactly where and how deep the fish was when it hit our targets.

That afternoon, at dockside, we met in the conning tower to discuss the test fires.

"Did you guys get all the film you need?" the skipper asked.

I turned to Black Jack and Riku, standing next to me. "Well fellows?"

"Yes, sir," Jack responded. "That final shot of the torpedo coming right at the camera was great, even though you could clearly see we were in a harbor."

"My shots are okay, too," Riku answered. "They should piece together for a good segment."

Pulling a lever and raising the periscope to eye-level, Shapiro remarked, "Then I think it's time to sink those two old rusty scows for real. I'll have a tug pull them out to sea, into deep water, early tomorrow. Then we can attack them with live-fire torpedoes. According to specs, I have to make both a surface attack and a submerged attack to complete the test. That's the rub. From underwater, you guys can't get any pictures."

Moving over to the small eyepiece of the periscope, I asked, "Can we jury-rig the camera to your scope, sir?"

"No. I have to see through it to line up the target and fire."

Studying the backside of the scope, Corporal Riku asked, "Do you have a manual for this periscope, sir?"

Nodding, the skipper reached for the overhead intercom level. "Senior Chief Carson, report to the conning tower with the manual for the periscope."

A few moments later, with the Chief standing by, Riku had a thick, bound manual in his hand. He started reading it, with his finger quickly moving down each page.

"What's he looking for?" the Chief asked to no one in particular.

"An idea," Riku responded without looking up.

"Is he some kind of speed reader?" the Chief asked me.

"Nope. He has a photographic memory."

"Oh...yeah", the pudgy Chief replied, with disbelief on his face.

Finally, putting down the manual, Riku moved to the periscope and motioned for the Chief to join him.

"See this plate on the backside of the scope? It's a maintenance access plate to adjust the mirrors inside the periscope.

There are twenty-six different mounting brackets and cam shafts used to calibrate the mirrors, so it's quite delicate. But if we replace the bottom mirror with a two-sided prism, and if your machine shop can cut me a 47mm hole in the cover plate, with just the right threads, at just the right angle and height, I can screw my camera lens onto it and see exactly what the skipper is seeing."

"Wow! You got all that from the manual?" the Chief exclaimed.

"Yeah. And your periscope hasn't been calibrated since 1939, so I'll bet it's off by a few degrees."

Shaking his head in disbelief, the Chief was clearly dumbfounded by all of the information Riku had absorbed.

"Take care of what he needs, Chief. If we miss sinking those old scows, tomorrow, this boat will be the laughing stock of Point Loma," Commander Shapiro said.

Later that afternoon, in the wardroom (officer's mess), the skipper remarked to me, "That Corporal Riku is amazing with his photographic memory. They should make him some kind chief engineer or something."

Looking across the small table, with a steaming cup of coffee in my hand, I responded, "I think all he wants is to be respected as an American."

The next morning, the *USS Swordfish* scored two direct hits on the rusty old garbage scows, one from the surface and one submerged. The only loss of life was a few seagulls that had followed the stinky barges out to sea. Corporal Riku's jury-rigged camera-mount on the periscope worked great, and we got some excellent periscope footage.

We spent the next week putting together our materials. After viewing all the raw film footage, I wrote a short script and let Black Jack and Riku edit and finish the motion picture. While they were busy with the film, I worked on the manual. The completed movie was fifteen minutes long and the printed manual ran forty-six pages, using seventy-eight photos as illustrations. Combined, the film and manual had the official Navy title of 'Field Modifications for the Mark 16MS.' A real page turner, I thought. But I was proud of what we'd accomplished.

While the premier of our movie, held at Admiral King's headquarters, lacked Hollywood lights, it did have high-ranking officers in the audience. Waiting for them to find their seats and the light to dim, I was as nervous as any Hollywood producer.

After the showing, when the lights came back on, Admiral King gave me a nod and a wink from across the room. His gesture of approval made me feel I had just received an Oscar. Later I was told the manual had been approved as well, with just a few minor changes.

The first half of our assignment was now complete. The next part, documenting the modifications and results under battle conditions, was about to begin. The results of this part of our mission would determine whether the Mark 16MS would be distributed to the fleet.

Our orders were to take a dozen modifications kits, along with three copies of our instructional materials and make our way, via Catalina flying boat, to Pearl Harbor, Hawaii. Once there, we would hook-up with another submarine, the *USS Argonaut*, for a battle cruise to the South Pacific.

As we made our preparations to go overseas, Maggie called, volunteering to drive down and pick up the staff car to store in her garage. What few personal items we had were placed in the car's trunk for when and *if* we returned.

The three of us met Maggie and John Craft, her car guy, for lunch on the day of the pick-up. We had a wonderful time, although it was hard to dance around their questions about our mission and where we were going. We told them what we could, but in the end they seemed more confused than ever.

The afternoon before our departure, I stopped by the *Swordfish* to drop off a stack of snapshots I had taken with my spy-camera. Commander Shapiro greeted me warmly and was quite surprised by all the pictures. Over the months, I had developed a technique for concealing the Minox camera in the palm of my hand in such a way that no one knew their picture was being taken. These candid images proved to be revealing character studies of the people I encountered in everyday life situations.

After sharing some of the snapshots with other crew members, the Commander invited me down to the wardroom for what he called a 'farewell cocktail.' Seated behind the green felt table in the small compartment, he explained that the fuel used in the Mark 16 torpedo was pure alcohol. Taking a metal pitcher from the pantry, he poured two plastic glasses half full of a light-orange brew.

It was his tradition, he said, to say goodbye to officers, off on their first battle cruise, with a cocktail made from that very fuel, after it had been filtered through bread and mixed with pineapple juice.

Taking the cocktail in hand, I smelled it before taking the first sip. It was bitter...but with a bold kick.

Smiling across the table at my reaction, he said, "You'll be surprised how you'll get used to it, after a few months out of Pearl. A battle cruise is weeks and months of monotony, punctuated with a few moments of terror. My advice to you, Lieutenant, is never to let the men see any fear in your face. It can be highly contagious, when it starts at the top. And one more thing -- listen for the clicks."

"Clicks, sir?"

"Depth charges. They click before they explode. The louder the click, the closer they are."

Aloha

The next morning, at 0700, we reported to Hangar 3 at the south wharf. Inside this gigantic building, we found the Catalina flying boat that would take us to Pearl.

Our first order of business was to check in with the Chief Weigh Master, who calculated every pound taken aboard the airplane. Our twelve modifications kits, now packed in unmarked gray-painted wooden crates, weighed in at sixty-four pounds each.

After weighing the last crate the Weigh Master asked me, "What's inside the crates, Lieutenant?"

Remembering our security orders, I answered, "I'm not sure. I think its wine for Admiral Hoyt in Hawaii. Guess he won a bet from some army general in Europe."

The crates did look about the size of boxes full of booze, and my explanation seemed to satisfy the Chief.

Next, our camera gear weighed in at a hundred and thirty pounds, our three duffel bags at two hundred and eighteen pounds, and the three of us at five hundred and seven pounds.

While tallying up the results, he told us how important weight was if we wanted to make it to Hawaii. The PBY had a range of 2800 miles, and Pearl was 2300 miles west of San Diego. With that distance, the Catalina could only carry a payload of 4000 pounds. Finally, shaking his head, he noted 1635 pounds on the manifest and gave instructions to the ground crew about where to stow our cargo on the plane. What we were loading aboard took up forty percent of the total cargo allotment and, from the expression on the Weigh Master's face; he thought crates of wine were pretty frivolous.

The Chief's final instructions were for us to take care of personal business before departing, as there was only an open honey pot on the aircraft. He also suggested we pick up some sandwiches and Cokes at the canteen next door, as the flight over would take twenty-two hours, with a good tail wind.

At 0900, we walked to the flight line and boarded the odd-looking craft. On the tarmac, the Catalina flying boat looked more like a duck out of water than an airplane. It had a white boat-bottom, with a dark-blue top holding up a wing that spanned a hundred and four feet. At each wingtip there was a large pontoon that reached down to the water. The Catalina's were workhorses for the Navy, flying cargo, chasing subs, and carrying out reconnaissance missions throughout the Pacific.

Our craft had a crew of five who made the long flight to Hawaii and back twice a week. After we snapped on our Mae-West lifejackets and buckled ourselves into our jump seats, the plane started its two enormous over-wing engines and lumbered out into the harbor. After a few minutes of floating around in the bay, the pilot positioned the Catalina into the wind and revved up the powerful motors. The entire plane shook as it started, ever so slowly, to move across the water.

Looking through the small porthole next to me, I could see the churning white-water as we cut through the harbor. The sounds of the racing water beneath us filled the inside of the plane, while the fierce vibrations nearly jarred us out of our seats. As the PBY gained speed, it heaved from wave top to wave top, with loud thuds running under our feet. Finally, with the engine noise ringing in our ears, the massive plane started to lift-off above the sea and, a few heartbeats later, we were flying!

The long, violent, white-knuckle takeoff had been unexpected. After we were airborne, I sat, stunned, catching my breath. The inside of the plane was long, skinny and dark. The only cabin light spilled in from two large blister windows, one on each side of the fuselage, near where we sat, close to the tail. Our cargo and other crates were lashed down underneath a net in the center of the plane, with just enough room for people to move down the fuselage on either side.

After takeoff, the pilot squeezed back to us and introduced himself. Over the roar of engines, he shouted, "I understand you're taking some Napoleon brandy across to Admiral Hoyt that he won from General Patton. Do you know what they bet on?"

Shaking my head over how the story had changed, I shouted back, "Don't really know, sir. Might have been the Army/Navy football game."

"Oh. Yeah. Ain't war hell?" he snorted as he made his way forward again.

Other than the adrenalin rush from takeoff, the flight over was uneventful, uncomfortable and noisy. With the sun rising in the sky behind us, we splashed down in Pearl Harbor at 0520, local time, the next morning.

After commandeering some help and transport at the Naval Air Station, we moved our cargo to the submarine base across the harbor. Checking in at headquarters, I was directed to Admiral Hoyt's office, where I met him and his chief of staff. As ordered, his people would take possession of the modification kits, storing them in a secure facility. We were to take eight kits with us on the battle patrol, leaving four kits and one copy of the manual and film behind in case anything happened to the *Argonaut*.

"Was anyone curious about the cargo?" the chief of staff asked.

"Yes sir," I replied. "The Weigh Master asked, but I told him it was wine for the Admiral."

With a beaming smile, the Admiral remarked, "I only wish."

USS Argonaut

After the cargo transfer, we were issued security passes and assigned rooms in two transit barracks. Finding our billets, we stowed our gear and walked down to where the submarines were moored. The morning stroll was bright and rich with color and the smell of gardenias. With birds singing everywhere and the early breeze warm on our faces, it was hard to imagine the death and destruction that had happened here only months before. When we arrived at the submarine pens, we asked around and soon found the *USS Argonaut* taking on supplies and torpedoes, docked at Pier S9. Before going aboard, we stopped dockside, just to feed our eyes of her massive form.

She was long and sleek, with two six-inch deck guns fore and aft, and large SM1 letters scrawled on the conning tower. Her fresh, dark-gray paint glimmered in the early light. While she was an older type of submarine, commissioned in 1928, she had been totally refitted from mine-laying missions to special operations in 1942. The *Argonaut* was a long-range cruiser, bigger but slower than most attack submarines used in the Pacific. Commander Shapiro had told me that much, and he'd also told me that her skipper, Commander Sullivan, was a first-rate officer.

Standing by some crates on the dock, we could see her crew loading torpedoes on the foredeck, while others manhandled supplies down the aft hatch. The dock was full of trucks, and even a small crane was helping with the torpedoes. On the seaward side, a large barge was pumping diesel fuel into her tanks. The boat was a beehive of activity, preparing for a battle patrol. As we stood watching, I became aware that the men working aboard were watching us as well. At first, I thought the sight of three mud Marines on a submarine dock must seem unusual to them...or was that it? A few moments later, down the gangway came an officer who walked over to us.

"Good morning men. I'm Lt. Commander Keel, the Executive Officer. Can I help you?"

Snapping to attention we gave the XO a brisk salute, which he half-heartily returned.

"Good morning, Commander," I said. "I'm Lieutenant Clarke and these are my men. We're here to report in to Commander Sullivan."

Taking a slow peek at us, he said, "The skipper is down at the supply depot, but he should be back in few minutes, Lieutenant. If you wish, you can wait in the wardroom."

"Thank you, sir...but if it's all the same to you, I'd rather wait here. We just got off the Catalina from San Diego and, standing here, the air tastes fresh and the sun feels good."

Nodding with a grin, he said, "Suit yourself. I did that flight once, myself, and I understand." He turned to return to the boat, then stopped and turned back to us again. "I'll have the steward send out some coffee while you wait."

"Thank you, sir."

Half an hour later, the skipper arrived back at the boat and, after talking to the XO, walked down the dock to where we were sipping java.

Snapping to attention again, we gave the full Commander a salute, which he returned sharply.

"I'm Commander Sullivan. I understand you're looking for me."

Introducing myself and my crew, I reached into my pocket and handed him our orders. He stood there a moment, reading the document, grunting now and then. Commander Sullivan looked as Irish as his name, with dark-green eyes and neatly trimmed reddish-blond hair. He was long and lean, with a strong chin and a fair, almost red complexion. There were no freckles but I was sure that, in his younger days, his face would have been full of them. I placed his age around thirty, and from all appearances he was just as Commander Shapiro had said: a man of action.

Finally looking up from the orders, he asked, "Clarke...is that English?"

"Scandinavian, sir."

"Sergeant Malone...now that would be Irish. Always nice to have another Irishman aboard," he remarked with a crooked smile.

"And Corporal Togo," he said, glaring at Riku. "Well, we know you're not Irish. But that's okay. We always like having an international crew."

"Yes, sir," Riku answered.

"Where is your gear?"

"Back at our billets. We were assigned quarters in transit barracks, this morning, sir," I replied.

"We shove off at 0700 tomorrow, so you and your gear should come aboard at 0600. I'll see that the XO gets you and your men squared away."

"Our gear includes eight wooden crates that will be sent over from headquarters, sir."

The skipper paused, making eye contact with me. "I want to ask what's in the crates, Lieutenant, but I have a feeling you won't tell me."

"No, sir."

"I like secrets as much as the next guy...but not on my boat! Lieutenant, walk with me. I think we should talk."

We moved down the wharf, out of earshot from everyone else on the pier. Commander Sullivan had a strange look on his face, part anger and part curiosity.

Standing in the bright sunshine with his eyes fixed on mine, he said, "I received an encrypted briefing about this mission, a few days ago. Seems we are going to sea to test some improved weapon system. You and your men are going to train my crew on the system and then report back with the results when we return. Is that correct, Lieutenant?"

I explained that he was right to a point, but that part of reporting back also included providing photos and film of the results.

"So you and your crew are really just photographers, here to document the testing."

"Yes, sir."

"Well, that's just dandy," he said, with a flash of anger on his face. "What moron made up your crew?"

I met his gaze levelly, saying nothing.

"Now, don't get me wrong. Personally, I don't care what color a man's skin is. But when it comes to my boat, it matters. Living in the close quarters of a submarine for months is a delicate balance of personalities, and having colored folks aboard is asking for trouble. Before I go to Admiral Hoyt and put a stop to this madness, I'll ask again what idiot made up your crew."

Reaching into my breast pocket, I retrieved the XKO Order and handed it to him. "This might explain, sir."

When he opened the envelope, I watched his eyes get as big as silver dollars, and he mumbled to himself while reading the short message. I wanted to state the obvious -- that Secretary Knox was the 'idiot' in question -- but I didn't.

Slowly, he put the paper back into the envelope and handed it to me.

"Thanks for the heads-up, Lieutenant. I want to make the Navy my career, after the war. It's nice to know where not to step. I'm on the beam now...but that doesn't mean my crew is." He shook his head, and I watched a flash of determination cross his face as he concluded, "I'll have a 'Come to Jesus' meeting with the crew this afternoon, so there shouldn't be any trouble."

"Yes, sir."

That evening at the chow hall, which was normally segregated between officers and men, I ate dinner with my crew. This sight caused some raised eyebrows -- two enlisted marines eating with an officer was unusual enough, but my two marines were also different. After finishing, we disposed of our trays and were heading for the door when I noticed Commander Sullivan giving me the high sign from across the room. Telling my guys to go on ahead, I walked over to the skipper's table to see what he wanted.

Looking up at me from a bowl of ice cream, he told me the wooden crates had come over from headquarters, and that the meeting with the crew had gone okay, but that there were still some hot heads aboard who didn't like our presence. He advised us to watch our backsides before we shoved off.

Thanking him for the information, I said good evening and hurried to catch up with Jack and Riku.

The sun was low and warm in the sky as I walked briskly between the barracks on my way back to my quarters. A few buildings down, I made a turn...and saw Black Jack and Corporal Riku standing up against a barracks, with four sailors surrounding them. Standing just next to the group was a young Ensign who looked my way as I approached.

"What the hell is going on here, Ensign?" I shouted.

"It's none of your affair, Lieutenant," he answered angrily.

Arriving at the scene, I looked over to Jack and Riku, who had their backs to each other, forming a V against the building. Black Jack winked at me, with a broad smile showing his bone-whites. Of the four guys standing in front of them, I recognized three from the *Argonaut*. Confronting Black Jack was the biggest, a brawny Second-Class Petty Officer with a bald head, a beer gut, no neck and black, hairy arms. Next to him was a stocky, short seaman with a bull-dog face and a rough complexion. On Riku's side were two young sailors, much taller than he was but of lean stature. They all had angry faces and fists clenched. One thing was for sure these guys weren't in the alley for a taffy pull.

Sometimes you notice the oddest things, in a tense situation. In my case, it was a radio playing Hawaiian music from an open window not far down the row of buildings.

I ordered, "Tell your men to back off, Ensign."

"Screw you sir," he muttered.

"Well then, I feel sorry --"

"Don't be sorry. We ain't going to kill' em. But the nigger and the Nip aren't coming on the cruise."

Shrugging my shoulders, I said, "When you disturb a beehive you get stung. So I don't feel sorry for them, Ensign. But I do feel sorry for your men."

"Back off, Lieutenant. It's not your problem."

"If you have a problem with my men, then you have a problem with me."

His gold bar was crooked on his khaki collar and he looked young, about my age, with features that were square, clean and athletic. He tried to stare me down but I had already done that with a grizzly, so it didn't work. His face slowly flushed with rage, and then he took a swing at me.

I saw it coming and moved my head to one side, but not in time. I felt something sharp glance across my eyebrow as he stumbled in front of me with his near-miss. At that moment, all hell broke out between the barracks buildings. Raising my arm like a club, I brought it across the Ensign's back as he flew past me. The blow struck hard enough that he fell to the ground.

I looked over to see that the first punch thrown at Riku had missed and had instead hit the building wall, with a loud crunch. The young seaman cried out in pain and fell to his knees, cradling his hand.

I didn't see Black Jack's first punch, but he must have gotten the chief in the gut, since he was doubled over, staggering backwards. The short guy landed a punch to Jack's kidneys, but that was all. With a right jab, Black Jack sucker-punched him in the face with so much power I heard a bone break from twenty feet away.

When I turned back, the Ensign was again on his feet, charging me like a bull. This time, I moved fast enough to trip him as he went by. When he fell down on all fours, I quickly spun around and dropped-kicked him like a football so hard that he flipped up in the air and landed on his back, groaning and groggy.

Looking back at Riku, I saw the second seaman crumpled up on the grass like an accordion. The Corporal stood over his two attackers in the classical Korean Judo position, ready for anything more they might offer. Next to him, Black Jack now faced the last man standing, the fat Chief, who had recovered from the blow to his gut.

"You son of a bitch. No nigger touches me," he muttered, red-faced with anger.

In the dim light, I saw the fat man reach into his pocket and retrieve a knife. Then he pressed a button on the handle, and a long narrow stiletto blade came into view.

"He's got a shiv," I shouted out.

Nodding, Black Jack reached into his back pocket and pulled out his sap. "Come on, fatso. You can do better than this."

The Chief stood there for a moment, grumbling, tossing his knife from one hand to the other. Then he lunged forward.

Jack jumped the opposite way, swinging his arm around, and the sap found its target on fatso's head. With a loud groan, he went down like a sack of potatoes.

Rushing over, I stopped Jack from striking a second blow to the semiconscious Chief. The entire brawl had taken less than a minute, and five sailors no longer stood.

With Arthur Godfrey strumming his ukulele in the background, I panted, "Let's get the hell out of here, before the SPs come."

Looking up from fatso, Jack's expression turned from anger to concern.

"You're bleeding, Dutch. Are you okay?"

Touching my hand to the side of my face, I felt blood tricking down. In all the excitement, I'd been unaware that the Ensign's ring had left a cut above my eye.

We double-timed it the long way around to my barracks. Once in my room, Black Jack rummaged through my duffle bag for the first aid kit while Riku cleaned the gash over my eye.

"We should go to the infirmary, Lieutenant. This cut is over an inch long."

"Nope. I'll sew it up myself if I have to. The last thing we need is to miss the boat tomorrow."

While we relived every blow of the brawl, Black Jack fixed up my cut well enough that stitches weren't required. None of us felt light-hearted about the fight, but we were proud that we had fought back to back and side by side, as a team. Grabbing my flask of brandy I passed it around, hoping we would soon be dealing out damage to the real enemy.

At 0600 the next morning, we stood at the bottom of the *Argonaut* gangway and asked the OD for permission to come aboard. After receiving it, we saluted the flag and walked up the gangway, where we were greeted by the XO.

"Commander Sullivan would like to see you in the wardroom, Lieutenant. Stow your gear here until we get everything squared away."

Leaving the guys and gear topside, I made my way down the aft hatch closest to the wardroom. To get there, I had to pass through the galley, and I was surprised to see Fatso, with a large bandage on his head, sitting alone at one table. The other two young seamen from the fight, one with his arm in a sling, were seated at a separate table. With gloomy expressions on their faces, they didn't look up as I passed through.

When I reached the wardroom, the door curtain was pulled closed, so I knocked on the side panel before going in.

"Enter," the skipper yelled.

Inside, I found the Commander seated behind the green felt table, holding a mug of coffee. Standing at attention in front of him was the Ensign from the brawl.

"Good morning, Lieutenant." Glaring up from the table, he continued, "Have you met Ensign Skinner yet?"

Glancing at Skinner, whose gaze was fixed on the bulkhead above the skipper, I answered, "No, sir...not formally."

"He graduated from the Academy last year and has just come over from Supply for his first battle patrol. This morning, he tells me an outrageous story that I'm having a hard time with. Maybe you can help. The story goes that he and four other crewmembers were jumped by three Marines last night, after chow. These Jar Heads caught them off-guard and kicked the shit out of them. One sailor is in the hospital with a broken jaw, another has a broken hand, still another has a near-concussion, and the Ensign has some cracked ribs. Would you know anything about this, Lieutenant?"

"Yes, sir...but I think the question is who jumped who. Three Marines jumping five sailors sounds pretty stupid to me...sir."

"That's what I was thinking. Sounded stupid to me, too. As you can see, the Ensign here isn't the brightest bulb on the boat, but he's my bulb. That is, unless you want me to call the Shore Patrol. I can have him and his comrades cooling their heels in the brig until we return for a formal court-martial. It's your call, Lieutenant. Just say the word."

I turned my attention again to Skinner. He had a twitch in his left eye, and a small bead of sweat running down the side of his face.

"I don't think that will be necessary, sir. Sometimes a bulb can burn brighter with the right amount of voltage."

Looking almost disappointed, the skipper replied, "And sometimes they burn out and have to be replaced." Now he faced the Ensign with a steely glare. "Okay, mister, you have dodged a bullet, compliments of the Lieutenant here. But you're still on report for the bilge-water you tried to pass. Since you love to roll in the dirt with the men, I think you should sleep with them. Remove your gear from Compartment D and relocate yourself to the aft torpedo room, which will be your quarters for this cruise."

Finally finding his voice, and looking more than a little relieved, he replied, "Aye, aye, sir."

"And one more thing, Ensign. If there's any more trouble on this boat, whether you're involved or not, I'm holding you personally responsible. If that happens, mister, your next cruise will be to the brig and then to Leavenworth. Are you on the beam, Ensign?"

"Yes, sir."

"Dismissed."

The little wardroom seemed to brighten with the hurried departure of Ensign Skinner. Commander Sullivan got up to pour himself some more coffee and, as he did, he closed the green curtain even tighter.

"Sit down, Lieutenant. What happened to your eye?"

Reaching up to my bandage, I answered outrageously, "I cut myself shaving, sir."

With a chuckle, he said, "I had a short phone conversation with Commander Shapiro this morning, after hearing the Ensign's story. He vouched for you and your crew. If Sam Shapiro says you're okay, then you're okay in my book." Moving to the seat across from me, he continued, "But mark my words -- this color problem is going to be divisive and cause trouble for the submarine service."

"Yes, sir..."

"You'll take Skinners place in Compartment D and bunk up with Lieutenant Handratty, our navigator. There are three berths in the companionway, next to D, that your men can use. Use the third rack for your camera gear. Space is limited on the boat and I understand you have lots of equipment. And, Dutch -- I'm going to call you Dutch, since that's what Sam called you -- I hope this mission is worth the trouble."

"So do I, sir."

New Georgia Sound

Twelve hours out of Pearl, as required by standing battle orders, the skipper removed the sealed operational orders from the wall safe in his small stateroom. I had been invited in because the orders concerned our mission, and also so that I could witness that the manila envelope had not been tampered with before opening. Like the rest of the boat, the skipper's little compartment smelled of diesel and stale tobacco.

Breaking the seal in the dim light, Commander Sullivan read the three-page order, using his desktop lamp while grunting now and then. After he was done, he twisted the lamp my direction and handed me the orders, saying, "I always tell the crew the short version. That way, they have some idea of what's happening."

As he lit a cigarette, I read the single-spaced document. After I finished, I slid the papers back across his desk, not really grasping all the submarine terminology.

Reaching for the intercom key just above the desk, the skipper announced, "Now here this. This is the Captain speaking. I have just opened our operational orders and they are as follows:

1. We are to search out and destroy enemy shipping.

2. Our assignment patrol area is 23 Zulu.

3. The Marine detachment aboard will train our torpedo crews on how to make certain modifications to the Mark 16 torpedoes that will render them effective at shallow depths.

4. We will fire these modified torpedoes at enemy barges in Area 23.

5. The Marine detachment will evaluate how effective these new torpedoes are.

6. After their evaluation, we will transfer the Marines to Motor Torpedo Squadron 3 on Wagina Island. There, they will test-fire and evaluate the modified torpedoes from the decks of PT boats.

7. One week later, we will return for our Marines and then proceed directly back to Pearl."

Placing his free hand next to one ear as if waiting to hear something, he finished, "After reading the *Argonaut* operational orders, it is my conclusion that this battle patrol will be completed in six to eight weeks. That is all."

A loud roar of shouts and yelling echoed down the companionway as the crew celebrated the shortness of the mission. Most patrols lasted three months or more, and this one was shaping up to be what the crew called a 'milk run.'

Finishing the last drag of his cigarette, the skipper remarked, "A happy crew is an effective crew. They liked that part about a short cruise, while I liked the part about the shallow torpedoes. If the 16MS works, it will be a windfall for boats like ours."

"Yes, sir." I hesitated. "Can I ask where Area 23 Zulu is?"

"Sure. It's in the northern Solomon Islands and includes an area called the New Georgia Sound, which should be rich with mule traffic. The Nips had their butts kicked off Guadalcanal, so now they're trying to reinforce other islands in the Solomon's. The Navy's not going to let that happen. That's why your mission is so important. The PT Squadron on Wagina is in the middle of the battle, working hard to keep the Japs out of the Sound. It's a hot area, so dropping your crew off isn't going to be easy."

Leaning back in my chair, I reflected on the orders; they seemed to have good news for everybody. That was pretty unusual for the Navy.

Later, Handratty showed me on the charts exactly where we were going. Area 23 Zulu was 2,900 miles southwest of Pearl. At a cruising speed of fifteen knots it would take us seven days to get into position. We could have made the distance in six days, traveling at 18 knots, but the skipper wanted to conserve the boat's diesel fuel. As it was, we would expend sixty percent of our fuel supply just sailing to and returning from our patrol area. The *Argonaut* had a crew of ninety, of whom eight were officers, and it ran like a fine-tuned clock. All the men stood watch on a schedule of twelve hours on and twelve off. There were only forty-six crew births on the boat, so the men 'hot bunked' with one another on different watches, while the officers shared small compartments. When the horn sounded for battle stations, which it did at practice drills once or twice a day, every crew member would report to a pre-determined position on the submarine. My station was in the conning tower, Jack's was in the forward torpedo room, and Corporal Riku was assigned to the engine room. This is where we would fight or die.

On the second day out, the XO gave a lecture to all crew members on surviving and exiting the submarine from underwater if the boat was unable to surface. It was a gloomy prospect that he spun as doable, using special breathing gear stowed throughout the boat. The only problem was that, if the boat was deep, the pressure from the water would cause what he called the 'bends' and would kill anyone trying to swim to the surface. The second part of his lecture was just as disturbing, as it dealt with the natives of the Solomon Islands. If for any reason a crewmember ended up on a local beach, they should avoid contact with the locals, as most of the natives had not taken sides in the war and would kill Yanks or Nips. Also, many of the inland people were thought to be cannibals, so it was critical to avoid them. Both prospects sounded frightening to me but, from the looks on most of the crew's faces, they had heard this lecture before. They knew that escaping a sinking submarine was a pipe dream, and safely landing on a local beach a fantasy.

After the XO had finished, I followed the skipper's orders and showed our training film and explained, in general terms, the modifications to the Mark 16 torpedo. I was surprised by how interested the crew was in our mission. As they asked questions and talked amongst themselves, I found out that most of them had been on cruises where they had missed targets by firing fish that swam too deep. As a result, they were excited about the prospect of the 16MS.

Over the next few days, we worked with the torpedo crews, showing them how to install the modification kits. As luck would have it, the fat Chief from the brawl was a member of the aft torpedo crew, so he was one of our twelve pupils. At first, I thought this might make for trouble, but I soon found out that he was all business when it came to torpedoes.

To start our sessions, I had Black Jack and Riku do the modifications on the first torpedo while the crew watched and followed along with the manual. As we performed each step, Riku gave a running narrative of what was being done.

About an hour into the demonstration, at the delicate point where the new guidance module was installed, Fatso interrupted by

Brian D. Ratty

asking, "Every word you're saying, Corporal, is identical to what's written in the manual. Did you write the manual?"

Looking up from the rear of the Mark 16, Riku answered, "No, Chief, I didn't. The Lieutenant here did...I read it for the first time last night."

As usual, a look of disbelief crossed the faces of our students. Fatso nodded and grunted, "Yeah, sure you did."

Moving down the long torpedo, I stood in front of the crew and remarked, "He's telling you the truth. He has a gift -- a photographic memory. He can read any document in seconds and tell you exactly what it said."

My comments did not erase their disbelief but I could tell they were thinking about it. Later, Black Jack told me that at chow that afternoon Fatso walked up to Riku and asked him if he knew anything about tuning up a Ford flat-head V8 engine. The Corporal said no, so the Chief handed him a copy of Mechanics Illustrated and asked him to read the six-page article on the subject.

Riku realized that Fatso wanted to test him, and hesitated at first, but then sensed that other crewmembers were watching. Taking the magazine in hand, he went through the article, using a finger to peruse its text. A few seconds later, he handed back the magazine and asked the Chief what he wanted to know.

After leafing through the pages for a moment, Fatso asked, "What's the compression ratio?"

Without even thinking, the Corporal answered.

Looking down again to the article, Fatso continued, "What's the correct spark plug gap?"

The Corporal answered.

"How many degrees off is the timing?"

The Corporal answered.

"What is the correct bore and stroke?"

Shrugging his shoulders, the Corporal answered again.

"I'll be damned! The little Nip got it right," the Chief exclaimed. "Ain't that the funniest damn thing I've ever seen? How did you get this photographic memory? Where can I get me one?"

That evening, I stood under the sail bridge hatch and asked permission to come topside for a smoke. The XO was on watch, and he shouted down his approval. Climbing the cool steel ladder, I was soon standing next to Lieutenant Commander Keel, who was busy working with Handratty, shooting an evening star with a sexton. There was a strong, warm breeze on the bridge as the boat churned up white phosphorus foam, cutting through the sea. With lookouts posted in the tower above us, I scanned the horizon while reaching for my cigarettes. The sun had just set and there was still a beautiful scarlet glow in the west that reflected a long narrow strip of light glimmering off the water. Soon, my gaze drifted down to the bow of boat, where I could see Corporal Riku standing next to the forward deck gun. There was something strange about this view that I couldn't put my finger on...

Then it dawned on me: he was smoking. As long as I had known Riku Togo, he had never used tobacco, because he felt it was unhealthy and a dirty habit. Scrambling down an outside ladder, I walked down the wooden deck slats to join him.

He glanced my way as I approached, then back out to sea. Placing a cigarette in my mouth, I turned my back to the breeze and used my Zippo to light it. Then, turning forward again, I remarked, "Good evening. Didn't know you were a smokin' man."

He took a last puff, then flipped the butt overboard. "I'm not, and they taste like shit."

There was a distant, almost angry look on his face, as if there had been trouble and he had come topside to cool off.

"What's going on, Corporal?"

With his black hair flapping in the wind, he glared at me for a moment and then gave in to my question. "To this crew I'm just another Jap! Lieutenant, did you know that the radar operator is named Kurt Muller? The crew calls him Kraut Muller. They love the guy. I heard him talking about his family. His folks live in New Jersey and are originally from Hamburg, Germany. His dad works for the railroad, his sisters go to public school, and his mom makes strudel every weekend. They have a normal American life...while my family has lost everything and lives in a filthy relocation camp. It just ain't right."

"You're right," I responded. "But I hear that you dazzled the crew with your memory. That's a step in the right direction."

"Sure. With that and a nickel, I could buy a cup of coffee. Hell, if I fell overboard, no one on this crew would throw me a line."

"Black Jack and I would."

With a bittersweet smile, he said, "I know that...but it just ain't right."

When we finished our work, we had four torpedoes modified. Two were loaded in Tubes 1 and 2. The remaining two were in position for reloading into the same top two tubes. The four lower tubes were loaded with standard Mark 16 torpedoes, for any deep-draft targets we might encounter. Riku had also jury-rigged a camera plate on the periscope, as he had done on the *Swordfish*.

All of our activities had been documented on film and we were confident the crew now knew the correct procedures for the 16MS. The final days of our journey to 23 Zulu were full of boredom, punctuated by daily drills. Because we didn't stand duty on the boat, the rest of my time was spent reading, playing pinochle and listening to Tokyo Rose on the radio. Her broadcasts were always the same: the President had lied to us, the war was started by American corporations, and we couldn't possibly win the war. Then she would play what we all enjoyed -- music from home.

On Station

Something was shaking me out of my deep sleep. Opening my eyes I saw a shadow looming over me. Over the soft murmur of the engines, a voice floated down to my ears. "Dutch...wake up."

It was the Skipper, dressed in a lightweight jacket, with his hat on. "Radar has a contact, and I thought you might want to watch the hunt."

I blinked as his words penetrated, and in a flash I was totally awake. "Yes, sir."

"I'll be on the bridge. You come on up after you get dressed," he said, and exited my compartment door.

Throwing off my blanket, I sat up and set my feet on the cold deck, then glanced at my watch. It was 2:25 AM.

Looking across the room, I found that Handratty's bunk was still made up. We had arrived on station three days ago and hunted the New Georgia Sound area without any luck. Pulling on my shirt and trousers, I hoped that this would be the morning our luck changed.

Hurrying down the companionway, I realized the boat was still dark and quiet. When I reached the control room, Handratty and the XO were huddled over the chart table, plotting a course. They smiled and nodded at me as I rushed toward the ladder to the conning tower.

As I stepped on the lower rung to go up, I heard Muller, the radar man, say in a soft, controlled voice, "Target still bearing 180...twelve miles out, sir."

Next to me was the radar station where Muller was hunched over a round scope, its pale green light reflecting on his face and headset. As the radar signal fanned his scope and hit the target, it would sing out with a muffled beep that almost sounded loud in the quiet room.

Scrambling up the ladder to the conning room, I found it only illuminated with red lights. As my eyes adjusted, I could see the Chief of the boat and three other seamen working the submarine's upper controls. They paid me no mind as I walked to the hatch for the sail bridge and asked permission to come topside. The skipper's face was faintly visible in the dim, amber light as he looked down the ladder at me and nodded his approval.

As soon as I was on the bridge, he handed me a headset so I could hear his communications. Just before slipping it on he said quietly, "Here's what we got... Radar has a target. From its size, it looks to be a single mule, hugging the coastline of Amayan Island. It's slowly moving south and we think it's trying for Santa Isabel, where the Japs still have a few garrisons. At our current speed and direction, we should intercept them in about half an hour. This should be a perfect target to try one of your new fish in a surface attack."

I was about to reply but the intercom interrupted. "XO, sir. Do you want me to sound battle stations?"

"Yes...but battle stations quiet. I don't want any noise drifting across the water. Also, have the gun crews stand by, in case these new fish don't work and we have to sink her the old-fashion way."

Flipping his voice switch off, he turned to me with a smile. "Sorry, Dutch, but I have to protect our butt."

"Can I get Sergeant Malone topside with his film camera, sir?"

"In this darkness, what the hell is he going to film?"

"If the fish works and we blow up the target, we can get some great footage, sir."

Flipping his voice switch on again, he ordered, "XO, have Sergeant Malone report topside with his film camera."

"Aye, aye sir."

As the skipper scanned the horizon with his binoculars, I turned and looked above the sail bridge. Through the darkness, I could see a lookout on each side of the conning tower, scanning the moonless night. Other than some starlight and the white foam from our wake, it was so dark that it reminded me of looking for a black cat in a coal bin. How we could search out, find and then destroy a target in this darkness was way beyond my pay grade.

Just after 0300, with Black Jack standing on the other side of the skipper, the radar operator said we were within five thousand yards of the target. Keying the intercom headset, Commander Sullivan ordered the engine room 'dead slow.' In an instant, the boat stopped its noisy vibrations and glided through the water as quiet as a tomb.

Soon, I thought I heard the sounds of a muffled engine in the distance. Then, within a few heartbeats, we all did. Finally, one lookout whispered down, "I have her, sir, three points off the starboard quarter."

Looking in that direction, I couldn't see a bloody thing, only black. Then, slowly, out of the darkness…a dim, low-to-the-water silhouette appeared.

"Engine Room, give me five knots. Maneuvering, come right fifteen degrees and standby for a turn to port. XO, ready Tubes One and Two and have the deck crews man their guns quietly," the skipper calmly ordered into his mouthpiece.

We moved parallel to the target for about ten minutes. Then, when the skipper was satisfied with our position, he pulled up the sail-bridge scope, which would give him the range and bearings to the mule.

"Maneuvering, come left to 96 degrees."

As the boat made its 90 degree turn, he bent down to the scope and sighted the target.

"Left to 94 degrees, steady as she goes. Range 2800 yards. We will fire at 2000. Stand by, Tube One." He looked in my direction and grinned. "I don't have to set the depth with these fish."

As I peered through the night, the silhouette that had looked so far away a few minutes ago now seemed to loom just in front of us. The shadow looked to be sixty feet long, with only about ten feet of her superstructure above the water line.

Still hunched over and looking through the scope, the skipper ordered, "Torpedo Room, stand by. Five...four...three...two...fire one. He paused. "Deck crews, stand by."

Over the intercom, the XO's voice rang out. "Thirty seconds to target...twenty seconds...ten seconds."

Before he could say 'zero,' the night sky in front of us lit up with a yellow-red glow. A heartbeat later, a god-awful earsplitting explosion almost blew us off the bridge. We could actually feel the heat as the blast changed night into day.

The two lookouts showed their approval with a loud "Yes!"

When my eyes adjusted to the scene, I could see men, most of them on fire, running and jumping overboard, their death shrieks echoing across the water. Those distant screams were as piercing as a knife blade and made me tremble. There were many secondary explosions as the inferno reached the onboard ammunition. As the smaller blasts rolled over the mule, it pushed the air our way, laden with a hot, mushy stench of burning flesh which hung over the *Argonaut* like a shroud.

Within ninety seconds, the whole thing was over, with the target sunk and only a flaming oil slick was left floating on the water.

I looked over at Black Jack, who stood with his teeth gritted. He removed the camera from his eye and stopped shooting, but he still gazed out across the water, where a few shadows still thrashed about in the water. The look on his face spoke a thousand words. At first, I wondered if we would pick up any of the survivors, but the Captain closed down the bridge scope and said, into the intercom, "Come right to 180 and give me flank speed. And, XO, tell the steward to start breakfast. I'm hungry."

Turning to me, with the oil fires sparking in his green eyes, he remarked, "Your fish worked, Lieutenant. That was a troop mule and, because of your efforts, a lot of Nips died for the Emperor tonight. Congratulations. Let's go eat."

I stood, stunned, for a moment. It had been a gruesome event to watch, but war is always horrible for spectators. But what stunned me most was the cold-blooded reaction of Commander Sullivan.

After a breakfast that I mostly didn't eat, I returned to my bunk to grab some shut-eye. I tossed and turned for almost an hour, reliving every detail of the morning's attack. From afar, I had watched men die a fiery death, with their screams still lingering in my consciousness. With these images in my mind, I wondered if I could ever kill, eyeball to eyeball, face to face. The violence and destruction had been both frightening and exhilarating...and that contradiction would haunt me for years.

Thirty-six hours later, while we were traveling a hundred miles north of our night-attack area, radar picked up multiple targets. This time, it was daylight, so we approached with great care. With the crew standing at battle stations, only the Skipper and two lookouts were topside as we moved at flank speed towards the targets. Through the intercom, Muller kept feeding out our position and the bearings to the target as the boat sped northwest across the Sound. Radar had three blips -- known as bogies -- moving five knots an hour, heading southeast two miles off Choiseul Island. From the size and speed of the bogies, the skipper was sure they were more mules. My battle station was in the CIC or Combat Information Center, standing next to the chart table, where I could watch Handratty plot out our course and speed. At the other end of the cramped room, next to the ladder to the conning tower, was the radar station. In between were a half dozen other stations that controlled every aspect of the boat's operation. The hatch up to the sail bridge was open, so fresh air spilled down through the conning tower and then down our hatch. It smelled sweet and good.

"I'm still getting those ghost images, sir," Muller said over the intercom.

"I'll check it out," the XO answered into his mouthpiece.

Sliding down the ladder from the conning tower, the XO was soon standing above the radar station, watching the little green screen.

"It just doesn't look right, sir. The blips should be sharp, but they keep going in and out of focus," Muller explained, using his finger to point out the bogies.

The XO stood there for a few minutes, watching, then quickly disappeared up the ladder. A few moments later, the Captain slid down the ladder and towered over Muller's screen, mumbling.

I heard him ask, "What's the distance to target now?"

Muller answered, "Ten miles, sir."

Turning to the station next to Radar, he asked, "Sonar, do you hear anything unusual?"

"No, sir."

"Are you locked onto the targets?"

"Yes, sir."

Bending down to use Muller's headset, he ordered, "XO, let's dive the boat and come to periscope depth. Engine Room, give me full speed on the electric motors. Helmsman, stay on this course."

With the drive horn blaring, the skipper stood up and turned to the room. "Lieutenant Handratty, plot me a new course to the target at eight knots. Lieutenant Clarke, join me in the conning tower."

With the submarine diving downward, the Captain hurriedly turned and scrambled back up the ladder again. With the XO and the lookouts descending into CIC, I waited for them to come down; then I joined the skipper, up in the conning tower.

Here, the Chief of the boat and a few seamen worked the fire control systems. Just as I pulled myself onto the upper deck, Handratty shouted from below me, "Estimate intercept in forty-six minutes, sir."

"What time is sunset?" the Skipper shouted back.

"2022, sir."

"Very well. Stand by."

"Twenty-six feet, sir," the Chief of the boat said.

"Up periscope" the Captain answered.

Standing to one side, I watched as the skipper slowly twisted his optics 360 degrees. When he had finished, he pulled the lever next to the periscope, causing it to slide back to the 'down' position.

Looking at me, he remarked, "We'll try a couple of your new fish from a submerged attack, just at dusk. With any luck, we should be able to sink two of the targets...and maybe many more."

"More, sir?" I asked.

"Yep. I think the Nips have set a little trap for some unsuspecting submarine or PT boat. I think those ghost images Muller saw are really a destroyer, slowly cruising just on the other side of the mules. Radar can't quite pick it up because the other boats are blocking the signal. If we attacked from the surface, we wouldn't have much time to dive before the destroyer came out and was on us. So, instead, we'll fool'em with a hat trick."

I nodded my head, indicating that I generally understood his strategy.

"Can I get Corporal Togo up here with the periscope camera, sir?"

Nodding, with a grin, Commander Sullivan answered, "Why not? You're always looking for family pictures. He ought to fit right in with our friends out there."

Flipping on the intercom, the skipper said, "XO, tell the Torpedo Room that, when I get into position, I'm going to fire out of sequence."

It had taken just a few minutes for Riku to mount the film camera on the periscope and check its alignment. The camera had a fresh hundred-foot load of film which could record just over two minutes of action. Because of the optics, Riku couldn't view what the Captain was seeing, but the camera would...so it was all about timing.

"Six thousand yards to targets, and closing." The sonar operator's voice cracked, on the intercom.

Pulling the lever to raise the periscope, with the Chief of the boat standing by, the skipper said, "Primary setup."

Moments later, as he peered through the scope, he added, "Bearings mark...range mark...angle on the bow mark."

Looking just above the Captain's eyepiece, on the opposite side of the periscope, the Chief shouted out the readings, which were then fed into the fire control processor by another seaman.

Lowering the scope again, the Captain flipped on the intercom lever. "XO, I'm going to fire Number 1, then Numbers 3 and 4, and finally Number 2. With any luck, we'll get the leading mule with 1, while 3 and 4 swim under the second target to get the destroyer, and then 2 will hit the last mule. If this works we'll surface, and take care of the remaining mule with the deck guns."

"Aye, aye, sir."

Looking at his watch, he waited a few seconds, then raised the periscope again.

"Shooting setup...bearings mark...range mark...angle on the bow mark...set depths on 3 and 4 to twelve feet...Stand by."

"Torpedoes ready, sir," the Chief shouted back, seconds later.

Looking over to Riku, I nodded my head, and he pushed the camera's start button. With the quiet hum of the camera rolling, the silent room waited several heartbeats.

"Fire 1." A long pause. "Fire 3...Fire 4." Another long pause. "Fire 2."

"Fish running straight and normal," the sonar operator reported.

"Twenty seconds to target," the XO's voice chimed in. "...Ten seconds... Contact."

The boat shook as one dull thud rolled underwater. Seconds later, we felt another thud -- but that was it. Only two hits.

"Shit" the Skipper shouted a few seconds later, still hunched over and looking through his eyepiece. Standing up abruptly and pulling the lever to lower the scope, he hurriedly ordered, "Dive. Bring the boat to two hundred feet and come right to 180. Rig the boat for silent running."

Looking my way, he continued, "I missed with 3 and 4. The destroyer is coming out and wants to play. It was a blind shot, but I should have gotten him."

And 'play' the destroyer did. Every time I heard the sounds of the tin can's screws above, and the splashes and clicks of its depth charges as they armed themselves underwater, I would think of what Commander Shapiro had told me: 'The louder the clicks, the closer they are.' The explosions rocked the boat, making it heave from one side to another, and the noise was god-awful, prompting most of us to cover our ears and open our mouths on each pass of the destroyer. Those of us who were standing would hang on to whatever was available, as the submarine pitched and rolled, with the clicks getting closer and closer.

At one point after a pass, with the room dead-silent, waiting for another attack, we heard a flip-flip-flip sound.

"What the hell is that noise?" the skipper asked.

Sheepishly, Riku looked his direction and answered, "It's my camera, sir. I forgot to turn it off."

"Well, turn the damn thing off and tell your relatives we don't want to play anymore."

Looking around the room, all the crew had grins on their faces. It was odd that anyone could feel light-hearted at such a time, but they did.

Even scarier than the explosions and noise was the utter darkness when our lights went out, leaving the room in a gloom so deep that it reminded me of iron coffin. Luckily, the lights kept coming back on, just when I was about to give up hope. For the next hour, I grasped the pipes above me as each minute dragged by like an eternity. Then reports started coming in regarding damage and leaks in different parts of the boat, and what was being done to control them. Part of me was in panic mode, thinking we were sinking, while another part could not forget: Never let the men see fear on your face. It can be contagious.

The skipper did what he could to maneuver the boat between attacks. After each pass, he would change direction and speed, setting a new depth and then hanging onto the down periscope, wait for sonar to report the destroyer's movement.

It was a painfully slow process, and soon the air in the boat got hot and stale. Most of us were dripping sweat, which added to the stench.

"She's coming around again, sir, on our port quarter," Sonar reported.

"That's it!" the Captain said harshly. "I'm done. I don't want to play anymore."

Splash...click...

Splash...click....

Everything went black.

CHAPTER SEVEN

Seabirds returned in flocks after the typhoon. There had to be thousands of them with their high-pitched shrieks, flying around the rocks and cliffs of our forbidding island destination. Rowing with a stiff breeze in my face, I kept asking myself where they had gone during the gale.

After yesterday's storm, the morning had dawned bright, clear and promising. We had shoved off early but not before taking advantage of the gale-force winds of the day before that had littered our atoll with coconut pods. We had collected seventeen of them, which I then cut open to harvest the inner nut. With our raft loaded and sprits high, we had departed for Gibraltar.

In the bright morning sun, my mates looked and sounded refreshed, with their faces shaved, clothes washed and fresh water in our canteen. The gloom of the storm had only brightened our prospects of finding a way to survive our ordeal by making landfall on Gibraltar. Here we could rest, eat and plan for our rescue, if there were no Japs on the island.

There was a warm breeze out of the south that caused a wind chop on the channel of two or three feet, but it was one that we could handle. With two of my mates on each side of the raft, rowing, and me in the rear using my oar as a rudder, we were making good time, crossing in a southwest direction. To the east, we could see the string of atolls we had leapfrogged up. Those tiny green specks of sand had saved our lives with nourishment and shelter, and would not be soon forgotten.

By midmorning, we had drifted and rowed to within a few hundred yards of the northern tip of Gibraltar. It was at this end of the island that its jagged, volcanic twin peaks came together and rose up into the sky, well over fifteen hundred feet. Looking through the mist that hung on top of the mountains, we could see patches of green foliage growing out of the crags. Below the peaks, we now had a clear view of Gibraltar's granite cliffs, which sheared off the mountains and fell over five hundred feet, almost straight down to the ocean floor. Looming just in front of the coastline, and grouped together, were three gigantic rocks pointing out of the sea, hundreds of feet high. On top of each of these haystacks were patches of green with white stains from the droppings of the seabirds that buzzed around. At the waterline, there was another dirty-white stain from millions of years of the rising and falling tides. From a distance, this stain looked as if God had painted a white outline around the rocks to make them stand out from the coral-green ocean.

The seascape was breathtaking but dangerous, with the jagged outcroppings and crashing surf. Landing our raft on this part of the rugged and dramatic island was out of the question.

"Keep an eye out for a lagoon or a strip of beach," I shouted as we rowed by the high sentinels.

Most islands in the South Pacific have coral reefs that help protect the land from the winds and sea, but not Gibraltar. As this island sprawled south, the land leveled out from the mountains, with a jungle-like landscape still atop granite cliffs high above the water's edge. As we reached Gibraltar's southern-most point, these cliffs were much shorter, with the green foliage only fifty or sixty feet above the channel waters. It was there that I hoped we could find a place to beach our raft.

"The current is drafting us away from the island," Jasper shouted.

"Everybody row on the port side. Let's turn the boat into the current and try to go around the other side," I shouted back.

After an hour of hard rowing, we were able to find slick water on the leeward side of the island. We had hugged the coastline all the way down and around without finding a beach and we were determined to find one, even if we had to circumnavigate the island. With the sun now high in the sky, we rowed even closer to the southern shore, scanning its line for sand.

Finally, Sergeant York stood on the rafts floats and pointed, yelling, "There! After that outcropping. I can see a beach!"

Jumping down from his perch, he joined us in rowing towards the rocks.

A few minutes later, we could all see the cove he had been pointing to. The beach was small, only a few hundred feet wide, nestled between huge rocks and backed by a fifty-foot rocky cliff. With its southern exposure, the sun lit up the barren little inlet as we rowed headlong into the shallow beach.

Pulling the raft out of the surf and up to the base of the cliff, we surveyed our choices. The cove wasn't much -- only a strip of sand that more than likely would be underwater at high tide -- but it was dry now and solid land. Walking around the base of the cliff, we looked for a game trail up to the jungle but found none. Forty feet above the beach were scrub trees and bushes growing out of the crags, and the rocks looked as if they could be climbed. But a climb up would take a great deal of effort, with a sure foot for finding just the right way.

Standing at the base of the cliff with bright sun reflecting off the granite, I turned to my pals. "I'll take the ropes and scale the rocks, then tie it off on one of the trees on top. I need to reconnoiter the area to see if there are any Japs. If we're clear, you guys can join me, using the ropes to pull yourselves up."

"I'll go with you," Jasper remarked.

I shook my head. "Look at your boots, Padre. They wouldn't make it up the sharp rocks. Mine are still in fairly good shape. I'll leave the canteen behind but I'll take the knife. You guys stick by the raft, in case we have to make a fast exit."

With two ropes tied together and around my body, I started the climb. The first twenty feet were easy, with good toe-and-finger-holds. The next twenty feet were slow going, as I had to move from side to side to find little cracks in rocks just to move up a few more inches. At one point, I was reaching up with one arm and searching blindly for a handhold when a bird pecked my hand and flew off the ledge with a loud shriek. The stinging pain and the loud sound scared the shit out of me, and I lost balance and almost tumbled back down to the beach.

A few moments later, I pulled myself up onto the bird's ledge and found a nest with two small eggs, which I carefully dropped down to my pals, standing below me.

I shouted down with a smile, "I'll take mine over easy!"

"Keep an eye out for breadfruit. Do you know what it looks like?" Jasper shouted back.

"Yeah, I know."

Kicking the nest off the ledge, I had a place to stand. Now I was only a few feet below a large tree growing in the crags. Taking the rope off my back, I tried throwing one end around its base, and on the third try I succeeded. Using the dangling lines, I pulled myself up the rest of the way and tied off one end of the rope to the tree.

As I finished the knot and threw the loose end down, I shouted, "You guys stay loose. I'll be back in a while." Using the tree stump and other scrub brush, I scrambled up the remaining few feet to the jungle.

Finally, getting to my feet, I walked just a few yards into the forest...and realized how dense and dark the trek would be. Taking the bayonet, I cut a big notch at the base of one of the palm trees, to mark my trailhead. This I would do every few yards so that, when I returned, I could find my way back to the rope and beach below.

Fifty or sixty yards inland, I found a rough game trail that seemed to head north, towards the mountains on the other end of the island. With the sounds of birds filling the air and the stench of decaying foliage in my nostrils, I quietly moved down the irregular path. The way weaved in and around groves of massive mangrove and eucalyptus trees which, with other tropical foliage, blocked the sunlight into perpetual twilight.

The jungle reminded me of the rain forests of British Columbia, only steamier and more vivid. Below the green canopy of trees, the forest floor was littered with dead and dying snags with long strains of moss. Next to these snags grew tropical ferns and plants of all sizes and descriptions, many of which had large, colorful flowers. In the hot, still air, the trek was hard going, as I had to move over and under many snags that blocked the way. As I moved down the path, I searched for any signs of human presence, like cigarette butts, footprints or other waste, but I found none. Maybe, I thought, there are no Japs on this island.

Ducking under a low snag that blocked the trail, I stopped to wipe the sweat out of my eyes...and then it hit me. It was like someone kicking me in the gut -- dysentery. We all had it, 'the trots' we called it, and it had only gotten worse since we started to eat again. The timing of this excruciating knot in my gut made me mad because I knew from experience that I had to find some relief, and soon. Walking off the trail, I cut some palm leaves and found a snag that I could crouch over.

As I slipped my trousers down, my thoughts were with the business at hand, and I was totally oblivious to my surroundings. Just as I looked up from using the last palm leaf, I felt the cold, sharp blade of a Japanese sword pinch my chest. Slowly looking up its long blade, I was terrified to find a large, jet-black man holding it. His chiseled face had bold features with a flat nose, and across his forehead was a crudely painted white strip. In the shadows, the whites of his manic eyes gleamed at me with a look of annoyance.

Next to him stood another, much smaller and younger black man, pointing a bamboo spear in my direction. The man with the sword moved the blade from my chest to under my chin and put pressure on it, as if to tell me to stand.

Slowly reaching down for my trousers, I pulled them up as I got to my feet.

As I buckled my belt, the painted man grunted. "Ugh."

Petrified, I replied, "How embarrassing."

Farewell *Argonaut*

My first recollection was of the low hum of the boat's motors, and then the malodor of diesel fuel mixed with human sweat. When I opened my eyes, it took a few moments for my vision to become clear. When it did, I could see the shadow of a man sleeping in a chair, next to my bunk, backlit by a reading lamp on a desk behind him.

Letting my eyes focus more clearly, I finally realized I was lying in my compartment aboard the *Argonaut*. And I had a headache, a big headache. Slowly moving my upper body, I reached for my head with one of my hands.

"Dutch, is that you? Are you awake?" Black Jack's drowsy voice reached me from the shadows.

"Wow. What the hell happened? My head is on fire."

"It was the last pass of that Jap tin can. The explosion from the depth charge blew you off your feet, just as the lights went out. When they came back on, they found you passed out on the deck, with a big welt on your head. You must have hit something on the way down. Anyway, the Pharmacist Mate thinks you might have a concussion, so you're supposed to take it easy."

Pulling myself up in the bunk and resting my back against the bulkhead, I felt the lump on my head under a big bandage. "How's the boat?"

"We're fine. Some damage forward and a few leaks, but the crew has it covered."

"What happened to the destroyer? How long have I been out?"

"Almost ten hours. We found a thermal layer in the water, where the tin can's sonar couldn't pick us up, so skipper thinks they just gave up. We were lucky."

Looking through the shadows directly at Jack, I remarked quietly, "I was scared, Black Jack. Scared shitless. My hands are still sore from holding onto the pipes above me in the control room. I've never felt panic before. What the hell's wrong with me?"

"Dying chews on a man, and anyone who says they weren't scared last night is either a liar or dead. There's no shame in fearing, only shame in not fearing. Forget it."

The little room fell silent for a few heartbeats as I strained my eyes at the shadow and said softly, "Thanks for being my friend."

A few hours later, I was up and around. While I still had a deep, dull ache on the top of my head, my eyesight was okay and I had no speech problems. With these positive signs the Pharmacist Mate said I was fit for duty.

Late that afternoon the skipper asked to see me in his cabin.

"Come on in, Dutch, and close the door. Are you feeling better?"

"Yes, sir. It's only a lump on my head."

"Good," he said with a wide smile, an unlit cigar clenched between his teeth. "Have a seat. You scared the hell out of us.

Can't get you a Purple Heart for the lump on your head, but I can pour you a shot of Irish whiskey for the pain."

"Thank you, sir."

Commander Sullivan, seated behind his small desk, reached into a compartment drawer to retrieve an unopened bottle of whiskey. Taking two small water glasses, he poured each half full and passed one across to me. "The British Navy still gives out rum rations to their men. That's one of the good traditions our navy didn't adopt. But rank has its privileges, so I bring along one bottle of good Irish whiskey for times like these."

Reaching down to a stack of papers, he also passed a single typewritten sheet to me.

"That's a copy of my report on your Mark 16MS. As far as I'm concerned, it's a big success. We've fired three and made three hits on our targets. Can't get any better than that."

"So we got two of the barges last night, sir?"

"Yep. I saw them go down just before the Nip destroyer came out. You should have it on film. It was a good run. I only wish I'd gotten the tin can so we could have finished off the third barge. It's all in my report." He waved his hand at it. "I want you to keep a copy for your records."

"Aye, aye, sir."

Leaning back in his chair, he sipped the pungent brew. "That brings us to the second part of your mission, testing the 16MS from the PT boats on Wagina Island. We've finished our repairs and, after nightfall, we'll surface and head in that direction. We should have you and your crew there by twelve hundred tomorrow. But that's when it gets tricky."

He pulled out a navigational chart and unfolded it on his desk top.

Turning the map in my direction, he used his finger as a pointer while saying, "Our battle orders say that MTB RON 3 is headquarted here, in a small bay on the southern tip of Wagina Island. And that's the rub. We only took the island last month and, according to this chart, there's only 45 feet of water at the end of the pier in the cove. That's way too shallow for us to approach from underwater."

The chart showed a crude outline of the southern portion of the island, and a small harbor with a long dock that extended out from its shore line. The map also had typewritten numbers in all the surrounding waters, showing the depth at low tide. Those numbers must have been in fathoms, because the number '7' appeared at the end of the pier.

"There's no more than sixty feet of water anywhere in the cove. That is, if you believe this chart. Take a look at the date on it. That chart was made by the Germans in 1908, when they were looking for coaling stations. Hell, the chart's older than I am. That's the problem. Down here, we don't have any updated charts we can count on, and most of these old ones are wrong."

"So, what do we do, sir?"

"We will lay off the island submerged, out in the sound, and then surface and approach the cove. But that'll be a two-mile run with our asses sticking out. This is a hot area. If there are any Jap planes in the vicinity, we could get hit from the air, and if there're any shore batteries on the island, we could get hit by friendly fire. It's a lose-lose proposition."

"Don't they know we're coming?'

"We have no direct communications with the station. We told Pearl this morning that we would be there tomorrow, but we have no way of knowing if Pearl relayed the message to Wagina. It's a crap shoot."

"How about dropping us off in one of the rubber life boats, and we can row ashore?"

"I thought about that…but the currents down here are so strong and you guys have so much gear that I'm afraid you wouldn't make it. No, we'll enter the cove with the stars and stripes flying, the guns manned, and Handratty using the signal light to tell them we're friendly. Then we'll pray that there're no planes, and that the dumb bastards ashore know how to read Morse code. Could be a wild ride…but here's my point. I want you and your men ready to get off the boat the minute we touch that pier. I'm not tying up, and there aren't going to be any long goodbyes. The second you're off, we're heading back out for deep water."

"Aye, aye, sir."

As the skipper reached across the desk to sweeten my glass with another shot of whiskey, his expression turned somber. "And one more thing, Dutch. I'll be back to pick you up, seven days from tomorrow, at twelve hundred hours. If I look through my periscope and don't see you sitting at the end of the pier, waiting, I'm not risking coming back in to find you. You'll be on your own. Are you on the beam?"

"Yes, sir."

Hoisting his glass in the air towards me, he concluded, "And, contrary to what I thought back at Pearl, it was worth it. Your guys are first-rate, and I'd ship out with any of you again!"

MTB RON 3

It was a wild ride into the cove. When the *Argonaut* surfaced off-shore, the lookouts were posted, the guns manned, and a large American flag raised on her mast even before the decks were dry. Then, with the skipper on the sail bridge and the XO in the control room, calling out depth readings, the submarine started its approach to Wagina Island.

With the boat's diesels turning at half-speed, it would take twenty minutes for the Captain to navigate the shallow, uncharted channel into the cove. As the boat started its run, Black Jack, Riku and I moved all of our duffel bags, camera equipment and the four remaining conversion kits to just under the aft hatch. The skipper was concerned that, if we were strafed by a Nip plane or shelled from shore, the equipment might get damaged, so we were instructed to wait before loading the gear up the ladder. Standing just below the open hatch, we were speculating about how we could carry the heavy gear up when Fatso approached us and offered to help. Just next to him were the two young seamen from the ally brawl, also offering to help.

I was both surprised and impressed by the offers, and I accepted their help.

Just as I did, the XO's voice rang out over the intercom, telling me to quickly join the Captain on the bridge. Scrambling up the aft hatch, with my eyes adjusting to the bright sunlight, I carefully made my way over the wet deck to the outside ladder up to the sail bridge. Crawling up, I found Handratty standing next to the skipper, working the signal light. As I got to my feet, the skipper handed me his binoculars and said, "Use these big eyes. You read the same sea orders I did. Didn't they say that RON 3 was in this cove on Wagina Island?"

"Yes, sir…"

"Well, take a look. I don't see one damn PT boat in this miserable little bay. All I can make out is a deserted cove with a long, ragged concrete pier and a few old buildings on shore."

Looking through the glasses, I saw that we were still in a narrow channel, a good half-mile from the cove. Other than a few deserted buildings, a long pier and palm trees the skipper was right -- it was empty.

Handing back the binoculars, I remarked, "Where the hell did everybody go?"

Just then, the XO's voice shouted out from the control room hatch, "We've only got twelve fathoms under the boat skipper."

BOOM!

The deafening sound of an explosion came from less than two hundred yards in front of us. Cold seawater sprayed the bridge as all three of us ducked for cover. The submarine heaved up into the air a few feet, twisted, and then came crashing back down with her diesels still turning.

Groping for words, I asked, "What the hell was that -- a mine?"

"No, a shore battery. I can't take evasive action because of this damn narrow channel and I don't have enough water under the bow to dive. Shit!" the skipper blurted.

BOOM!

Another deafening blast fell some three hundred yards behind us. This time, at least, the boat stayed on course and in the water.

"They'll have the range with the next shot," the skipper warned. Turning to Handratty he demanded, "Are you giving those guys the right message?"

Handratty, his hands shaking, didn't look our way. He just kept signaling, while answering, "Yes, sir…at least, I think so. My Morse might be rusty. I saw the muzzle flash from the last shell, halfway up on that hill behind the buildings, and I'm signaling in that direction."

With our eyes fixed on the island and our ears still ringing from the shelling, we waited for more…but it didn't come. Then, just as we entered the cove, there was a flash from atop one of the buildings. At first I thought it might be another gun going off, but the skipper exclaimed that it was a signal acknowledging our messages. With relief in his voice, the skipper said to Handratty, "Ask them if MTB3 lives here…and ask them nicely."

A few moments later, we were signaled in the affirmative.

Looking over at Handratty, who now had the signaling light at his side, I said, "Good job, sir. Your Morse Code must not have been so rusty."

Forcing a smile, he replied, "Don't be so sure. For all I know, I could have been talking to the Japs."

Calling for reduced speed, the skipper positioned the boat for docking, while the XO told my men to get the gear topside. As we pulled to a few feet from the end of the pier, one of the crew jumped down to the boat's bail tanks and then leaped across to a ladder attached to the dock. Scrambling up it, he was thrown a line for the *Argonaut*, which he loosely secured to the pier. Then he slid two planks he found on the dock across as a gangway, and Fatso and his friends started unloading our gear.

With the submarine's motors idling, the skipper turned to me with a smile and said, "Get your ugly face out of here, Lieutenant. I've had enough excitement for one day. I'll see you next week…and don't be late!"

Giving both him and Handratty a salute, I answered, "Aye, aye, sir."

Standing on the pier, we watched the *Argonaut* slip back out to sea with Fatso and his friends still standing on her fantail. As the boat turned into the channel, through the layer of black diesel exhaust that hung in the air, we saw them give us a seaman's wave. Then, just before she got out of earshot, Fatso shouted back, "We were wrong about you guys. You're okay. Good luck. See ya next week!"

Black Jack and I raised our hands and returned the wave. Riku didn't.

Soon, the end of the dock fell silent, with only the sounds of birds and lapping water. The long, concrete pier was pockmarked with what I guessed were shell holes and scars of all sizes and shapes from battles gone by. While the dock looked serviceable, it was empty of all boats or supplies. On the beach end of the pier, surrounding two large, rusty, corrugated-tin buildings were the burned-out, skeletal remains of other structures. Above those ashes, and stretching north as far as the eye could see, were the island's hills and mountains, covered with thick jungle vegetation. Obviously, we had been plunked down into the middle of a war zone, on a pier in the middle of nowhere, overlooking an empty, menacing cove that was quiet...too quiet. With my hair standing up on the back of my neck, and Handratty's joke about talking to the Japs ringing in my ears, I wondered where everyone was.

A few moments later, I heard, before I saw, the low rumblings of a Willys engine. The sound was coming from the other side of the old buildings at the end of the pier. Then, out of a dust storm, a Navy jeep came into view.

As it navigated through the pot holes down to the dock, I could see two Americans riding in the front. They were a strange-looking pair, as neither wore a uniform. The driver was wearing a Hawaiian shirt with a baseball cap, while his companion had a straw hat over a khaki shirt with no sleeves. As the jeep squeaked to a halt in front of us, I was still trying to grasp the sight of these two strangers.

"Who the hell are you guys?" the man with the straw hat asked, with a sour look on his face.

"I'm Lieutenant Dutch Clarke and this is my crew. Can you direct us to the commanding officer of RON 3?"

"Why? And where in the hell are your weapons?"

"We have orders to report to him, and we don't have any weapons...sir."

At my reply, the driver's expression turned to a grin, while his companion started shaking his head in disbelief. "Marines without weapons...now ain't that something to behold? Lieutenant, what moron sends three Marines into a combat zone without weapons?"

Being questioned by these two civilians was starting to get to me, and so, with anger in my voice, I answered, "Admiral James King, with special orders for the commanding officer of RON 3. Would you please direct us to him?"

My reply caught both men off-guard, and their expressions turned on a dime.

Glaring at me from under the shade of his straw hat, the passenger stated, "I'm Lt. Commander Jacobson, Commander of RON 3, and this officer next to me is Lieutenant Dudley, my XO. I'll ask again, who the hell are you?"

All three of us snapped to attention and saluted. With our hands in the air, I took a good look at Commander Jacobson. Below his cut-off khaki shirt, he wore white tennis shorts and canvas shoes...and across his lap he carried a Thomson submachine gun. His body was trim and dark brown from the tropical sun. His face, while young, had a square jaw with bold features. His XO, the driver, also had shorts on, with a shoulder holster striped across his colorful shirt. These two guys looked more like Hawaiian cowboys than naval officers.

"Didn't Pearl tell you we were coming? And I'm sorry, sir. We didn't know you were officers," I finally responded.

Half-heartedly returning our salute, he answered, "No, I guess you wouldn't. Stand at ease and no more saluting. The Nip snipers target the officers, so we don't do much of that military shit out here. We haven't heard from Pearl for over a month. They just keep sending us torpedoes and we just keep sinking Japanese shipping. What's your mission, Lieutenant?"

Reaching into my pocket, I gave the Commander a copy of our sea orders, which he scanned as I verbally outlined our mission. After I had finished, he took a good long look at my crew, with special interest directed to Corporal Riku.

Shit, I thought, here we go again. I'd better get out the XKO Order.

But it wasn't necessary. Instead, the Commander shrugged his shoulders and said, "Ok, Mac. You guys jump in the back and we'll take you to our little oasis." He also told us that he would send a truck back for our gear and the conversion kits.

As the jeep moved down the dock and across the dusty, bumpy road, he went on to explain that the squadron had moved, a few weeks ago, to another cove about a mile away. It seemed that where we'd landed had gotten too hot, with almost daily attacks from the air. After hearing this, I told him that I was concerned about the safety of our kits and gear, but he told me not to worry -- air strikes always came in the early mornings or at sunset.

"You could almost set your watch by the bastards. We'd be standing by with our weapons ready and here they would come, out of the sun. We shot a couple down and never lost a boat but they sure the hell pockmarked the dock. Finally, we just got tired of playing their game, so we moved to Smuggler's Cove, on the windward side of the island, for better protection. It's a lot cooler and quieter there."

A few minutes later, we pulled into a cove that was just a small bay surrounded by high rocks and jungle. Here, under camouflage netting, were moored the twelve Elco class PT boats assigned to RON 3. The boats were grouped in twos and threes, tied up in shallow inlets, with each group having its own small wooden pier. The dense mangrove trees grew right up to the water's edge and so, with the netting, the boats were invisible from the air.

Commander Jacobson explained that Wagina Island had been a thriving Dutch rubber plantation before the war, so it had become an important target for the Japanese war efforts. A large garrison of Japs had occupied the island ever since January of '42, but six weeks earlier elements of the 2nd Marines Division had landed and kicked most of them off. The fighting had been bitter hand-to-hand combat with an enemy that was determined and well dug-in. RON 3 had moved in and setup shop right after the southern end of the island was secured. What remained of the Nips, on this part of the island, were starving; they roamed about, killing and looking for food.

To compound the problem, the few natives that remained on the island would steal anything that wasn't tacked down. There was still an Army Infantry Regiment on the north end of the island, cleaning up the last pockets of resistance, so this little oasis was a dangerous place, and all personnel were required to carry weapons.

Just up from the water's edge was the old plantation house; it had been commandeered as a headquarters and mess hall. Nestled around this dwelling, under the shade of tall trees, were several dozen tents for his crews and support personnel. As we walked up the rickety stairs to the front porch of the old house, he stopped and pointed out towards the sea. "For the most part, we yacht at night, with three groups of three boats on patrol. We keep a fourth group in reserve for maintenance and squadron protection. We don't go after that many mules because we know our fish can't sink them, and it can be a bloody brawl with only our small arms and 50 cal's…so if you can help, you're welcome on our little piece of paradise." Turning to Lieutenant Dudley, he concluded, "Send some guys out for their gear and get them set up in the Bamboo Room. And get them some weapons. We don't want anything happening to them before they work their magic on our torpedoes."

Dudley nodded, grinned, and departed as we walked through the front door.

The lower floor of the house held the kitchen and dining areas, with the squadron office and officers' quarters upstairs, overlooking the cove. As we moved up the stairs, I noted how grubby the building was, the walls were cracked and stained, and the floorboards squeaked under our feet. This grand old house had seen better days and was now just a dirty shell of what must once have been a magnificent plantation home.

The Commander's office fronted the cove, and one end of the room had large wooden-shuttered doors that opened onto a small veranda. While the area was spacious, after the cramped quarters aboard the *Argonaut*, it was also musty and cluttered with papers, empty beer cans and personal items. The furniture was tattered, ripped and dirty. The commander's desk was nothing more than two empty fifty-gallon oil drums with wooden planks across. 'Marine clean' it was not.

After opening the veranda doors, Commander Jacobson slipped behind his makeshift desk. "Take a load off, boys, while we have a chat."

After removing some old newspapers and maps, Blackjack and Riku found a spot on a couch without any cushions, while I plopped down in a wobbly chair next to the commander's desk.

Reaching down to the floor, Jacobson picked up a large bottle wrapped in a wicker basket and placed it on top of his desk. "One thing the Nips left behind was lots of sake. We found a whole storehouse full and, of course, we commandeered it for our medicinal needs."

Opening the bottle, the Commander poured four paper Dixie Cups half-full and slid three over to me. Reaching over, I passed two cups on to Jack and Riku, who looked a little bewildered.

Lifting his cup into the air, Jacobson exclaimed, "Here's mud in your eyes. Drink it fast, boys, before it eats a hole in the paper."

All of us downed the potent wine in one gulp and made sour faces. All of us, that is, except Riku, who swirled his around in the cup and took three or four loud sips.

"Now down to business," Jacobson continued. "How long will it take to make the conversions?"

"Two or three hours per fish, sir," I replied.

"Okay. I'll get your guys set up with the torpedo crews, and tomorrow I'll get on the horn and see if any of the coast watchers have any mule sightings. If I understand this right, you want to film our attacks to show the brass back at Pearl, right?"

"Yes, sir," I answered.

For the first time, Jacobson took his straw hat off and placed it on his desk. As he did, he looked at me, his emerald-green eyes keen and alert.

"Dutch, drop that 'sir' shit. The men call me Jake, and my XO is Dud. We're not part of the real Navy, we're just yachtsmen with guns. Every man here is a volunteer. We eat together, drink together, fight together and some die together, so we're all on a first-name basis. Now, if you want to take pictures, I'm assuming you'll need daylight."

"Yes, sir...I mean 'Jake.' But we can shoot at night, if we have to."

Leaning forward and rubbing his temple with one hand, he remarked, "That will mean changing our routine but that'll be okay. Oh, and one more thing -- I don't want your guys roaming around camp after dark. Stay close to the Bamboo Room and keep your flap closed." Looking straight across to Jack and Riku, he continued, "In the dark, one of you could be mistaken for a native and the other for a Nip. The last thing I need is enemy-recognition problems. I have no idea what wise man sent you to me, but I'll be a hell of a lot happier when I see you leaving my oasis, all in one piece."

The dust-filled room fell quiet, with Black Jack and Riku staring back at the Commander.

"What's the Bamboo Room?" I asked, breaking the silence.

"It's our VIP tent, down by the swamp, next to a stand of bamboo trees. You shouldn't have any problems there. Most of the men know it's only for the brass, so they don't go near it."

Black Jack cleared his voice and remarked angrily, "You know, Commander, we're not leopards. We're members of the United States Marine Corps, here to do a job -- a job to help you defeat our enemy. And all we ask in return is a little respect. If your guys can't tell the difference between a Marine and the enemy, then our country is in a lot worse shape than I thought."

I wanted to applaud, but I didn't. Instead, I watched Jake's expression turn from puzzlement to determination as he answered, "Don't get your dander up, boys. There's nothing personal in what I said, just facts. Two years ago, I was a sailboat bum, having fun off the coast of Nantucket. I couldn't tell the difference between Japs or Krauts, Negroes or Wops, and I couldn't have cared less. Then the Navy convinced me that 'the boats' were my calling and put me in charge of this outfit. That makes me responsible for twelve PT boats and over two hundred men. So, when you stood on my dock this morning that made me responsible for you. I still couldn't care less 'what' you are, but I sure as hell care 'who' you are. So take my advice or ignore it. That's up to you."

The sea spray blew across my face and tasted salty as I stood, holding the radar mast for balance. With the decks vibrating under my feet, PT44 headed northwest towards Rob Roy Island, some forty-five miles over the horizon. Jake, the boat's captain, held the vessel at normal cruising speed, just under thirty knots, while the boat's three Packard V-12 engines laid out a mile-long, phosphorescent wake. Rain had swept in from the west about noon, and now the sky was completely overcast. But the ocean was still relatively calm, with a slight chop that actually aided the boat, allowing the hull to break surface tension and lift smoothly up on the step, with only its props and rudders submerged.

Low in the cloudy sky behind us, I could still make out the dark green outline of Wagina Island slipping out of view. The eighty-foot PT boat was armed with four torpedo tubes, one twin .50-caliber machine gun on each side of the helm, a stand-up machine gun on the bow, and a new 20mm cannon mounted on the stern. The crew said that the 44 boat was fifty tons of fighting fury, and that it had seen lots of action in and around the northern Solomon's.

Black Jack and Riku were below, loading the cameras and checking our gear, while eight other crewmen were busy preparing the boat for our third mule hunt. Running next to us on the port side was the 37 boat, and on the starboard side was PT41. They had been our shadows on each of the two unsuccessful hunts. This afternoon, before departing, the skipper had talked on a shortwave radio to an Australian coast watcher who had assured him that mules were traveling on the windward or ocean side of Rob Roy Island. There had been rain squalls there all day, and the Nips were using the bad weather to help hide the barge traffic. We were hopeful that today's hunt would have better results than our last tries. Standing just next to the captain, on the other side of the helm, was Lieutenant Dudley, his XO. Gone now were the cowboy outfits; both officers were all business when they were out 'yachting,' as they called it. All of us were now wearing blue Navy life jackets, gun belts and heavy flack helmets, and we were armed with pistols or rifles for further protection.

Turning to the skipper, I shouted over the rumbling engines, "I'm going below to check on my guys."

He nodded back and I headed down the wooden gangway to the small compartment below.

The passageway reminded me that these boats were also called 'sawdust coffins,' as they were nothing more than fast-moving pieces of plywood and glue. Jack and Riku were seated behind an oblong table across from a tiny galley, with our camera gear spread out on top. Just aft of this area, and nestled next to and under the gangway, was a closet-sized room where the radio/radar operator worked. His door was open, and I could hear the muffled sounds of his radio working over the noise of the boats motors.

Just forward of this compartment was the sleeping quarters for the crew. There were eight bunks but none of the crews slept on the boats, which were too hot and muggy and lacked ventilation. Taking off my helmet, I poured myself a mug of coffee. Then sat down at the table and reviewed the plans for photographing the attack.

There were two 16MS loaded in the forward torpedo tubes, while the aft two tubes had standard fish for larger and deeper targets. Riku had screwed metal plates onto the deck of the bow, to fasten down both his film-camera tripod and himself in order to get footage of any quarry and the fish being fired. Black Jack's position was just behind the new 20mm cannon to get still pictures of the results of our fast moving attack. My position, with the spy camera, was on the bridge, to get whatever action shots I could. We had been forewarned that the boat would be making abrupt maneuvers that could result in being thrown overboard if we weren't holding on, so safety was Job One.

An hour later, and ten miles off the coast of Rob Roy Island, the weather closed in on us. The visibility dropped to less than a half mile, with rough seas, then intermittent rain squalls. With the heavy weather, the skipper dropped the boat's speed to five knots, only using the power of the center engine, with the two wing units running, but out of gear. We could hear him talking to the radar operator over the intercom from the bridge, looking for any targets in the cloudy muck. With the boat bobbing in the choppy waters, the skipper called for general quarters, and we made our way topside to get into position. Standing next to the helm, I could hear all the conversations between our boat and the other two PT's, now behind us. Thirty minutes later, a target bogey popped onto our boat's radar screen, vague and misty at first, then more solid, fifteen hundred yards out. From its size and shape, the operator was certain it was a Japanese barge hugging the shoreline so that probing radar pulses would be diffused against the nearby jungle background and the bad weather.

Ten minutes later, we were still moving at near-idle speed, shadowing the target, with the skipper and Dudley both glassing the shoreline with their high-powered, light-collecting binoculars. The rain had eased off some, with all the crew now drenched while standing at their battle stations. The gunner in the turret next to me cleared his .50 cal weapon, with that sharp, distinctive crack of metal locking in. The sound pumped up my adrenaline and brought a strange copper taste to my mouth. Reaching into my pocket, I pulled out my weapon -- the Minox camera -- and stood ready.

"There it is," Dudley called out quietly. "Two-nine-zero degrees, about fourteen hundred yards out."

Jake swung his glasses around until he picked up the target. He stared for a moment and then, without lowering his binoculars, barked, "Standby for a port torpedo run."

Dud passed on the order to all of the gun crews while Jake let his glasses fall to his chest and started turning the helm to port. The boat continued slowly for a few hundred yards; then the skipper hit the engine throttles, and all three Packards roared to life. In a heartbeat, the boat trembled as its stern dropped down sharply, with the props grabbing the water. A huge rooster-tail erupted off the stern, and the boat surged ahead with all three engines howling. Within seconds, the PT went from five knots to forty.

With the bow crashing through the high seas, the boat gained fast on the mule now some eight-hundred yards directly in front of us. Putting the spy camera to my eye, I started taking pictures just as three bright lights came reflecting across the water from our target. These spotlights from the low-silhouetted barge were the prelude as the evening abruptly filled with tracer rounds -- odd-looking red and orange bullets being fired towards us but all going high. Then the sounds of the guns roared across the water with a hard, spaced chatter.

With my heart racing and my adrenaline pumping, I turned my camera towards the skipper just as he raised and instantly lowered his right arm. The PT's two turret and bow machine guns opened up with long bursts of fire, creating horrific noise. Hot, spent shells flew to the deck as their tracers slashed straight lines across the mist to the barge. Over the bombastic noise, the skipper shouted, "Fire one," and the port-side torpedo leaped into the water with a loud, dull swish. "Fire two," he called, and the starboard side fish did the same.

Now the boat snapped into a sharp turn, with Jake spinning the helm wheel. All the crew held on as the PT made the abrupt maneuver and then recovered. As the boat came out of its turn, it was running parallel to the mule. The 20mm gun immediately began firing: whop, whop, whop. The enemy barge was right off our port quarter and less than two hundred yards away when I noticed the first fish bouncing atop the water and missing the mule's stern by over 50 yards. Turning to my right, I saw the second torpedo do the same, missing the target's bow by only a few feet.

"Shit, they ran wild!" I heard the skipper shout as he abruptly turned the boat away from the battle. Holding onto the gun turret next to me, I looked behind us.

All guns were still firing. The 20 mm canon shells were rocketing out balls of white fire as the .50s tore into the barge, making sharp flashes as their hot tracers bounced off its metal plating. Then a cannon shell hit the top side of the mule, creating an intense sunburst of light.

The Nips retuning fire lowered their aim and began homing onto our boat. Bullets snickered past. One struck the base of the port turret, while others slammed into the cockpit, throwing wood splinters and sawdust. One shell exploded just above our stern, lighting up the sky with a starburst of red and orange, then raining shrapnel in our wake.

A few heartbeats later, the 20mm cannon stopped firing, and then the machine guns, as we moved out of range. The skipper ran out for a few more seconds and then reduced speed as we watched the 37 and 41 boats follow down the gauntlet of our wake. By the time they joined us, we could see small fires burning out of control on the barge. We had mauled it but not sunk it.

With the last sign of twilight in the western sky, the boats grouped together, and the Skipper got on the radio for a battle report. We had been lucky: no major injuries or damage, other than the 37 boat having fuel-pump problems. With the boats bobbing in the heavy swells, Jake ordered the 41 boat to take the 37 under tow so they could work on the problem as we made the long, slow trek back to base.

"I couldn't have missed at five hundred yards out. The torpedoes just ran wild. So what the hell happened?" the skipper asked in the galley, with the cabin lights on and the blackout curtains closed.

Rain had started again, with some of the crew sprawled out on their bunks, while others stood in the compartment doorway, waiting for answers.

"I have no idea. They worked just great in all the other tests. There was just something different tonight," I remarked.

The galley shook as the boat crashed through some waves, with loud thuds rumbling up from her keel.

"It was the swells," Black Jack said from behind the table, unloading his camera.

"The swells?" I shot him a look. "I don't understand."

"Think about it, Lieutenant. In all our testing, we've been shooting in the calm waters of San Diego, or in the New Georgia Sound. We've never had swells any bigger than three or four feet. Tonight they were ten to twelve feet high. It was just like when we took off in the PBY for Hawaii. We got up on a wave and then heaved to the next, and then the next. Well, that's what our fish did, too. And each time they heaved forward, the next wave jarred them off course a little. That's why we missed."

"Well, that's just great," the skipper commented darkly, "if you're fighting a war on a nice, calm day."

"So," I said to Black Jack, "you think the fish were swimming too high in the rough water?"

"Yeah. They were on top of it, more than swimming in it," he answered.

"Is there a fix?"

"Hell, I don't know, sir. I'm no engineer. I just know what I saw in my viewfinder."

Sitting next to Jack, Riku had his eyes closed, with his lips silently moving. I had seen this before and knew what he was doing.

Watching me and then Riku, the skipper scowled. "I hope we're not keeping you awake, Corporal."

"He's reading, sir," I answered back.

"Reading!" Jake exclaimed with a surprised look on his face.

With a hypnotic expression on his face, Riku finally opened his eyes and lifted his gaze. "Page 47, paragraph four, of the engineering specs that came with the modification kits says that the gyro, M37B, installed within the guidance module, Z45B, is specified to work with the redesign thirteen-degree fins to keep the Mark 16MS shallow. If the fins are not installed and calibrated properly, the 16MS has a tendency to sink one foot for every hundred yards of firing range." Pausing for a moment, he nodded, smiled and then finished, "Therefore, I conclude that if we hadn't installed the new fins, our torpedoes would have run deeper and not been thrown off-course, tonight."

The little compartment fell as quiet as a church on Monday morning, with all the crew staring at him.

"That's scary. How the hell did you do that, Corporal?" Jake asked with disbelief in his voice.

"He's got a photographic memory," Black Jack answered back.

Still with a puzzled look, the skipper asked, "Okay...but how do you prove this conclusion?"

"Simple" I replied. "We use our last two kits, one with full modifications and the other without new fins, and then find another target in the same sea conditions."

In the harsh cabin lights the skipper's face contorted. "Let me see if I understand this. You want to use my boat and crew as guinea pigs to prove the Corporal's theory. Is that right?"

"Yes, sir. That pretty well sums it up."

Jake had said he wanted to sleep on my idea, but by the time we got back to Wagina Island, he had made his decision, and it was a go.

The next day, we used our two remaining kits as planned, and loaded the modified torpedoes into the forward tubes of the 44 boat. For three straight days, we hunted for just the right target in just the right sea conditions. On the final day, just before we were to leave, radar picked up a bogey trying to clear some shoals just south of Bikolia Island, in heavy weather and with a strong rip tide.

It was late afternoon by the time we got into position for the attack and, as before, the 37 and 41 boats had fallen in behind us to make the run. This time, the Skipper ran at the mule at full speed from over two thousand yards out. As we pulled close, there was that strange copper taste in my mouth again, as if my body was warning me of danger.

Just then, we began taking small-arms fire from the barge but, because of our guns firing, for the most part the Nips kept their heads down. Crashing through swells of over twelve feet, we got to three hundred yards out, and Jake fired both fish, then made the same sharp portside maneuver.

With bullets zinging by me, I held my breath. The first fish, with the new fins, crashed from wave to wave, mostly on top of the water. The other, without new fins, was just visible under the swells.

The first missed.

The second didn't. With a loud, bright explosion, the mule lifted up into the air a dozen feet or more, split in half, and then came crashing back down. The horrendous noise echoed off the water, while the shock wave rocked our boat. In thirty seconds she disappeared into the sea, leaving only a fiery oil slick with a few Jap survivors and debris floating in the water.

With all of our guns now silent, the port turret gunner shouted down, "Permission to strafe the Nip survivors."

As Jake turned the boat back into the battle area, he yelled at me, "It's your kill, Dutch. Do we kill off these slant-eyed survivors?"

His question caught me off-guard, and I fumbled for a response. "Nah," I replied. "Let the sharks have 'em."

Jake frowned at me, then looked up to the gunner and shook his head no. I could tell he was disappointed with my decision but I just wasn't as blood-thirsty as I'd thought I would be.

Mission Report

We had proven Riku's conclusions, and it was important information that had to be communicated back up the line. By the next morning, I had completed two copies of a handwritten, three-page report outlining changes that had to be made to the manual in order to use the Mark 16MS successfully in heavy seas. With this report and our films, the brass could still salvage the program and distribute the modification kits as planned. I inserted one copy of the report into a Navy envelope, addressed to Admiral Hoyt, and placed it with other outgoing dispatches. The other copy I added to the report done on the *Argonaut*.

Commander Jacobson drove us back to the cove where we had been dropped off exactly seven days earlier. As the jeep squeaked to a stop on the pier, I checked the time: 11:38 AM. Grabbing our duffle bags and camera gear, we stacked them at the end of the dock and returned to the jeep to say our goodbyes.

"Skipper, I added my mission report to your outgoing dispatches. It's important and has to be sent up the line. Will you see to it, sir?"

Looking up at me from under his straw hat, he said, "Sure. You can count on it, Dutch." With the three of us now standing next to him, he extended his hand for a shake and continued, "You guys are okay. Like I said, what you are is of no importance, but who you are is. Your visit to our little oasis was enlightening. We'll take two dozen kits ASAP. And I want you guys to keep the weapons we gave you, as a little token of our appreciation. We robbed them from the Marines, so I guess it's only fitting that you get a few back."

After shaking hands, he started the jeep, backed around and then stopped and shouted, "How long before you think the kits will be available, Dutch?"

"I have no idea, sir…but I'll put you at the top of the list," I shouted back, waving.

In a cloud of dust, he was gone and we were alone on that silent pier again.

A lot had happened in a week. My sea legs were still wobbling and my mind was still reeling. We were packing iron, we were in the middle of a war zone, and we were real Marines fighting a real war. Standing next to our gear, I took out a cigarette and lit it while I waited.

By thirteen hundred, I knew something was wrong. By fourteen hundred, we moved our sea bags and gear off the dock to one of the burned-out buildings on the beach. By fifteen hundred, we knew the sub wasn't coming and that we were on our own. During these hours, we had gone from reflection to apprehension to concern. Finally, loading up our gear, we started the mile-long walk back to Smugglers Cove.

Had the *Argonaut* been sunk? Did she have battle damage, or had bad weather or mechanical problems prevented her from picking us up? We had no idea and no way of finding out. All I knew was that we had to get off Wagina Island to deliver our report.

Commander Jacobson told us that the only other way off the island was via Black Cats that flew into the cove twice a week from Guadalcanal. These PBY flying boats brought in supplies and took out the wounded. If there was room, maybe we could hitch a ride back. From Guadalcanal we might get a flight to Australia, and from there to Hawaii via the Fiji Islands on a Pan Am Clipper that he had heard was still flying the route. Our other option was to wait for a supply ship, which could mean weeks of cooling our heels in the Bamboo Room.

Two mornings later, we stood again at the foot of the pier, watching a PBY come in for a landing on the entrance channel. This plane was just like the one on which we had flown from San Diego, with the exception that she was painted black on the top side and a dark blue-gray on the bottom, hence their name Black Cats. This one was also armed with twin .30 caliber machine guns sticking out of a bow eyeball turret, and two single .50 caliber guns showing out of each waist blister window.

As the Cat taxied towards the dock, I was surprised at all the activity on the pier. Next to us, an empty flatbed truck waited for supplies, with three guys standing-by to help the plane tie up. On the beach end of the dock, two Army ambulances were parked, with their drivers smoking and talking.

After the PBY was moored, one of the waist blister windows opened and members of the flight crew started handing out supplies. These crates looked to be artillery shells and perishable food. In the evenings, we had often heard the roar of the cannon fire coming from the north end of the island, and we knew the Army was still fighting it out with the Nips up there.

As the last crates were placed on the truck, a Navy Lieutenant JG appeared from the window, armed with a clip board. Standing next to the load, he did a final count and then had the driver sign for the supplies. Moving a few feet closer to him, I asked, "Lieutenant, are you the pilot?"

Handing the driver a copy of the receipt, he answered, "Yeah. What can I do for you?" He was young tall and lean. If he used a razor, it was only for show, as his blond hair was lost in his fair complexion.

"I'm Lieutenant Dutch Clarke," I told him, "and my crew and I need a lift to Guadalcanal. Can you help us out?"

Finally looking our way, he said, "I don't know, Lieutenant. We can only carry ten and I don't know how many wounded there will be. And, from the looks of your crew and all your gear, I'd have to count you as four."

"It's of the utmost naval importance that we contact Pearl as soon as possible," I replied.

Doing a double-take back to Black Jack, Riku and our gear again, he asked, "What are you guys? I didn't think any mud Marines were still stationed on Wagina."

"We're not. We were dropped off by submarine over a week ago and she didn't make it back to pick us up, so we really need your help."

Just as I finished, a navy nurse pulled herself through the Black Cat's window and dropped to the dock. In the bright sunlight, her auburn hair glistened, and even in her baggy flight suit we could see the outline of her shapely figure. This unexpected sight lifted our eyes and brought smiles to our faces. To say we were speechless would be an understatement.

"That's Ensign Nurse Pratt. She's really hell on wheels, boys. I'll check with her on the wounded while you guys cool your heels here for a few minutes."

As it turned out, they had five stretcher cases and three walking wounded for the flight back. After they loaded, however, the pilot told us he had been short one waist gunner on the flight up, so if one of my guys would man one of the waist guns, he would take us, even if he was overloaded. Black Jack volunteered right away, so we stowed our gear aboard, took seats next to the aft guns, and waited to depart.

A few minutes later, looking out the blister window just as the plane was about to push off, I noticed an Army jeep screeching to a halt at the end of the pier, with its horn blowing. With the waist window reopened, the pilot was summoned for a powwow with the jeep's occupants.

Seconds later, I was beckoned, as well. As I approached the jeep, I saw that a full Army Colonel and a Major stood next to it, each caring small valises.

"Lieutenant Clarke," the pilot said, "the Colonel and Major here need to bump two of your guys off the plane so they can get to a meeting. Sorry, but I'm already over the limit."

Looking over to the Colonel, I braced myself and gave him a salute, which he sharply returned. Under the eagle on his campaign cap was the weather-beaten face of an older officer, with a large nose, short gray hair and dark-blue eyes that cried out for respect. He wore a fatigue uniform, with pearl-handled guns in shoulder holsters. He was as spit-and-polished as if he was going on parade.

"Good morning, sir," I snapped. "It's imperative that my crew and I get to Guadalcanal to file a time-sensitive mission report back Pearl Harbor. It's of the utmost importance to the Navy, sir."

He chuckled sarcastically, and then snapped back, "I don't give a shit what the Navy needs. As far as I'm concerned, they're only in the transportation business, while I'm in the killing business. This little birdie on my hat tells me I'm getting on the plane, and that your guys are coming off, and that my decision is not up for discussion. Do you understand, Lieutenant?"

Reaching into my pocket for XKO Order, I answered, "Yes, sir." Unfolding the paper, I handed it to the pilot while remarking, "You might want to look at this, sir."

With a warm breeze on my back, I watched the Lieutenant JG read and then reread the document. Finally, looking up at the Colonel, he handed the paper to him while saying, "I'm sorry, sir. It seems Lieutenant Clarke has priority, after all."

With frowns on their faces, both the Colonel and Major read the general order.

The Colonel's eyes held a gelid stare as he shot back, "I don't give a good goddamn what this paper says. I'm full bird Colonel, so who the hell cares what the Secretary of the Navy says?"

Reaching across, the JG gently removed the paper from the Colonel's hands and passed it back to me, saying, "I do, sir. He's my boss and I am the captain of this plane. The Lieutenant and his crew stay. It's my decision and it's not up for discussion." Turning to me he concluded, "Get aboard, Lieutenant. The Navy will provide you with some *transportation* to Guadalcanal."

The looks on their faces were priceless. Turning, I walked back across the dock and crawled into the plane, leaving the Army brass flat-footed and fuming, with the JG just behind me. As the pilot closed the blister window, the Army Colonel screamed, "You Lieutenants will hear about this! You Navy people will not treat me like this! I've got your number and your asses are mine!"

"Yes, sir," the pilot yelled back, and latched the window. Turning to me, he continued with a smile, "Thanks, I needed that. I never did want to make the Navy a career. Let's get the hell out of here."

A few moments later, the pilot yelled 'Clear!' out his window and cranked up the twin 1200-horse Black Cat engines. With a deafening roar, the plane vibrated across the water and slowly lifted off the coral-green runway. As the plane circled around the cove to gain altitude, out the blister window I could see the Army jeep, in a cloud of dust, making its way back up the beach road.

The morning was bright and crisp and, as the PBY tipped its wings again to head south, we could view all of Wagina Island, from its rugged, jungle-covered mountains in the north to Smugglers Cove in the south. This little strip of land looked peaceful, clean and beautiful from the air, covered in bright green foliage, surrounded by the sparkling blue Pacific. But it was a deceiving view, as we all knew; this tropical oasis was full of death and destruction.

Black Jack had taken his position, manning the left waist gun, with Riku seated in a jump seat next to him. Across from them was the right waist gunner, a freckled-faced sailor named Henry. He told us that the flight back would take almost three hours.

I was sitting next to Henry, in a small jump seat. The two plastic blister- or bubble windows that the waist gunners used had 180-degree views left to right, up and down. Their .50 caliber machine guns were mounted on a swivel tripod that could be pushed forward and could then fire with the window open. As Henry instructed Jack on the finer points of being a waist gunner, they opened their windows and cleared their weapons by firing a few rounds. Hot, spent casings rattled and swirled to the flight deck and rolled around, while the fuselage filled with the bitter smell of cordite. Then, closing the eyelid-type windows, they continued talking about the different ways of holding off enemy planes, and the types of Nip aircraft that were in the area.

Leaning back in my seat, I turned my attention to the center of the plane. Here, in the dim light, I could see Nurse Pratt working with the wounded. On the left side, there were a number of racks that held the stretchers cases, and on the right was a row of jump seats for the walking wounded. In the space between, the nurse gently cared for and chatted with the men.

Other than muffled voices over the roar of the engines, I was surprised by how quiet these guys were. They reminded me of my decision not to strafe the Nip survivors in the water. Was I too soft for combat? Why did I show mercy? Where was my boot-camp grit? I had been wrestling with my decision for days and, after seeing these poor bastards, I wished I could change it now. Resting my head on the side of the plane, I pondered these unanswerable questions until, finally, I dozed off.

Bam…bam…bam.

I was startled awake by the noise of bullets zinging through the fuselage, and Henry shouting, "Open your window! Meatball coming around!"

Then Black Jack's gun started firing: *yak…yak…yak.*

It took a few heartbeats for me to realize that we were under attack. Jumping to my feet, I caught a fleeting glimpse of the Nip plane as it flew from under us, out the left side, with Jack's tracers trying to follow.

Seconds later, Black Jack yelled, "He's turning around and coming back."

"What kind of plane is it?" Henry shouted from his window.

"Hell, I don't know. One with guns!" Jack shouted back as he opened fire again.

Crouching just next to Black Jack's blister, I watched his body wave with the recoil of the machine gun, as hot brass burped out of its breach. Then bullets and shrapnel from the Nip's plane ripped through our fuselage again.

Just then, our pilot tipped the right wing sharply down in an evasive move, and all of us lost our footing and hung on.

"He's coming your way," Jack yelled.

But there was no answer.

Turning, I looked across to find no one at the other waist gun. We had not heard a sound, over Jack's gun, but Henry was gone. He must have been sucked out or had fallen out through the window during the steep maneuver.

Stumbling across, I took his position just as the Nip came roaring out from under us. Grabbing the gun, with the wind through the open window whirling around me, I started shooting, but I missed the plane badly.

The low-wing, single-engine enemy flew out a few thousand yards and banked again for another pass. This time, I laid my fire well in front of his approach. With my tracers showing the way, I kept my fingers wrapped tightly on my gun's trigger: *yak...yak*. A burst of sunlight reflected off the Nip's cockpit window, like a flash bulb going off, as he came racing straight back to my position. *Yak...yak...yak...* And then I saw the faint signs of black smoke coming from under the cowling of his engine.

Bam...bam...bam... My right hip buckled like a nut beneath a hammer's blow, and my left arm felt like fire. With my adrenaline pumping, I ignored the pain and kept firing while moving the gun downward. "I think I nicked him. He's coming your way," I heard myself shout.

Black Jack's gun opened fire, as I lost the plane under us and stopped firing. Turning on my left heel, I watched Jack's tracers follow the meatball out...and then it exploded in midair.

The shock wave from the explosion shook our plane, causing us to pitch and roll. Then it recovered. Black Jack turned his head towards me and flashed me one of those million dollar smiles as he yelled, "We got the son-of-a-bitch!"

I tried to answer, but my tongue suddenly weighed a ton. With my sleeve wet with warm blood, I tried to take a step out with my right leg, then tumbled forward onto the flight deck, passing out as I fell.

What came next was all in foggy bits and pieces. I seemed to remember Nurse Pratt hovering over me with a big syringe in her hand...and then blackness. After a while, there were balls of sunlight glaring in my eyes as strange, hooded ghosts stood around me. My mind was playing funny tricks, with sounds and images flashing by. In slow motion, I watched Henry, the waist gunner, fall out of his window, screaming as he tumbled towards the sea. Next, there was the face of the Jap pilot, smiling through his cockpit window as his bullets raced straight for me. Then, in a flicker, I could see the distorted face of Commander Shapiro, and hear his voice echoing, "Listen for the clicks, Dutch." After a while, he was replaced by Commander Sullivan, saying, "Radar has a contact, Dutch," and lastly Commander Jacobson, screaming, "It's your kill, Dutch...Do we finish off the survivors?"

"Shoot 'em! Shoot 'em all", I yelled at the murky images as I started running towards them...but then they were gone.

Tap...tap...tap...

"I can't quite make that out," I shouted. "What is it? What the hell is it?"

Step by Step

Slowly opening my eyes, I felt a cool breeze wash across my face. As my mind reached for reality, I could hear that *tap...tap...tap...* and, after some time, I realized it was an open window next to me, with a breeze rattling the half-closed curtain.

As I moved my head around, my eyes started to come back into focus, and I saw that I was lying in a hospital bed in a drab, pea-green room. Next to me was another empty bed.

I tried to pull myself up for a better view...then stopped as excruciating pain flared from my hip and from my left arm, useless in a sling. Giving up, I collapsed back onto the bed, staring up at the ceiling. What the hell has happened to me? I wondered.

Just then, the door near the foot of my bed opened and Black Jacked appeared.

"Look who's awake! Glad to see you back," he said as he moved to the side of my bed.

I was groggy, searching for my words. Finally, I blurted, "Where are we?"

Reaching for the bottle of water next to me, he placed the straw to my lips. "You're at St. George Hospital in Sydney, Australia. The doctors repaired your hip yesterday, so you're just coming out of it."

The water tasted sweet to my cotton-dry mouth. After Jack moved it away, I asked, "How long?"

"Since you got shot? Five days, more or less. The nurse on the plane stopped your bleeding and saved your life. Then the doctors on Guadalcanal patched you up and had you flown here, to the best orthopedic doctors in the country. Yesterday, they did surgery, replacing some of your damaged hip bone with metal plates. You'll be okay."

Dazed, I was having a hard time absorbing what he was saying. He had to repeat it a number of times before, finally, I got it and understood.

By then, my memory had begun to work. With my head raised and my eyes blinking, I mumbled, "Our mission... What about our mission?"

"Relax. Three days ago, I gave our film and your mission report to the pilot of the Pan Am Clipper flying to Pearl. He signed for it and gave me his word that he would personally deliver it to Admiral Hoyt. It should be there by now."

Relieved, I let my head fall back on the pillow and grinned. "Thanks, Black Jack." I had to stop for a minute, while a wave of dizziness passed. Then I asked, "What about everyone else on the plane?"

"They're all okay...except Henry. He made me put on my safety harness when we took off, but he didn't wear his. He said it restricted his shooting. Whoosh, the kid was gone. Damn. I wish he'd used it."

"Yeah. I didn't even see or hear him fall. Hell of a way to go."

Black Jack sat down in a chair next to me, frowning. Finally, he said, "Dutch, I've got bad news...and bad news. The doctors don't think you'll ever walk quite right again. Your hip just took too much damage. The Navy wants to ship you to the States for rehabilitation and then, if you don't recover, they're going to kick you out of the Marines or give you a desk job. It's a lose-lose."

His words stung me to my core. The image of me stumbling around with a cane in civilian clothes was unacceptable. Firmly, I answered, "I can't let that happen. I'll recover, Jack. I know I will."

"I agree. We can't break up our team now, so I have a plan...if you're up to hearing it..."

The Navy doctors were willing to give me a few weeks to recover from my surgery; then they planned to put me on the first available hospital ship bound for the States. Black Jack used his best salesmanship -- and our special orders -- to persuade them that this wouldn't be what the Secretary of the Navy wanted. He begged and borrowed ninety days for me to make a full recovery while staying at St. George Hospital. He even convinced them to assign him as my personal trainer and rehab specialist. Then he got Corporal Togo assigned, temporarily, to a Navy photo lab down on the docks of Sydney.

Next, he worked with the doctors and hospital staff, securing their help in getting me back on my feet. Hell, he even persuaded them to let him move in and use the bed next to mine. Jack was like a bull in a china shop; he used his influence, my influence, and even the Secretary of the Navy's influence to get what he needed. The nurses started jokingly calling him the 'Admiral,' because he was so determined and resourceful.

In the uphill battle I'd taken on, I couldn't have had a better ally.

We started, two days after surgery, with the complete removal of all my feeding, medical and relief tubes. Jack put me on my own, and to say that I was helpless would be an understatement. At first, he had to carry me to the toilet, shave me, and even help feed me. It was humiliating and frustrating but, with Jack's good natured attitude and his contagious will for me to succeed, we started down the road.

He would rub both of my legs for hours to keep the muscle tone built-up, and then slowly move the right leg up and down until I cried out with pain. He showed me the x-rays of my hip, before and after the surgery, and talked about how a steel hip is stronger and better than Mother Nature's original -- a hip we now had to train to do what we wanted. He got a radio and had music blasting in our room, nonstop, and if I started feeling sorry for myself, he would get into my face and talk me out of it. Being around him was like listening to a football coach at half-time, with the Aussie nurses as the cheerleaders. It was positive this and positive that -- there was no room for failure.

At the end of the first week, I could put some weight on my right leg and, with Jack's help, hobble around the room. By the beginning of the second week, the doctors removed the bandage from my arm. A piece of hot shrapnel had swirled into my shoulder, leaving a six-inch crooked scar just under my bear tattoo.

It had taken sixteen stitches to sew it up, and Jack said it added an air of mystery to my tattoo story.

At the end of the second week, with my sling gone, I was up on crutches, struggling down the hospital corridors. The staff and doctors of St. George couldn't have been better. They loved us Yanks, and showered us with encouragement, compassion and an occasional pint of whiskey to help take the edge off my pain. Those pints were supplemented with cans of Victory beer that Black Jack purchased at a Navy commissary and hid under his bed. Many a night, we would lie on our bunks, drinking warm 'boilermakers,' talking of friends, home and photography.

I knew Black Jack was special, but never more so than at these times. One evening, he told me how much he loved Australia, as there didn't seem to be any prejudice. He said that strangers would go out of their way just to come over and say hello, and that the local gals kept giving him the eye. He wasn't sure if it was him or the uniform, but he loved the Aussies. I told him he should ask one of the local girls out, and he was astounded.

"You mean you wouldn't care if I dated a white woman?"

"Hell, no. Would you care if I dated a colored gal?"

"You'd never date a Negro."

"I sure the hell would if she was as beautiful as your girlfriend back home."

My true statement set Jack back on his heels, and he chewed on it for a long while. To me, the only difference between the two of us was that he could walk. And that difference, with his help, would soon dissolve.

The rehabilitation process was one difficult step at a time. Jack took white tape and marked the hall floor in front of our room. Each day, he would move the mark a little farther down the corridor, and I would have to walk to the tape without using my crutches. Then we would go down to the hospital swimming pool, or use their gym. Here we would spend hours, sweating and exercising. It was slow, painful going but, after a wobbly start, my bum hip started working. At the end of six weeks, I was walking -- or limping -- on my own, with only the help of a cane. The doctors were surprised by my progress and attributed it to my young age and the tenacity of my personal trainer.

To celebrate my near-recovery, Black Jack and Riku took me out to one of the local pubs for drinks and dinner. Here, for the first time, I was introduced to an Aussie beer called Fosters. It was far superior to the Falstaff brew I had enjoyed for years. The pubs in Australia were like extended living rooms for the locals, who would gather together for pleasant conversations about war and politics. These were friendly people who, as Black Jack had said, would go out of their way to say hello and buy you and your mates a schooner of beer. They enjoyed life and loved the Yanks -- and why not? If it hadn't been for America, they would have fallen to the Japanese, just like the Philippines and Malaysia, so they showed their thanks with warm hospitality.

During our dinner conversation, Riku told us about his work at the Navy Lab. It seemed the Ensign that ran the darkroom didn't like having a Nisei working for him, so he stuck Riku in the semi-dark print room to make proofs from poorly exposed negatives. For eight hours a day, he worked in the safe-light environment, cranking out hundreds of black-and-white prints. But he said he didn't mind the duty, and every time the Ensign came into his area, he would start murmuring 'banzai,' the Japanese word for a 'battle cheer,' under his breath.

With a big grin on his face, he concluded, "Beats slinging hash...and I love watching the Ensign's face as he beats a speedy retreat. But what are we going to be doing six weeks from now?"

That was the question.

The next week, I started to make inquiries about USMC outfits in Australia. I soon found that the 2nd Marine Division was retraining, re-supplying and refitting, over in Melbourne. When I started calling them, they kept passing me from one person to the next, since no one seemed to know what to do about three Marines without orders. After numerous calls, I finally got an appointment to meet with a Colonel Conway, the Commanding General's Adjutant.

Taking the night train, Black Jack and I made the eleven-hour journey to Melbourne. The train ride was long, slow and stuffy, as the only seats we could get were in a second-class day coach. Unlike American trains, the day coaches were really little compartments with three-person bench seats that faced across from one other. Finding our assigned compartment, we took the seats in front of the window. At first, we thought we might be alone in the little room, but we were soon joined by a middle-aged, motherly woman who sat on Jack's side, and by a young Aussie Army Private who sat next to me.

These two people were delightful company for the first few hours of the trip. We talked family, country and war, typical subjects on the home front. By ten o'clock, the lady next to Black Jack fell asleep, with her head bobbing against her headrest. Half an hour later, the Private faded away, leaving just Jack and I talking, across from one another.

In the dim light, Black Jack reached into the blouse of his uniform and retrieved a small silver flask. After taking a swig, he passed it over to me. "Are we going to use your special orders when we meet with Colonel Conway?"

I took a drink of the whiskey and passed the flask back. "I'm don't know. The orders could do more damage than good, if he thinks we're spies for the Secretary."

"So you hope he's just going to welcome us as Marines and leave it at that?"

"Yeah."

Looking over to confirm that both our traveling companions were sleeping, Jack asked, with one of those serious looks, "How did you get those special orders? They are really something to have. When you were out of it, on Guadalcanal, I showed them to the Navy doctors, and all of sudden you were on the top of their list for surgery, and given priority for St. George."

"I told you that Admiral King gave them to me."

"Yeah…but I want the real story," he said with a grin. "I just can't see how an up-start Lieutenant became pals with a powerful Admiral. What really happened?"

His question caught me off guard, but I figured he had a right to know. "Turns out my Uncle Roy has been chums with Admiral King for years, and he used that friendship, without my knowledge, to pull a few strings. That's how I got my gold bars and ended up at OWI. Then I met the Admiral, and he took a shine to me and gave us our first assignment and those special orders."

Leaning back in his seat and taking another swig, Jack remarked, "Sounds like your uncle is a rich, powerful white guy if he can pull those kinds of strings."

"Yeah...he is," I answered quietly.

Cocking his head to one side, with a funny look, Jack then quietly asked, "Does that make you the same?"

He didn't know, and why should he? I hadn't told anyone about the money. But he wasn't just anyone. He was the one got me walking again, so why not?

I slowly nodded my head yes, saying, "I'm white, not so powerful and rich...maybe."

He looked across at me for the longest while, then said, "I guess I'm not surprised, with all you've spent on camera gear, and loaning us money between paydays... but how rich?"

Smiling back at him, I put four fingers in the air and then realized the lady sleeping next to him had one eye open, looking directly at me. She had eavesdropped on the whole conversation.

It took a few seconds for Jack to get my drift, and then his eyes lit up like headlights as he exclaimed, "Four million!"

I shook my head yes for the benefit of the lady next to him, who now had both eyes and her mouth wide open.

The next morning, we hired a cab and rode twenty miles out to the countryside where the 2nd Division was encamped. Here we met with Colonel Conway in one of the command Quonset huts.

The Colonel had a round face, with a small nose and short hair that was brown but streaked with gray. He was pleasant enough as I explained our situation. I told him about our temporary assignment to Admiral King's staff and, in general terms, about our mission on both the *Argonaut* and on Wagina Island. I described how the submarine had failed to pick us up, and then recounted the skirmish in the PBY. Assuring him that my limp was only transitory, I went on to explain that it had been months since our last pay call and that, if the Division didn't need us as photographers, we would take combat duty. Anything to get us back into the war.

He listened carefully and even made notes on a pad, but he wasn't encouraging. Yes, the 2nd Division had a combat photography unit and yes, they might welcome more photographers, but we didn't have any paperwork. He explained that Marines without papers were like a cabbie without a cab: going nowhere. And the fact that we were attached to a Navy Admiral's Staff back in the States, even temporarily, made it more difficult.

In the end, he took down all of our personal information and said he would send it up the chain of command to get the ball rolling, but he then went on to tell us that it would take weeks to get new orders cut, and that he couldn't even start the process until the doctors released me for duty. His comments were vague, and he kept trying to put us off by saying he'd get back to us.

Finally, I showed him the only paperwork we did have, the XKO order. While I hadn't planned on showing it, I wanted to light a fire under him, and I thought it might do the trick.

He read the order carefully, writing down its contents, staring at the Secretary's signature. Then, sliding it back across his desk, he said, "Lieutenant, I assure you that we will contact you, through St. George Hospital, as soon we have a disposition of your situation."

Leaving his office, all I could think of was that dreaded word: snafu.

Returning to the hospital, Jack and I redoubled our efforts on my rehabilitation schedule. We worked at it seven days a week, ten hours a day, in the pool, in the gym and on the Aussie football field across the street. We were determined to get me walking and running again without a limp.

Slowly, ever so slowly, I started to improve. Gone were my wobbly legs, replaced with muscles I hadn't even known I had. And the bum hip, while still stiff and painful at times, started feeling natural again. There were days of frustration and times of failure, but they were short-lived, thanks to Black Jack.

Five weeks later, on my twenty-third birthday, a Navy doctor by the name of Captain Ray Foster came out to the hospital, and Jack put me through an hour-long program to prove my recovery. After swimming ten lengths of the pool and then running two miles on the field, I finished with fifty deep knee bends, all without a limp. Then we showed him my x-rays before and after the surgery, and film taken just the day before. He was astounded by my progress, and he released me for duty on the spot.

After signing my release order and agreeing to send a copy of it to Colonel Conway, Doc. Foster reached into his pocket and handed me an envelope. He told me that a Marine Lt. Colonel had visited his office, the day before, pumping him for details about my medical condition, and had then asked him to deliver the note to me only if he released me for duty.

Looking down at the plain white envelope, I saw my name and rank typed there, along with the words:

`'Private & Confidential.'`

Two days later, with my release in hand, we said our goodbyes to the doctors and staff of St. George. Through their hard work, along with the determination of Black Jack, I had recovered, but at a painful price I would discuss with no one. Gone were my days of running the obstacle course like the wind, along with nights without soreness and pain in my hip, but the price was worth paying. If I had to grab onto that .50 caliber machine gun again and relive it all, I would, secure in the knowledge that any good Marine would do the same.

Appropriate Mission

On a cold, rainy day after the Doc released me for duty, I hired a cab and rode to the address I had found in the confidential note. It had been a strange message and, while it told me to report to a Lt. Colonel Flag, and gave me the time and address, it also instructed me to come alone and to destroy the note after reading it.

As thunder rolled across the sky, the cab finally pulled up -- not to a government building but to a commercial warehouse. Peering out through the water-splattered window, I asked the Aussie lady cab driver if this was the correct address on Wharf Roadway. She said yes, and added that we were now in the warehouse district on the waterfront.

As I paid off the fare from the back seat, the cabbie turned her head my way and remarked, "Watch yourself, Yank. Lots of dock rats down here."

Pulling up the collar of my raincoat, I stepped out into the weather, and she quickly pulled away. Standing there in a downpour, I could see the right numbers tacked across a large wooden door that had a sign above it that read, 'Kings Heights, Moving & Storage.' There was no overhang or cover in the front. Looking down the vacant roadway, I saw similar brick buildings crowded together on both sides.

With large drops of rain pelting me, I walked to the old garage door and looked for a bell or buzzer. When I found none, I started banging on the wood.

Moments later, one half of the door slid partially open to reveal a fat, elderly Aussie man wearing dirty blue coveralls.

With the downpour now blowing sideways, I shouted, "I'm here to see a Colonel Flag. Could this be the right place?"

He eyed me for a second, then looked up and down the deserted roadway before saying, "Yeah, mate. Come on in out of the rain and follow me."

I hurried inside and took my hat off, shaking it dry while I snuck a quick look around. The old building was dark and damp, stacked with wooden crates from floor to ceiling. There was a stench in the room, the smell of grease and gun oil. Following the old man down an aisle towards the back, I noticed that all the boxes had long black numbers stenciled on them, and that the floor was covered with the kind of wood-shaving strands typically used as packing material. Obviously, this was some type of government or military warehouse.

As we reached the back of the building, the old man pushed open a metal door with a window and continued through a small, glass-covered atrium. Reaching the other side, he took out a key and unlocked another metal door, this one windowless, and held it open for me. "You'll find the Colonel's office at the end of the corridor. Go right in. He's expecting you, Lieutenant."

When I stepped inside, I found a wide, well-lit, brightly painted hallway. Moving down the corridor, I passed an open area on the right that contained a room full of radio equipment, with two operators. On the left, there was another open area that had four or five desks with Navy clerks working behind them. As I walked by, it seemed to me that one of the yeomen looked vaguely familiar, but he didn't glance my way, and I moved on.

At the very end, I found a door marked 'G2 CO.' Knocking on the hatch, I reached down and swung the door open. Inside, I found the Colonel behind his desk, talking on the telephone. He looked up, waving me in and pointing to a chair in front of his desk.

I moved across the large, bright room, noting that its walls were full of maps and black-and-white photos of different islands. Just behind the Colonel was a bank of windows that looked out over the harbor. Even in the gray weather, I could make out the shadows of a few ships at anchor. Just after I took my seat, he hung up the receiver, and I jumped to my feet again, bracing myself. But before I could say a word, he told me to sit back down.

"Let me find your file. It's here somewhere."

As he shuffled through some papers, I had a chance to take a good look at him. Colonel Flag wore Marine camouflage battle fatigues that had his name tag sewed just above his right breast pocket and his silver oak leaf neatly pinned to his collar. His shoulders were large and square, connected to a lean and trim body. He looked like a sun-browned college tight end, his brown hair boot-camp short across his scalp.

"Here it is. Yeah, you're the rich kid that thinks he's a spy."

His comment caught me off-guard and set me back on my heels, "I'm sorry, sir. You must have the wrong file."

He seemed to be watching my reactions closely as he answered, "Nope, says right here that you carry some special order from the Secretary of the Navy and that your personal net worth is somewhere in the millions. Do I have that wrong, Lieutenant?"

How could he know this? Then it dawned on me -- the Aussie Army private that sat next to me on the train to Melbourne was also the Navy yeoman I had just seen out front. That was why he'd looked familiar!

"I think you may have misunderstood your information, sir. Were you having me followed?"

Leaning back in his chair, he clasped both hands together, exercising his fingers.

"That's what we do here, Lieutenant. We are the intelligence office for this theater of operations, and we've known about you and your crew for months. I make it my policy to get to know the people we're dealing with...so we did a little investigation."

The room went silent for a moment as I absorbed his comments. He made me mad as hell -- he'd had no right to send someone to eavesdrop on my conversation with Black Jack.

Stiffly, I said, "As you probably know, sir, I went to Melbourne to talk to Colonel Conway of the 2nd division and offer our services as combat photographers. He should be processing our orders as we speak, so I'm not sure how you would be dealing with us."

Pulling himself back up to his desk, he shuffled through more papers…and, to my surprise, unearthed the handwritten notes that Colonel Conway had made.

"I wouldn't count on those orders, Lieutenant." His sarcastic grin revealed a gold cap on one of his front teeth as he continued. "You're still attached to Admiral King's staff and, in their wisdom, they're not letting you go. They are, in a way, attaching you to me."

Reaching down next to his desk, he rummaged through a briefcase and brought up two manila envelopes, one large and letter-sized, the other small and thick. He slid the letter-sized one across to me, saying, "Here are your official orders. Basically, you and your crew are being assigned as photographers to the *USS Heed*, a converted minesweeper that's doing charting and topography. Under the table, however, you'll be doing some missions for me."

Stunned, I picked up the envelope. "I'm confused, Colonel. I thought Admiral King was in charge of procurement. What does that have to do with all this cloak-and-dagger stuff?"

"He was…but now he's the Chief of Naval Operations for the Pacific. Hell, he's above Admiral Nimitz and General MacArthur, and reports directly to the President. Most importantly, he's our boss."

This news rolled around in my head like a handful of loose marbles. "Good for the Admiral…but why the *Heed*? If you want us to work for you, why not just come out and say so?"

"The *Heed* is a place to park you and your crew, and it's good cover. Besides, down the road I may need some information that you just might run across while working on her. As to you and your guys working here, your 'look' would just stand out too much. Anyhow, it wasn't my decision."

Glancing down at my envelope, I knew there wasn't anything I could do about the orders. They were what they were: orders. I looked up to find that the Colonel was shoving the fat envelope and a piece of paper across to me.

"Here's the back pay for you and your crew. There's a little over a thousand bucks here, so count it and sign for it."

Opening it, I found it full of new twenty dollar bills, along with a few fives and ones.

As I spread them out on the desk for the count, the Colonel kept talking. "I'll give you a little free advice, Lieutenant. Never say anything out loud that you don't want heard. There are people like me always listening. My G2 office is the best in the world. We move like the wind, we're as silent as sand, and we see like hawks."

Glancing up at him, I didn't know whether to laugh or cry at his statement. Maybe he had just seen too many movies. Then I realized that this guy was a real spook and believed every word.

"And one more thing -- you will tell no one, including your crew, about this meeting, and you will never come to this office again. I'll give you a card with a phone number on it. If you need to reach me, use it."

After I counted the money and signed the receipt, Flag went on to tell me that the *USS Heed* was due back at Berth M7, some ten blocks south along Wharf Roadway, on the following Monday. We were to report to her skipper, a Commander Parks, at 0800 on that day. He also told me that the billeting officer for the district had secured us temporary quarters at the Usher Hotel, but that we should spend the next few days looking for something more permanent and closer to the *Heed*. Reaching into his desk, he gave me the business card of a local realtor and told me to call him. Housing was hard to come by in Sydney, and what little Navy housing had been available was filled up.

I asked him if he had any news about the *Argonaut* and her crew. He said he didn't but that he would check on it. Walking me to his door, he finished, "Enjoy your new duty station. You'll only hear from me again when we have an appropriate mission."

As I walked out and passed the familiar yeoman, I looked at him and said, "Good day, mate."

Later, I read all the paperwork the Colonel had given me. It was pretty much as he'd said, except that I found that Black Jack had been awarded a USMC Combat Action Ribbon and Riku had received the USMC Air Combat Ribbon for their actions in the skies above the Solomon Islands. I was pleased that my guys had finally received some official recognition from the Navy, and I looked forward to their reactions. Reading a little further, I was humbled and gratified to learn that I had been awarded both a Purple Heart and a Bronze Star for the same. Also all of us had been given the Marine Good Conduct Medal. Inside the envelope, I found a short note from Admiral King that simply read:

```
     Dutch, pleased to hear of your recovery.
And thanks for your work in saving the 16MS
program. Your report and film were invaluable.
Enjoy your duty on the Heed -- she's a great old
ship that I severed on in WWI. Colonel Flag will
let you know when I have your next appropriate
mission.

     Admiral James King

     PS: Congratulations on your Purple Heart.
Wish I could have been there personally to pin it
on, but don't get any more or Roy will have my
hide!
```

Folding the note, I had the feeling I had just been sent back to purgatory.

That evening, I took the guys out to a local pub. There, I passed out their back pay and orders, and we settled up our loan accounts. Then we celebrated that the team was back together again. I didn't share my feelings of disappointment or any information about my meeting with Flag. Instead, I painted the new assignment as a reward for our actions.

USS Heed

The moaning sounds of the engine made it difficult to hear as the pilot shouted, "Six thousand, heading due north, mark."

From the rear seat, I waved my hand back at him as I peered down and through the viewfinder, waiting for the leading edge of Utupua Island to come into view. A few seconds later, I could see the southern coastline as we started the third pass over our target. Pressing the shutter release button, I felt the focal plane shutter move across the film and started counting in my head: one thousand one, one thousand two… As I counted, I reached down alongside the massive Fairchild K-1 aerial camera and twisted the film advance lever, which also re-cocked the shutter.

The air from outside rushed up at me from the opening in the floor of the old DeHaviland seaplane. Inside this hole was my Gimbal mount, which held my camera level, plum and square to expose the eight-by-eight-inch film. One thousand seven, one thousand eight, Fire. Then I would start the process all over again, until I had made the last exposure of the northern shore of the island. After that, the plane would fly out a ways and turn back south to make the next run over Utupua, trying to overlap the last run by fifty percent. It would take ten such runs and fifty-eight exposures to complete the mission.

Making aerial maps was partly technical (air speed, altitude, and camera position) and partly luck (lining up landmarks, weather and line of flight). The concept was basic enough; shoot as much film as possible from a controlled attack or constant elevation so that, back in Sydney, the Navy topographers could piece together a photographic mosaic map of the target island. These photo maps would then be converted to printed maps for navigational charts. For small islands and atolls, this could mean just a few frames of film, while for big islands it could take hundreds of sheets. Each target landmass posed its own set of problems and solutions, but one thing was for sure: we would never run out of targets because there were thousands of these islands dotting the landscape. And, as Commander Sullivan had pointed out aboard the *Argonaut*, most of the islands had few or no charts for navigational use. Our mission, while boring and mundane, filled a genuine need, and I knew that what we were doing was worthwhile. After my ambivalence about killing the Nip survivors, I had convinced myself that shooting aerials maps was better than shooting Japs.

As we made the last pass over Utupua, I saw two of our four sounding barges working in a small cove on the eastern coastline. Their job was just as difficult as ours; they had to position themselves off the shoreline, at specific points, and make depth soundings of the surrounding waters. These soundings, in fathoms and calculated for low mean tide, would be used in the final navigational charts of the island.

"Beer Barrel, I'm done. Let's head back to the barn," I shouted as I removed the heavy twenty-inch camera from the Gimbal mount and closed the floor hatch.

Chief Aviation Pilot Ted Williams, or 'Beer Barrel' as we called him, banked the old seaplane to port and headed for the small speck below us that was the *USS Heed*. Our DeHaviland was newer than our ship, as it had been built in 1929 while the keel of the *Heed* was laid in 1916. Hell, even the K-1 camera I was using was older than me. The tools we had been given to work with were old, older and very old. The plane was a high-wing, single-engine seaplane that had seen service up in Alaska before the war. We called her the 'blue goose,' as she was painted light blue under her belly and wings and a dark blue on top. Just like her namesake, she was graceful in flight but awkward on the ground. The cockpit was closed-in and could carry four passengers, with a small cargo area just behind the rear seat. Her top speed was only 120 MPH but she was built like a tank and almost flew herself.

A few minutes later, Ted banked the plane and buzzed the fantail of the *Heed* to alert her pickup crew that we were landing. As we came around to land, I had a good view of the old minesweeper. She was Navy gray and on her bow, in white letters, was painted CAM-54. The C designated 'converted,' the AM was the class of minesweeper, and 54 was her hull number. She was just under two hundred twenty-five feet long, with a beam just over thirty-two feet. Originally, she had been a coal-burning two stacker but in 1941 she'd been converted to diesel and now had only one funnel. With a top speed of eighteen knots, she had a complement of ninety-six, including officers, sailors, sounding engineers, photographers and our one pilot. Her armor and armaments were light, with a single three-inch gun forward and two 40mm cannons, port and starboard, amidships. On her stern, they had removed all the old minesweeping gear and replaced it with a large crane for aircraft and barge recovery.

The CAM class of ships had been converted for North Atlantic convoy duty but, because of their small size and the rough seas of the convoy routes, this hadn't worked out as planned. Most of these types of ships had been reassigned to utility missions such as ours. The *USS Heed* was old, small, hot and uncomfortable, but it had been our home, every other month, for the past half-year.

Skimming across the water while slowly losing altitude, our two underside pontoons finally made contact with the sea, sending loud thuds through the fuselage. As it did, ocean spray rolled up and out, glistening in the sunlight. With the throttle back, the resistance of the water brought down the weight of the plane, sinking our pontoons ever deeper into the sea. A few seconds later, we were floating.

The DeHaviland could take off or land in just a few hundred yards of water, which made her ideal for our kind of work. Beer Barrel brought the plane to a near-stop before throttling it up again to maneuver towards the stern of the *Heed*. This was always the tricky part, as the aircraft had to come within fifty feet of the fantail so that a line could be attached from the crane. On days with heavy swells and winds, it often took many attempts to safely attach the line without allowing the plane to crash into the stern. But on this day, with its long-reaching swells, the maneuver looked remarkably simple.

As we got close to the stern, Beer Barrel reached up and unsnapped a hatch plate just above his seat. Then, standing on the seat, he squeezed his massive frame through the hatch to help guide the line from the crane to our pickup hook. Once we were secured, the crane started dragging the plane across the water, and Beer Barrel cut our engine. Now we waited and watched as the seaplane was ever so slowly pulled towards the stern and then lifted out of the water.

As I waited, I reached down the length of the twenty-inch K1 camera barrel and unscrewed the red lens filter, placing it into its protective pouch. The development and use of this filter had been another one of Black Jack's innovations, to improve our aerial images. Before we'd started using the red filter, our black-and-white negatives had been flat, without much contrast. This made the Topographers' task more difficult, as they couldn't make out some changes in the landscape. The red filter added contrast, making the blues a deeper gray, with the greens and yellows a lighter gray. Our filtered images provided more detail and, therefore, better maps.

The crane pulled us out of the water and lifted us above the stern, then swung around one-hundred-eighty degrees and deposited us on the deck. While the recovery crew lashed the pontoons and wings to the hold-downs welded onto the deck, Beer Barrel and I exited the plane.

Black Jack and Riku were waiting by the rail for us. "How did it go, Lieutenant? See anything of interest?" Riku asked.

Handing the film magazine to him for reloading, I answered, "Green, green and more green. Damn, there's a lot of jungle out here. There's a long beach on the windward side, but it has a barrier reef that we should get some images of, and a small plateau just inland on the leeward side that might be flat enough for an airstrip. I think we should put some boots on the ground, this afternoon."

"What's G2 saying about Utupua?" Black Jack asked.

"It shouldn't be hot. They think there might be one or two small native villages on the island, although I didn't see a thing. But we'll go in armed." Turning to Ted, I continued, "That means you, too, Beer Barrel. I want you to draw out a Thompson with half a dozen magazines. You and I will back up Jack and Riku while they do the photography."

"Yes, sir," the pudgy pilot replied.

In truth, having Beer Barrel as backup in a fire fight was a crap shoot. In the air, he was a good enough pilot. He was even giving me flying lessons. But on the ground he was big, slow and clumsy. In port, he had a propensity for Aussie beer and, at sea, for the ship's ice-cream machine. While he wasn't a cupcake yet, he was getting there.

As we stood there, talking, one of the recovery crew walked by and said, "Beer Barrel, I watched you trying to slip that hog body of yours through the recovery hatch after you landed. If you don't watch your girlish figure, they're going to take your wings away."

"Go screw yourself," Beer Barrel replied.

Ribbing the pilot about his weight was a mission the whole crew enjoyed. Somehow, he had become the brunt of all the jokesters and pranksters aboard ship. While my crew and I did call him by his nickname, we didn't otherwise rib him, since we knew he didn't like it and we had to work with him.

Turning to the guys, I said, "The Captain says we're heading back to port after he recovers all of the barges, this afternoon, so we should take off right after noon chow. Jack, you use the Leica. Riku, take the film camera. And draw out your side arms, both of you."

"Yes, sir."

That afternoon, with me flying co-pilot, the four of us flew back to Utupua Island to shoot detailed photos of special points of interest. We always put boots on the ground on any strip of land that had potential military use. We looked for anchorages, beaches that could be used for landings, areas where airstrips could be constructed, fresh-water sources and any other special features. This was the dangerous part of our mission.

Many of the islands we were charting had been skipped over by our military, leaving units of starving Japs. G-2 called these islands 'hot,' so we wouldn't put boots on the ground and were cautious even when flying our mapping missions. But G-2 wasn't always right. On two separate occasions, we had drawn sniper fire on 'cold' islands, so we always went in armed. There were also the locals or natives to deal with. Some were friendly, some were not. If we spotted big villages from the air, we were fairly confident we would be welcomed, but there had been stories of cannibalism, so we always proceeded with caution. On this particular island, on this particular day, we didn't see a living soul. We did find a deserted three-hut village on a small, fresh-water creek, and other signs of fishing and hunting campsites, but no people. We noted these locations and took photos of our finds, which would be included in my final report. Three hours later, we were flying back to the *Heed* with our mission accomplished.

That evening, with the *Heed* steaming south towards Australia, I walked to the bow for a smoke and to reflect on our third mission as aerial photographers. It had been hot and stuffy all day, all week, all month. The cooler breeze that whipped through my hair and across my face, created by our fifteen-knot speed, had the salty-sweetness of the sea. The sun was low in the sky, about to rest behind the horizon, and its rays sparkled across the vast ocean. It reminded me of that evening in Malibu and the wonderful dinner I had enjoyed with Maggie. I had to write her again... I was two letters behind, and I didn't want to lose her to time.

Turning my back to the wind, I used my Zippo to light my cigarette, then gazed past the three-inch deck gun to look up to the bridge of the ship. In the low, warm sunlight, she looked bigger and more powerful than she really was. To call her a warship would be a stretch, but she had been good to me and my crew, and had provided better duty than OWI. We had spent Thanksgiving on her, and the cooks had done a marvelous job of making chicken taste like turkey.

As I turned forward again, my mind raced to spending Christmas in Sydney. Using Colonel Flag's realtor contact, we had rented a three-bedroom flat with a small terrace overlooking the harbor. It was a walkup third-floor unit, completely furnished, that rented for the considerable sum of fifty-five dollars a month. It was old but spacious, with skylights and windows that made the drab walls seem brighter than they were. It was also within walking distance of the Navy photo lab where we spent most of our time while in port. Shore duty was consumed with processing film, making prints, helping the topographers with the mosaic maps, and writing reports. By the end of this cruise, we would have completed fifty-four aerial surveys of islands and atolls in and around the northern Solomon Islands. And in all those months, I hadn't heard from or seen Colonel Flag again; we must have been lost in his priorities or paperwork, and I was resigned to our duties on the *Heed.*

There had also been time to enjoy Sydney, with its diverse landscape and culture. The city was the international gateway to all of Southeast Asia and had a flavor much like San Francisco. There were shops and stores, galleries and theaters, restaurants and pubs, all stretching down long, clean streets inhabited by colorful and friendly people. Riku had searched out and made friends within the sizable local Japanese community, and spent most of his free time with them. Black Jack had fallen for the night life and spent much of his time escorting Aussie ladies to the many nightclubs for drinks and dancing.

I, however, had found this nightlife a little too crowded and noisy for my taste. Most of the pubs were full of Navy personnel, dressed in their white uniforms with Dixie Cup hats, making fools of themselves with too much booze and too many broads. Usually, I would beg off from these 'buck nights,' preferring instead to stay around the flat, reading and writing. We called them 'buck nights' because, with our strong currency exchange, we could go nightclubbing, including cab fare, drinks and food, all for a dollar. It was a deal most Yanks couldn't resist.

Flipping the butt of my cigarette overboard, I knew that spending the holidays in the tropics would be a new experience for all of us. I would have to do something special for my crew...my friends.

When we arrived back in Sydney, the news was humming about the fighting on Bougainville and the recent amphibious landings on Tarawa. In just seventy-two hours of fighting, the Marines had wiped out the entire Japanese garrison of five thousand, but at the shocking cost of forty-four hundred wounded and dead leathernecks. The Navy had just released some photos of dead Marines on the beaches of that godforsaken atoll.

As we looked at the gruesome pictures, we knew it was a place we should have been and a job we should have done. With this in mind, none of us was in the mood for a traditional Christmas celebration. While the spirit of the season was not lost on us, it was a difficult time of reflection.

Still, I wanted to do something to ease our thoughts, something for my friends, so I planned a Christmas dinner. Talking with a local butcher, I secured the main course for our meal: a turkey, which he would purchase on the Black Market. In this part of the world, there were no turkey farms. The bird was not indigenous to Australia. The only country in the South Pacific where you could find turkeys was New Zealand, and theirs were wild and protected. But, like everything else in war, if you had enough money and the right contacts, you could buy whatever you needed on the Black Market.

Finding a turkey turned out to be easy; finding cranberry sauce was the real mission. The Navy cooks wouldn't or couldn't help, so finally, after many phone calls and lots of shoe leather, I bought the last can of cranberries at -- of all places -- a Chinese market.

The menu was set. Now all I had to do was find just the right gifts for Black Jack and Riku. Walking down a wide boulevard lined with palm trees and Christmas decorations, I thought about how unusual it was to be shopping for Christmas in the blistering summer sun. It was as if everything had been turned upside down. Maybe that was why Australia was called 'the land down-under.'

Stopping in front of a pub, I thought about a beer, but then, for some reason, my eyes were drawn across the street to a record store. The flat did have a player, and Jack did like music. Inside, I found rows and rows of wooden bins filled with 78 rpm record albums. Most of the selections came from the US, with artists like Benny Goodman, Peggy Lee and Harry James. In one bin, I found a record by the Negro singer Nat King Cole. I grinned, because it had just the title for Jack: 'Straighten Up and Fly Right.'

It was then, standing there and reading the album cover, that I saw it. The used records were just next to where I stood, and the first row was open to an album with a familiar ring: 'Bourbon Street Blues' with Lilly Malone!

I couldn't believe my good fortune. Halfway around the world, I had found a recording by Blacks Jack's mother. Picking up the dog-eared album, I saw a picture of Lilly for the first time. She was a beautiful colored lady with the same delicate facial features, including the bone-white teeth, as her son. There were faint signs of gray in her otherwise straight jet-black hair, and the twinkle in her eyes was bright and inviting.

The back of the jacket cover said she had recorded the music in 1938 with Decca Records. I was sure Jack didn't know anything about the album, as he had never mentioned it to me. This was a great find, the perfect gift; I purchased both albums and looked forward to Black Jack's reactions.

The next day, after a long search and with Bing Crosby singing 'White Christmas' in the background, I found Riku's gift. It was in the window of an antique store on King's Road. My plan had always been to buy something Japanese, something with meaning for him. But finding Nip gifts, with the war on, had been a problem. There were lots of Jap swords, guns and other items taken off dead Nips, but these were definitely not what I wanted. What I sought was something more cultural, with roots in Japan's history and her people. That's why I got so excited when I discovered my find, a ten-inch, hand-engraved, bronze wakizashi. The proprietor told me that the dagger had been used by Samurais, Japanese noble warriors, to kill an especially brutal and corrupt Emperor in the eighteen-hundreds. The Japanese writing on the sheath and blade told the story of the deed and how and why the Samurais liberated the people of Japan. The story was part folklore and part history, but all Japanese. The tale illustrated the struggle of good over bad, which made it the ideal gift for Riku.

On Christmas Eve, we shared our meal and a good bottle of wine together. The turkey turned out okay but, just as the butcher had warned, the dark meat was too gamey to eat. The baked yams were good and the canned cranberries were both bitter and sweet. While the meal wasn't much like Grandmother's, it was passable for three young bachelors halfway around the world.

Afterwards, I passed out my unwrapped gifts to my friends. As expected, Black Jack was floored with my find; he'd had no idea his mother had ever recorded the album. He stared at his mother's image for the longest time and then, with watery eyes, turned to me.

"Of all the gifts, from all the people, in all the places, this is the best. Thanks, Dutch."

Smiling back across the table, I remarked, "I'm pleased that providence let me find it and that it makes you happy. Boy, did your mother get the looks in your family!"

Riku was just as pleased with his present. Taking the dagger in hand, he gleefully read us the inscriptions and story of the Samurais. As he did so, he provided historical background about the history and struggles of the Japanese people. It reminded me that the land of the rising sun had been through troubled times before, and that maybe she could survive again...but at what cost?

"I'll treasure your gift for life," Riku said with sincerity. "It will always remind me of this epoch and the both of you...my friends."

CHAPTER EIGHT

"Do you guys speak English? I'm American. We're...friends."

As my words floated in the air, the ugly guy was still holding the cold, pointed edge of his Nip sword to my throat. He was tall and big, about six feet and probably two hundred pounds. He had a coal-black, horrifying face with sharp features and fury in his eyes. The little guy next to him, shorter and younger, looked to weigh only around a hundred and thirty. His complexion was rough and light-chocolate brown. As he stepped forward to remove my bayonet from its scabbard, he threw his spear, pointed-end down, between my feet. Removing my knife, he handed it to the big fellow and then moved behind me.

Using what felt like rawhide, he tied my hands together. After my hands were secured he said some more gibberish, and the big man lowered his sword from my windpipe. As the little man reappeared in front of me, he reached down, pulling out his spear. Then, from behind a bush, he picked up what looked like a basket of food.

The ugly one stepped forward and, staring at me with his manic eyes, tied a long piece of rawhide, with a slip knot, around my neck. My knees trembled and my mind was in panic mode as I watched these two black natives talk for a moment. Then, using the rawhide like a leash, they started pulling me back along the path from where they had come.

As they dragged me, I began frantically using my fingers to search for the knot that restrained my hands, but with my wrists bound on top of each other, it was difficult to find. After a few steps, the path turned into a well-used trail that meandered through the fetid jungle. Soon, the trail gave way, through some jungle brush, to a wide, sandy beach with a large, blue lagoon. As I was dragged into the sunlight, I could tell by the shadows that we were now on the east side of Gibraltar. This was the cove we had been looking for. We had just searched on the wrong side of the island.

Down the beach was a long, crude dugout canoe which we walked towards. Stopping by its side, the little guy placed his basket inside the boat.

I tried again. "Do you guys speak English? I'm American."

The chiseled-faced black man, watching me, moved to the boat and took a large husk out of the basket. Then, using my bayonet, he made one powerful swing of the blade and cut its top off.

As the top of the pod fell to the sand, he and the little guy started laughing. As they laughed and talked, both of them reached over and felt my thigh. Their message was clear: that fruit was my head, and I was a slab of meat for their cook pots. With sweat spouting from every pore, and my fingers still searching for a knot, I knew I had to control my panic or I would die.

Soon the big fellow started cutting chunks of fruit from the husk and eating them, passing a few bites to his friend. After a few moments, he cut a new chunk and, using the pointed end of the knife, brought it up in front of my face. Dangling the food in front of me and staring at me, he said something, with an expression that almost looked magnanimous.

Did he want me to eat it? If I moved my face towards the fruit, I was afraid he would jam the knife down my throat, so I did nothing.

He looked at me with his head twisted, then dropped his gaze to my neck. Pulling the blade back, he consumed the chunk of fruit and then, using the knife point, pulled my dog tags out from under my shirt. With his other grubby hand, he grabbed the condom tied onto the chain.

Shit, I thought, I can't let this SOB take my rubber.

He held the condom, with his head cocked inquisitively. I knew he was about to pull it off my neck, and there wasn't a bloody thing I could do about it!

Just then, shouts erupted from out on the lagoon. Looking up, I saw two more natives in another dugout, rowing towards us. When he spotted them, the big guy let go of the rubber and turned to the cove. Waving and shouting back to the men on the boat, he dropped the bayonet into the food basket and picked up his sword. Then, saying something to the little guy, he turned and started dancing and hollering towards the water's edge, waving his sword in the air. Meanwhile, the little man had his spear pointed right at my body.

Watching what was happening, and with my hands hidden from view, I finally found the rawhide knot. I contorted two fingers and started, slowly, to untie the noose. With the big guy gone, I knew it was time to make a break. I looked over at the little guy, who was watching me but glancing out to the water, as well. I worked...and worked... and finally the knot came undone and the rawhide twine fell to the sand behind my legs.

The water's edge was just a few yards down from us. Just as the dugout reached the small surf, the little guy turned his head, shouting something to the other men. With that copper taste in my mouth, I knew this was my chance. I reached out, grabbed the pointed end of his spear, and jerked it -- and him -- towards me.

As he stumbled my way, I swung my left fist with all the power I could muster, and clipped him right across the forehead. When my blow landed, he collapsed like a sand castle at high tide. Reaching over to the canoe, I grabbed the basket of food, with my bayonet inside, and ran like hell towards the jungle.

Stumbling at first, I quickly moved from the bright sand to the dark bowels of the jungle. Going as fast as my bum hip would take me, I ran uphill, dodging under and over snags that blocked my way south. Within moments, I could hear the natives behind me as they pursued my path. With patches of diffused sunlight sweeping my face and the jungle birds singing a laughing song, I searched for the tree markers I had cut. My mind was racing with terrified, murky thoughts. All I could think about was getting off this island, and fast.

Finally I came upon one of my markers, and then another. Within a few seconds, I emerged from the jungle, staggering onto the cliff above our little cove. Nearly out of breath, I screamed, "Get the raft in the water now!"

Down below, I could see Sergeant York's surprised facing looking up at me.

I dropped the basket down to him. "Get the raft in the water. Move it. Move it!"

In one fluid motion, I bent down, grabbed hold of the grass rope, and started repelling myself down it. A few heart beats later, I was stumbling on the sandy beach, where my mates were just starting to carry the raft towards the water.

"What's going on?" the Padre yelled. "Are the Japs after you?"

"No, but we have to get the hell out of here now", I shouted as I joined them in packing the float.

Just then, from the cliff above us, three of my pursuers started yelling and throwing down spears as we stumbled towards the surf. As we dodged this hail of bamboo, my mates realized the severity of the problem and picked up their pace. By the time we got to the water's edge, the three natives had reached the cove floor. Picking up their spent spears, they ran towards us.

Splashing through the water, we pushed the raft ever deeper into the surf. When we got waist-deep, everyone but Bates -- with his bad arm -- pulled themselves onto the float and frantically started rowing. With Bates hanging on, we got out a ways. Then the Padre and I reached down to drag him aboard.

By now, our assailants were running in the surf behind us, screaming bloody murder. Just as we pulled Bates up onto the raft, a spear found its mark, penetrating his bum shoulder. As it hit, he let out a loud moan, and his face twitched with pain. Reaching down, I quickly pulled the spear out, and we hauled him the rest of the way into the raft.

Within seconds, we were finally out of range and out of danger. Looking back, we could see the angry men still in the surf, yelling gibberish, their raised fists shaking in the air.

Looking over, the Padre asked, "What did you do to those guys to make them so mad?"

With scorn in my voice, I answered, "I stole their dinner."

He gestured toward the basket. "That?"

"No," I answered with grim satisfaction. "Me."

Call to Duty

Somewhere inside a sweet dream, I was lost. Gardenias filled the air and I could hear music and see a beautiful bright light coming my way. Suddenly, that light steered my slumber and I was back in bed in my quiet drab bedroom, with the early morning light shining across the room. Laying there for a moment, I wondered what time it was and reached for my watch on the bed stand. Trying to get my eyes to focus on the little dial, I sensed there was something wrong; that gardenia smell was now cheap aftershave. I knew I had pulled the shades, the night, before so why all this light? Looking down at the watch face, I thought, *7:13...early, too early. I don't need to be aboard the Heed until 0900, so I have another hour before I have to get up.*

Putting my watch back on the stand, I pulled myself up further in the bed and looked around the little room. Both window shades were up. Had I forgotten to close them? As my gaze slowly turned to the other side of the room, it stopped at a darkened corner where I could just barely see a shadowy figure sitting in a chair. Startled, I about jumped out of my skin. "What the shit?"

The figure moved until just his face was in the light. It took me a second of surprise to realize it was Colonel Flag.

"What the hell are you doing there, Colonel?"

He scooted his chair out from the shadows. Now he was visible, in his neatly pressed utility uniform. "Watching and listening, Lieutenant."

With my back now fully upright and my mind as clear as the morning, I shot back, "Watching and listening for what?"

"You. I wanted to see if you walked or talked in your sleep. That can be a big problem for security, so I like to know."

"Well, did I? And how the hell did you get in here?"

"No. You didn't. Sergeant Malone came in a few hours ago and he forgot to lock the front door. Of course, it wouldn't have mattered if he had locked it. I could have gotten in, anyhow. I needed to see you."

Pulling my legs from under the covers and reaching for my trousers, I asked, "About what...sir?"

"A little job I have for you."

As I dressed, he explained. The *USS Heed's* new assignment area for January was a small chain of islands a hundred miles north of Bougainville called the Green Islands. He warned that some of these islands were still hot, so we should proceed with caution, but that the islands he was interested in were the Tulun group, some ninety miles southeast of the Green Islands.

"Tulun is really just a group of nine atolls that form a horseshoe around a shallow lagoon that runs north-south. Han Island is the largest and highest of the chain, on the southwest tip of the horseshoe. Because of the high ground, that's where we think the Japs are setting up a new early warning radar station. If they are, it's going to be a problem, because they could pick up all our air and sea support coming up the Bougainville Strait. We need film of these islands, with special attention to Han."

"So why not send a recon flight out of Bougainville, or send the *Heed* there, sir?"

"That's just it. We don't want the Nips to know we have a special interest in Tulun...and we might be wrong. They already know we're mapping most of the islands, up there, so I want you to fly over from the Green Islands to get the pictures. That way, it'll look just like a routine mapping mission."

"That shouldn't be a problem. Have you cleared it with the Skipper?"

"No, not yet, but I'll talk to Commander Parks this morning. For security reasons, though, I don't want the whole ship to know what we're doing. We want as few people as possible to know about our interest in Tulun, so it's up to you to get over there and get the shots."

Now fully dressed, I stood bare-footed in front of the Colonel and replied, "My pilot and crew will know, and the guys in the radar shack that track all of our flights will know. It's hard to keep a secret on a ship as small as the *Heed*."

Looking up at me with those steel blue eyes, he answered, "Then improvise a cover story, and don't tell your pilot any more than you have to. Chief Pilot Williams talks too much when he drinks, and he drinks too much to trust."

Moving to the adjoining bathroom, I kept the door open, relieving myself while saying, "I'll try getting in low over the islands and shooting some additional shots with a second camera.

Maybe, if the light's right and we're at the right angle, we can get some good pictures. Say, Colonel, have you heard anything about the *Argonaut* and her crew?" Pulling the chain, I flushed the toilet and returned to the bedroom. It was empty; Flag was gone. Maybe he was as silent as sand.

Tulun Islands

Three weeks later, we had just about completed our survey of the Green Islands, and I knew it was time to tackle Colonel Flag's job. During this tour, I had told both Black Jack and Riku about our hush-hush secondary assignment but had not yet talked to the Skipper about it. One afternoon, finding him in his sea cabin, I broached the subject.

"Did a Colonel Flag come and talk to you, before we departed for this cruise, sir?"

Commander Parks had been fair with me and my crew, a little stand-offish and a little cool but a good Skipper. He was older, and I was sure he was a WWI retread. Looking over some old navigational charts on his desk, he answered my query without looking up. "Yes, Lieutenant, he did. He told me about the mission he wanted, and that you and your crew were going to do it. The operative word here is 'told,' not 'asked.' The more I thought about it, the madder I got. Where does he get off, telling me what to do with my ship and crew? So I've decided the hell with him. The mission is off!"

Watching him a moment, hunched over the desk, I wasn't sure how to reply.

Finally finding my voice, I said, "I don't know the Colonel very well, but he can be quite direct. I'm sure he didn't mean any disrespect, sir. He just has a job to do, and his boss is a long way up the food chain."

A small black fan pushed warm air around the small compartment as he stood up and met my eye. His uniform was wrinkled, and there were sweat stains under his arms. He looked old and tired. "I could care less about who his boss is. Mine is the Secretary of the Navy, and he made me the captain of this ship. I'm responsible for all the men and equipment aboard, and I'm not sending them off on some unauthorized mission."

Looking into his droopy gray eyes, I could see his deter-mination, and I realized in some ways he was right. He had no written orders, and sending us off to Tulun could be dangerous.

"I have the same boss you do, sir. Let me show you my orders." Reaching into my pocket, I retrieved the XKO Order, unfolded it, and handed the paper to Commander Parks.

With the little fan working the cabin and making swishing sounds, the skipper read the order with a scowl on his face and then handed it back to me. "I should have known," he said. "I ask for one signalman and they send me three Marine photographers. And what a crew -- one mulatto, one Nip, and you, a guy who went through the ranks faster than a warm knife through butter. Hell, Lieutenant, you're not even a ninety-day wonder. It just didn't make any sense, until now. How long have you been spying on us?"

"We're not spying on you, sir. We were parked here until an appropriate mission came along, and I guess Tulun is it. But you're the captain. We'll do whatever you order us to do, and if that's not doing the Tulun assignment, that's fine. I would just like that order in writing, to protect my butt...sir."

Flopping down in his desk chair, he rubbed his forehead with stiff fingers. He was mad and confused. I had caught him off guard with my special order and my request for his decision in writing.

In an angry voice, he finally replied, "No, you do your mission, Lieutenant. I didn't like being told what to do by your colonel, but when Frank Knox asks, I obey. Is there anything else?"

"Yes, sir. We don't want the whole ship to know about our assignment. Can you arrange for a temporary radar malfunction for tomorrow morning?"

Shaking his head in rueful disbelief, he answered, "Okay...but that's it! And for the record, Lieutenant, I don't like spies, so after this tour, you and your crew will have to find a new billet. Dismissed."

That evening, I told Jack and Riku about my turbulent meeting with the skipper, and that we had been fired. Shrugging their shoulders, the guys took the news in stride, and we got down to planning our mission. Our only remaining obstacle was the pilot.

Black Jack thought I should have a heart-to-heart talk with him, but I wasn't convinced. Deep down, I agreed with Colonel Flag that he was a security risk. Therefore, I decided to ditch him on some outer island.

Black Jack put up the loudest protest about my idea, since he wasn't sure I could fly the Blue Goose alone. Riku disagreed. He had been with us many times when Beer Barrel had given me flying lessons, and he was confident of my skills. After some discussion, and a little joking around about crashing into the sea, we all agreed that Chief Williams would cool his heels while we flew our mission.

The next morning, at 0800, the old DeHaviland took off from the stern of the *Heed* while her crew went looking for some radar parts that had mysteriously disappeared overnight. As the loaded Blue Goose gained altitude, I told Beer Barrel to head south for the last small island on the southern tip of the Green chain. As we flew in that direction, I went on to tell him that we were going to put boots on the ground, and that he and I would be covering the guys as they did the photography. Twenty minutes later, circling just above a small island named Hump, we found a safe place to land just inside the break-water of the reef that surrounded it. We had done our aerial mission over this island some days before, and I was confident it was a cold, safe place to ditch our pilot. As Beer Barrel nosed the plane's pontoons up to the beach and switched off the ignition, I told him that we would get out and do a quick look-see while the guys got the equipment ready. As we disembarked, I retrieved our rifles and a small knapsack from the cargo hatch behind the seats. Then we walked through the shallow surf and up onto the shore.

Looking around the little cove, I spotted a large outcropping of rocks, up the beach. I told Beer Barrel to climb up one of them for a better look into the jungle on the other side. Before he departed, I handed him one of the rifles and my knapsack, telling him that there was beer in it for later. His eyes lit up, and he had a smile on his face as he started trudging down the shoreline. As he moved away, I turned and walked back towards the plane, giving my crew the high sign. By the time I was standing in ankle-deep surf, Jack and Riku were pushing the plane into deeper water and starting to turn her around. Looking back, I saw Beer Barrel reach the summit of one of the rocks, but he still hadn't turned our way.

Placing one of my hands beside my mouth, I shouted, "Beer Barrel, we got an emergency radio call. A pilot has gone down and we're going to check it out. We'll be back to pick you up later."

Finally, he turned our way and placed one of his hands next to his ear. I screamed the message a second time, only louder. He nodded his head but stood there, flat-footed, as the message filtered through to his beer-brain. By now, the guys had the plane turned, in deep water and rebounding her. Splashing through knee-deep water, I joined them and entered the plane, for the first time, on the pilot's side.

With Blackjack now in the co-pilot's seat, I switched on the ignition, adjusted the throttle, and hit the starter button. My hands were shaking, and I was as nervous as a groom on his wedding night. I thanked the Lord the day was clear and calm. On the second crank, the warm engine came to life, and we slowly started moving away from the island.

As I faced the plane into the light wind, I noticed that the controls felt different on this side of the cockpit. Turning the wheel back and forth, and pushing the pedals in and out, I found that the controls seemed looser and easier to feel. As I got into position, I throttled up the engine, and we started moving with greater speed across the breakwater. With my knuckles white and my heart racing, I reviewed in my head all the instructions Beer Barrel had been giving me. Soon, ocean spray engulfed the fuselage from the pontoons breaking through the water as the plane bounced from one wave to the next with loud thuds.

As we reached the correct air speed for lift-off, I glanced over to Black Jack, just as he asked, "Do you know what the hell you're doing?"

"I hope so," was my reply as I gently pulled back on the wheel.

A few heartbeats later, we were airborne. As I pointed the plane's nose gently up, I banked her back over the cove. Looking down, we could see Beer Barrel standing on the beach, staring up at us with his middle finger in the air.

Black Jack gave me one of those toothy smiles. "I don't think we'll be on Chief Williams' Christmas list this year!"

Turning, I set a course for Tulun. While I gained altitude and watched my horizon line, there was an exhilarating feeling about being in control of the old DeHaviland. As we slipped through the air, Riku retrieved the K1 camera from the cargo area and, opening the floor hatch, attached it to the Gimbal mount. While he worked, Black Jack opened his knapsack, took out the Leica, and changed the lens and viewfinder to a telephoto. Then he double-checked that the camera was loaded and working properly. Other than these activities, the little cockpit was quiet, its silence broken only by the roar of our engine.

Seventy-five miles later, from six-thousand feet, we spotted Tulun off the starboard quarter in the low, bright sunshine. From the air, this group did look like a crude, upside-down horseshoe, with milk-white beaches. Turning the plane a few times, we approached Tulun from the south. There were three large atolls and six smaller ones forming a horseshoe around a large blue-green lagoon. This bay looked to be about three miles long and two miles wide, with a big opening to the sea. On the left, was Han Island, the largest in the group; on the right, Piul Island had a long, flat dog-leg shape. At the very top of the horseshoe, was Iolasa Island, which curved around the bay and sprawled roughly from east to west. The other, unnamed atolls were interconnected with the large ones, separated only by small channels of water that fed into the lagoon. These nine islands made up the Tulun group.

Maneuvering the plane to the eastern side of the group, I dropped down to our attack altitude of four thousand feet. As we approached the southern tip of Piul, I reduced our airspeed to ninety knots, raised my hand, and shouted, "Four-thousand, heading due north, mark."

From the rear, I heard Riku make his first exposure and start the count. Next to me, Jack opened his window and hung his camera out, waiting for any shots of interest. A few minutes later, we had covered the length of the eastern shoreline, and I turned to make a second pass over the same side, heading due south. Working our way back and forth, it took us half an hour to complete the aerial shots, with forty-six eight-inch frames exposed.

As we flew out over Han Island for the last time, I turned to the west and shouted, "Did anyone see anything? I've been too busy flying to look."

"Not a damn thing. They look deserted to me," Black Jack shouted back.

"I couldn't see anything," Riku added from the rear.

"Okay, I'm going to drop down to two thousand and make one last pass, with Han on your wing, Jack. Maybe we can get something if I'm a little closer."

Guiding the Blue Goose some five-hundred yards off the seaward shoreline of Han, I made another pass, just for Blackjack's camera. As I reached the northernmost point, I banked the plane around the tip and followed the lagoon-side of Han back south. After I finished the maneuver, I had just started heading back out to sea when Black Jack yelled, "Let's do that one more time from five hundred feet. I think I saw something up on that hill in the center of the island."

"Five hundred feet? That's low, Jack. But okay, one more time."

Swooping down, we approached Han again from the seaward side. Keeping one eye on where we were flying and another on the little hill, I searched for what Jack thought he had seen, but I spotted nothing. With Jack hanging out the window, taking pictures, I flew us alongside the little mound of jungle in the center, so close that we could have reached out to pick a cocoanut.

Zing...zing...zing.

"What the hell was that?" I shouted, turning to look at Jack.

In a flash, Black Jack had his butt back on his seat, with camera in hand, as he shouted, "Son-of-bitch someone is shooting at us!"

Turning to look to the rear, I found Riku with a ghost-white face, pointing to a bullet hole in the window glass next to him. There were two other small holes in the fuselage just behind his seat. Turning forward, I reached for the throttle and gave the Blue Goose full power while pulling up on the wheel for altitude. As I did, the plane began to shake and fall backwards. Realizing that she was stalling, I pushed the wheel forward again and regained control, but not before our right wing was struck by a few more bullets. Luckily, those hits only ripped the fabric of the wing, leaving jagged, quarter-sized holes.

In a gentle turn, slowly gaining altitude, I headed out to sea. With my heart racing, I yelled, "Is everyone okay?"

"I'm okay," Riku called, "but that slug missed me by inches."

Jack added, "Yeah…and I got the shot. There's some kind of antenna on top of that hill. They have it camouflaged between two trees, but I saw its outline and got the picture."

As we got to four-thousand feet, I changed course again and headed for Hump Island. As we flew back and our adrenaline rush ebbed, we went over our cover story.

By the time we picked up Beer Barrel, he was as mad as an old hornet, not just because we'd left him behind but because of all the bullet holes in his beloved DeHaviland. As he flew us back to the *Heed*, we explained that we hadn't found the downed pilot but did have a run-in with a Jap patrol boat that was also searching the area.

He didn't give a shit about our story. All he kept saying was how he was going to tell the Skipper about our escapade -- which he did, but what could the Skipper do, fire us twice?

The boat ride back to Sydney was long and hot, and our only joy came from watching Beer Barrel being ribbed about losing his plane to three mud Marines.

As the *Heed* tied up to Berth M7, back in Sydney Harbor, I half expected to find Colonel Flag standing on the wharf waiting, but he wasn't. Cleaning out our lockers, we filled our sea bags and, with the exposed film safely packed away, said good-by to the *USS Heed* and walked towards our flat.

When we arrived home, we found the Colonel sitting at our kitchen table, drinking coffee spiked with my scotch. For the first time, Black Jack and Riku met the shadowy figure who pulled the strings of their future. At first, he was all military, cool and distant, but as I explained our mission results and Black Jack handed him our film, he warmed. We told him about what we'd seen and photographed on Tulun, and about the antenna on Han. He seemed pleased with our report and asked lots of questions. Then I told him about my run-in with Commander Parks, and about us getting fired.

He just shrugged. "I already heard. Don't worry about it. The Skipper's from the old school and doesn't like Jar Heads telling him what to do. I'll find a new station for you in the next few days."

Then, holding up my bottle of scotch, he asked us to join him. Boy, did this guy have gall! Moments later, as the guys and I were distracted around the coffee pot, we looked up to find Flag gone. As usual, his entries and exits were damn dramatic.

Three days went by before we were summoned to Colonel Flag's warehouse office for what we speculated would be our reassignment orders. Moving through the warehouse with the same old Aussie worker, I was surprised to find that it was now empty. Gone were the crates and boxes, leaving only barren racks, with even the floor spotlessly swept. When we walked through the locked door from the atrium, I found the offices twice as full of men and equipment as it had been on my first visit. Obviously, the intelligence business was improving.

We entered the Colonel's office and found him standing by a large, round table stacked with black-and-white photo prints. Glancing up, he told us to join him. Here on the center of the table we found a large composite print of the topographical map made from our aerial images of Tulun. The print had written call-outs, in grease pencil, all around the outer edges of the atolls and, in the center, pasted over the lagoon area, smaller pictures had been blown up from our negatives. The whole composite print looked to be forty-by-forty inches.

Standing there, absorbing the information like a blotter, I marveled at what the topographers had wrung out of our negatives. On Piul Island, there were two areas circled with the call-out 'Gun Emplacement,' with small close-up photos pasted over the lagoon showing defensive positions made out of logs on the atoll just north of the same. On Iolasa, there were call-outs and photos of tents, supply huts and other gun emplacements hidden under and around the jungle with camouflage netting. But the big prize was a small building, antenna and gun emplacements hidden by palm trees on Han Island itself. Everything we were looking at we had seen before, but hadn't really seen. Only through the magic of photography had Tulun come to life.

Finally, Colonel Flag said, "You guys did a great job. We got more details from your pictures than we ever thought possible. They confirmed our worst suspicions."

Looking up, I asked, "So what's next, Colonel?"

Reaching down, he picked up a stack of 8x10 prints and shuffled through them. Finding the one he wanted, he turned it our way so that we could see it. The picture was a side view of the antenna on the hill, the last shot Black Jack had taken just before the shooting began.

"See the shape and size of this antenna? We haven't seen anything like this in the Pacific Theater. The normal Jap radar beacon is smaller and a different shape. So I radioed a copy of the print to some radar experts on Guadalcanal, and they say it looks like a modified German Funkgerat/Wassermann WF-5000 design."

Black Jack reached over and took the print from the Colonel's hands. "So are you saying the Nips are using German radar now?"

"That's just it -- we don't know. We could send some B-17's up from Bougainville and wipe Tulun off the map, but we still wouldn't know what the Nips are up to. That's why I sent for you guys."

Jack glanced my way with a half-grin while I asked, "What can we do for you, sir?"

Moving across the room, the Colonel asked us to sit down in three chairs pre-positioned in front of his desk. As we took our seats he continued, "We are planning a recon and raiding mission on Tulun. From your pictures, we estimate there is just a small garrison on the island for protection of the radar station. What we need is a company of Marine Raiders and photographers who know the lay of the land, know how to read Japanese, and can take close-up pictures of the equipment the Nips are using before we blow it up. Once our experts get a good look at the photos, they'll know exactly what to expect from our enemy's new system. It's an in-and-out mission, but a hot mission. Do you guys feel up to it?"

Was the Colonel kidding? What he offered was the treasure I had searched for ever since joining the Marines: a combat mission. I jumped at the chance, and so did Jack and Riku.

Flag went on to tell us that we were being sent up to Guadalcanal, where we would be given a crash course on how radar worked. With this knowledge, we would know exactly what to photograph when we got onto Han Island. While we were busy in the classroom, he would put together the fighting force and transportation needed to move us onto and off of Tulun. The raid was planned for February fourteenth, St. Valentine's Day. Smiling to myself, I thought we could have our own massacre for the history books.

As we got up to leave, Flag handed us our typewritten orders and said he would meet us ten days hence, up on Guadalcanal. With a vague, condescending smile, he told us that he never questioned whether we would volunteer for the mission, but that, if we hadn't, we would have gone anyway.

As we got to the door, I asked about his empty warehouse. He told me that it was the depository for all the equipment needed by the coast watchers and guerillas fighting in the jungles all the way up to the Philippine Islands. He assured me that, by my next visit, it would be filled again.

"Whatever they need, we get. Then, somehow, sometime, somewhere, by plane or sub, we deliver it to them as quickly as we can."

Watching his face, I could see the pride in his eyes. He was doing a good job, an important job, and for the first time I was pleased to have him as my boss.

Raid on Tulun

On the PBY flight up to the Canal, we talked about our new assignment. With our first true combat assignment looming, I wanted to know what my friends were thinking.

Their responses, in some ways, surprised me. Riku was concerned about his ability to read Japanese fluently. He explained that what he had written and read over the years had been more conversational than technical.

"What if we get there and it's all written in such a way that I can't read it?"

"Hell," I replied, "when we get there, it's more than likely going to be written in German."

Blackjack, on the other hand, had more practical concerns. "The Colonel said we might join the battle by submarine. Another sub ride is not something I look forward to." As Jack talked about his concerns he didn't make eye contact. Instead, he was staring down at his lighter as he flipped it over and over in one hand.

"Submarines...I didn't know you don't like them," I answered.

"The quarters are too close for me, and they smell worse than the grease pit back at the canteen. After the war, no more submarine rides for me."

Leaning back in my jump seat I glanced over at one of the blister windows and studied the gunner as he stood watch. The scene caused a rush of memories of that day in the skies over Wagina Island and Henry. I had dreamed about that day more times than I wanted to admit.

While I had asked my pals about their concerns, they never asked me. And my fears ran deep, so deep that I wasn't sure I would have talked about them if they had asked. There was a battle going on inside me as to whether I had the guts to kill, eyeball-to-eyeball. We had seen death from afar, we had heard its screams and smelled its pungent odor, but could I face it man-to-man?

When we arrived at Guadalcanal, I was surprised by how large a facility it was. It had gone from a battle field to airstrips, bivouac areas, hospitals and warehouses in less than a year. And down on the waterfront was a big Navy port. Here we met with a full Navy Captain by the name of Rollins. He and his staff ran a large network of radar stations in and around the secured islands of the Pacific theater of operations. They were the experts, they were our teachers.

The first three days were spent in the classroom, learning the history, principles and electronics of radar. These basic principles were the same in all systems, American and foreign. From the books, we learned about vacuum tubes, transformers, resisters and what radar could and couldn't do. Rollins and his staff were floored by the near-total recall Riku had from the books used in the classroom sessions.

Next, we were sent to one of the outer islands, where there was a large, modern radar station. Here, we had hands-on instruction about the operations and maintenance of all the electronic components. Working with some real whiz kids, we learned how to disassemble and assemble the inner-workings of different types of Radar systems.

As it turned out, the basics of radar are really quite simple. There is a power supply that runs the whole show, an oscillator that sends out an electronic signal over an antenna, a receiver that processes this signal as it returns and, finally, a picture tube that displays the returning signal to an operator. Four simple components: each complex, each mysterious. It was our job to know what the components looked like and then to know what to photograph in the new Japanese system. By week's end, we had taken some test shots, using a new Leica macro lens the Navy had commandeered for us, and we were confident that we could find our way around whatever system the Japs had.

When we returned to the Canal, we were informed that Colonel Flag's arrival would be delayed by twenty-four hours. Cooling our heels in a transit tent, we used the time and our battle orders to obtain new tropical combat gear, which included camouflage uniforms, K-Bar knives, cartridge belts, haversacks and Colt .45 automatic pistols as side arms. Also, after much haggling with the supply Sergeant, I was able to trade in my M1 carbine, given to us on Wagina, for a new, out-of-the-crate, M1A1 Thomson sub-machinegun. Black Jack and Riku elected to keep their M1's, which were lighter, because they would be carrying a lot of gear.

Our next stop was the Base photo lab, where we processed and reviewed our test shots. After looking at our pictures, we talked about taking a C6. After much discussion, however, we decided the camera was too heavy and bulky for the mission. We were able to secure new metal cases for both the Leica and Bell & Howell camera systems. These cases were water resistant and would provide protection for our equipment, as well as being easier to handle than our old rucksacks. The photo lab also offered us some battery-powered lights that could be used for the close-up work, inside the dark electronic components. These 12-volt systems were large and cumbersome. Therefore, we elected to take just one unit on the mission. The final item on our shopping list was film, and we took all we could carry. By the end of our supply day, we looked every bit like combat Marine photographers ready for our next mission.

That evening, a few of the guys from the photo lab stopped by our tent with some beers. With everyone sipping suds and sitting around on hard canvas cots, the conversation soon turned to photography. As the guys talked shop, I went to work, using my sewing kit to stitch compartments into the hem of my new fatigue shirts. In them, I would carry, wrapped in small, rubber film bags, the Minox Camera and two metal canisters, with extra 16mm film. With the spy camera safely tucked away in my shirt, I would have free hands to help the crew with all of our gear.

Early the next day, when the Colonel arrived from Sydney, we all moved to a new bivouac area down by the docks. With dusty, dirt roads, and brown army tents with wooden floors, here we would stay for another week as we trained and planned the raid.

Late that morning, I caught up with Colonel Flag in his command tent, and told him about the results of our radar training and the new photographic equipment we had secured. He patiently listened to my report and then expressed his doubts about the upcoming mission.

"I asked for a company of Marine Raiders, but they're sending only two platoons, since the regiment is in the process of being dissolved. I asked for two submarines to insert the troops, and they're only sending one. I asked for air support, and instead we'll have only one destroyer as backup. This whole operation is turning out to be a FUBAR." (Fucked Up Beyond Any Repair)

I was taken aback by his candor with a junior officer like myself. He either respected my opinion or was beating his gums out of frustration.

"When do the Raiders get in, sir?"

Moving to the open flap of his tent, he gazed outside and then turned my way, answering angrily, "They should be here this afternoon. I want your guys to get some pictures of them arriving and getting set up. I want to document this raid from start to finish. That way, if we end up in the tank, we'll have filmed proof of what the Navy didn't give us."

That afternoon, the *USS Bush* (DD-529), a sleek Fletcher-class destroyer, tied up at the end of Pier 3 and off-loaded two platoons from Company B of the 3rd Marine Raider Regiment. With Black Jack and Riku taking pictures, ninety-eight men walked down the gangway in full battle gear and formed two groups on the dock. In front of each group was the platoon Officer and Sergeant, watching the men form up. Walking towards the ranks with the Minox in hand, I wanted to get closer. As I approached from the back side of one group of leaders, the Sergeant yelled, "Attention."

Seconds later, the officer standing next to him started barking out instructions. He hadn't gotten two words out of his mouth before I froze in my footsteps. I couldn't yet see his face, but I knew that voice. It was Sergeant Nelson, now 2nd Lieutenant, my old DI and friend from Camp Pendleton.

Waiting quietly in the background, I let him finish his spiel. When he was done, the two Sergeants took over, shouting out marching orders to the men. As troops marched off, down the dock, I walked up behind Dick. Disguising my voice, I roared, "Sergeant Nelson, give me the fifth general order!"

Instantly, Dick came to attention, raising his hand for a salute as he turned my way on his boot. As our eyes met, the sober expression on his face melted away to a grin.

Still with his hand in the air, he asked, "What the hell are you doing here, Dutch…I mean, sir?"

"Take that damn hand down. I'm here waiting for you…Second Lieutenant Nelson. Congratulations."

"Thank you, sir. You knew I was coming?"

"I knew they were sending us some of the best Raiders the Marines had, so I'm not surprised to see you leading them."

"You're going on the mission with us?"

"Yep."

"Woo, that's great. Did you hear…they're breaking up the Raiders?"

"Yeah, I did. That's the shits."

Just then, the Company Commander, a Captain Reed, came over to where we were talking. Dick did the introductions while I saluted and shook hands with him.

Reed told Nelson to break off the gab fest and help get the platoon squared away, so we agreed to meet up again after chow.

As Dick walked away, my mind was racing about all the changes to Sergeant Nelson. He looked tired, and skinnier, with his eyes deeper in their sockets. And that smile didn't seem as bright as I remembered. But with those new gold bars, he could still walk and talk with a true Marine presence. In some ways, the Marine recruiting poster had just gotten older and a little tattered. And, whatever the changes, I was excited to have him on the raid and next to me on my first combat mission.

That evening, as sand crabs scurried along the shoreline, Dick and I strolled down the beach next to the docks. Here, with the shadows long and the sands still littered with burned-out skeletons of yesterday's battles, we caught up. Our talk, like our walk, started slowly; about our current mission, his men, and other battles they had fought. He told me about the raid on Puruata Island near Bougainville, and how Company B had lost four landing craft during the initial assault. When he got ashore, his platoon and the platoon next to them had no officers or senior NCOs still standing. Taking charge, he led both platoons through the jungle havoc for the next ten days. During that time, he was given a battle-field promotion to Second Lieutenant.

In Dick's quiet and unassuming way, he related the tale of that battle and promotion in matter-of-fact terms down-playing his role while praising the heroics of his men. When their objectives were finally achieved and they were relieved, they had lost over 30% of the company. Most had been killed during the initial landings and during hand-to-hand combat with fanatical Nips making banzai charges. Reading between the lines, I was sure that it was because of the actions of Lieutenant Nelson that the battle had been won.

Changing the subject, I asked if he had heard anything about my pals from Camp Pendleton. He said that he had run into Jim Wilson, the comedian, drunk as a skunk in a bar in Waikiki, just before shipping out for our mission. Jim told him that Hank Marks, one of the guys from Ketchikan, had been killed on Tarawa with the 2nd Marine Division.

This sad news stopped me dead in my tracks. I was shaken to the bone. Hank had been a good friend, and his loss was hard to fathom. "What about Kurt?" I asked.

"Jim told me that he and Kurt had made it off Tarawa without a scratch, and that they were being shipped back to the States to help start a new Marine Division, the Fifth. You okay, Dutch? You look a little pale."

Slowly moving a few yards up the beach to a burned-out tank sunk in the sand, I put my back to it and reached for a cigarette. The news about Hank was still racing through my body. Dick joined me and, using his lighter, lit my smoke.

"Hank was a good guy," I said, exhaling. "I'll miss him."

"Bad things happen to good guys. I've seen that a lot, down here. Have you seen much action?"

I told him of my experiences in sinking Nip barges from the decks of the *Argonaut* and PT44. About what I'd seen, what I'd heard and what I'd felt. Then I told about my run-in with the Jap Meatball in the skies over Wagina Island, and my months of recovery at St. George Hospital.

As I talked, Dick took a knee next to me and lit a cigarette, then started doodling in the sand with his K-bar knife. As I finished my story, I let my body slip down the side of the rusty tank to a sitting position, with my knees up.

Staring out into space, I concluded, "The fact is, I haven't killed eyeball-to-eyeball yet...and I worry about my grit. Any advice?"

Looking my way, Nelson thought a moment, and then threw his knife to the ground, slicing a nearby sand crab. "All I can say is that who you were, where you've been, what you did, who you loved, or who loved you...is all gone out here. If you live in the past, you will have no future. There is no humanity out here. In battle, it's not about winning or losing, it's not about apple pie, and it's not about home. It's all about your buddies, the guy next to you, the guy in front and the guy behind. The only thing you think about is not letting your buddies down. The fighting part comes instinctively, from all your training."

"Are the Japs like that, too?" I asked.

"Don't know. The only Japs I've met were dead. But one thing I can tell you, forget all that chivalry shit. They offer no quarter, and you offer none to them. They fight with no rules and they die with no rules. If you hesitate for an instant, they live and you die. There're good enough soldiers, but there're all fanatics and only worth killing. At the end of the battle, we win because we fight as a team, with better equipment and better buddies."

Sitting quietly, I let his words sink in like an anchor in a harbor. He had the savvy and courage that I looked for, and I hoped some of it would rub off on me.

Looking down at his watch, he stood up. "I better get back and get my guys bedded down."

As we walked towards the pier, a large grin raced across his face. "Say, Dutch, whatever happened to you and that movie star? You know, the Marine Sweetheart. She and you had something going, so what's the poop?"

Smiling back, I knew Dick had been enamored with Carol and didn't need all the details. "You got the pictures I sent of you and Carol didn't you?"

"Yeah. Thanks. My mom made copies and passed them out all over town. For a time, I was a real local hero. But what happened between you two?"

"Carol turned out to be like sandpaper, silky smooth on one side and rough on the other. Anyhow, I was way out of her league."

Dick abruptly halted and put one hand out to stop me. Turning to me, he said, "That's not true, Dutch. She was out of your league."

The next morning, the three officers and senior NCOs from the First and Second Platoons of Company B met with Colonel Flag and my crew for a review of our raiding plans. What the Colonel laid out was simple enough. On February twelfth, a submarine would leave the Channel and transport our raiding party to a position just north of the Tulun Islands. At 2200 hours on the thirteenth, the 1st Platoon, under the command of Lieutenant Nelson, and my crew would be inserted via rubber boats at the northern tip of Han, where we would lay low until the next day. While we were getting into position, the submarine would transport the Second Platoon, under the command of Captain Reed, to the southern tip of Piul. There, in the early morning hours of the fourteenth, the Second would start making a noisy attack up Piul Island towards Iolasa Island. This loud offensive was a diversion to draw enemy defenses away from Han and Iolasa, to the other side of the lagoon. Once most of the defenders from Han had moved off the island, we were to close the door behind them and begin our assault on the radar station. After killing off any remaining guards, we would take our photographs and then blow up the equipment, after which we would make our escape to the southern tip of the island, where the submarine would pick us up. Once the Second Platoon heard the explosions of the radar station, they would break off the battle and begin their escape to the southern tip Piul, where they would be recovered by the *USS Bush*.

As planned, the operation would have boots on the ground for less then twelve hours, just enough time to get in, get our pictures, blow up the station, and get the hell out.

After the Colonel's presentation, everyone stood around our aerial map, asking questions and making comments. Originally, Flag had planned for three platoons to make the assault up Piul, so could only one get the job done? What if the enemy garrison on Iolasa was larger than expected? What would happen if the troops on Han were not fooled and drawn off by the diversion across the lagoon? How big was the radar equipment and what types of explosives would be needed? Were there enough rubber boats for the two landings and extractions? How close-in could the Bush come with covering fire as the Second Platoon escaped to the sea? Lots of questions, lots of speculation.

In the end, it was decided that one squad from the First Platoon would be used to reinforce the Second, and that the keys to the operation were timing, communications and the success of the diversion. Watching the Raiders talk amongst themselves, I detected few doubts and no grumbling. What I saw was only the spirit of teamwork and getting the job done. This professionalism was a positive sign in the face of what Colonel Flag thought was a FUBAR.

We spent the next six days refining the plan, setting up communications and working together on maneuvers. We found a shack, just off one of the active runways, that was about the same size as the one on Han. Here, with Corsairs roaring overhead, the First Platoon, minus one squad, and my crew launched daily mock assaults. As we worked on one side of the Channel, the other

Raiders trudged through the scrub jungle, practicing their loud attack on Piul. By the end of these maneuvers, the five squads of the Second Platoon could make every bit as much noise as a full company charging up the atoll. These sounds would help with the illusion of the diversion.

As February twelfth approached, we were told that the submarine had been delayed and that we would be transported, instead, by the *USS Bush*. With our plans now changing, it was decided that the destroyer would rendezvous with the submarine on the evening of the thirteenth, just north of Tulun, where we could be off-loaded. Transferring men at night down the side of a destroyer onto a bobbing submarine on the high seas could be a tricky proposition. But the Navy said it could be done, if the seas were light and the moon bright. With this first obstacle resolved, we departed Guadalcanal.

Avoiding the Bougainville Strait and the Nip radar eyes, the Bush cruised at flank speed up the western approaches of Bougainville Island and around the Green Islands to its northern position off Tulun. But when we arrived at the rendezvous point, there was neither sight nor sound of the submarine. With the men standing on deck in full battle gear, we waited for the better part of two hours before realizing she wasn't going to show up. After some discussion about the sea conditions, the moonrise and the tides, Colonel Flag and Captain Reed decided the mission was still a go, with the Bush doing both the insertions and the recoveries. However, this would mean that the First Platoon would have to hold its position on Han while the Second was being recovered off of Piul. Then the destroyer would move to our side and pick us up. Still, with the guards killed and the radar station destroyed, we figured that this holding position shouldn't be a problem.

An hour later, under cover of darkness, the *Bush* moved to within half a mile of the Tulun reef. Using binoculars, we watched the low, shadowy outline of Iolasa slip by, as we crept at a dead-slow speed past the two small connecting atolls towards the northern tip of Han.

As we moved, the First Platoon made its final preparations. Each man checked and rechecked his buddy's gear and the camouflage makeup smeared across all the white faces. These dark strips would help hide us in the moonlight. As I was checking Black Jack, I noticed that he didn't have any on. When I handed him a stick, he smiled and said, "Thanks...don't need any."

Grinning back, I said, "Okay, but don't smile when you get on the beach. Those Pepsodent teeth will be a dead give-away."

The last thing I did was pin my Lieutenant bars onto the backside of my collar. This was the custom of all American officers, so they wouldn't be targeted by enemy snipers.

Our insertion had been timed for high tide so that we could float across the small barrier reef without fighting any heavy surf. As the destroyer came to a stop, a cargo net was dropped over her side, and seven rubber rafts were lowered to the sea. Each small boat would carry six men, their equipment and one *Bush* sailor for recovery and reuse for the Second Platoon.

As we approached the rail to start loading, Captain Reed had one final comment. "The moon comes up in thirty minutes and sets at 0131. You have just three hours to find your assigned positions and hunker down. We will start our attack at 0800 tomorrow. Until then, avoid the enemy and stay quiet. How you perform in the next 12 hours will either be worthy of your uniforms or an embarrassment to history. Good luck and good hunting."

With the seas calm, my stomach tight, and a sour taste in my mouth, we scrambled down the nets to the black holes of the bobbing rubber boats. As planned, once all the boats were loaded, Lieutenant Nelson's raft led the way towards Han. Our boat was Number Six and, with every man rowing, we followed Number Five. Within minutes of departing the *Bush*, her camouflaged superstructure disappeared from view and we were alone on the open sea. The night was pitch-black, so we had a difficult time just keeping in visual sight of the line of rafts in front of us.

Fifteen minutes later our boat rolled up on the beach in light surf. Jumping into the shallow water, we removed our gear and quickly made our way to the vegetation line. As we arrived, I looked back just in time to see the rafts being rowed back out to sea by the sailors and disappearing in the murk. With our lifeline to the outside world gone, we grouped together in some sea-grass, waiting for the moon to rise.

The first raft had the scouts aboard. After landing, they searched our perimeter, looking for any Jap sentries. By the time they returned, the moon was just starting to show. Reporting to Lieutenant Nelson with hand signals, they gave the 'all clear.' Dick then moved down the line of men, breaking us up into squads to begin moving to our preplanned positions.

The first squad, with my crew, was to make their way around the northern tip of the island and then move down on the lagoon side. Once we were parallel with the radar station, we would climb the small hill that held the antenna, then hunker down.

The second squad was to move down Han on the seaward side until they were parallel with the station.

The third squad was to remain where we were, covering the low-tide causeway that led north to Iolasa. This was our backdoor. They were to allow any Nips moving north towards the diversion to leave, but stop any that were moving back towards Han during the raid. After we blew the station, they would fall back and act as our rear guard as we made our way to the southern tip for recovery.

The three squads numbered thirty seven men and so, with my crew, we had forty Marines on Han.

With one scout out in front, the first squad started making its way towards our position. In the tree line just up from the sea-grass and beach, we would creep a few hundred yards then stop, wait for the 'all clear' from the scout, then move a few hundred yards more. It was a slow process, and we had over a mile to our destination. My crew and I were in the middle of the line, reacting to every instruction we were given with hand signs. As we got midway down the other side of the island, we found a large stand of mangrove trees that grew out of the lava, right down to the water's edge. From our aerial images, we knew that this grove blocked the beach for almost two hundred yards, and that the radar station was just west of the outcropping. Quietly moving from tree to tree, we crept through the grove until, about fifty yards in, the squad came to an abrupt halt, suddenly aware of the faint sounds of music hanging in the air.

Frozen in our tracks, it took a few moments before we realized that it was coming from the station, now less than a few hundred yards inland. Slowly starting to move again, we soon discovered a well-used path that led from the station down to the lagoon.

Peering down this path in the moonlight, I was surprised to see a small harbor carved out of the granite. Here, under the cover of the tall trees, the Nips had built a wooden dock that extended fifty or more feet into the cove, with the water of the lagoon just beyond. Our aerial images had not shown any of these improvements.

Moving again down the path, we came to the base of the hill that held the antenna. Here, with Lieutenant Nelson and a scout in the lead, my crew and I scrambled up the mound towards the top. As we moved out, the rest of the squad set up a defense perimeter at its base.

Creeping up the hill, we found a ledge of rocks just a few yards from the palm trees that helped conceal the radar tower. With Nelson and the scout giving us hand signals, we crouched between two large boulders and quietly arranged our equipment. Here we would stay until the battle started. From this vantage point, we had the station on one side; while on the other, we could look out over a tree line and across the lagoon to Piul.

With a tap on my shoulder, Lieutenant Nelson motioned for me to follow him to the rocky shelf just above our target. As I crawled over to it, he handed me his binoculars. Peering down, I could see faint lights shining through the open windows of the radar shack, and still hear the twang of the music coming from it. Moving the big eyes around, I found that the compound was bigger than I had expected. The hut itself was twice the size of the one we had trained around, back on the Channel, and across from it were two more darkened shacks about the same size. Putting the eyes down for a moment, I looked to my left and up to the tower next to us. In the inky shadows, I could just make out a second tall radio antenna, alongside the radar beacon. A month ago, this tower and the other shacks hadn't been there. The Japs must have made those improvements since our flyover.

Turning to Nelson, I shook my head and made the expression of surprise. Then, using the big eyes again, I looked out and across the lagoon to Piul. With the last rays of the moonlight shimmering off the water, I just could make out the low silhouette of the atoll.

Just as I was about to hand the eyes back to Dick, we heard laughter mixed in with the music. Twisting around, I watched the outline of two figures staggering across the compound. Each was carrying a large bottle in a wicker basket; they stopped once for a swig and then continued up the steps of the radar shack, all the while laughing.

Shaking my head again with a smile, I handed the binoculars to Dick and crawled back between our rocks. Resting with my back against the boulder, I reflected that I didn't like what I had just seen. The new dock, the new radio tower and the other outbuildings were all shockers. What else didn't we know?

Taking a deep breath and trying to relax, I thought about how quiet it was -- almost too quiet. We had infiltrated Han without being detected, and at this very moment the reinforced Second Platoon was doing the same on Piul. Looking down at the luminous face of my watch, I saw that it read 0113. In seven hours, with speed, surprise and overwhelming fire power on our side, we would know 'what else.'

I wanted a smoke to quiet my nerves but, of course, I couldn't.

I must have dozed off, because the next thing I was aware of was an elbow poking me. Lifting my head, I found Black Jack pointing towards the first signs of an amber sky to the east. Shaking the cobwebs out of my head, I moved over to his position, where I could hear the faint sounds of airplane motors. Cupping one ear, I tried to pinpoint the direction the sounds were coming from, and a few seconds later I saw a seaplane as it flew just above the surf, approaching the lagoon from the south. At first, because of its size, I thought it was a PBY but moments later, through the muddy twilight, I recognized the red rising sun painted on its dark fuselage. It was a big four-engine job, with blister windows full of fire power. As it touched down, I crept back through boulders and crawled out on the ledge that overlooked the station. Nelson and his binoculars were gone but I had a good view, with the brightening sky, of the compound.

Just as Jack crawled next to me, I saw five or six soldiers run out from one of the darkened shacks and form ranks in front. Soon they were joined by another man from the radar shack. This Nip shouted out orders, and the group turned, marching off towards the dock. Through the trees on our right, we could just make out the plane as it taxied across the lagoon and into the small cove. With the plane's loud roar ringing around the bay, the crew from the compound helped it dock; then the motors were switched off.

As we watched, Lieutenant Nelson reappeared and crawled on his belly to join us. Putting his mouth next to my ear, he whispered, "That's what we call an Emily. It's an H8K Jap seaplane. They were all over us on Bougainville, and they're trouble. Which way did it come from?"

Raising my hand, I pointed south, and he shook his head in disbelief. Using the big eyes, over and through the tree tops, we watched the plane's door open. The first to exit was a pudgy officer carrying a satchel, who was greeted by the leader from the compound. These two talked for a short time, with the leader continually bowing, and then they turned and walked towards the station.

The next out of the Emily was a full squad of Nip soldiers. While these men formed ranks, Nelson handed me the eyes and I turned to watch the first two men, now walking across the compound. From what I could tell, both of these Nips were officers, and the one from the plane looked to be an admiral. Handing the eyes back to Nelson, I pointed down to them and made a hand gesture, urging him to take a look-see.

After doing a double-take with the eyes, he put the binoculars down and whispered, "What the hell is an admiral doing on this rock? And those troops aren't garrison soldiers, they're Imperial Marines. What kind of shit hole have we fallen into?"

Shaking my head, I pointed down to my watch, which read 0620, and whispered back, "We'll soon know."

Crawling back between the big boulders, I noticed that Riku hadn't stirred from his slumber. He had to have nerves of steel to sleep on a morning like this. I thought about kicking him and giving him the news, but what the hell could he do about an admiral and Imperial Marines? Instead, I closed my eyes and tried, without success, to rejoin him in slumber.

At 0800, all hell broke loose, across the lagoon. The first sounds were those of mortar fire, followed by grenades and small arms as the Second Platoon made its planned noisy attack up Piul. With the earsplitting sounds of battle echoing around the lagoon, I crept out again on the ledge that overlooked the compound.

A few seconds later, Black Jack and Riku joined me. Looking down, we soon saw an officer come out of the radar shack and cross to the middle of the compound, where he blew a high-pitched whistle that beckoned soldiers from the two huts in front of him. As troops poured out of the shacks and formed ranks, the Admiral reappeared from the radar hut, carrying his sword or shin-gunto. Strolling across the grounds, he made some remarks to the troops while waving his sword in the air. The soldiers responded by screaming back banzai and waving their rifles in the air.

After the short pep talk, the troops came to attention and, turning right, marched off towards our backdoor. At least these troops looked like the standard garrison soldiers, and I breathed a short sigh of relief. Turning to my guys, I gave a thumbs-up; this part of our diversion was working as planned.

Moving back to our gear, we checked and double-checked our equipment. Now all we had to do was nervously wait for our phase of the raid.

At 0959, the second squad moved from its beach position and assaulted the radar hut. At first, all we could hear was a few muffled *pop...pop...pops* as the few remaining operators were killed inside. Just as this was happening, the first squad surprised the two troop shacks, supply tents and outhouses with the blaring sounds of Thomson machine guns. In less time than it takes to cook an egg, the compound was secured and Lieutenant Nelson was giving us the high sign to move from our position. As we did, we stopped at the base of the beacons, taking both film and stills of their designs and connections to the station. Then we raced down the hill to the radar shack. Lugging our camera cases across the grounds, we drew some sniper fire, which immediately answered from three Marines now posted around the perimeter of the shack. With the smell of gun powder in my nostrils, and my ears ringing from rifle fire, we rushed into the hut to find two raiders, carrying satchel charges of TNT, standing over three dead

Japs. Another dead Nip was still slumped over the radio console, with blood and brains splattered all over the equipment. For a fleeting second, this sight and the strong stench of fish and garlic turned my stomach, but I shook it off and got down to business. On one side of the narrow room was the radar gear. On the other side was the radio equipment and, connected behind, a larger room with desks and sleeping cots. This looked to be the officers' quarters.

As we got in and started to set up, the Marines dragged the dead bodies away from the equipment and into the room behind. With only the sounds of a few rifle shots outside, we mounted the film camera on the tripod and set up the battery light. Within seconds, Riku began filming the exterior of the radar equipment, with Jack holding the light. As they did, I moved to the radio station, taking pictures of the gear with my spy camera. Looking down, I found a handful of handwritten Japanese papers that looked to be incoming or outgoing radio messages. Moving them closer to the window light, I took a close-up image of each note.

At one point, the radio receiver came alive with loud static and dots and dashes of code. This sudden burst of noise about scared the shit out of me. Finishing up, I reloaded the Minox and slid it back into my hem pocket, then went across the room, taking the light from Jack so he could start shooting stills of the outside of the radar gear. While he worked, Riku reloaded the film camera. After the last image of dials and knobs, I turned the light off and began snipping the connecting wires with side cutters, and unscrewing the components from the racks. Pulling each part out, Riku filmed the interiors of the units. When he finished, Jack took over with the still camera. Riku then unloaded his camera, handing me three exposed rolls of 16mm film, which I put into my rucksack along with the single roll of film from my spy camera.

Looking up from the portable light, I said to Riku, "Snoop around back and see if you can find anything else of interest."

Just as he turned, Lieutenant Nelson busted through front door, shouting, "Hurry it up, guys. We have to blow it!"

Looking over to Dick, I raised my hand with five fingers in the air. He nodded and returned to the outside. Moments later, with Black Jack reloading the Leica with his third roll of film, Riku shouted out from the room behind, "Dutch, I need you."

Screwing the portable light onto the film tripod, I left Jack to finish up with the radar pictures. Just as I made my way into the backroom, mortar shells starting raining out front, in the compound area. *Boom...boom*! The whole building shook as the concussion waves swept past. The Japs had realized the diversion and had started shelling their own station.

Staggering into the room, I found Riku sitting behind one of the desks with a stack of papers in his hands. His almond eyes were as big saucers. Holding the papers in the air, he looked up at me and shouted, "Found these in the Admiral's case. They're the detailed battle plans for an air attack on the Panama Canal, sometime this spring. From what I can make out, the attack is going to be made with planes flown off of some new secret type of aircraft submarine called an I-400."

The sound of his words filled the room but my mind was having a hard time grasping them. If the Nips knocked out the Panama Canal, I knew it would be a big setback for the Pacific war. And the idea of planes flying off submarines was beyond my imagination.

"Why would the Admiral be carrying papers like that here on this rock?"

"I'm not sure, but I think he was on his way to Rabaul, to recruit some veteran fliers for the raid. I can't read the papers fast enough to get all the details!"

Boom...boom! The building shook again, with dust flying all around.

"Grab the whole damn briefcase. We'll take it back to Colonel Flag."

Just then, the shack was riddled with machine gun bullets on the north side, blasting out one of the front windows. Falling to the floor, I crawled around one of the Nip bodies, back to where Jack was.

I found him kneeling in broken glass, behind the equipment, calmly reloading his camera.

Looking up, I shouted, "Are you done?"

Smiling, he handed me the last roll of exposed film. "Yeah...but we have to get packed up."

As Jack slipped the camera around his neck, the front door fell to the ground under the force of Lieutenant Nelson's body weight.

"Everybody out," he shouted. "Set those satchel charges. The whole damn Nip army is breaking through our back door. We'll cover your backside down to the pickup point. Move it! Move-it!"

Getting to my knees, I looked at Black Jack. "Screw packing up. The only thing I care about is the film. Let's get the hell out of here!"

With explosions and gunfire raining around us, Riku and the briefcase were the first out of the shack, with me close behind and Jack next. We ran south, across the clearing, thirty yards to some cover at the base of the little hill. There we stopped and watched as the two remaining Raiders set fuses to the TNT and then leaped out of the building, running towards us.

The first Raider made it to our position. The second didn't. He was gunned down not twenty feet from where we knelt behind some trees. As he ran towards us, his gaze was fixed on mine. When the machine gun's bullets ripped through his back, it twisted him around like a corkscrew. Then he collapsed to the ground, moaning. We could see his back covered with black-red blood, and hear him gasping for air and sobbing, "Mommy! Mommy, they shot me."

In the snap of a finger, this hardened Marine had been transformed into an innocent little boy, calling out for his mother. His words rushed through my body, and I started to move out towards him, but was pulled back by Jack just as another burst of gunfire strafed his now-limp body.

Black Jack's stoic face told the story as he shouted, "He's dead, Dutch. We have to get the hell out of here."

I looked back, but I couldn't see any more signs of life, and I knew he was right. But what about his body?

Ka-boom! The ground rocked as the radar shack exploded from the TNT. The fireball rose in the air for what looked to be a thousand feet. Then a shock wave bent the trees and about threw us to the ground. With building parts and metal raining down all around us, I knew that our troops on Piul would see and hear the explosion, and break off their battle for recovery.

Turning, I saw Riku and the first Raider take off down the path, heading south toward our assembly area. Getting to my feet, I took one last look at the hole in the ground that use to be the radar station, and the dead body of my fellow Marine. Part of me wanted to drag his body back, while another told me to run.

I ran.

The path we were on went around the hill on the seaward side of the island. Every now and then, in front of me, I could see the backsides of Riku and the Marine, roughly fifty yards ahead, darting in and out of the underbrush. As I ran, I could hear Jack's footsteps behind me as we navigated the snag-littered, crooked trail. With my throat dry, my heart pounding, and that bitter copper taste in my mouth, I staggered down the path. The sun was hot, and my clothes wet with sweat as I came to a sharp bend in the trail.

Just as I turned it, out of the corner of my eye I saw a figure jump up from behind some sea grass. In an instant, I twisted around, bringing my Thompson up finding a Nip solider with a grass-covered helmet pointing his rifle at me. I pulled the trigger...and nothing happened. The damn safety was still on! As I fumbled for the release, the Nip hesitated for a heartbeat. Then I heard the shot and felt the bullet. But the shot came from behind, and the bullet I felt raced by my ear as Jack's slug found its mark, right between the eyes of the standing Jap.

The Nip looked at me for a second with surprise in his eyes, still blinking. With a small clean round black hole in his forehead, he then fell forward, dead.

Standing there, flat-footed, I was stunned and shaking as Black Jack ran up to me.

"You okay, Dutch?"

It took me a second to find my voice, as I fought not to vomit from fear. "Yeah..." I rasped. "Thanks."

"Let's get going. We have to keep moving."

Trying to compose myself, I replied, "Yeah, I'm right behind you."

As Jack took off again, I walked through the grass and kicked over the dead Nip body so that I could see his face. With his helmet now lying beside him, I found a young man with his eyes still open, staring sightlessly up at me. He had no whiskers, and his yellow skin looked as soft as cream. He looked more like a schoolboy in uniform than my feared enemy. As I looked down at him, a thousand thoughts raced through my head. Why did he stand up? Why did he hesitate? Why am I still alive? Jack saved my life!

From down the trail, I heard Jack call, "Come on, Dutch. He might have buddies!"

Looking up at Black Jack, I waved my hand and started racing down the trail again. We still had a half-mile to go…a half-mile to recovery and safety.

Ten minutes later, I came to the end of the path. Just as I emerged from the jungle, I ran past two Raiders who were behind a sand dune, covering the trail.

"Anyone behind you, Lieutenant?"

Stumbling past their position, I shouted back, "No…not that I saw."

A few yards down the beach, Riku raised his head up from behind another mound of sand, waving to me. Running in his direction, I slid over the top of the dune and found him, along with the Raider from the shack, with their weapons at the ready. They were alone behind the dune, cut off by the sea.

Out of breath and still shaking, I tried to collect my thoughts. Looking east, I could see and hear the *Bush* just across the lagoon, lobbing shells with her five-inch guns. She was laying down protective fire for the Second Platoon as they made their way to be recovered. Soon, she would be moving to our position to pick us up. We had made it this far. All we had to do now was wait.

Slipping the rucksack with the film off my neck, I reached for a cigarette and breathed a small sigh of relief. As I lit the smoke, I could hear the sounds of our battle still raging up-island. Could we hold until recovered? As I took a long drag, my mind raced back to what I had seen: all that violence…all that death…all that destruction. What had I expected? Dick had been right; humanity was lost, out here.

Exhaling smoke, I tapped Riku on the shoulder and asked, "Where's Jack? Have you seen Jack?"

"Yeah, he raced by and told me he was going up the lagoon side to get some pictures."

Startled, I shouted, "Pictures of what?"

"I wondered the same thing, Dutch…but I guess that's what a combat photographer does."

Rolling over with my back to the sand, I stared out to sea. Riku was right -- that was what they did, but not here and not now! With the information we'd found, our mission had a lot more importance than any pictures of combat. But Jack didn't know about the briefcase. In the excitement, he hadn't asked and I hadn't had time to tell him.

Flipping my cigarette away, I turned to Riku again. "I'm going to get him back. You stay with the film and the satchel."

"I'll go with you, Lieutenant," Riku answered, starting to get up.

"No, you won't. That's an order. This film and that briefcase have to get aboard the *Bush* and into the hands of Colonel Flag. Understand?"

Riku just stared at me for a moment. I'm not sure I had ever given him a direct order before...but he knew I was right.

"Okay...but you have to get back here, Lieutenant. That destroyer is not going to wait around for you guys."

"We'll be back. You just get your ass on that ship and don't worry about us."

As I got up to leave, I looked back to the Corporal and gave him a half-hearted salute. Smiling, he looked up and returned it, and then I took off running.

Just around the point, with small-arms fire echoing off the lagoon, I came across another Raider carrying a wounded buddy, fireman-style. As he stumbled by in the sea grass, I asked if he had seen a guy with a camera.

"No, sir...but there is a hell of a fire fight going on, just up the beach. Is the recovery area secure?"

Nodding yes, I pointed in its direction and continued running. A few moments later, Han begin to shake as the *USS Bush* started laying down covering fire on the hill next to the radar station. The shelling came in threes, *boom, boom, boom,* from her five-inch guns.

Looking to my right, I could see the destroyer with her turrets flashing, recovering the Second Platoon up her cargo nets. I knew it wouldn't be long until she moved to our side of the lagoon to pick us up. With her shells roaring over my head, I would stop and drop waiting for the explosions. After one three-shot volley, I got to my feet and looked up to the hill to find that the antennas were gone, with only smoldering broken sticks of trees still remaining. A few hundred yards further up, I found three Raiders behind log snags, holding off some Nips who were trying to make their way down the beach. Recognizing the corporal in charge, I crawled in next to him, with enemy fire pelting the logs and sand around his defensive position. The Japs were hard to see, as they hid in the jungle and behind the sand dunes with sea-grass for cover. *Pop...pop...pop*! The Marines fired wildly in their direction, keeping their heads down.

"Have you seen Sergeant Malone?" I screamed over the noise of the firing carbines.

Shaking his head yes, he pointed inland and up to the base of the hill. "There's a Nip pillbox up there that shot a lot of our guys. Lieutenant Nelson tried to take it out and got hit. Your Sergeant Malone took some grenades from us and went to rescue him -- and in the process he took out the pillbox. The last we saw, he was dragging the Lieutenant into a bunker for protection from shelling, and throwing out dead Nips from the inside." Staring at me, with sweat rolling off his camouflaged face, the Corporal continued, "We're all that's left of the first squad. When should we fall back to the recovery area sir? What about the Lieutenant and your Sergeant? What about our buddy's bodies? Who will pick them up and bring them home? I don't know what to do."

Boom...boom...boom! Three more shells crashed down around us. Looking to my right, I could see that the *Bush* was on the move. In ten or fifteen minutes, it would be over to our rallying point.

Grabbing the shoulder of the corporal, I yelled, "Give me covering fire and five minutes to get up to the pillbox to help Jack with the Lieutenant. Then you guys fall back, double time, to the rallying point. We'll be right behind you."

His eyes blinked yes, and I started crawling towards the tree line for my dash uphill to the pillbox.

Just as I got to my feet, the three Marines started laying down my cover and I took off running. Zigzagging from tree to tree, bush to bush, I covered the fifty yards up the hill in no time. As I ran, I doubled-checked that my safety was off and my Thompson ready. The last fifty yards would be across open ground. Pausing for a moment, I looked up at the bunker with its log-and-sandbag-covered roof, and screamed out to Jack that I was coming in. From behind the bunker's darkened gun opening, I could see Black Jack's pearly whites smiling back as he shouted that they would give me covering fire.

Taking a deep breath, and with my legs trembling, I took off across the open ground. There were dead Nip bodies scattered on the ground in front of the bunker, and I could see two rifles flashing from the inside, giving me cover.

Just as I jumped over the last body and was about to dive into the gun hole, the sand and logs around me came alive with bullets. Looking up, I found half a dozen Japs charging the pillbox from the opposite flank. My instincts kicked in and, without thinking, I brought the Thompson up. It came to life, burping out loud, short bursts of deadly gunfire. With my white knuckles holding back the weapon's recoil, the gun battle was like a slow-motion film playing out, frame by frame.

My first burst caught the two lead Japs with such a force that they stood straight up, their eyes budging as they screamed in pain. Instantly, their jungle tunics turned crimson, and they fell to the sand, dead.

My second burst literally blew the face off the solider just behind them, but his faceless torso didn't stop running until it tripped over his dead comrades. That moving, faceless image would stay vivid in me for all my life.

As my victims fell, firing from the Raiders below and from inside the bunker stopped the remaining attackers. In a few heartbeats, the attack was over, although I emptied my magazine into the dead bodies just to make sure.

Boom...boom...boom! I dove through the log hole in the pillbox for protection from the shelling. While sand shook through the roof from the explosions, I landed on my belly at the base of the front log wall. Quickly turning over, I looked up to find Jack and Dick staring down at me.

"Glad you could join us," Black Jack said with a grin.

Stumbling to my feet, I surveyed the room. The bunker was small, only about eight feet long and five wide. The three log walls were barely five feet high, with the back wall fashioned from the rocky soil of the hillside.

Smiling back, I answered, "I like what you've done to the place."

Lieutenant Nelson was leaning against the front wall, with his carbine resting in the gun port and the bloody calf of his left leg extended out into the room. Jack was on the other side of the opening, with his camera still strapped to his neck and his weapon at the ready.

"We've got to get the hell out of here, boys. The *Bush* is on the move."

"I took one in the leg," Dick said with anguish as he tried to move it. "I'm not sure how fast I can run."

"I'll carry you, while Jack covers our ass. But we have to get out of here now!"

Boom...boom...boom! Three shells fell just above us, buckling some of the logs and causing a sandstorm inside.

"They're coming back," Jack called from the opening.

With three of us now at the gun port, we held back a second charge with massive gunfire. This time, we counted only four attackers, but we had no help from the Raider position on the other side. They must have moved to the rallying point.

Boom...BOOM!

The last shell must have been a direct hit, as it lifted the log-and-sandbag roof right off the bunker and tossed it into the air. The concussion and the raining debris stunned us as we were all thrown to the ground.

With my ears ringing and my eyes unable to focus, I was still dazed, moments later, trying to figure out what the hell had happened. Finally, I regained my composure and eyesight. Looking around, I found that roof logs and sandbags had fallen back into the pillbox, pinning us against what remained of the front wall. Using my arms and shoulder, I rolled a log off my body and then went digging for Jack and Dick.

Next to me, I found Black Jack. As I started removing debris from around him, he came alive and started to help. On the other side of the room, we found Dick under a log and broken sandbags. He, too, came alive as we moved debris off his body. At last, we were free, but it had taken precious minutes to accomplish it. Just as we started to drag Dick and his bum leg out of the bunker, I looked up to find three Nip soldiers standing on the hillside of the pillbox, with their bayoneted weapons aimed straight down on us.

Hell on Tulun

Boom...boom...boom! We heard another round of shells coming in and half-ducked our heads, but this time the rolling barrage had moved a few hundred yards down the beach. Our Jap captors didn't flinch. Then one soldier called out something in Japanese, and an officer carrying a shin-gunto joined the hillside group.

We were frozen in place, with them glaring down at us. Our weapons were still buried in the sand, and I feared that at any second they would open fire. They talked amongst themselves for a moment, and then the officer waved his sword, motioning for us to come up and out of the collapsed bunker.

I was the first to crawl out. Then, reaching back, I dragged Dick up, with Black Jack pushing from below. Soon Jack and I stood with our hands raised in the air, while Dick sprawled on the ground.

The Nip officer with his gaunt, weedy face approached me, glaring as he flipped up my shirt collar. Looking at my rank, he smiled. Then, crouching down, he did the same to Dick. Two captured officers -- this seemed to please him. Then he moved to Black Jack, whose Sergeant stripes were clearly visible. But the officer wasn't interested in his rank, he was interested in the camera. Grabbing it, he yanked it from around Jack's neck.

Turning to his men, he shouted out orders, and we were immediately searched from head to toe. They stripped us of everything from side arms to knives, helmets to gun belts, canteens to cigarettes, watches to lighters. The last item they plucked from my pockets was our special XKO Order. All the small items were placed in one of the helmets and then handed to the officer. He glanced through contents for a moment before handing off the helmet to a Sergeant that had joined the group.

Taking his sword and pointing it our way, he barked out more orders. Using gun butts, two of the soldiers next to him motioned for us to start walking. Reaching down, Jack and I each grabbed

Dick by a shoulder and helped him get to his feet. With us working as a crutch on each side, the three of us slowly started stumbling forward. Dick gasped with pain a few times but we soon found a rhythm to our march.

As we moved north, the noise of the battle from the south suddenly stopped. We knew it meant that the *Bush* had made her recovery and was steaming for home without us.

With a sinking feeling I had never experienced before, I knew we were alone and were soon to die.

Along our march, we passed what just a few hours before had been the radar station. All that remained were the charred remnants of buildings and equipment, littered with corpses rotting in the sun. As we passed, the soldiers behind us began ramming their gun butts hard into our backsides. They, too, were looking at our work, and I feared they would start using the bayoneted end of their weapons.

This continued until we arrived at the northern tip of Han. Here we waded through the watery causeways and across the two small atolls that connected to Iolasa Island. As we marched down the sandy path, we passed some troops making their way back to Han. These soldiers looked at us with hatred in their eyes and fingers on their triggers, spitting on us as we staggered by.

Half an hour later, we stumbled into the main garrison compound on Iolasa. It was big -- bigger than I would have ever expected. From the size, I guessed we had fought not garrison troops but a company of Imperial Marines. A short dirt road ran parallel with the island, east and west. On the seaward side, there were three large log-and-bamboo huts. Behind these huts was a bivouac area with rows of tents. Across the road were two more long, low, log huts with bamboo-and-dirt roofs that had been dug deep into the sandy soil. These buildings looked to be supply sheds for the compound. Next to one of those sheds was a large mangrove tree some sixty or seventy feet tall. Under the shade of this tree, we were deposited by our captors.

Jack and I helped Dick slip to the ground, with his back to the tree trunk, and we were then motioned by our guards to sit next to him, with our hands behind our heads. As we complied, the officer barked out a few orders. Then he and the Sergeant, carrying the helmet filled with our personal belongings, walked across the dusty street to the center hut, which had a small, log, front porch.

The march to this point, helping the Lieutenant, had been long, hard and hot. My head and hair were wet with sweat, which stung my eyes as it dripped down my face to where I could taste its salty solution. Sitting next to me, Black Jack's face looked like mine felt.

It took a few moments for me to dry my face by shaking my head. As I did so, my eyesight and composure returned. That's when I first felt the bulge on my backside. It had been there all the time, but my mind just hadn't focused on it. During our search, the Japs had missed my spy camera, which was still concealed in the hem of my shirt. But what good will this do? They'll more than likely find it when they search us again…if they search us again. It was a double-edged thought. Might they kill me for having it? But then, I didn't expect to live past sundown anyway, so I let the thought go.

For the better part of an hour, we sat there and watched beleaguered Nips returning from the battle. Just across from us, next to the building with the porch, was a hut that had to be an aid station or infirmary. Here a solitary soldier sat on a bamboo chair behind a crude wooden table, examining wounded troops as they filed by. His medical opinion was short and fast. Soldiers who appeared before him without help from others and with only superficial wounds could enter the station. On the other hand, if they needed a buddy to help them to his table, or if they were carried in on a stretcher, they were quickly sent down the path next to the infirmary to the circle of death.

Lieutenant Nelson had told us about this practice, but I was shocked to see it in action. The Japanese Army had convinced their troops that, if they were wounded badly, the only honorable thing to do was to die. 'The circle of death' was where they went in order not be a burden to the Emperor. The worst cases, the ones close to death and on stretchers, were placed in the center of the circle, while the wounded that could still walk and those that could still drag themselves around were placed on the outer edges. As the men died in the center, the soldiers from the outer edges would drag their dead bodies out of the circle and stack up the corpses like so much cord wood. For the most part, the non-wounded troops would stay away from the circle, but sometimes soldiers would walk through, looking for buddies. If they found them, they would more than likely shoot their friends, to hurry death.

It was a gruesome practice that showed how little respect the Japanese had for life. What amazed me was how no wounded soldier protested the life-or-death destiny being handed out like aspirin. They were given nothing for their pain, no hope for recovery, but still they did not cry out for help or complain of the decision. They would just nod in obedience and somehow drag themselves, with or without help, to the circle. It was the saddest thing I had ever seen.

At one point, we heard a commotion coming from the other end of the road. Looking that way, we saw the chubby Admiral, still carrying his sword, and squads of troops emerge from the path that lead down to Piul. As they marched towards the compound, other soldiers and the wounded along the way would stop what they were doing and bow down, while screaming out some Japanese phrase. It was as if the army of the conquering hero had just returned.

The Admiral marched his troops to the front of the center hut, brought them to attention and then, after yelling out orders, dismissed them. As he moved to the porch, he stopped, glanced over to where we were sitting, and scowled. The look on his face sent chills down my spine, and I cussed the darkness.

Just behind this group of troops, other soldiers staggered into camp in small groups of twos and threes. One group had two more Raider prisoners that had been taken captive. As they were brutally pushed and shoved towards us, I recognized them as being from the Second Platoon. The first was a PFC that I had seen around camp, but I didn't know his name. The second was a Corporal by the name of Silverman or Silverstein...I wasn't sure. As they reached our position, they both were forced to the ground, still holding their hands above their heads. There were five of us now, with the two new guys sitting in the semi-circle on the other side of Dick, who still had his back resting against the trunk of the tree.

The Corporal looked across to me with a face full of fear, shaking his head 'no'. The PFC next to him just stared at the sand, his whole body trembling. Their captors bowed to our guards, said something, and then crossed the compound to the bivouac area. As they walked away, I noticed how both Nips were pigeon-toed. It was a strange observation for a strange time.

As the shadows grew longer, and the line of wounded shorter, we grew more concerned about our fate. The two guards watching us had relaxed somewhat and were leaning against the wall of one of the supply huts, talking. Most of the other troops were now back in camp and a quiet hush seemed to hang in the air. An afternoon breeze had freshened up from the south, and I could hear it rustling in the trees and feel its cooling power. Maybe, I thought, just maybe, I'll wake up to find this is nothing more than a bad dream.

But I was wrong. Looking up, I saw the door of the center hut open, and the Sergeant that had escorted us came out. He yelled across the way, and both of our guards came to attention. Slowly, he walked in our direction, reeling off angry orders or instructions that I couldn't understand. When he arrived on our side, he walked over to our guards and slapped both of them hard across the face, still shouting at the top of his voice.

Then he turned to our group. Moving to the Corporal, he hovered over his reposed body, still yelling out angry Japanese words. Even from where I was sitting, I could smell the alcohol on his breath and see his bloodshot eyes.

The Corporal looked up at him, not knowing what to say or do. The Sergeant then reached into the holster on his hip and retrieved his Nambu pistol. At the sight of the gun, a quiet gasp arose from our group. The drunken Nip said a few more words and then...*bang*... shot the Corporal in the forehead, causing his instantly dead body to fall backwards.

As the shot rang out, all of us twitched in shock and fear.

Taking two steps sideways, he next stood above the PFC, who still had his head down and his lips moving in a silent prayer.

My body was shaking from panic and my mouth as dry as cotton...I could not believe what I was watching. The Sergeant said some more words and then...*bang*...he shot the lad in the top of his head, blowing away the back side of his brain. Like an accordion without air, the young soldier's body collapsed to the ground.

Three more slow steps sideways, and now the Nip Sergeant was facing Lieutenant Nelson, who was looking up, watching his every move.

Dick's eyes were on fire and he stared directly at the Sergeant. Taking his hands down from above his head, Dick screamed, "Shoot me, you son-of-a-bitch, and I'll see you in hell. God bless Amer…"

Bang…bang. Without saying a word, the Jap shot the Lieutenant twice in the chest, the force of the bullets throwing his body against the tree trunk. He let out a small groan and softly finished the word America, then was still.

Frowning down at the Lieutenant's limp body, the Sergeant mumbled a few words. With smoke still billowing out of his gun barrel, he then side-stepped to Black Jack.

Twisting around, I looked into Jack's face to see a tear rolling down his cheek. We knew that our last breaths were upon us. With the Nip's trigger finger tightening, our eyes met in a silent good-bye.

CHAPTER NINE

"**D**o you really think they were cannibals?" Jasper asked, looking back at the natives who were still dancing and shouting at the water's edge.

Frantically working my oar, I answered, "One thing is for sure...they didn't want me for my pleasing personality."

Paddling, Jasper thought for a moment and then replied, "Maybe they just didn't understand that we meant them no harm. If we went back, I'll bet we could reason with them."

"Sure, Padre," I shouted back. "But you didn't see the look on their faces when they sized me up for the cook pot. I think the only kind of 'reason' these guys understand is white meat or dark."

Jasper was always thinking about the good in his fellow man. Even after what we had been through, he had a hard time believing there were bad people on God's earth. The Padre was well suited for his chosen profession.

A few hundred yards out, the current took over and started drifting us south-west. As we stopped rowing, we turned and watched Gibraltar slip off our stern. What lay behind us was our last hope of survival and rescue; what lay ahead was open water and despair.

"I don't feel so good," Corporal Bates slurred.

Turning to him, I saw that he didn't look so good, either. Moving over, I asked him to turn around with his back to me. Helping him remove his frayed shirt, I took my fingers and explored the area the spear had struck. There was a small puncture wound close to his old bullet hole, but there wasn't any bleeding. The spear had broken his skin but hadn't lodged any deeper than half an inch into his shoulder. It looked clean but I took a few coconut shells of seawater to clean it out even further.

Helping him back on with his shirt, I said, "You'll be okay. The spear broke the skin but there's no bleeding."

Turning back around to me, he whispered, "I'm on fire. Can I have some water? I'm really thirsty."

"Sure."

Thirty minutes later, Corporal Bates died. After he had taken a few swigs of water, he had propped himself up against the float and seemed to doze off. He looked so peaceful, with his head bobbing around with the motion of the waves, that we didn't pay him any attention. We had no idea he was close to death. At one point, he opened his eyes, looked around the raft and, with labored breathing, shouted, "I hear you, Mom...and I'm coming. I won't be late." Then he closed his eyes again. Within moments, with a slight grin on his face, he passed away.

We were shocked and stunned by the quickness of it all. The only explanation for his death that we could come up with was that the spear had been dipped in some kind of poison. There could be no other reason, unless being chased off the island had caused him to just give up. No...it had to be poison.

After we regained our composure, Jasper said some words over Corporal Bates's remains. Kneeling next to the body, with a soft breeze blowing across his weather-beaten face, his eyes sad and sunken, the Padre simply said, "Lord, have mercy on our brother's soul. He was cheery in all conditions, never refused a task, and never took your name in vain. May he reside with you in your kingdom for all time. God bless Corporal Humphrey Bates. Amen."

The shortness of his prayer surprised me as much as the quickness of the death. But I could tell that Jasper had been shaken and was having difficulty finding words. The Padre had presided over so many deaths during the years that it should have gotten easier, but instead it had got harder. Who comforts the comforter?

After a few moments of silence, we had to face the grim reality. We would have to lower the body into the ocean or, in the hot sun, it would rot in place. But we had no way of weighting the body down, so it would just float away and become so much shark bait. This idea was repulsive to all of us but we could think of no alternatives.

Then there was the matter of what Bates owned. Was there anything we needed? His clothes were just rags, his shoes simply pieces of leather held together by the treads. Other than his belt and dog tags, there was nothing we wanted or could use. The sum of a man's belongings...one belt.

It was a gruesome task but, an hour later, we rolled the Corporal into the sea. Then, taking our oars, we quickly rowed away from his floating corpse until he was out of sight. When we stopped paddling, the raft remained silent for the rest of the afternoon and through the night. Each of us was lost in his own thoughts of the pasts and of the dismal future that lay ahead. With Gibraltar gone, hope was gone.

Wits

Click. The Nip Sergeant's firing pin fell on an empty chamber. Mumbling something under his breath, he took his free hand and released the spent magazine from his pistol. As it dropped he fumbled inside his pocket for another. Black Jack and I sat there, frozen in place, watching this half-drunken bastard search for his next instrument of death. As I glanced at Black Jack, with my hands still held up and behind my head, my stomach was sour, and I thought I might piss on myself. Out of the corner of my eye, I could see the two guards, with smiles on their faces, standing over the bodies of our three dead comrades.

Then I heard the sound of metal on metal as the Sergeant slid in another magazine and cocked his pistol. Twisting my head, I found his eyes wild with hate as he loomed over us. As his gun pointed right at Black Jack's forehead, I watched the Sergeant's finger drift towards the trigger. Then, from behind him, came some yelling in Japanese.

Looking around his towering body, I saw the Lieutenant that had captured us standing on the hut porch, screaming at the Sergeant. At first, the Sergeant was frozen in place, just staring down at us. Then, slowly, lowered his pistol and carefully moved the guns safety into position.

At first, we didn't comprehend what had happen. Then, in a few heartbeats, we realized we had a stay of execution.

The Sergeant barked out a few orders and our guards, using their gun butts, got us up onto our wobbly feet and pushed and shoved us across the road and into the center hut. As we stumbled through the doorway, we found ourselves entering a small room with enlisted men working behind a few desks. Towards the back was a long wooden table, and behind this table were two officers, sitting and drinking. The one on the left was the Lieutenant who had just saved our lives. On the right was a Major in a shabby and dirty Imperial Marine uniform. In the center was a third vacant chair.

Behind these officers was another room that was walled off with bamboo matting and a draped doorway. In front of the table were two empty chairs, where we were forced to sit, with our guards standing, rigid, behind us. The room was hot and stuffy, smelling of sweat, booze and garlic.

The officers glared at us from across the table as they continued sipping their sake from little white porcelain cups without saying a word. Finally, the Lieutenant looked my way and spoke. It took me a second to understand what he asked in Japanese: "Do you speak Japanese?" Riku's tutoring was paying off. I almost shook my head yes, but thought better of it and just stared back at him. He asked the same question again, this time looking at Black Jack, with the same results. Turning to the Major, he said something about us not understanding.

If he talked slowly, I could catch about one word in four, just enough to have an inkling about what was being said. Then, from behind the beaded curtain, the pudgy Admiral appeared, carrying the helmet with our personal effects. The two officers across from us jumped to attention as the Admiral came into the room. He took the chair in the middle and, as he sat down, poured out the contents from the helmet. With the other two officers taking their chairs again, the Admiral searched through the items.

With my head held low, I sneaked a peek at his chubby, pock-marked face. There was dried blood on his uniform collar, and his slant eyes were deep-set and close together. Finally, grabbing the Leica camera, he pushed it across the table, lens first, towards Black Jack. Then he reached again into the pile for my special order envelope and, after opening it, shoved the open piece of paper across the table to me. Turning back to Jack, he said something so fast that I couldn't understand a word. He waited a moment, then repeated what must have been a question. Jack just sat there, not understanding, staring at the camera on the table. The Admiral gave a slight nod, and the guard behind Jack took his gun butt and crashed it down on the top of his head.

Black Jack rolled off his chair and went crashing to the floor. As he hit the deck, he let out a soft groan. Then the room fell silent. Turning to me, the Admiral asked the same question, and this time I thought I understood two of the words: "…take here?"

Looking up, I shouted out my name and rank, and got through half of my serial number before the guard behind me did the same. His wood-and-metal gun butt grazed my left temple and eyebrow, cutting the skin. My head and upper body was forced forward as the blow sent me sprawling across the tabletop with a thud. Dazed and disoriented, I just laid there for a moment, with pain shooting from my head to my toes. Then I pulled myself upright in the chair again, still with my arms raised. As I did so, I could feel warm blood trickling down the side of my face. Looking across the table, I had trouble focusing on the three officers. My eyes played tricks as pain pulsated through my brain. Then the Major shouted orders to the guard standing over Jack, and he was lifted back into his chair. The Lieutenant said something to the Admiral about us not understanding Japanese, and then shouted out some orders to the men at the front of the room.

As the room grew quiet again, I peered over to Jack, who was breathing heavily next to me. He seemed okay but his sweaty face was now caked with dirt and sand from the wooden floor. Seconds later, a Nip Corporal rushed through the front door and braced himself at one end of the table. He was a skinny, short kid with buck teeth, in a wrinkled uniform wearing wire-rimmed glasses. He looked every bit like the stereotypical image of the average Japanese soldier that the US news liked to show. As the Admiral said a few words, the kid kept bowing, never once looking up at the officers. Then he turned our way and slowly said, "I English speak."

The Admiral pointed to the camera again and spoke loudly to the translator.

He bowed again and then turned to Black Jack. After a few moments of searching for the English words, the boy asked, "Why here you? What you take?"

The Corporal's English was as bad as my Japanese. Watching the frantic Admiral, I was sure he was worried about his battle plans in the satchel. Had they been destroyed or had we taken them? He wasn't sure. Jack looked up and stared at the translator for a heartbeat, then down at the camera, and then over to me. He slowly smiled, showing his white teeth through the grime on his face, and stated his name, rank and serial number.

As I watched the Admiral fume I thought about how crazy this was: We're getting the shit beat out of us, and Jack doesn't even know the reason why.

Just as the guard behind Jack was about to take another swipe, I threw up my arms and shouted, "Wait! I'll tell you anything you want!"

The officers were startled by my outburst and turned their attention to me. The Admiral threw up his hand, stopping the guard from hitting Jack. Out of the corner of my eye, I could see Black Jack glaring at me as if I were Judas himself.

The skinny kid turned to me and said, "Yes...slow."

Taking my arms down, I reached slowly across the table, picked up the paper with our special orders, and started a line of bullshit -- my gamble for our lives.

"Frank Knox, the Secretary of the Navy, sent us here personally." Gesturing with my other hand towards the camera, I continued, "We took pictures of your oscillators and diodes, which we teleported directly to him, using our new ray gun!"

Some of this double-talk came from my favorite comic strip, Dick Tracy. I was sure most of my words would be over the head of our translator. And I was right. The kid stood there, flat-footed, with his mouth hanging open while the three officers looked directly at him for the translation. He knew a few of the words, and I heard him repeat them to the officers: Frank Knox's name was repeated, and navy and photography were translated. Then he shook his head and admitted that he didn't understand the rest of what had just been said.

At that, the Admiral reached across the table and jerked the paper out of my hand. He stared at it again, while saying, "Hai...Frank Knox." The room went quiet, with the three officers glaring curiously across at us. They weren't sure who we were, why we were there, or what I had just said. One thing was for sure, though; they couldn't smell good old-fashioned Yankee manure. If they killed us, any information we might have would be lost. And if we lived, they would have to take us to someone who could understand. They were faced with a dilemma.

Moments later we were marched out of the office and tied to the posts on the front porch. Our special orders had saved our bacon again...thank the Lord and Admiral King.

With evening upon us, Black Jack and I sat at one end of the porch with our hands tied together around a post, back-to-back, in silence. From my position, I could see our two guards. Finally, one of them left and returned shortly with two bowls of rice. He and the second guard then moved down to the other end of the porch to eat their chow.

With them out of earshot, I whispered, "You okay, Jack?"

"Yeah...but what was all that bullshit about ray guns?" he whispered back.

"Another diversion. But it's not going to work for long. Pretty soon, they'll find somebody that understands, and our goose will be cooked."

"What are they worried about? We're just photographers. How's your face? Did it stop bleeding?"

I didn't get a chance to answer. The door of the hut suddenly opened and out walked the Admiral and the Lieutenant. They shouted some orders to our guards, who spilled their rice bowls as they jumped to attention. We were untied from the post and then retied with our hands behind our backs. Then we were marched off behind the two officers, with our guards in the rear, heading in the direction of the burned-out radar station.

Half an hour later, as we waded through the last causeway to Han, I glanced west to see the sun about to drop behind the horizon. The sky was richly colored, and the coral-green ocean shimmered with a thousand points of light. Inwardly, I smiled and rejoiced. It was sunset, and we were still alive -- a fate I would have not believed, a few short hours ago.

The waist gunner stood guard duty over us as the Emily picked up the speed necessary to take off on the waters of the lagoon. With the last rays of light in the sky, we had been loaded onto the Nip seaplane and tied up in the rear, close to the blister windows. Jack was across from me, with his hands bound high through the plane's frame. My hands were the same, and we both sat on the deck of the seaplane.

As the plane sped and bounced across the water, I wondered why she had been overlooked by the first squad. True, she had been an unexpected target, but she should have been destroyed during the battle. Obviously, that hadn't happened.

The Admiral and a squad of Imperial Marines occupied the front part of the darkened aircraft. From what I could eavesdrop, our destination was Rabaul, a Japanese stronghold on the northern tip of New Britain. As the plane gained altitude, the last signs of light gave way to a moonless night. The view down the fuselage was as black as the inside of a cheap cigar, and smelled about the same. Jack tried to whisper something across to me, but the gunner standing over us heard him and gave him a hard kick with his boot. With silence as our companion, I let my head lean against the skin of the plane and tried to rest. Sleep was out of the question, as my head still throbbed and my mind was racked with fear and anticipation. But I closed my eyes and listened to the air as it rushed by, and did my best to dream of Laura and better days.

When I opened my eyes again, some hours later, the rising moon had cast a faint blue glow of light inside the plane. Moving my head away from the skin and resting it on one of the frames, I observed the Jap gunner nervously standing watch by both blister windows. He was young and lean, standing above us, ready to defend with his machine guns. At one point, he reached to his belt, removed his canteen and took a drink.

I felt like I had a cotton-ball stuck in my throat, and I knew my body was dehydrated from sweating buckets. Cautiously, I moved my foot to his boot and nudged it. Taking the canteen away from his face he glared down at me, thought for a moment, and then shook his head no. I did it again, this time silently moving my lips. He turned away and looked out the window, then slowly turned back and looked down the inside of the darkened plane. Finally, he bent down, put the canteen in front of my face, and let me have a big swig of the water.

As he pulled it away, I nodded across to Jack. The guard shook his head no again, and again I nudged his boot. Staring up at him, I pleaded with my eyes. He thought a moment more, then quickly did the same for Black Jack. As he stood back up, he slid the canteen onto his belt again and gazed out the window.

I wanted to thank him with another nod but he never looked down on us again. Maybe, just maybe, I thought, there is some humanity out here.

Our Limit

With the moon still in the sky, we reached Rabaul sometime in the early morning. After the Admiral and the troops disembarked, two soldiers entered the plane, carrying flashlights. From their arm bands, I knew they were Japanese Military Police. We were untied from the frame and then handcuffed with our hands behinds us. After exiting, we were loaded onto the back of a small, open truck, with both guards sitting next to us. Before we pulled away, we were blindfolded and told 'hi to-ku" -- no talk.

We bounced over dock planks for a while and then turned onto some paved streets. A few minutes later, the truck came to a stop. Here we were dragged out and marched up some steps and through a narrow doorway. Out of the bottom of my blindfold, I could just make out the beam of light from one of the Nip's flashlights. After another doorway and a short hallway, we were forced to stop. Standing there, I could hear metal-to-metal sounds coming from the hands of one of the guards, and then the loud opening of iron doors. I was shoved forward and felt the handcuffs being removed. Then the door slammed behind me.

Listening to the retreating echo of footsteps, I reached up and untied my blindfold just in time to see a beam of light exit through a closing door. Where I stood was as black as a crude oil wellhead, and the only sound I could hear was my breathing.

"Are you there, Black Jack?"

Nothing…and then just a whisper. "Yeah."

His voice, while next to me, sounded far away. Holding my arms out, I started searching around the room, blinking my eyes in an attempt to see. Just behind me was the barred locked door I had just entered. On each side were iron-barred walls. At the far end was a brick wall and, by the time I found it, my eyes could see a soft glow of starlit sky coming from a small, barred window high up on the exterior wall. The jail room was tiny, only five or six feet across and eight deep. Slowly, my un-swollen eye started adjusting.

"I've got a small window, high up the front wall. I can just see the sky outside. Do you have one?" I whispered back.

I heard some stumbling, then the thud of something next to me.

"Yeah, I have a window, and I just tripped over an empty wooden bucket in one corner. Must be our piss bucket. Where the hell do you think we are?"

Feeling around on my hands and knees, I answered back, "Some jailhouse on Rabaul. I have a bucket, too, and there's a rolled-up mat on the floor in the other corner. It'll be light soon. Then we'll be okay. Try to get some rest."

"Yeah…sure. I don't' like this, Dutch. It's like an oven in here, and it's the middle of the night."

He was right. I had sweat pouring out of me like a water faucet. Unfurling the mat, I took my shirt off and rolled it up on the floor. With my back and swollen face resting against the coarse, slightly cooler brick wall, I got some relief and tried to rest.

I must have dozed off, for the next thing I remember was being dragged out of my cell, with sunlight just visible outside my window. The two guards pushed and shoved me down a short hallway and into a totally darkened room. In the middle of the room was a table that held a burning oil lamp. This small flame provided the only light, casting long abstract shadows around the tiny area.

In front of the table, the guards forced me to sit on a small wooden stool, with my forearms and hands lying on the tabletop, palms up. There I sat for what seemed like forever. Sensing the guards hovering just inside the shadows behind me, I tried to calm myself. It was spooky, like waiting for Saturday Inspection back at boot camp, making you think of all your weaknesses and faults. Finally, I heard a door open, and out of the shadows stepped a Nip officer.

Slowly, sitting in a chair in front of me, he placed a flashlight and a brown folder on the table. Opening the folder, he gazed across at me.

"I'm Captain Kyoji. I'm Kempeitai. Do you know what that is?" he asked in near-perfect English.

Staring back at him, I didn't respond.

After a few seconds, a curious grin raced across his face, and he nodded his head. From behind me I heard a whistling sound, and then a bamboo stick came crashing down from the shadows, landing across the palms of my opens hands with a loud '*clap.*'

Pain raced through my arms and body, and I winced with the blow. The stick had slits which created the sounds in the air and then the loud noise of the slits coming together with the blow. I realized that it had startled me as much as hurt me.

"That will happen every time you do not respond," he said. "Kempeitai is Japanese secret police, much like German Gestapo or your FBI. I tell you this so you will know that you aren't dealing with any farm boys here. I was educated in your country and I know your Yankee culture. There are only two ways for you to leave here -- dead or alive. If you live, we will transfer you to one of our many POW camps. This is up to you, Lieutenant. Do you understand?"

I responded with my name and rank, and I had just started on my serial number when the next 'whistling' and 'clapping' struck my open palms. My hands felt like they were on fire, and I could already see them puffing up in the dim light.

"This will be quite painful for you, Lieutenant. If you cooperate, we can have a doctor fix that gash on your face. If you don't, then you will die. Do you understand?"

Staring across at him, I could see the determination in his eyes.

I nodded.

Leaning back in his chair, he reached into his breast pocket and retrieved a cigarette and lighter. Then, watching me across the table, he lit the cigarette.

Through the flickering light, I could see that the Captain's uniform was neat and pressed. He was small but had square shoulders, with an older face and a black pencil mustache. Behind his rimless glasses were manic eyes tight to his skull that gleamed with anger.

Watching the smoke roll off the tip of his cigarette, I prayed for courage.

Picking up the flashlight with his free hand, he turned it on and aimed its beam onto my face. "Now, what is all this about ray guns and teleporting? I read Dick Tracy and Flash Gordon, too, so don't try your bullshit with me. If you lie to me, it will be your last lie. So why the deception, Lieutenant?"

With the beam of light right in my eyes, I looked down and softly replied, "Your men didn't seem to know about the Geneva Convention. They had just murdered some prisoners. They didn't seem to understand the rules."

The room fell quiet for the longest moment. Then, with my head still low, I heard him say, "Ah...the rules. The Geneva Convention."

From behind, one of the guards grabbed my hair and forced my head up and my eyes into the beam of light.

"Japan never signed the Geneva Convention," he said, "as our soldiers never surrender. The only rules we have are our rules. Do you understand that, Lieutenant?"

With my hair still held tightly, and the light still in my face, I slowly nodded.

The guard released his grip.

Captain Kyogi drew on his cigarette and let the smoke escape slowly. "So let's talk about your raid on Tulun -- and I warn you that I will have the same talk with your Nigger Sergeant, so don't lie to me..."

That was how it started. A few hours later, after the whistling stick had bloodied my palms and forearms, I was dragged back to my cell and deposited there. Then the guards took Black Jack, before we could say a word to each other. Sprawled out on the mat,

I feared for his life. I hoped he would talk and be spared. While I hadn't told them anything, it had cost me. My fingers hardly moved, and my hands and shoulders had swollen up like blimps. My mind was fogged with pain, and I drifted in and out of consciousness.

Sometime later, Jack was dragged back, looking like I felt. He winked at me through the bars as they threw him to the floor. Then they dragged me out for a second session with Captain Kyoji.

This time, the whistling stick was used on my back and thighs. It continued for hours, with blood dripping down the back of my t-shirt, and my legs so wobbly that I kept falling off the stool. Finally, mercifully, I passed out.

When I came to, Jack was just being dragged back from his second session. Watching the guards throw Jack into his cell, I feared that I would be next again. Instead the guards locked his door and walked away. In the waning daylight, I dragged my body to the bars that separated us, and looked at Jack. I could see his rolled-up body breathing and hear him moan, but he wasn't conscious.

Dragging myself back to the mat, I pulled my swollen back up the wall to a sitting position. Here again, the cooling bricks seemed to help. We had taken twelve hours of torture and we looked like so much raw meat for our efforts...

I wasn't sure I could do it again. In some ways, I prayed for the fate of Lieutenant Nelson. At least he was at peace and without pain. How could man do this to man...?

With my head hung low, I quietly sobbed. I wanted water...I wanted relief...I wanted death.

Sometime in the night, Black Jack came around and dragged himself over to whisper through the bars. "I didn't tell them a thing, Dutch....no, not a thing...but I can't take anymore. God help me...no more."

The dark cells were silent, and I knew he was right...but what could I say? In my foggy mind, I searched for the right words. All I could come up with was, "Maybe it's over."

On the second morning, I was rousted out first and taken to Captain Kyoji. As I was dragged into his chamber, I knew he had changed his torture tactics. Gone were the blackout curtains over the windows; now the room was bright. Gone, too, was the little stool in front of the table. The guards, one on each side, made me stand in front of the table and wait for my tormentor. With my lips parched and swollen, I stood there, gazing around the little room. It had a wooden floor, and a tin roof covering brick walls on each side. The wall behind the table was made out of wicker and bamboo panels. The chamber was bare and smelled of sweat from the day before. As I stood there, the room seemed to be spinning, and my body was racked with pain. With my wobbly legs, I felt that I might pass out at any time. Then the door opened and Koyji entered the room, carrying his file, and took his seat behind the table.

Opening the folder, he looked up at me and flashed that sadistic smile, "You don't look so good, Lieutenant, but then you and your Nigger Sergeant showed us your courage yesterday. I respect you for that, but today will be different. Today you will talk...or die."

Reaching into a side pocket, he pulled out a small line of wire. Working with the strand, he made a loop with a slip knot, while he continued, "Most Americans are plowboys or cowboys. Do you know horses, Lieutenant? Do you know what a 'proud' stallion is? I think you might know them as geldings. Do you know this type of horse?"

Slowly I nodded my head.

Taking the loop, he slid it around two of his fingers. "Good. In Japan, we use piano wire to remove the stallion's testicles. If we remove just one, he will still have energy and spirit. If we remove both, he will be lazy and useless. I have often wondered if it would be the same with humans. That's what we will find out today." He paused, gazing at me. "If you talk, I'll give you water and food. If you don't, we will watch you bleed to death, with your balls on the floor."

As he finished speaking, he pulled the loop tight around his fingers while eyeing me across the table. Then he nodded at the guards. One quickly moved behind me, putting his arms around my neck in a choke hold, while the other reached down, unbuckled my belt and pulled my trousers and shorts to the floor.

I struggled but to no avail. For the longest moment, the Captain's manic eyes just stared across at me. My heart was throbbing and seemed about to explode, and my mind couldn't believe what he was saying. Then he reached across the table, handing the wire to the guard.

I watched with horror. I was so scared, so thirsty. I would rather lose my life than my testicles, and I couldn't think of a worse way of dying. Before the guard could turn back to me, I stammered, "I'll talk...I'll talk."

Koyji sat there for a moment, enjoying the terror on my face. Then he nodded again to the guard, who handed back the wire and pulled up my pants. The stool was placed in front of me, and I collapsed onto it, mumbling, "Water...please...water."

The Captain reached under the table, bringing up a canteen and tin cup, which he poured half full. Grabbing the cup, I spilled half the liquid before I got it to my lips. Then I drank the cool, sweet water.

"You will tell me everything, every detail. And if your Sergeant confirms your story, you just might live through this day."

For hours I sat there, talking in a near whisper with tearful eyes, telling him names, units and plans. Who we were, what our mission was, why I had the special orders, where I was trained, and about my background. I told him about everything... everything except about the satchel. I would have told him that, too, but since Black Jack didn't know about it, he couldn't confirm it, and I was afraid that might mean death for the both of us.

The Captain fished for information about the war plans without really asking, as he didn't want me to know what he was searching for. He asked about what we photographed, what we saw, what we took...without ever mentioning the briefcase. In the end, I think he was confident that he had all of my information.

As I was lead back to my cell, my heart sank to a new low. Forty-eight hours before, I had been a solider, a Marine. Now I was a traitor. Should I have allowed myself to be castrated? For what -- names and old battle plans? I just didn't know.

As my cell door opened, I cried out to Black Jack that I had told them everything. He had to know, so that he might be spared the wire, and confirm my story. As they lead him away, he eyed me, looking for my inner soul, the reason why I had given in. After he left, I curled up in a corner and bawled like a baby, until, out of exhaustion, I fell asleep.

Sometime later, the guards returned Jack to his cell. After they left, he crawled over next to my corner, looked at me through the bars, and told me he understood.

"That 'proud' stallion shit was enough to make any man talk", he sobbed. "We didn't know anything worth our nuts. God help me, I told them everything, too."

Then, with tears rolling down his cheeks, he slipped one of his hands through the bars. Taking it, I clung to it for a moment as we looked at each other. We had both been broken and humiliated; we had been tortured beyond our endurance.

Surprisingly, true to Captain Koyji's word, we were given food and water that afternoon. One bucket was half-full of fresh water, which Jack and I shared. The other was full of seawater, to wash the sweat, grime and dried blood from our bodies. The food was a tin plate of rice and a few pieces of fish.

We ate every morsel. Then, after washing out our t-shirts in seawater, we put them back on, wet, and then our shirts. The warm seawater felt good on our welts, and our shirts held in the moisture. We didn't say a dozen words to each other all afternoon, both of us lost in our own private hell, reliving what had just happened.

Early that evening, we were removed from the jailhouse and taken, blindfolded, to the docks. After removing our blindfolds, the guards took us aboard an old, rusty barge, where they chained us to the boat's ribs on the lower deck. As the guards departed, we watched them climb a ladder and give the keys and paperwork to an officer, topside.

Standing below the open deck, we looked around to find that the mule was full of equipment and supplies, with a small compliment of sailors who paid us little attention. After nightfall, its motors came alive, and we slowly started moving north, out of the harbor of Rabaul.

We would spend three nights and two days shackled to the frame of that barge. There was great fear, aboard, about being spotted by American planes, PT boats, or submarines, so we only moved at night, and always north. During the days, we would seek refuge from the American danger by hiding in the small coves or inlets of the different islands. Our iron chains were long enough so that we could find shade during the hot days and take some comfort during the chilly nights. But we both knew that, if the mule was attacked and sunk, we would go down with her like an anchor. It was a chilling thought, realizing that some of the barges we had sunk might have had POWs aboard. But then, being a prisoner of war was as dangerous as being a Nip.

We were given two bowls of rice a day, and a couple cups of water. The sailor who brought the food and water would sometimes drop his half-smoked cigarette on the deck in front of us so that we could pick it up and finish it, which we always did. And slowly, over the days of the voyage, we gained back some of the strength and resolve that we had left behind on Rabaul.

Camp Ireland

Early on the morning of February 19th, we arrived at the port city of Kavieng, on the northern tip of the island nation of New Ireland. This information was ascertained by overhearing the sailors talking as they prepared to make landfall. From memory, I knew we were some two hundred miles north of Rabaul, and roughly four hundred miles northwest of Bougainville.

After the barge was moored, two Nip guards came aboard and released us from our chains. As we were marched off the mule, untied and without blindfolds, I noticed the sorry condition of the docks and piers along the waterfront. Most of the warehouse buildings on the bay, as well as half of the six piers, were nothing more than the charred remains from air strikes, some of which were still smoldering.

We marched through the little town behind the waterfront and saw that many of the wood-framed buildings bore scars from fire damage. The town, with its bomb-riddled main street, looked every bit like a war zone. Slowly we continued to march down dusty streets, passing small homes, and then out through the countryside. A few miles outside of town, we came to an encampment with a main gate, tall barbed-wire fences, and guard towers. The compound itself was small, only a few hundred yards square, with rows of ramshackle bamboo huts on a hillside.

Just outside the fence were other framed buildings that looked like barracks for the Japs. Here we stopped. After our guards talked to a Corporal through the wire, the front gate opened and we were lead into the camp. Standing in the hot, early morning sun, just inside the gate, we watched our guards give the Corporal some papers and then depart.

The Corporal then moved our way, raising his gun butt in the air and screamed in pigeon English, "Bow all Japanese soldiers speedo...speedo"

We bowed. Glaring at us, he finally smiled and then led us across a dusty open area in front of the huts. At one side of this area were three metal boxes dug into the ground. Each box looked to be three or four feet square, about three feet above ground. The tin pillboxes were roughly ten feet apart, in a straight line. As we walked by them, I wondered what their purpose might be.

Just beyond the boxes, we stopped at one of the front huts. The Corporal yelled something through the darkened, open doorway, then turned and walked away. A few moments later, a skinny man in a tattered khaki shirt appeared in the opening, pulling up a pair of shorts.

Looking at us with surprise, he mumbled, "What the bloody hell...? Who are you guys?"

Thrilled to hear English again, we introduced ourselves and found out that the skinny guy was Major Dunn of the Royal Australian Army, the ranking POW officer for the camp. Hearing his rank, both Jack and I braced and gave him a salute, which he returned. He was a short fireplug of a man, with a confident grin and a firm handshake.

Staring at us for a moment, he said, "You boys look like dung. Come on in and get out of the sun."

Walking through the door, we found a large room with a handful of wooden beds at one end. The men that occupied these racks were just getting up and getting dressed. The walls were made of loosely woven grass and bamboo panels. Dots of sunlight spread throughout the room from all the holes in the thatching. There were windows on each side, covered with other woven panels. As these panels were raised open and fixed into position with sticks, the room flooded with sunlight. The floor was earthen, and at the front of the room was a small, rickety table with four chairs; here we were told to sit.

The other men were so curious to see a couple of Yanks that they were all soon standing around the table, wanting to hear our story. With the Major's approval, I told them in general terms what had happen to us.

As I finished, the Major asked, "So you guys came in on a barge, early this morning?"

"Yes sir," I replied.

"A barge hasn't made it up from Rabaul in over two weeks. Your bombers have had this little port buttoned up for months. You're very lucky blokes!"

Just then, one of the other men stepped forward and introduced himself as Captain Ross, the regimental surgeon. He asked if he could take a look at us. We nodded and took off our shirts. As the doc examined our cuts, welts and bruises, the Major sat down and told us their story.

When the war started, the Major was the executive officer for the 14th Royal Engineering Regiment, building docks and piers in the Dutch East Indies. Early in 1942, the Japs invaded that country, after which a short but gallant and bloody campaign ensued. When the battle ended, over half of their men in the Regiment had been lost, including their commanding officer. What remained of the Regiment finally surrendered on March 8th, 1942. In all, the Japs captured 256 officers and men, but now, after two years and three POW camps, only 157 still survived. They had lost over a third of their surrendering ranks to torture, disease and friendly fire.

Looking up from examining Black Jack's welts, the doctor added, "Our mates drop like flies around here. Cherish your good health while you still have it. I see you had a run-in with the Nip 'singing stick.' It's their favorite tool of torture. You're lucky though -- your wounds look worse than they are. See me after chow, I have some crankcase oil I can put on them. It will help them heal in this blazing sun."

Just then, another officer stepped forward and extended his hand for a shake. "I'm Captain Jasper Young, the Regimental

Chaplain. Welcome to hell. If the slave labor, dysentery or bad food don't' get ya, then the boxes will." He nodded towards the front of the compound and continued, "Our little yellow brothers call those bakkin kou or penalty boxes. These are the tin ovens the Nips use to cook our guys -- and sometimes their own soldiers -- for the slightest infraction of the rules."

After the Padre finished, all the other officers stepped forward and introduced themselves. As Jack and I got to our feet to shake hands, my mind shut out all they were saying. I was stunned by what I was seeing and what I had just heard. We had fallen from one shit hole into another. These men were nothing more than walking skeletons, with loose skin, hollow cheeks and deep-set, almost black, eyes. Their uniforms were rags, their living conditions appalling, but their sprit still lived.

Just then, the shrieking call of a whistle filled the air.

"That'll be morning enlightenment," the Major said, looking up, "You guys stick close to me and do what I do. Afterwards is chow, and I'll see that you get something to eat. Then we will meet up with the Doc over at his infirmary, to get you greased up for the day. Padre, why don't you join us so we can get these Yanks squared away?"

'Enlightenment' was something to experience. The prisoners formed three ranks, in front of the tin ovens in the open yard, and roll call was taken. The Major told us that we faced the boxes as a Nip reminder and that, when men were inside them, the stench was unbelievable.

Then the main gate was opened, and guards marched in to form another rank to our left, also facing the boxes. Soon, just over two hundred men were standing in the hot, early morning sun, facing the bakkin kou that had a small bamboo platform in front. Moments later, a fat Nip Sergeant wearing a sword and a clean uniform walked through the main gate, ascended the platform, and addressed the group in Japanese. He was a bull throated mug with a round face frozen in a perpetual scowl. His talk was short, but delivered with a demeanor of great animation. On our side, we bowed, knelt, chanted and stood again. The only words I understood were 'spirit,' 'faith,' and something to do with the Emperor. Then he abruptly stopped, raised his sword in the air, and screamed, "Shugyou" or 'discipline.' At that, all the men, guards included, formed into small groups of three or more and started slapping each other across the face! Our group of Aussies, including Major Dunn, had grins on their faces, and their slaps were soft and half-hearted. The Major told Jack and I to slap each other, which we finally did, gently.

The whole thing was crazy and seemed to be some kind of game. But then I looked over and saw that the Nip guards were slapping each other with zeal. The sounds of open hands on skin echoed across the yard. If what I was watching hadn't been so pathetic, it would have been humorous.

Then the whistle blew again, and we formed back into ranks. The fat Sergeant just stood there for a moment, looking at the group, and then said in pigeon English, "Work details half-hour, all men draw out tools." Then he directed his gaze right at Black Jack and myself, while concluding, "New men see Colonel Hisachi, this morning. No work today. You rest. Tomorrow work." Then he stepped down from the platform and walked back out through the main gate. Morning enlightenment was over.

After a morning meal of some type of rice gruel that tasted like dishwater, we walked over to the infirmary. The hovel was about half the size of the officer's hut, with only six beds, two of which were occupied. As we took off our shirts for treatment, the Doc explained that 'Nip Rule One' was no food to those who didn't work. Therefore, staying in his hospital was an option of last resort for the men. The Major added that all officers and men were required to work, seven days a week, ten hours a day, down on the docks and piers. What our bombers were destroying, his men were to rebuild. With all the air strikes over the last few weeks, this had been a losing proposition; still, the Japs demanded their sweat.

"But there is one good side to this labor," he added. "We work down around the water, where we can sometimes find things like canned food and shellfish that we hide and bring back to camp. Also, the Nips allow us to have a small garden outside the gates, although the guards take most of our crop. And the Doc here is allowed to treat the people down the road at the internment camp. For his services, they give him things that he smuggles back to camp. Somehow, between what we grow, smuggle and steal, we get by."

As the Doc smeared on the gooey motor oil, he went on to tell us that the internment camp held forty-six women and children detainees. They were Australian and New Zealanders who had lived in Kavieng before the war. While their living conditions were a little better than those at our camp, it was still a hell hole for the women and children.

The Padre added that the Doc was also allowed to treat the local town's people twice a week. Seems the Jap doctors didn't want to dirty their hands helping the local natives, as they felt they were inferior people of color. The natives gave the Doc jewelry and other trinkets for his services, which he traded on the black market for his limited medical supplies.

"Nip Rule Two," Jasper said. "Bow, and bow low, to all Jap soldiers or you will end up in a box. Your brain will fry inside those ovens. Two of our mates have died in them, so bow, and bow low."

As the Doc finished the grease job, he added, "Nip Rule Three, death to you and nine other prisoners if you try to escape. This island is crawling with IJA (Imperial Japanese Army) so there's no place to run. Don't even think about it, for your sake and ours."

The room fell quiet. I asked, "Any more rules?"

"Yes -- Aussie Rule One. Survive," the Major said, with a grin of determination.

"What was all that slapping about this morning?"

The Padre shook his head and answered, "Its bushido, or warrior code. These blokes really believe in this code of obedience, and they show it by slapping each other around. If it wasn't so sad, it would be funny."

"Are there any other Americans in camp?" Black Jack asked.

"No, and we're surprised," the Major answered. "We've seen some of your planes get shot down, and we've watched the parachutes float to earth. But none of those flyboys have ever been brought into camp."

"That's because they've killed the poor saps," the Doc said, wiping his hands of the oil.

I tried not to dwell on that. "What about this Colonel Hisachi? Anything we should know?"

The three Aussie officers stared at me for the longest moment before the Major answered, "Watch yourself. Don't trust the yellow devil. He speaks perfect English and he's one sadistic Dandy."

"And he's a Sheila as well," the Padre added. "He's had the same Korean boy as his orderly for years, if you know what I mean."

"I don't understand. What's a Dandy? What's a Sheila?"

"I think you Yanks call Dandies 'neat freaks.' And a male Shelia is a queer or homosexual. The Colonel's both, so watch yourselves. And stay clear of Sergeant Yoshio, the fat guy from this morning's enlightenment. He's the worst bugger of them all," the Major answered with a scowl.

Just then, a whistle blew, outside.

"That will be work call," the Major said, and then turned to the Doc. "Get them set up with a mess kit and canteen. Then have the Lieutenant move in with us, and the Sergeant with the other NCOs in Hut Three."

As the Major and the Padre got up to leave, I stopped them. "If it's all the same to you, sir, I'd rather stick with Sergeant Malone." Reaching over, I patted Black Jack on the shoulder. "He's my lucky charm."

The Major answered, "Suit yourself, Lieutenant. Doc, get them both set up in Hut Three. We'll see you guys, this evening."

All the huts in camp were built on open ground, with no vegetation around them. Hut Three was long and narrow, with a dirt floor and a tin roof, and it was located just behind the officer's hovel. The thatched walls had windows on each side, with bamboo panels that were propped open so that fresh air could move around.

The Doc found two bunks next to the rear door that Jack and I could use. Next, he set about scrounging some kits and two dirty blankets that we could stretch across our bamboo beds. Looking over what he found, I realized that it was all dead-man's gear. Finally, he walked us down to the latrine, which was nothing more than an open slit trench on the lower level of the compound.

After that, we walked up a path to the opposite side of the compound, where a small stream flowed through rocks from the hillside just behind the camp. This was where we were to get our drinking water. He explained that the water was full of parasites and would have to be boiled each evening, before we drank it. He said our mates would show us the right way to treat the water.

Kneeling down, he filled our canteens and then dropped three white pills into each. These water purification pills were hard to come by, but they would make our water drinkable for the day. As we walked back through the camp, he explained other sanitary rules that we were to follow. Disease was rampant, malaria, cholera, dysentery, and he had little or no medicine with which to fight it, so we had to take every precaution in our effort to stay healthy.

When we got back to our hut, a guard arrived, gesturing impatiently, wanting us to follow him to Colonel Hisachi. The Nip Corporal carried a bamboo stick, and the three of us bowed low to him. Then the Doc wished us luck and disappeared.

Just outside the main gate, across from the guards' barracks, was a wood-framed house, built three steps off the ground. It had a small porch which overlooked the compound and was the only building to have a shade tree growing in front.

After the Corporal knocked on the door, we were lead inside to a front office and told to stand facing a large, vacant, teak desk. Just behind this desk was a low credenza, also made of teak, above which a Nippon flag hung on the wall. Both the desk and credenza were highly polished and devoid of anything on top. The room, which smelled of incense, was spotlessly clean and had two large windows overlooking the guard barracks. The windows had real glass panes, and the sunlight flowing in illuminated the desk like a spotlight.

Glancing around, I could see rice-paper scrolls hanging on other walls, and the wood floor had woven mats. Two chairs were the only other furniture in the room, next to the opposite wall. We stood there for a long while before a wall panel slid open at one side of the desk. First through the doorway was Sergeant Yoshio, still dressed in his neat uniform and sword. Next to enter the room was Colonel Hisachi.

Both Black Jack and I bowed low before I could get a good look at him. While our heads were still down, the Colonel took his seat behind the desk. The Sergeant stood at one end of the desk while the Corporal moved to a position just behind us. I feared we were about to receive another treatment with the singing stick.

The room went silent. Then the Colonel said, "You may look up."

As we did, Hisachi reached into a desk drawer and retrieved a small silver dagger. He positioned it in the sunlight so that it would reflect a beam across the desk, into our eyes. As he talked, he moved the beam from one of our faces to the other. Staring at me, he began by saying, "Lieutenant Clarke, USMC." Then he moved the beam to Jack. "And Sergeant Malone, also USMC. Our first American prisoners. How nice."

The Colonel's voice was high-pitched, as if he were still in puberty, but his face showed maturity. Hisachi looked very much like a store clerk you might find back home. His English was impeccable. He was slender, with rounded shoulders, a round face and small hands. The dress uniform he wore was clean and freshly pressed, with a single row of battle ribbons. Not one black hair was out of place, and his fingernails looked manicured and polished.

He continued, "Here, you will work or you will die. Here, you will die with nine others if you try to escape. Here, you will bow to all Japanese soldiers or you may die in one of my boxes. We are superior. We did not surrender and bring shame upon ourselves, as you did. Make the best of what I have to offer...and you may live through this time." Placing the dagger on the desktop, the Colonel glanced to the Nip Sergeant and continued. "This is Sergeant Yoshio. When he talks, he speaks for me. Obey him or you will die. Do you understand?"

We bowed again, saying, "Yes, sir."

"Good. Sergeant Malone, Corporal Shozo will take you back to your hut. I will talk to your Lieutenant in private."

Turning back to Sergeant Yoshio, he said something so fast that I couldn't comprehend it. The Sergeant braced himself, bowed, and turned on his boot heel to leave the room.

Black Jack just stood next to me for a moment, not sure what to do next. I nodded my head his way, and he started to bow, just as the Corporal brought the stick singing down on his back.

"You will bow when leaving the presence of all Japanese soldiers," the Colonel remarked with a sour look.

With his head hung low, Black Jack back-stepped two paces and then turned to leave with the Corporal. With my heart racing, I heard the front door close as the three men departed. Bringing myself to attention, I wondered what brutal fate was in store for me now, and why I was alone with Colonel Hisachi.

The Colonel got up from his seat and moved around to the front of the desk, saying, "Lieutenant, do you know San Francisco?"

His question caught me off guard. Finally, I replied, "Yes, sir."

"Good. Did you live there?"

"No, sir. I did photography assignments there."

"Oh, yes," the Colonel said, resting on the corner of his desk. "You are a photographer. I learned photography when I lived there from 1936 to 1939. I wish I had my pictures with me to show you, but they are in Japan. I worked for a bank, back then, and I still have many friends living in the area. I plan to return to San Francisco after our victory. Do you have friends there?"

Like a chameleon, the Colonel had changed and now talked as if we were accidental tourists. I fibbed, "Yes, sir."

"Good. Do you smoke, Lieutenant?"

His face was sincere, his eyes friendly, but I still expected some kind of a trap. "Only when I can get them, sir."

Reaching into a side pocket, he pulled out half a pack of Camels and handed them to me. "Take these. I have plenty. In the next few days, you and I will have tea and speak more about San Francisco. It is the most clean and beautiful city in the world. You are dismissed, Lieutenant."

Taking the cigarettes, I bowed. "Thank you, sir."

As I stepped backwards, he said, "I'll have Sergeant Yoshio find you some clean clothes for our tea. Please shave and wash up. You look shabby."

When I walked out of the Colonel's office, there were no guards to escort me back. The front gates were open, with no one around. As I strolled through the deserted camp, my mind replayed the bizarre conversation with Colonel Hisachi. What was all this 'tea' shit about? And that part about clean clothes and washing? He was creepy, and he scared the hell out of me!

Walking into Hut Three, I found it empty, so I called out Jack's name. From outside in the rear, I heard his response. Walking out the backdoor, I found Jack sitting in the shade of the building, his back propped up against the hut wall. As I approached, he looked up at me angrily.

Sliding down next to him, I asked, "You okay?"

He stared directly at me. "No. I'm not. That Colonel Hisachi is a real piece of work. We have to escape from here, and soon."

"We can't do that. If we do, nine others will die."

"What the hell do I care about these Aussies? They're nothing to me."

Black Jack's face was full of rage, with something deep down inside gnawing at him.

"That's just not like you, Jack. We still have our balls. Let's not lose them now."

Finally, he let it out. "I'm no field nigger, bowing to my masters. If one of those Nip bustards lays a hand on me again, I'll kill him. If I don't escape from here, Dutch, I'll surely die."

My mind searched for a way to temper his anger and reason with him. Reaching into my pocket, I pulled out the pack of Camels. "The Colonel's not so bad. Look what he gave us."

Shaking his head without a smile, Jack answered, "Hell, Dutch, we don't even have any matches to light those damn things. They've taken everything from us. We have nothing."

With my other hand, I reached behind my back and slipped the spy camera out of my shirt hem. As I brought it up, I removed it from the plastic sack. Holding it in front of me, I said, "They didn't get this, and I think we should take some pictures of this hell hole before we go."

Jack's jaw just about dropped to the ground. "What the hell...! You still have the Minox! Is it loaded?" he demanded, with the sparkle returning to his gaze. "How did the Nips miss that?"

Finally, Jack had something he could sink his teeth into -- a photo assignment.

CHAPTER TEN

The sea was boiling with forty-foot swells, and the wind was howling like a band saw. The waves had grown from small hills to towering mountains in less than an hour. Our little cork raft was rocking, up and down, side to side. We would get trapped in a trough and then the wind would push us up to the crest, where white water would curl over us. On top of the waves, we could look out and see breaking whitecaps all around us; then we would tumble back into another valley. The setting sun was having a hard time penetrating the black veil of clouds. Thunder rolled across the sky like bowling balls down an alley, with lightning piercing the darkness with bright sharp flashes. The wind was roaring so loudly that we had to scream to be heard. Another typhoon was upon us, and this time we didn't have the safety of land. My fear was that the raft would capsize.

"If we flip over, swim back and hold onto the bottom webbing. It's our only hope," I yelled into the whirling wind.

Seven days had passed since we lost Bates and watched Gibraltar slip from our stern, and it had been a couple of days since we'd used up the last of our food and water. Each morning, I took the bayonet and made a mark on the side of the float. This morning's mark was the sixteenth. Sixteen days ago, we'd escaped...sixteen days of freedom and fear.

A seventeenth mark didn't seem likely.

"I've got a couple of short pieces of rope. Should we tie them to the raft so we have something to hold onto?" Sergeant York shouted.

Nodding yes, I sloshed over and tied one while he tied the other. "Hold on as best you can," I yelled to no one in particular. "The last thing we need is to be in the water."

We were all scared, and why not? We were dueling against the torments of Mother Nature, with no way to fight back. We had come so far, been through so much, and now she would have the final say.

"It's getting dark," Jasper yelled.

"Yeah. Pretty soon it will be as black as Hisachi's heart," I answered, forcing a smile.

Just then, a gust of wind caught us, pushing us up the side of another mountain of water. As we got to the summit, a second blast lifted us right off the crest, into the air.

The ride was short and high. As we came down, we flipped, scattering all of us into the water. I lost sight of everything except bubbles alongside my face. I tried to scramble back towards the surface of the water, but something kept holding me down. Finally, I made it to the top and took a mouthful of air, only to be pulled back down again.

Suddenly, it dawned on me that the problem was my boots. My legs were too weak to carry them, full of water. Reaching down in the churning water, I blindly untied my boots and let them drop. Then I popped to the surface again, just as another curl of white water came crashing down on me.

Splashing and choking on seawater, I recovered again. With my head above the surface, I looked for my mates and the raft, but saw…nothing.

As I floated up the side of another swell, I frantically turned, looking and praying. Then, as if the Lord had turned on a flashlight, a point of light broke through the black clouds, focusing its beam on the raft, atop of a wave just behind me. Swimming in its direction, I lost sight of it as I tumbled down into another trough. Down it would go, up I would go. I caught new glimpses of the raft every now and then, but I didn't seem to be making any headway toward it. Still, I kept trying, struggling, swimming. Adrenaline pushed my body forward, but my arms and legs soon felt like cement blocks.

Just as I was about to give up, a wave came crashing down on me, carrying with it the upside-down raft. Grabbing one of the ropes, I pulled myself close to the float, and then up on top of it. With my fingers gripping the webbing, I sat atop it, screaming my mates' names.

Nothing.

I tried again, with the same results. Then, in the last rays of daylight, I saw the shadow of a head swimming towards me. Its progress was slow, thrashing in the water. Grabbing the rope, I jumped back in and swam in its direction. As I extended my arms as far as I could, we finally touched. Pulling the swimmer closer to me, I looked down to see the Padre's exhausted face. With wind and waves still curling around us, I dragged him back to the raft and pushed him on top, then lifted myself next to him.

We said nothing. We were too tired, too spent. From our perch, we searched the water for any more swimmers, but there were none, and soon the night turned as black as the typhoon.

Survival

We heard them before we saw them, the sounds of planes reverberating off the harbors waters. Stopping work underneath the pier, I looked out to where three Nip freighters were anchored, a mile out in deep water. With the waterfront of Kavieng in shambles, the freighters had to be off-loaded out in the harbor, using barges. These ships made perfect targets. The B-25 Mitchells came in, one at a time, surprisingly low from behind the targets. Soon we could see their payloads dropping, and the bright red and yellow flashes as their bombs found their marks. Then loud booms echoed off the waters as more explosions rained down. As the first Billy (B-25) finished its run, it turned and headed straight for us with its guns at the ready.

Seeing what was about to happen I began to move for cover but the Major stopped me. "Not until the whistle blows or you'll end up in the box."

Looking across the harbor at the incoming bomber, I screamed back, "That's crazy."

"Nippers' rules," answered the Major.

Just then, the whistle did blow and we all ran for cover. All nine Billys made the same single pass over the waterfront with their guns strafing hot steel. When it was over, I crawled out from my cover and looked back to the harbor to find two of the freighters sinking and the third on fire. It had been a glorious show of American air power.

Then the whistle blew again and we returned to work.

That evening, as we marched back to camp, the Major reminded all the men to keep a sharp eye, the next day, for any wreckage that might be littering the shoreline. There we might find edible or useable items. For us, scrounging had become a way of life, a way to survive.

The next morning, after enlightenment, Sergeant Yoshio called out two of the men from the ranks. As the Corporal and a Private walked towards the platform, a quiet hush spread across the yard. Stepping down from the platform, Yoshio had the two Aussies turn and face the assembled ranks, with their heads lowered.

"You are all cowards for surrendering, but these two are bigger cowards, as yesterday they ran before the whistle. Today and tomorrow they will spend in bakkin kou."

The Aussie Corporal turned to Sergeant Yoshio, pleading, but was rewarded with a 'clap' across his face. He stumbled backwards from the singing-stick blow with blood dripping down his nose.

The ranks let out a gasp. Tension filled the air as the guards braced themselves. I started to step forward but was held back by Jasper's hand on my belt. "It'll do no good, Lieutenant," he whispered.

Guards rushed forward and dragged the screaming men to the boxes, while other guards opened the tin lids. Within seconds, like deflated accordions, the men were crammed into the ovens and the lids were secured. When the dust cleared, guards with bayonets fixed surrounded us, waiting for any trouble.

Standing there, I looked beyond them and through the open gates, where I spotted Colonel Hisachi watching the event from his front porch. He didn't even have the courage to show his face.

Then the whistle blew for work. There would be no food this morning.

Work proceeded on the docks in all weather conditions, during and after attacks. Both Jack and I were assigned to the 'Black Gang,' which dismantled the charred and damaged structures. It was hot, dirty work, but neither of us complained. The 'White Gang,' commanded by Jasper and a few other junior officers, cannibalized other buildings that the Nips had no use for. Long gone were the town's only church and half of a two-story building. They took everything: wood beams, planks, nails, even doors and windows, so that the 'Yellow Gang," commanded by the Major, could reconstruct the waterfront to the Nips' specifications. But it was a losing cause, as what they built one day was often destroyed the next. Eventually, either Kavieng would run out of building materials or the gangs would die working.

On our third morning, Sergeant Yoshio announced that there would be no work, in honor of a Japanese holiday. Further, the Emperor had called for a day of forgiveness, so the men in the boxes would be released. To our great delight, we were dismissed until evening roll call.

After helping the Doc take the two men from the ovens back to his infirmary, I started back towards Hut Three. Just as I approached the front door, I heard Corporal Shozo call out my name. Turning and bowing, I saw him walking towards me with his arms full.

"Report to Colonel Hisachi at sixteen hundred. Wear these clothes and shave."

Looking up as he approached, I saw anger in his face. Bowing again while taking his bundle, I answered, "Hai."

With a hateful look, he turned on his boot and walked away.

Inside, I found Jack talking to one of our bunk mates, Sergeant York. When I put the bundle on the bed and unfolded it, I found a clean khaki shirt and a pair of cut-off pants, along with a straight razor and a bar of soap.

"What the hell" York exclaimed. "Where did you get that stuff? We haven't seen soap or a razor for months."

Shaking my head, I told them about having to report to the Colonel at sixteen hundred.

"It's tea time," Black Jack said with a wide grin as I had told him of my first encounter.

"Tea time! You're having tea with that Shelia...God help you...Lieutenant!"

"It's not my idea. And it's not about tea, it's about San Francisco."

"Yeah, sure," the Sergeant replied, shaking his head.

Walking through the front gate just before reporting, I felt like all the eyes in the compound were on me. It gave me a creepy feeling. And even though I was clean for the first time in weeks, I still felt dirty. Why me? The guards outside the fence paid me no attention, although, I thought I could see smirks on some of their faces. Walking up the steps, I knocked on the door. From the inside, I heard the Colonel call, "Raikou" (enter).

Inside, I found Hisachi behind his desk, working with a stack of papers. Marching up to his desk, I braced myself and bowed.

He finished what he was doing before stating, "Stand at ease, Lieutenant." He finally looked up and gazed at me for a moment, then smiled. "Don't you look fine." Checking his watch, he added, "Where has the time gone? We will have tea in my quarters."

He showed me through a paneled sliding door and into a room where there was a seating area on one side and a small, square lacquered table, only two feet high, on the other. Here we crossed our legs and sat down, using pillows on the floor.

Snapping his fingers he said, "I enjoyed our little conversation about San Francisco. It brought back so many good memories."

Just then, another panel slid open and the Korean boy carrying a tray entered the room. He wore a white jacket with a pair of black slacks, and looked to be in his late teens. As he crossed the room, I noticed how tidy the Colonels' quarters were. There were a few rice paper scrolls on the walls, and the wicker furniture sat atop polished wooden floors with tatami mats as rugs. Looking up, I could see a long, large mat hanging sideways from the ceiling, moving back and forth. This mat acted like a fan to cool the room, and was operated by a native laborer sitting outside, pulling ropes. The Colonel had the same set-up in his office.

"This is Toby, my orderly," he said. "He has been with me for years. He takes care of my needs and I have taught him English. Toby, this is Lieutenant Clarke. He is an American."

The Korean boy glared at me and then bowed as he set the tea pot and cups on the table.

"Let me pour, Dutch. May I call you 'Dutch'? That is your Christian name, isn't it?" Hisachi asked.

Watching Toby stand and huff back towards the door, I replied, "Yes, sir."

"Toby, bring us some of your rice cakes. The Lieutenant will enjoy them."

I could tell that the Korean kid didn't like me...but why? Did he see me as a rival?

Oblivious to everything, the Colonel started talking about San Francisco again as he poured the tea and then sat and sipped it. He rambled for the better part of an hour about the city, its people, its places and his photography. I found the tea bitter, the cakes sweet, and the conversation boring. He must have loved to use his English, as he did all the talking.

"What kind of pictures did you take in the city, Dutch?" he finally asked me.

Thinking for a moment, I answered with a half-truth. "Mostly of movie stars...sir."

"Movie stars! Would I know of any of them?"

I reeled off the celebrity names from the USO bash. The Colonel had only heard of Hope and Crosby from their movies, and seemed impressed that I knew them. "Have you ever met Clark Gable? He's my favorite."

Thinking back to reporting in on the Paramount lot, I answered, "Yes, sir...but only in passing."

Toby reappeared with more cakes, placing them on the table as the Colonel continued, "I haven't seen *Gone with the Wind* yet, but I've read the Mitchell book. It's all about the South and freeing the slaves. What a mistake that was. The Negroes are mongrels and their race is impure. Like your Sergeant, they're only worth owning."

With a sour look on his face, Toby turned to leave, just as the Colonel grabbed my arm and said, in loud, superior tones, "Just like the Koreans."

His hand on my arm gave me a creepy feeling and I wanted to push it off.

Instead, I glared across at him and said, "Things have changed since you lived in America, sir…and some of us think the changes have been for the better."

For a heartbeat, he stared at me with his cold-blooded eyes. Had I gone too far?

Taking his hand back from my arm, he grinned and replied, "No politics at tea. Next time, we will talk of your movie star friends. I've always loved American movies."

Then, reaching into his side pocket, he removed two packs of Camels and a silver lighter.

Sliding them across to me, he said, "Here are more cigarettes. I even found one of my old lighters that still works. I know how valuable tobacco is, here in camp." Like a child, he now had a friendly look on his face.

"Don't you smoke anymore, sir?"

Moving from the table, the Colonel answered as he got to his feet. "Only at private times. It's really a filthy habit."

Taking the smokes from the table, I jumped to my feet. He walked back to his office with me following. As he took his chair, I braced myself in front of him and bowed. Just as I started to step backwards, he raised one hand, without looking up, to stop me.

"Things are going to be changing around here soon, so I've found better work for you, Lieutenant. Starting tomorrow, you're off the 'Black Gang' and moved to doctor's assistant. I'll have Sergeant Yoshio get you a pass so you can move around freely with Captain Ross."

Then he did look up, staring me right in the eye. "I might be the best friend you have here, Dutch. But don't confuse kindness with weakness. Do you understand?"

Bowing, I answered, "Yes sir."

Black Days

Her skin was silky soft, and her long, skinny legs were bronze from all the sun. She had blond hair that framed a round face, with big blue eyes that twinkled. When she talked, she made a funny 'hissing' sound, as one front tooth was missing. "Are you really an American?" she asked with a curious smile.

"Yes, one hundred percent Yankee," I said, and smiled back.

"I've never met an American…but then, I've never been off this island."

Gently holding down one of her legs, I watched as the Doc wrapped a bandage around her sprained ankle. Anna was seven, and her mother was in the next room with two more just like her. They were a Kawai family that had ended up in the internment camp right after the Japs invaded New Ireland. Her father had joined the New Zealand Army and marched off to Europe in 1941, thinking his family would be safe on this remote, tiny island. Now they were enslave and he was half a world away.

"Okay, young lady, you're done. Watch where you run or next time I might have to saw your foot off," the Doc said with large grin as he finished the bandage.

I enjoyed working with Captain Ross, and had come to respect him as a caring, loving physician. He was older than most of the guys back at camp, somewhere in his forties. He had graying temples with black hair above a gentle face. He did what he could for his patients, and worked hard, making his 'calls' from town to internment camp and back to our camp. There was little or no medicine to fight all the tropical diseases but he did the best he could. He seemed to like having me as his assistant; if nothing else, I could help him smuggle out his 'fees.'

It had been a week since my visit with Colonel Hisachi, and I was sure by now that the bamboo telegraph had told the whole island what kind of low life I was. The guys back at camp were having a great time ribbing me about having tea with a male Sheila, and how Toby was jealous. I took the ribbing with a smile, but deep down I detested Hisachi and all that he stood for. After my tea, Major Dunn had rushed up to me, pleased that I had befriended the Colonel and wanting the scoop. I had told him everything, including the Colonel's comment about things changing.

"I know what that means," the Major had said. "We will soon be leaving here. I'll bet the Yanks will be on the beach within the week, so the Nips will have to get us out of here before they come."

"I don't know, sir. Hisachi didn't seem very concerned," I answered back.

"They never do. If they did, they would have to admit they're losing."

With rumors of invasion rifling through camp, Black Jack and I made plans to take photos with the spy camera. We agreed not to tell any of our mates about the Minox and only take pictures as what we called 'palm-shots.' This was a method of concealing the camera upright in the palm of your hand while pointing it, and using the thumb to trip the shutter and advance the film. Using this technique correctly, we could get very close to our subjects without being detected. Jack had already taken a half roll of film in camp and down around at the docks.

On this day, I had brought the camera with me and taken a dozen shots of the women, children and guards of the internment camp. It was a hot, dirty, wretched environment for the internees, and my pictures were intended to show the Japs' complacency.

Late in the afternoon, we started walking back to camp, with the Doc explaining all the different medical problems of his patients. Captain Ross worried about each and every one, and made a verbal wish list of the medicines he needed to fight their problems. With any luck, he could trade for a few items, down on the waterfront, with a corrupt Nip Sergeant that seemed to run the entire black market for New Ireland. He hated dealing with this sleaze-ball, but the man was the only source available. As we strolled along, I thought about the word "corrupt" and how funny it was, because the Doc's case was full of vegetables that we had just smuggled out of the internment camp. I guessed, in war, that everyone becomes a little corrupt.

As we approached camp, Doc was the first to comment about the two guards standing over someone sitting under Hisachi's shade tree. From a distance, they were just shadowy figures. As we got closer, the image came into focus, and I realized it was Black Jack on the ground, with his hands tied behind him. Picking up the pace, and with my heart in my mouth, we soon reached Jack.

One side of his head was red and raw, with blood oozing down his face and neck. His left eye was swollen shut and his shirt was caked with mud and ripped to shreds. As we started to kneel down, the guards used their weapons to push us back. Jack looked up at us and, with a pained grimace, slowly shook his head.

"I'm the doctor," Captain Ross thundered, "and this man needs help."

Then we heard the voice of Sergeant Yoshio, from the front porch. "Stay away from the prisoner."

With my mind racing, I turned. Walking towards the Sergeant while bowing, I asked, "May I see Colonel Hisachi, please?"

From inside the open doorway, I heard the Colonel shout, "Hai."

Yoshio backed off as I walked up the steps and into Hisachi's office. He was standing next to his desk, putting on his sword as I approached. Bracing myself while bowing, I asked, "What's all this about, sir?"

Looking at me, red-faced and angry, he scoffed, "What's this all about? It's about your nigger Sergeant almost killing Corporal Shozo." Finishing with his sword he reached across to his desk and picked up a black sock with a large knot tied at one end. "This is full of iron washers. He used it on my Corporal. If three other guards hadn't pulled him off, the Corporal would be dead. As it is, he has a broken arm and a concussion, and he is in the hospital. Your Sergeant dies in five minutes, Lieutenant, and there is no reprieve."

His words smothered me as I searched for my reply. "I'm sure the Corporal provoked it, sir...but don't kill him. Put him in the box. He's worth more alive than dead."

The Colonel walked towards me, slapping the sap between his hands. "Provoked! You Americans started this war, and you stand there blaming Corporal Shozo! No, Lieutenant, he dies. And if you cause trouble," he yelled in his falsetto voice, "you will join him."

"Sir, I ask that you reconsider. You talked about coming back to San Francisco after the war. Well, I have money, my family has money. I can set you up…whatever you want. All I ask is that you reconsider and let Sergeant Malone live. I beg you as a friend, sir."

By now, he stood just next to me. I could smell booze on his breath, and his cold-blooded eyes were twitching wildly.

"You insult me with offers of money that you won't have after the war. You ask for mercy as a friend, but your Sergeant showed no mercy to Shozo. No, Lieutenant. The nigger dies. But I will grant two concessions. He will die at the end of my sword, like a Samurai. And even though some of my soldiers believe the liver of a black man is sweet, I will not allow them to desecrate his body. Now go and say farewell to your Sergeant." He paused looking at his watch. "He has four minutes to live."

I was about to say something more, but Hisachi stopped me with an angry shake of his head, then turned to the doorway, motioning for Yoshio to usher me out.

Rushing down the steps, I knelt next to Jack, with no interference from the guards. He was semi-conscious, still dazed from his beating. Slowly lifting his head, he looked at me with the one good eye. Soon the Doc knelt down next to me and started washing off Jack's face with a wet cloth.

"They're going to kill you, Jack…and there's nothing I can do about it," I mumbled in a near-whisper.

Licking the cloth as it went by his lips, he slowly answered, "I screwed the pooch, Dutch. Shozo came after me with his stick and I just couldn't take it anymore. I told you I would die here."

"What have I done, Black Jack? You should be back at your canteen, not out in this hell-hole. Forgive me!"

His good eye stared at me for a heartbeat. Then, with unexpected power in his voice, he answered, "Wouldn't have missed this dance for the world. My only regret is that I didn't make more of a difference."

"But you did," I said softly with my heart sinking. "Back on Tulun, Riku found battle plans for a raid on the Panama Channel. After we blew the station, he took the plans to Colonel Flag. Because of your actions, we may have saved Panama."

With a forced grin on his lips, he replied, "So that's what those bastards were looking for…and why they didn't kill us. Thanks. I needed to know that."

"It doesn't change what's going to happen…"

"Yeah, it does," he answered back in a whisper. "Use what I taught you. Use the Minox. It's the only weapon you have. Show the world what's happening here."

"Move away from the prisoner. Your time is up," Sergeant Yoshio yelled from the porch.

Instantly, the two guards behind us moved forward, using their rifles to push us back. As I got to my feet, I looked at Jack's mangled face and said, "I love you like a brother. I'll never forget you, and I will tell the world. You have my word. God bless you!"

He nodded and, with his one good eye, winked at me. Then, from the porch, I heard Yoshio blow the whistle for assembly. As the guards shoved the Doc and me through the main gate and into the yard, I kept looking back at Jack. But he had his head down, lost in his final thoughts.

Most of the men had already been milling around the yard, knowing something was up. When the whistle blew for the second time, it only took a few moments to form ranks. As we did, I reached behind my back and slipped out the spy camera. Concealing it in my right palm, I joined one of the front ranks. Within seconds, Major Dunn broke into the same line and stood on my left, with the Padre on my right. Neither said a word. Then two Nips dragged Jack through the gate and towards us, with his hands still tied behind his back, his legs sliding across the dirt. As they did, other guards with bayonets fixed surrounded our three ranks.

Walking just after Jack came Sergeant Yoshio and Colonel Hisachi. As Jack was made to kneel in front of the platform, Hisachi stepped to its top and turned to the group.

"This American pig struck Corporal Shozo, today, so he will die. He made a weapon and then used it on Shozo. Any POW that touches one of my guards will die."

As he rambled on, I took my first picture. *Click.*

With my body shaking from fear, and tears rolling down my face, I stood there, trying to clear my mind. I had to think clearly, to make the images that I had promised Jack. Then Hisachi barked out orders in Japanese, and one of the guards behind Black Jack moved forward with a blindfold.

"No blindfold, you cockroach. And fuck you, Colonel," Jack shouted, looking up at the platform from his kneeling position.

Hisachi stared down on him for a moment and then slowly drew his sword from its scabbard. *Click.*

Stepping down, he shouted, "Okay, blackie, have it your way." He stood above Jack and slowly raised his blade. Click. The Colonel's face was distorted with rage as he yelled, "I honor you like a Samurai and you insult me...Banzai!" *Click.*

Jack's head was high, his body twitching as the blade came down. I looked away and heard a sound like a snapping towel. *Click.* A loud moan rolled from our ranks, while the guards let out a loud cheer. Forcing myself to look back, I watched the Colonel kick Jack's headless body over. *Click.* With blood spurting from his torso, it fell onto his head. I felt faint. *Click.*

Then the Colonel looked straight at me. "All huts and prisoners will be searched. Lieutenant Clarke, step forward."

The men around me let out a gasp as I tried to regain my composure. Was I to be next? I had to find my grit. With all eyes on me, what could I do with the camera? Faking a stumble I fell to my right, onto the Padre. As I did so, I slipped the Minox into his left hand. Out of the corner of my eye, I watched his expression turn to surprise as he felt the small metal object. In a heartbeat, he recovered and took it. Regaining my balance, I moved to the Colonel, not twenty feet away. I wanted to look down at Jack's body, but I didn't. Instead, I stared right into the murdering eyes of Hisachi and, without bowing, approached him.

"Lieutenant Clarke is going to the box...for his own protection. Others will join him, or the dead Sergeant here, if we find more weapons or contraband."

Two guards stepped forward and searched me, while other guards opened the tin lid of the center box. As I was being patted down, I stood there, staring at the Colonel, daring him to look back at me, but he didn't. Then I was shoved towards the box and forced to get in. As I crawled in, I looked back to the ranks and made eye contact with Jasper. He nodded, as if to say the camera was safe, just as I squeezed down and the lid closed.

With my knees to my face in the hot, stuffy box, I listened as Yoshio shouted roll call. Moving my head around, I found a nail hole in the tin where I could see part of the yard. I watched with shock and grief as the men were searched as their names were called. One by one, they were then released to return to their huts.

From my view I couldn't see Jack's body still sprawled on the ground but I knew it was there. Soon the yard was vacant, and I rested my head against the metal wall and wept like a baby. With images of Jack's death rolling through my mind, I lost complete control, crying so hard that I soiled myself and, moments later, threw up on my legs. With the torment of Jack's headless body vivid, I found myself being sucked into a black sinkhole, deep down inside of me. As I tumbled ever deeper into this void, I heard sounds of banging, and then realized that I had been punching the metal box with my fist so hard that my knuckles were bleeding.

Shaking my head, I tried to force myself to think of Black Jack in better times, to hear his voice, to see his smile, to watch him teaching me photography under the zoo's shade tree, oh so long ago. He had indeed been the brother I never had. He had been my mentor, my friend. With his death, a good part of me died. Oh God, what have I done to this man? Why have you taken him?

Time seemed to stand still, but yet slip by…

The next thing I remembered, it was night and, while the box had cooled, my mind hadn't. My grief soon turned to hate, my thoughts to revenge. That night, the last vestige of my innocence was replaced with blind, uncontrollable rage. My anger was so violent, so deep, that it scared even me. I must have planned killing Hisachi a dozen different ways that night, using a dozen different weapons. There were guns, knives, his own sword, piano wire around his nuts…the list went on and on. Each plan ended the same way, with me watching his face as life slowly squished out of his body. I relished the plans and could not concentrate on anything else. The death of Hisachi was now my mission.

Inexplicably, the next morning after 'Enlightenment,' the guards lifted my lid and walked away. Doc Ross and the Padre rushed forward to give me water. As they helped me out of the box, I realized that I was all cried out, with only blood hate and contempt tugging on me.

Back at the infirmary, the Doc wrapped my knuckles and cleaned me up.

"What happened to Jack's body?" I asked.

"We removed it last night." He looked at me hesitantly. "We heard you banging. We buried him early this morning, not knowing you were going to be released," answered the Doc.

"We can have a proper funeral tonight," the Padre added.

Turning to Jasper, I replied, "I'll make the marker. You can say the words. What about the camera?"

Reaching inside his pocket, he handed it to me. "It's right here. You know, you scared the crap out of me when I felt it in my hand. How long have you had this?"

Taking the camera, I explained, "The Nips missed it when they searched me back on Tulun. Jack and I have been shooting pictures around here ever since. How did you get it by the shakedown?"

With a grin of pride, the Padre answered, "While the whole camp was watching you being stuffed into the box, I knelt down and slipped it into my boot. Nobody looks at a man's shoes, not even our dumb guards. But they did find and take your razor."

Shaking my head while relishing the thought, I replied, "Guess there's not going to be any more tea parties."

"Dutch, they'll kill you if they find that camera. I can trade it for you on the black market, if you want," Doc Ross said.

"I'll think about it. Right now, the film inside will vindicate me after I kill the Colonel."

"You're going to do what!" the Doc exclaimed, his jaw dropping.

"I'm going to kill that bastard, the first chance I get. I pledge this on the headless dead body of Black Jack Malone."

Seeing the rage in my eyes, they didn't dare doubt me.

"If you do that, they'll kill us all," the Doc lamented.

Then the Padre added, "Look for redemption, not revenge, Dutch. It's the only way you'll live through this."

I shook my head stubbornly. "I'll look for redemption after I've squeezed the life out of Hisachi, and not before."

After the Padre left for work, the Doc and I walked up to the graveyard. He helped me fashion a cross out of two bamboo sticks, and I placed it at the head of Jack's mound of rocks and dirt. The

Doc reached into his pocket, gave me Jack's dog-tags, and walked away.

I took one tag off the chain and slipped it into my pocket, then hung the remaining tag and chain on the cross. Then, kneeling by the mound next to the crude marker, I prayed.

Due to the rocky soil, Jack's grave was shallow, just like the others he had joined. It was a quiet place, just up from the latrine, and even had some grass and a few wildflowers nearby. After my prayer, I started adding small stones to his mound while I talked to him. I told him of my thoughts, how I felt, how much I loved him...all the things I should have told him in life. Then, standing and looking around at all the other mounds and markers, I pulled out the camera and took a picture, tearfully restating my pledge to show the world what had gone on here.

Late that morning, the Doc and I walked to town to see some patients. At first, he wasn't going to take me, but then he thought better of leaving me behind, given my traumatized mood. As we worked that day, I gained some comfort from having Black Jack's dog-tag inside my pocket. Somehow, having something personal of his close to me lifted my spirits.

The lines were long and the day hot as Doc Ross and a local nurse worked from a store-front clinic downtown. At one point in the afternoon, I stepped outside for some fresh air. As I was about to go back inside, I heard my name being called from up the street. Stopping and looking around, I saw Toby standing just inside an alley, across the way. Looking up and down the near-deserted street, he waved at me to join him. As I walked across and down, he slipped deeper into the shadows of the alley.

Something inside of me said this could be a trap, so I was prepared for anything. But when I turned the corner between the buildings, I found him alone.

"Lieutenant, you see guards on street?" Toby asked in clumsy English.

Looking both ways, I answered, "No."

"I overhear Colonel Hisachi and Sergeant Yoshio talk. There is trouble on wharf tonight, after work." The kid's young, soft face looked sincere, as if he was telling me a secret. "You and the Doctor should stay away. Big trouble."

"What kind of trouble?"

"Don't know. Don't understand all talk. Something about women and children up the road. You stay away…" He looked around furtively. "I leave now."

As he started to walk out of the alley I put my hand on his shoulder. "Why are you telling me? I thought you were friends with the Colonel."

Stopping, he turned and gave me a frenzied look. "That pig? I spit on him. I will piss on his grave! I am a prisoner, like you."

Rushing back to the clinic, I pulled the Doc aside and told him what Toby had said, then explained, "I've got to know what's going on down there, Doc. Can we hang around in town after the work detail returns to camp?"

He hesitated, his face full of concern. "That could be dangerous."

"We can't just walk away without knowing. These are your patients."

"Okay. I can stop off and see the Mayor's wife on my way back to camp, while you go take a look. She's having a difficult pregnancy so it will be good cover. But we have to be back before six o'clock roll call or we'll end up in the box." Reaching into his pants, he took out a pocket watch. "Here. You take this and make sure you're back to the Mayor's house no later than 5:45. You know his house, on the way back?"

"Yes. Where did you get this? I didn't think any of us knew the right time."

"The Mayor has a clock in his home. I'll keep an eye on it. I'm out of there at 5:45 with or without you so don't be late. That gives us just enough time to make roll call. Don't be late Dutch. I want that watch back. It was given to me by one of the women at the internment camp. It was her father's."

We heard the work gang march back towards camp at about four-forty, right after which I started making my way down to the piers. To get there, I snuck from alley to alley, across two streets and down three blocks, stopping between a couple of buildings that looked out over the docks.

On my right, the wharf was open and exposed, with only a few piles of cannibalized beams and planks that the White Gang had stacked for construction. The waterside of the wharf connected to the only three piers that still stood, after all the bombings. Floating just below the third pier down, in front of the skeletal remains of a warehouse, was a small barge. Aboard this garbage scow was the charred debris that the Black Gang had removed, earlier that day. Other than a few seabirds, the wharf and bay looked deserted.

Not knowing what to expect, I decided to hide and wait. Cautiously I moved down the dock until I was behind the stack of building materials. Then, crouching down, I found a good place to hide between two rows of beams with some view of the wharf. As I got into position, I clicked open the pocket watch to check the time. It read just before 5 o'clock. It would take fifteen minutes to reach the mayor's house and another fifteen to get back to camp, so I would have to leave the wharf no later than five-thirty.

Replacing the watch with the spy camera, I checked my light. The sun was low in the sky and behind my left shoulder, good light for anything I wanted to see or photograph. Taking a few deep breaths, I tried to get my body to relax as I settled down to wait.

It was so quiet behind those beams that I soon started having doubts about Toby. What the hell would he know? He was just a Sheila. The whole thing could be a set-up, engineered by Colonel Hisachi to test what we would do. Why was I here? There was nothing I could do but take pictures, even if there was trouble...

With my mind lost in grief and doubts, I waited.

Half-hour later, just as I was preparing to leave, I heard the sound of motors rolling down the wharf at the far end. Looking up from my thoughts, I found three trucks moving my way. The first truck was open in the back and carried a dozen or more guards, while the last two trucks had canvas covering their cargo areas.

The front truck rolled right up to where I was hiding and stopped. From the passenger side of the cab, Sergeant Yoshio jumped out, barking orders as the guards dismounted. They were so close to me that I recognized most of them from our camp or the internment camp.

The last two trucks came to a stop on the other side of the guards' truck, which partially blocked my view. From the rear of those trucks, I could hear the loud sobs of women and children. I watched as some of the guards moved down to the pier next to the garbage scow, while others moved behind the covered trucks. The guards started dragging out some blindfolded internees, with their hands tied behind their backs. Women with infants had their hands free, holding their babies in their arms, but they, too, were blindfolded. As small groups were dragged out of the trucks, they were forced to move down to the pier. Soon, the evening air filled with sounds of fear and confusion, with the children screaming, women weeping, guards yelling.

Because of where Yoshio's truck was parked, I couldn't quite see what was happening on the pier. Frantically, I looked around for a better vantage point. Just down the wharf, I spotted a better place, inside the old warehouse. But getting there would require moving in the open for some forty or fifty feet. With my heart racing and not really thinking, I made the dash across the dock towards the charred warehouse.

The run only took a few heartbeats, before I slid behind the remains of a burned-out wall.

I was lucky; the guards were distracted by the prisoners, and no one noticed me. The wobbly wall had a few boards missing, which opened my view down to the pier. It was then that I realized what was going on. At first, I couldn't believe my eyes, and I had to force myself to point and shoot the camera. The small groups of women and children were forced to kneel at the edge of the pier, facing the garbage scow. Standing just behind the group was Sergeant Yoshio, with his sword waving in the air. He would scream out orders and guards would come up behind each hostage, one at a time, where, using wire lines, they would brutally strangle the internee. As their bodies went limp from the strangling, Yoshio moved over and stuck his sword through their torsos, then used his boot to kick the dead women and children over and onto the floating barge. Woman with babies had the infants ripped out of their hands and killed first, while the guards tied the mothers' hands and then killed them. Some victims did nothing, while others resisted, but to no avail.

The barge soon had bodies sprawled across the blackened debris. Traumatized, I watched as the next group, with little Anna, her sisters and her mother, were pushed, blindfolded and tied, from the trucks to the pier. Her mother screamed and begged for mercy, but she and her family were forced to kneel dockside.

As the guards approached the family from behind, I looked away. I could not take any more...see any more...hear any more. The camera was shaking in my hands as I pushed the shutter without watching. Mercifully it was the last frame of film, as my fingers could no longer advance the lever. With tears running down my face, I slipped the camera into my pocket and searched for an escape route.

I really don't recall how I got off the wharf. The next thing I remember was running towards the mayor's house. I felt so helpless, so useless. There had been nothing I could do to help those women and children. I had to just sit there, watching the brutal slaughter. In less than twenty-four hours, I had seen Black Jack murdered and now this...all without lifting a finger to stop it.

What kind of people could do this? As I ran and cried, a voice deep inside me kept screaming back, 'Buck up! Buck up! You have to live!'

Turning the corner to the mayor's house, I saw Doc Ross jogging towards the camp, just ahead of me. Running as fast as my bum hip would take me, I caught up.

"You're late Lieutenant," the Doc panted angrily as we ran.

Jogging next to the Doc without a sob or a tear, I blurted out what I had just seen and photographed. As my story unfolded, I saw the Doc's face wince and his eyes moisten at my description of the deaths.

He said not another word, and he let me finish before he abruptly stopped, grabbing onto my arm. "We can't tell this story to our mates or they'll panic. The Nips must be afraid the invasion is coming, and we might be next. Don't say a word until I have talked with the Major."

The Doc's sweat-filled face was red with anger and worry. Handing the pocket watch back to him, I nodded my agreement. Then we turned and resumed running.

We made it back to camp just as the gates were closing for evening roll call. After chow, Jasper conducted a grave-side service for Jack. Almost the whole camp gathered around the little cemetery. Standing on the hillside in the fading light, the Padre gave a sermon and prayed with the men. I really can't remember a word he said, as I was lost in my own thoughts of Black Jack and the massacre on the wharf.

When the Padre asked if I wanted to say anything, I shook my head no. There were no words that could express the pulsations of anger, hatred and revenge that were pulling at my soul. The Major and the Doc did say a few words, and then everyone filed away, leaving me alone. Kneeling next to Black Jack's grave, I quietly told him of the God-awful events of the day. With tears rolling down my cheeks, I swore to him that I would not forget or forgive. There would be retribution that I promised.

Walking back to my hut in the dark, I told myself that there would be no more weeping, no more sobs. I would live to see the dead bodies of Colonel Hisachi and Sergeant Yoshio lying next to each other.

Stopping behind my shack I unloaded the spy camera. The rolled-up strip of 16mm film was too bulky to fit into the black glass pill bottle the Doc had given me and so, unrolling the film, I ripped it in half. Then, carefully, I wrapped each half in foil from a cigarette pack, slid these two rolls inside the tiny bottle, and secured the bottle tightly with a cork plug. Once the vial was secured, I held it in my hand, thinking about its contents....

Someday, somewhere, somehow, I would develop this film and show the world.

The next morning, at roll call, we were informed that internees had been 'relocated' to another camp. Only the Doc, Major Dunn, Jasper and I knew about my film and this lie. The four of us had agreed not to tell the rest of the camp, as we feared we might be next. After chow, I walked to the infirmary, where I found the Doc and the Major talking.

As I approached them, I handed the Minox to Doc and said, "What do you think you can get for this?"

Quickly slipping it into his pocket and out of view, he answered, "Hard telling. As much quinine as I can get, and maybe some morphine."

Looking him directly in the eye, I added, "And a carton of cigarettes and a condom."

Both the Major and the Doc eyed me, startled by this strange request. "You plannin' a party, mate?" the Major shot back.

It took me a moment to understand what they were thinking, and how silly my request must have sounded. "No," I assured them, "the smokes are for the guys in camp, compliments of Black Jack Malone. He owned half of that camera. And the condom is for protection of the film, and to hang it on my dog-tag chain."

They both nodded their heads in solemn understanding, and it was agreed.

That evening, after stuffing the vial into a condom and tying it to my chain, I reminded myself how important it was to keep the rubber hidden under my t-shirt. If the Nips found it, I'd be dead. Then I walked around camp, handing out the cigarettes. At first, the guys were a little dumbstruck, receiving a smoke from a dead man, but they soon caught on to the spirit of the offer. Many thanked Jack and talked of his grit in calling the Japs cockroaches. Somehow, this simple gesture on his behalf seemed to help me with my grief.

Palau

The next evening, after roll call, we were told to gather up our belongings and prepare to leave camp. Later, as we moved towards the wharf, I feared our fate…but then realized that the guards marching us had full backpacks. If they were going to kill us, surely they would not have packed up. Once on the wharf, we were loaded onto three open barges, and after nightfall we started a long and dangerous trip north to the islands of Palau. There we would build and repair an airstrip outside of a town, on Peleliu, by the name of Goikul.

Conditions were deplorable; our camp was nothing more than ragged tents, with barbwire strung around its perimeter. The weather was hot and humid, with torrential rains almost every day.

One moment, you could be roasting in the hot sun; the next, you were ankle-deep in a quagmire of mud. Our food was nothing more than sub-standard rice and beans, with little or no meat. Soon we took to catching rats, bugs, and a few birds to add to our cook pots. With weight falling off my body like apples off a tree, my thoughts of revenge were soon replaced by thoughts of survival.

On the high coastal plains where we labored, there was nothing we could grow, smuggle or steal. The few pieces of Jap heavy equipment we were required to use were old, rusty and unreliable. The Aussies spent more time fixing the machines than using them. Our routine was simple: work and survive. Days melted into weeks, weeks into months. During our entire stay, we didn't see Colonel Hisachi. Only later did we learn that he had commandeered a beach-front bungalow in Goikul, where he spent his time in meetings. We did see Sergeant Yoshio a few times each week, but when the weather got bad or the work hard, we would look up and he would be gone. Finally, the Japs got so desperate to get the airstrip completed that our guards were forced to work beside us. At first, we thought watching the guards working in the hot sun would give us pleasure, but it didn't, as their living conditions weren't much better than ours. As they labored, their sad, sweat-filled faces told the story: they deplored Yoshio as much as we did. In some ways, I almost felt sorry for them.

By the end of July, we had repaired and lengthened one runway and built another. Soon the little airfield was filled with Nip planes and flyboys. With our work completed and rumors of another American devil invasion circulating, we were marched off the field and into trucks for transfer to another camp. As we pulled out, we prayed for the five souls we were leaving behind. Three had died from disease, one from an accident, and one at the brutal hands of Sergeant Yoshio. With the victims' names etched in our minds, we were herded into the dark, dirty, forward hold of a small freighter. Once the hatch cover was dogged down, we set out for an unknown destination.

Our Hell Ship moved slowly in a direction we could not determine. The freighter had been used to bring livestock for the troops on Peleliu, so the hold we were crowded into was littered with soiled straw and cow dung. To say it stunk would be an understatement. The forward cargo space was about fifty feet long and thirty wide, with a twenty-foot-square cover some thirty feet above us. The only light inside our darkened tomb came from a single bulb dangling just below the closed hatch cover. During the days, the tropical sun roasted our little space like the hot boxes back on Kavieng. At times, our hold reached over 120 degrees, with the metal plates as hot as irons. Our only relief was when the guards would open part of the hatch and hose us down with seawater.

Adding to this misery, we were given no drinking water during the entire voyage. Every day, when the guards rolled back a corner of the hatch cover to hose us down, we would scream up for drinking water, but we only received saltwater for our efforts. Our only food was a metal drum of cooked rice, once a day, which was rationed out by Major Dunn and Doc Ross. After the second day, some men took to drinking the little amount of urine their bodies could pass. Doc Ross advised against it, but they did it anyhow. On the third night out, I realized the prospects of living through this endless voyage were getting slim; if things didn't change, some of my mates would die.

The next morning, many of the men stopped moving around, stopped talking, and stopped caring. They just sat and stared into the darkness of the Hell Ship, lost in their own tormented thoughts. Each morning, the Padre would stand among us and lead us in prayer. His words were always full of comfort, love and redemption, but they seemed to do little for those who had given up and those who were about to. We were spent, we were thirsty, we were hungry, and we were lost.

Then, on the third day, when the guards removed the hatch cover there was no hose, no seawater. Instead, the entire cover was removed, and falling through the shafts of sunlight was rain…sweet, cool, wet rain. It took us a moment to realize the gift, but when we did, we all crowded under the open hatch with our mouths open. Soon there were over a hundred and fifty dirty, gaunt faces looking skyward, letting the rain wash away our grime, fill our parched throats and lift our spirits.

Then, from topside, one of the guards screamed down, "Welcome to Mindanao."

Mindanao

At first, I had no idea where Mindanao was. After talking with the Padre, I realized we were on the southern tip of the second largest island of the Philippines. After being offloaded from the freighter, we were marched through a town by the name of Davao. Some five miles later, we came into a new camp.

If Peleliu had been a hell hole, Penal Colony #502 was heaven. Before the war, it had held convicted civilian prisoners from all over the southern Philippines. After the war started, it held over five hundred American POW's as farm labors, until they were transferred to Manila in June of 1944. The facilities were large, constructed with cinder-block and tin roofs. The windows were still open and the floors still dirt, but we had barracks for the men, and a working latrine, with showers. There was even a covered assembly area for morning enlightenment.

The guards had just about the same kind of quarters, outside our ten-foot fenced-in perimeter. But the best news was that the fields around our camp were full of rice, fruit and vegetables, planted by the Americans.

Finally, we seemed to have caught some luck.

But what the Japs gave with one hand, they took back with another. Our job was to complete a narrow-gauge railroad that connected, some hundred and twenty-five miles north, to Butuan. The project had been started by a Nip engineering battalion, the year before, but then they, too, were transferred to Manila. What remained was a thirty-mile stretch of tracks cut into the sides of the mountains in the center of Mindanao. The jungle this roadbed snaked through was hot, humid and horrific, which made the work miserable, with terrible weather and demanding guards. We labored from sun-up to sun-down, and our only rest came on the train ride to and from the railhead. The only tools we used were what we carried: picks, shovels and axes. We were lucky to complete a few hundred yards of track a day, which was way below our keepers' expectations.

The Japs tried everything to increase our production. We were beaten, kicked and whipped, all to no avail. The 14th Regiment was just too weak and too sick to work any harder. Finally, after a month of this brutal treatment, Doc Ross convinced Colonel Hisachi to allow the sickest POW's to remain in camp, harvesting some of the food in the fields. These vegetables and fruits would be used in both the guards' and prisoners' cook pots. He also talked the Colonel into a shorter workday, more medicine, and -- most importantly -- dynamite to help us clear the roadbed.

Within a week of these changes, our production doubled, and the guards backed off their deplorable treatment.

We were luckier than most, as Hisachi needed the railroad completed by the first of December; if we all died while building it, he would be held responsible. Ever so slowly, with the increase of medicine and food supply, our energy heightened and our outlook brightened. By the end of September, we were confident that the narrow-gauge line would be finished on time. The Japs would have their rail link, connecting the port city of Davao north to the Mindanao Sea. This link would be used for transferring men and materials north for the expected invasion of the Philippines.

Most of my time on Mindanao was spent trying to stay alive, sane and human. In the first few months of building the railroad, the war had seemed to slip right by us. The only planes we saw were Japs, and the only soldiers were IJA. We had no idea what was going on outside our little hell-hole. There were no newspapers or radios, and if the guards knew anything, they certainly weren't telling us. All we had to go on were rumors, which ran though camp faster than dysentery.

One of these rumors was that the Japanese government had proclaimed that all POW's on the Philippines be executed if the Americans invaded. Only later did we find out that this rumor was true and that the Nips would kill thousands of POW's under the terms of this proclamation.

Towards the end of October, our war returned with the first bombings of Davao. Hundreds of carrier-based planes came swooping down, three days in a row. They targeted the docks, the warehouses and the shipping lanes inside the harbor. On the third morning, while riding the train to the railhead, we looked down from our mountain tracks and watched the planes making their runs. They were mostly dive bombers making large arcs in the sky and then plunging straight down at the targets. We could hear their motors squeal, see the bombs release, and then hear and see the yellow-red flashes from the explosions. We wanted to yell and scream our approval, but the sour expressions on our guards' faces forced us to think better of it. That evening, when we returned, the shoreline fires were still smoldering, and we could see two half-sunken ships out in the bay. It was a glorious sight, one that brought smiles to all of our faces.

That same evening, as I returned to camp, I was summoned to report to Colonel Hisachi. This would be the first time I had seen the Colonel close-up since Camp Ireland...but why now? As I walked towards his office, I wondered whether we would be alone, and whether I'd have the grit and strength to kill him. Was this the opportunity I had dreamed about?

When I got to his office and was admitted, however, I found Hisachi and Sergeant Yoshio beating an American flyboy with a singing stick. The young ensign had his hands tied behind his back, and he was sitting on a stool just in front of the Colonel's desk, with two other soldiers standing guard. The kids face was puffy red and smeared with blood. He wore a still-damp, oil-stained khaki flight suit, with a half-inflated yellow Mae West lifejacket around his neck. His brown hair was freshly cut and attached to a square-shouldered, well-fed body.

Looking up from his bloody stick, the Colonel said, "Good. You are here, Lieutenant. Your countryman was shot down, this morning, and we fished him out of the bay. He has great bushido and won't talk to us. But the Kempeitai will be here soon. I want you to give him the scoop...or he won't live out the night."

Bowing to the Colonel, I asked in Japanese for water and a cloth. Hisachi nodded and thundered out for Toby. Moving closer, I knelt on the floor next to the ensign to get a better look at his raw face. The young flyboy was scared, and when I put my hand on his head, I could feel his whole body shake. In a soft tone, I told him it would be okay.

Soon, Toby was standing by me, offering water and a wash cloth. When I looked up at him to take the bowl, he flashed me a grin, his droopy, sad eyes adding a thousand unspoken words.

As I started cleaning up the flyer, the Colonel told Sergeant Yoshio to go outside and wait for the Kempeitai.

"Ensign," I said loudly, working the cloth, "the Japanese never signed the Geneva Convention, since their soldiers never surrender. The only rules out here are their rules."

The flyer's moist blue eyes showed surprise at my overacted statement. I was just about to continue when the phone on the Colonel's desk rang. Answering it, Hisachi turned his back on us.

Leaning forward, I whispered quickly in the ensign's ear. "What's the news? We don't know what's going on."

A startled look raced across his face, and he whispered back, "MacArthur landed on Leyte, last week, and the Japs are on the run."

"What about Rabaul and New Ireland?"

"Cut-off and by bypassed."

"And Palau?"

"The 1st Marines landed in September and are kicking butts. Do you speak Japanese, sir? What are they going to do with me?"

Letting him drink from the bowl of water, I looked him right in the eye and whispered, "I speak a little Nip. The Japs coming to get you are bad sons-of-bitches. You were lucky to be picked up by the Colonel here. He likes Americans. Take as much punishment as you can from the Kempeitai, but in the end you should tell them what they want to know. If they respect your courage, you just might live. What's your name?"

The flyboy looked more confused than ever. "He likes Americans? He beat the shit out of me. That's not fair. My name's Asbow. Doug Asbow."

"Well, listen to me, Doug. There ain't nothing fair out here. If you want to live, tell them what you know."

"Lieutenant, what are you whispering about, down there?" Hisachi bellowed as he hung up the phone.

Jumping to my feet, I bowed in his direction and answered, "Giving the ensign the scoop, sir."

Moments later, Yoshio came back into the office and announced that the Kempeitai were outside, waiting. The Colonel handed the Sergeant some papers and then ordered the guards to remove the flyboy. As the ensign stood up, I caught his eye and tried to give him an encouraging look. But as he was shoved through the doorway, he still looked scared and confused.

I only hoped he would heed my advice.

With their exit, it dawned on me that I was finally alone with Hisachi. How was my courage? Turning to confront him, I found him standing right next to me, holding the silver dagger from his desk.

"You look like hell, Dutch...but I still miss our little talks. I wish I could trust you."

Squeezing my fist tight, I glared back at his cold-blooded eyes, "Will that be all, sir?"

He thought a long moment, with the stiletto in hand, and then scoffed, "You disappoint me, Lieutenant. All this over a dead Nigger? Dismissed."

Walking back to my hut, I thought about how Americans were plowboys and cowboys, but we were also flyboys. This notion lifted my spirits. With my updated war news, the camp buzzed like a beehive for weeks. Leyte was just three hundred miles north, and we all hoped that liberation would soon come. But after a few days, when the bombers stopped coming, we had to face the reality that Mindanao had more than likely been bypassed.

With the last spike on the last rail, and with no fanfare, the narrow-gauge line opened on December 2nd. We stood and watched in awe as car after car of troops and materials snaked their way over the mountains to defend the northern shoreline from the American devils.

Some of us felt bad that we had helped the Nip war effort, but what the hell could we do about it? In the end, the thirty-mile stretch of tracks cost three lives: two from accidents and one poor sap that just walked off into the jungle and was later found dead. The Doc never did figure out what killed him; we guessed that he just gave up.

With the rail line completed, and no more attacks on Davao, our next job was repairing the docks and piers from the October bombings. The work was much the same as on Kavieng as we worked in three gangs, tearing down, scrounging material and rebuilding. All the men were pleased to be out of the hot, steamy jungle, working waterside again. Soon we were stealing anything and everything we could find on the wharfs.

Our guards must have known about the battle raging on Leyte as, in the passing weeks and months, their treatment towards us turned more brutal again. In the middle of December, we were forced to build three bakkin kou inside the compound. The very next morning, three of the guys were stuffed into the boxes for two days. Their crime: not bowing low enough.

But, just like the wind, this attitude changed again on Christmas Day. At morning enlightenment, Colonel Hisachi made a surprise appearance and announced it as a day of rest, then ordered that Red Cross parcels be handed out to all of the men. The Padre told me that this was just the second time in three years that they had seen such parcels. And what gifts they were! Blankets, underwear, socks and khaki shorts and shirts were distributed, and each box also had cigarettes, soap, tooth powder and coffee or tea. Some even contained safety razors, shaving cream, aspirin, suntan lotion, foot powder and the biggest prize of all...toilet paper! It was, without a doubt, the biggest grab-bag of things we all needed but didn't have.

That night, with our guards looking the other way, we all sat in the assembly hall, drinking stolen sake, sharing and exchanging items. What surprised me was how the Aussies treated their mates. What one man needed, another would offer or trade. There were no arguments, no whining, just one bloke helping another. After three years of traumatizing captivity, the Australian soldiers remained uncommonly common.

The Last Voyage

Right after the first of the year, the bombers came back with a vengeance. Just like on New Ireland, what we built or repaired one day would be destroyed the next. While the Nips had fortified their antiaircraft guns, and tried to provide air cover with their own planes, our Navy just had too much might.

On some occasions, we could watch these great air battles from the questionable safety of bomb shelters alongside the harbor. Hundreds of American fighters and light bombers would swoop in from the south, dodging flak, depositing death and destruction. The explosions rocked the bay with so much force that buildings fell just from the concussions. The amber-red fireballs from the bombs would reach to the skies, with smoke plumes over five thousand feet high. What an awesome and frightening sight!

Soon, the harbor facilities were down from ten to two serviceable docks, and the bay was littered with sunken and half-sunk ships of every description. Our gangs worked long and hard down on the wharfs but, just like a dog I had as a kid, I knew we were only chasing our tails. It took weeks, but soon even the Japs realized that we, their slaves, were fighting a losing battle. What only months before had been a vital transportation link for all of Mindanao was now in ruins, and there wasn't anything that anyone could do about it. And, to add insult to injury, some of the local Filipinos had told us that MacArthur had taken Leyte and moved north to Luzon and Manila. It seemed like the Japs were on the run everywhere in the Philippines except where we were.

At the end of February, we were told that the Regiment was being transferred to the home islands of Japan. The trip, which would cover more than two thousand miles, was scheduled to depart the next morning, and we could carry aboard only personal items wrapped in a single blanket. If we tried to smuggle food, water, booze or any other contraband, we would be shot on the spot.

The next morning, before daybreak, we marched to the docks and were loaded into the rear cargo hold of a Hell Ship by the name of Nissho Maru. As I waited in line at the gangway, I noticed Colonel Hisachi supervising the loading of fruit and vegetables into the forward cargo hold. In the first rays of the morning sun, he looked down from his perch on the flying bridge and nodded at me.

I looked away. If I was going to kill him, I would have to wait until we reached Japan.

Glancing out to the bay, I saw other freighters and two destroyers with steam up, waiting for our departure. Our trip to Japan would be a small convoy...and a perfect target.

Moments later, I was crawling down a ladder to the deck of the aft hold. With the hatch cover still open, we could clearly see what would be our home for the next days if not weeks, until -- and if -- we reached Japan. At least the hold deck was cleaner than the last freighter had been, and the Nips had even provided some wooden 'honey-buckets' in one corner. What we couldn't find was any sign of water or food. We knew these provisions would only be provided at the whims of guards.

Half an hour later, the hatch cover was dogged down. Then with only a single light burning, the ship quivered, groaned, and slowly departed Mindanao.

The tomb in which we were entrapped was larger than the last freighter, and the Major soon had us organized into our work gangs. These groups would eat and drink in order, if and when the Nips provided us with food and water. During the day, the tomb was like an oven, and during the night it was a refrigerator. We thanked God and the Red Cross for our blankets.

After dark on the first day, the Nips sent down a drum of water and another full of a rice gruel, just enough for every man to have a half cup of each. During the day, I must have sweated two cups of fluid and pissed another, so half a cup of water didn't even come close to meeting my needs. It wouldn't take long before we were all dehydrated. And the food was full of Nip garbage. There were onion skins, fruit peels and other discarded pieces of vegetables mixed in with the rice. The guards must have thought they were slopping the hogs, as that was the kind of food we got. By the end of the first day, the men got edgy, fearing they wouldn't live through the long, slow trip. The Padre did what he could to reassure them, but his words couldn't fill a belly or quench a thirst.

We were three or four days out, with no one quite sure since time had been lost to our misery, when it happened. Sitting in the dark aft corner, I was listening to the thrashing of the ship's single propeller when all of a sudden its pitch changed and the boat abruptly turned. Placing my ear on the hull, I heard the vibrations quicken, and then detected a faint explosion in the distance. Seconds later, there was another explosion, but this one was close, real close. The convoy was under attack!

Jumping to my feet and moving inward, I screamed for the guys to move away from the hull and into the center of the hold. Just as my mates started moving, an explosion hit the iron plates, almost dead center on the port side. The concussion threw us all to the deck as the boat rocked from the blast. In a heartbeat, the hold filled with shrapnel that ricocheted around, blowing out our one light bulb and injuring some of the men.

Instantly, our darkened tomb filled with cries of pain and heavy black smoke. Slowly scrambling to my feet, I tried to get my bearings. As the smoke started dissipating, I could see a faint light and feel cool air rushing in from outside. Turning, I stepped over a few dazed mates and stumbled towards the opening. It was night out, and the jagged hole was big, about twenty feet around. Sea water was rushing in, as some of our deck plates were below the water line. Looking out, I could see one of the destroyers on fire and sinking, some two hundred yards beyond. The waters surrounding the mired boat were ablaze from oil and fuel. The light from those fires trickled into our tomb and revealed the death and destruction all around me. Through the haze, I could see the Doc and Major Dunn helping the wounded to the high, far corner of the starboard hold.

Boom…another explosion rocked the boat forward of our compartment. The Hell Ship was sinking, and we would all be trapped if we didn't get out. Turning back to the sea, I watched the bow of the destroyer slip under the water. Then, amazingly, a Nip life raft shot out of the water like a champagne cork. As it landed back on the sea's surface, the flickering oil fires showed it floating right side up, not a hundred yards away.

"What should we do?" one of the men standing next to me yelled, with firelight washing his scared face.

"This tub is sinking! I'm going for that raft," I screamed back while driving into the ocean and swimming away.

CHAPTER ELEVEN

"**D**o you believe in God, Dutch?" the Padre asked, with his body propped up against the side of the raft, and a breeze in his matted hair. He looked ten years older than he had, just the day before. His lips were swollen, his face gaunt, his clothes ripped to shreds. He looked the way I felt.

"I don't know...," I answered slowly. "I think so,"

Looking across at me with sadness, Jasper added, "I lost my faith five years ago, when my wife and baby died at birth. I fell apart, didn't know what to do...what to believe. Then I joined the Regiment and found my faith again through the men. Now they're all gone." He sighed. "Did you go to church?"

We hadn't said a word to each other since flipping the raft over, at daybreak. Now, however, the Padre was chatty.

"No. Didn't know you'd been married...sorry," I answered with a half lie. I had gone to church back at Camp Pendleton, and before that I lived in God's wilderness church in British Columbia. My faith ran deep, and while I might be questioning it now, it was just too complicated and I didn't have the energy to talk. The typhoon had taken it out of me. The night before, we had held on tight to the webbing of the capsized raft for what seemed like an eternity. With the ocean boiling, the wind howling and the night as black as hell, it had been a nightmare.

"That's too bad...I wish I had a church to go to right now...I need to know why."

He looked a little crazed as he talked, but then, he was dying. We both were dying. "Bricks and mortar don't make a church," I told him. "I think we're in one right now. Just look around...God's here."

Slowly, he nodded, forcing a small grin, then turned and gazed out towards the sunrise, lost in his yesterdays and praying for our tomorrows.

Watching Jasper for a while, with my throat swollen, I wondered why, too. Finally, my heavy eyelids found the marks I had made in the side of the raft. This morning would be the seventeenth, but I had no way of marking the event. Gone was the bayonet, the canteen, the coconut shells...everything. Hell, I didn't even have boots anymore. Grabbing the rubber hanging from my neck, I was relieved to feel it and know it was still there. But for what? Film that would never be developed...pictures that would never be seen...events soon forgotten.

It was then that I realized that my daydream had been a pipedream. The film, like me, was doomed and lost.

Crawling to the far corner of the raft, I propped myself up with my arms resting on its sides and looked to the sky. Soon I was lost in disjointed thoughts with fuzzy images. My mind kept playing cruel tricks on me. I saw my mother in the distance, motioning me to join her... Then there was Laura, holding her baby, shaking her head, saying, "Not now...Dutch, not now." Closing my eyes, I knew I was hallucinating.

When I opened them again, I found Black Jack sitting next to me, holding the film in one hand, roaring, "It's all here, Dutch! It's all here."

Startled I cried out, "Why?" But he disappeared.

How long I sat there, hours or days, I just don't know. What my last thoughts were or whether I said anything more, I don't know, either. I do remember dreaming of heaven, and angels, and a big white bird.

When this bird flew over me, its big wings blocked the sun, and I feared it was time for me to go. Then an angel knelt next to me, dressed not in white but in powder blue, holding my hand.

Somehow, I was soon in the belly of the bird, with other angels looking down at me. One of them reached towards the condom.

Jack's voice rang out in my head, "The film, Dutch!"

I grabbed for my chain and clutched the vial tight in my hand.

Then the angel said, "It's okay, Mac. You're safe. I just need to know your name. You're on your way home."

CHAPTER TWELVE

L ady Death had woven her long fingers through the hairs on my chest while whispering in my ear about forgiveness. Then she kissed me with that sweet taste of redemption. With her call, warm and seductive, this temptress was drawing me ever closer...

Why I closed my ears to her siren song, I will never know.

It was months later that I finally learned of the chain of events that led to our rescue. The typhoon we had lived through had swept across the Central Pacific, wreaking havoc with shipping. Many vessels were reported floundering or sinking. As soon as the weather improved, Catalina's out of the Marianas started flying lifeguard missions. Our PBY, Zulu-Henry-One-Five-One, was on her trip home after a second day of search duty, some three-hundred miles east of Guam, when they sighted our raft. They flew over us twice, trying to identify whether we were storm survivors or the enemy. After the second look-see, the crew talked on the intercom about leaving us behind, because they believed we were dead Japs on a Nip raft. Their mission was life-saving, not morgue duty.

Luckily, the pilot decided to land his plane in the sea next to us and send out a recovery boat. The first sailors to row over almost didn't check us for life, as they were so confident we were dead. But they did, and realized we were barely alive -- and white. Somehow, they got us back to the PBY and loaded us aboard, for the flight back to Guam. In a heartbeat, their mission had turned again to life-saving.

The date was March 28, 1945. We had spent nineteen days on the Pacific Ocean in an open life raft. We had lost three souls, and the two of us that remained held onto life by only a thread, but we had completed a feat some said was near impossible.

My recollections of Guam are as foggy as a summer costal morning. I do remember the angels on Guam were dressed in white, that they smelled of ether, and that a ceiling fan was always working above me, the few times I opened my eyes. Later, I learned that one of the nurses had tried to remove the rubber from my neck and, even though I was in a coma, I grabbed onto her hand with such force that she let go. The doctors must have told her to forget it, as the condom was still hanging on me when I regained consciousness.

Both the Padre and I were put in an isolation ward, as the staff worried about how contagious our tropical diseases might be. My medical records say that, the first time they weighed us, I came in at one-hundred-fifteen pounds, and Jasper at one-hundred-one. I had lost over fifty pounds since basic training, and the Padre was off nearly seventy pounds. We were nothing more than scarecrows, and what remained was a long list of symptoms the doctors and staff worked hard to treat. We suffered from exposure, malaria, dysentery, jaundice, dengue fever, and other aliments only described in books. We would be on fire one minute, with chills and shakes the next, and the night sweats were so bad that our bedding had to be changed constantly. For the first few weeks, we were mostly unconscious. We just lay in bed with all kinds of tubes sticking in and out of our bodies, unable to communicate. While I can't remember physical pain, I do recall my dark muzzy dreams of the dead. Not a day or a night went by without revisiting images of Black Jack and the women and children on the wharf. Through the hazy I could see their fear and hear their screams. Why had I lived? What was the purpose of it all?

My first clear vision came in the middle of April, when we were loaded into ambulances and driven to the docks. When my stretcher was removed from the back, I looked across the water and saw the biggest and most beautiful hospital ship I had ever seen, the *USS Relief.* Her sleek design, with a bold red cross painted on her white sides, glistened in the sunlight.

One of the sailors carrying me looked down and said, "There's your ticket home, Mac."

The Way Back

The first thing I remember about the *USS Relief* was that our ward was air-conditioned. That might sound trivial but, after years in the tropics, it was a luxury beyond compare. The doctors and nurses were top-notch and, even though we were stuck in isolation again, our care was outstanding.

As the ship started steaming towards Hawaii, I was sitting up and moving around a little. On the first day out, the ship received the shocking news that FDR had died. Lying in my bed, I thought about this great man and his vision for America. I prayed for our new president, Harry S. Truman, a man I knew next to nothing about. It would be years later that I had the opportunity to meet President Truman, and by then the world knew that, with divine guidance, one great man had replaced another. But, at this time and place, it was hard to imagine America without FDR.

Somehow though, I suspected the future was bright, even for the poor souls aboard this mercy ship. On the third day out, with my resolve lifted and my body recovering, I convinced the doctors to remove all my tubes and allow me to eat solid foods -- that is, if you consider Jell-O and soup 'solid.' By the end of the week, I was up and walking around.

Our ship was full of brave, wounded marines from the battle for Iwo Jima, and a few of MacArthur's boys from the battle of Luzon. We also carried POWs from all over the Philippines. Of these POWs, I was one of the lucky ones; all of the other guys in our ten-bed ward, including Jasper, were still drugged up and having a tough time. During the nights I would listen to them cry out and sob, as their minds relived their tragedies. These screams for help would bring on a hopeless feeling inside of me, because there was nothing I could do or say to help calm their fears.

My only escape was to get up and walk around but, because we were in quarantine, I couldn't venture far. The nurses limited my walks to our ward and a stretch of deck outside. Then, late one night, while walking the deck, I found an open hatchway that led below. Sneaking down the ladder, I followed a dimly lit companionway towards the aft of the ship. Finally, stopping by an open doorway, I looked into a bright, deserted room that seemed to be an officer's wardroom. On the sideboard, I could see a tray of sandwiches, next to a large urn of coffee.

The sight and smell of coffee and real food gripped my attention. Looking up and down the deserted companionway, I decided to go in and help myself.

Taking a sandwich and a mug of java, I slid behind the green felt table. It's hard to describe how tasty a peanut-butter-and-jelly sandwich with hot coffee can be when it's been years... I slowly chewed every bite, rediscovering flavors I had long forgotten.

Just as I was finishing, a young ensign, wearing a pea jacket and binoculars, came into the wardroom and poured himself a cup of coffee. As he did so, I straightened my blue bathrobe, hoping to conceal my hospital gown, knowing full well that I was off limits.

Taking a seat across from me, he looked at me over his steaming cup and said, "Good evening. Are you supposed to be here, solider?"

His question was on point, but his face looked friendly.

"Guess not," I admitted, "but I saw the sandwiches and smelled the brew, and I couldn't resist."

With the thrashing of the ship's engines in the background, he looked at me for a moment and then smiled warmly, "Don't worry about me. I won't tell. I've got the watch in a few minutes, so enjoy."

As he talked, I noticed that his gaze was affixed to my chest. Glancing down, I saw the reason why: my dog tags were exposed, outside of my gown.

The ensign grinned. "I know who you are! You're the Marine Lieutenant they call the Rubber Patient! The whole ship's buzzing about you."

"I've been called a lot of things," I said, smiling back, "but never that. What's the scuttlebutt?"

"Well, some say the bottle inside that condom contains dead Japs gold teeth. Others say it's diamonds you took from Nip officers' rings. The story is that, when a nurse tried to remove it from your chain back on Guam, you came out of a coma and almost killed her. Now, nobody will touch it. They say you've been through hell...and back."

The ensign was young and handsome, with a square jaw, a flat-top haircut and a face bright with curiosity.

"What's your name, Ensign?" I asked.

"Bernard. My friends call me Bernie...sir."

"Well, Bernie, what say you about this rubber?"

He cocked his head and thought a moment, all the while staring at me. "I don't know, sir. It's got to be important...some kind of secret."

Draining the last dregs from my mug, I replied, "You're close, Bernie. I have a question. Does this red-crossed angel of a ship have a darkroom?"

Looking surprised, he answered, "Yes, sir. Two decks down."

"Is it any good?"

"It better be. I'm the Photo Officer."

"Well then, I'd like to use it. Inside this condom is some film that needs to be seen. Will you help me out?"

At first, he hesitated, probably because I was in quarantine, but he relented after I told him how important the film was. After some discussion, we agreed to meet, the next evening, two decks down in the darkroom, just before his midnight watch.

The next evening, Bernie got me set up in his lab and gave me a refresher course on film development and printing. Then, after showing me where all the supplies were, he excused himself for his deck duty.

Four hours later, when he returned, my second sets of prints were dropping off the ferrotype plate from the print dryer. The two strips of 16mm film had processed out just fine, although I had lost nine images on the negatives to light streaks, mold and a spot where I ripped the film in half. Of the fifty-two good negatives, I made two four-by-five-inch prints of each.

While I worked a print trimmer on the first set of pictures, Bernie looked at each gruesome image as they dropped off the dryer's belt. Without looking up, he commented, "I have never seen anything like this before. Does the Navy know about these? Woo, how could man do this to man?"

At first, I didn't answer him. The prints had moved me to tears while making them in the darkroom, and I was still choked up. Finally, he finished looking at the prints and brought the new stack over to me for trimming. As he put them in front of me, I spread them out and started telling the story of each picture. Faces, places, names… As I talked, it all rushed back to me, like ghosts from the past. What I had seen, what I had done and, mostly, what I hadn't done. The sadness and anger welled up inside of me, and I realized I was telling my tale through tears.

When I finished, Bernie was standing next to me, his lower lip quivering and his eyes moist. Stepping forward, he put his big arms around me and hugged me. For the longest moment, we two complete strangers stood there, holding each other, sobbing.

Finally, as we stepped apart, Bernie said in a choked-up voice, "After the war, there are going to be war-crime trials, and your pictures are these bastards' death warrants."

Turning away, I slowly answered, "They're all already dead. They went down when our hell-ship was sunk returning to Japan…but I'll show the world what happened, with these pictures."

Watching me with his big, moist, blue eyes, Bernie remarked, "Sometimes it's better to let bad things go, and get on with life."

Looking over to him, I replied, "Not this time. I will never forget or forgive."

A few days later, and just over two years after my first battle patrol, the *USS Relief* dropped anchor in Pearl Harbor. All the wounded with tropical diseases were taken to a special quarantine wing of the Naval Hospital. This unit, ICUQ14, was big, with over two hundred beds. Our twenty-bed ward was run by a loud and demanding head nurse by the name of Miss Crabtree. She was big, older, and all business, with a face and personality to match her name. Like the Nips, she had her rules, and her rules were law. She and her staff ran the ward like Marine DI's, and God help those who didn't toe the mark.

When I first got there, I noticed that my recovery took a step backwards, and I soon realized it was from all the medication. Most of the time, the staff had us drugged up, cleaned up, and fed up with our slow recovery. One pretty young nurse by the name of Margi, who pushed most of the pills, was nice enough to explain what kind of medications they were feeding us. For the most part, what we took were drugs for all the different tropical diseases, but the 'cocktails' also contained powerful sedatives to help control pain, sleep and our emotions.

Soon, I started hiding these sedatives under my tongue and then spitting them out, not swallowing them. With Jasper's bed right next to mine, when he was finally put on solid foods, I told him what I was doing with some of the pills and suggested he do the same. He did and, amazingly, his recovery also started improving. Within days, half the ward was ditching the sedatives, and our drab little ward seemed to come alive.

At the end of the first week, the Navy sent in a team of WAVES to interview each man, bedside, and to update their military files. These ladies were all administrative and wanted only the facts from each patient, so they could get records in order and the men get their back pay. The lady sitting next to my bed was a sour-faced gal whose only concern was the form on her clipboard. Her questions were simple: name, rank, serial number, date of capture, place of capture, etc. As we went along, I tried to tell her other facts, gruesome facts, detailed facts, but she was as cold as a winter breeze and would have none of it. Reluctantly, at one point, I removed Black Jack's dog tag from my chain and tried to give it to her and tell his story.

Looking down on me, she commented, "I have no forms for a Sergeant Malone. Someone else will have to do that."

Then she told me that the people on my next-of-kin list had been sent War Department telegrams back in March of 1944, telling them that I was missing in action and presumed dead. She also added that my $10,000 life insurance policy had not been paid out yet, so I won't have to worry about returning it. For some reason, she seemed pleased about this point. As we finished up, she said the government paid for one ten-word telegram for each returning wounded solider but that, because I was a returning POW, I would be allowed two ten-word telegrams. Handing me her clipboard with a blank piece of paper, she instructed me to write out my message.

Looking at her cold gaze, I knew she would be of no help, and I didn't want her staring at me as I tried to write out my telegrams, so I came up with a distraction. Reaching into the ditty bag Bernie had given me, I pulled out some pictures of Black Jack's execution and handed them to her. I told her to take a look at my 'snapshots' while I wrote out my messages.

Hesitantly she agreed as I turned to her clipboard.

What do you say in ten words? In my state of mind, I couldn't even remember the mailing address for either Laura or Uncle Roy, so I just wrote out their full names, with the appropriate town and state, and hoped the local Western Union office would see to the delivery.

Then I simply wrote: Safe in Hawaii, thinking of you, will write soon. Dutch.

I wanted to say so much more, as I knew this telegram would come like a bolt of lightning, but I didn't have money for any extras words. Finally, turning my attention back to the WAVE, I passed her the clipboard. She stared at me, with tears running down her cheeks, and handed back my prints.

"Why did you show me those pictures?" she asked.

Eyeing her now sad face, I replied, "So you would know we're more than just names on paper."

Standing up from my bedside, she looked down at me and sobbed. "I'm so sorry...I had no idea what you had been through. Forgive me."

The very next morning, I awoke to find a full bird Marine Colonel, in a Class A uniform with a chest full of ribbons, sitting next to my bed.

"Good morning, Lieutenant. I'm Colonel Handover from G-2. I understand from a WAVE who interviewed you yesterday that you have some disturbing pictures. I'd like to see them."

Pulling myself up in bed without saying a word, I reached into my bag and handed him one full stack. Leafing through the pictures, he didn't twitch or reveal any facial expressions, but his eyes carefully read each image.

When he was done, he looked up and asked, "Who else has seen these?"

"Just an Ensign Bernard on the *USS Relief*, who helped me soup them, sir. There's a story behind each image, if you're interested."

"Oh, we're very interested Lieutenant. But afraid I'm going to have to confiscate these prints and the negatives."

Shock raced through my body as I protested, "Why? We took these damn pictures so the world would know the truth about what happened out there."

With a deadpan expression, he replied, "America's not ready for this kind of truth, and we don't want them shown around. That's a direct order Lieutenant. When you feel up to it, we'll debrief you, over at G-2. Is this the only set of prints?"

Glaring at the Colonel, I thought about Black Jack and his story. Should I give this Colonel his dog tag?

No. Handover was on a self-serving mission and wouldn't care.

Reaching into my bag for the negatives, I looked up at him and fibbed, "Yes, sir."

"Good," the Colonel said, as he put the negatives and prints into his briefcase.

As he got up to leave, I stopped him. "If you can get me out of here tomorrow, I'd be glad to tell you my story. And, Colonel, that man being executed also helped me take those pictures. He was a very good man...a very good Marine..."

Coldly, the Colonel interrupted, "We'll cover all that in the debriefing. See you tomorrow."

As the days fused into weeks, most of the men in our ward greatly improved in both body and spirit. The Padre soon had put on twenty pounds, with his color and attitude back in the pink. Most of the other guys were doing the same, with all our different tropical diseases apparently under control. Our recovery was not surprising, as the ward was full of young men, all of whom were in their late teens or early twenties.

Soon, these men got restless and bored, as I had been the only patient allowed to leave the facility, over the loud protest of Nurse Crabtree, and then only once for a few hours to G-2. Many days, the ward seemed more like a morgue than a hospital. While we could walk the grounds and did have a day room where we could play cards, write letters and read, that was our quarantine limit. Then, one evening while I was taking my nocturnal stroll, I came across a small, vacant Doctors Lounge. Inside, I found a glass cabinet stocked with pint bottles of pure grain alcohol, with a plugged in portable radio on top of the cabinet.

Smiling to myself, I 'liberated' two pints from the cupboard, unplugged the radio, and snuck the items back onto our ward.

The next evening, a few hours before lights out, I rang for a nurse. As luck would have it, Nurse Margi appeared.

"I need your help, Margi. If you look around, you'll see that there's something wrong in this ward, and I want to fix it."

Standing next to me, she turned her shapely body glancing around the room, trying to see what I was talking about. "I don't see anything wrong," she said at last.

"That's just it," I agreed. "It's inside these guys. They need some fun. The medication I'm prescribing for tonight is torpedo juice. What I need from you is two pitchers of ice and two large cans of pineapple juice. Will you help me out?"

She looked at me with her big blue eyes and then, with a silly grin, asked, "What's torpedo juice?"

"That's what the Navy calls pineapple juice. It's an old sailor's tradition, and really good for the soul. If you help me out, you can have some."

That's how it started, and what a party we had! While Margi went off looking for ice and juice, I removed the radio from under my bed, and the two pints from under my mattress. This booze I hid inside my bathrobe pockets. By the time Margi returned, I had Tommy Dorsey playing, with most of the guys sitting up in their beds, keeping the beat.

Taking over the tray of ice and the cans of juice, I started mixing the cocktails, carefully concealing the alcohol from Margi. With the guys watching, bedside, I spiked each pitcher and then walked around, pouring out drinks. Within minutes, there were smiles on every face, with jokes and conversations buzzing.

The last of my first run of cocktails I poured for Margi.

She took a swig from her glass and then exclaimed, "We didn't get much pineapple juice in Montana. It's very bold, but very good. But I wonder why the Navy calls it torpedo juice?"

With this, the whole room broke out laughing and applauding. Margi's lips curled a little, embarrassed, and then she downed the rest of her glass of juice.

With the music playing and my cocktails flowing, we enjoyed drinks and each other for the better part of two hours. At one point,

Margi started dancing with the guys. With her hips swaying to the rhythm of the music, and the men lined up to tap in, her white uniform twisted gracefully up and down the center aisle. As the men danced, Jasper stood on his bed, using a toilet brush as if directing the radio band. It was a sight to see, and I'm sure it was the most fun any of these guys had had for years. But all good things must come to an end. Just as we were finishing up the last round of drinks, the double doors to our ward burst open to reveal Nurse Crabtree.

Looking down the row of beds with a sour expression, she screamed, "Nurse Grace, what goes on here?"

Letting go of her dance partner, Margi turned to the room and said simply, "Parties over, boys, and I'm in trouble."

Turning down the radio, I glanced towards Crabtree and shouted back, "I know why they call you the head nurse. Because you clean the latrines."

The next morning, Jasper and I were kicked out of ICUQ14 and transferred to a convalescent facility on the windward side of Oahu. We never saw Margi Grace again, but I'll bet she'll never forget her first taste of torpedo juice.

Decisions

The place we were sent was called Palm Cove Convalescent Hospital. Before the war, it had been a seaside hotel and, before that, a Catholic monastery. It was a modest facility, with fifty beds in the main building and a dozen little cottages spotted around the grounds, next to a beautiful stretch of palm-shaded beach. It was commanded by a Navy captain by the name of Dr. Lovejoy. He and his staff of doctors, nurses and orderlies specialized in mental diseases. Yes, we had been set to a Nut Farm!

At first, Jasper and I resisted our orders, as we knew they were just revenge from Nurse Crabtree for the party. But the doctors and staff would have none of it, and put us through a battery of tests, interviews and group therapy sessions. At these gatherings, the Padre and I soon noticed that the poor saps in the hospital had big problems and needed their treatment, while we were only taking up space. As our tests results came back, the staff realized we were as normal as two ex-POW's could be, although Dr. Lovejoy told me that I had a lot of 'pent-up anger,' and they agreed that our transfer had been just another Navy snafu. After some discussion, we were assigned to one of the cottages on the grounds. Here, we could rest and continue recovering, while the Navy fixed the mistake and made other arrangements.

In the first few days of our stay at the hospital, the news arrived that Nazi Germany had surrendered. VE day prompted only a low-key celebration by the staff and patients, as we all knew that only half of the war was over, with Japan being the last obstacle to true peace.

Then, right after we were transferred to the cottages, my Navy paperwork and pay caught up with me. The pay envelope I was given seemed a little fat, even considering that it contained years' back pay. When I reviewed my paperwork, I found out why: I had been promoted to the rank of captain, effective 14 February 1944, the very day of the Tulun Raid. Also, I had been awarded the Marine Air Medal for our recon mission over Tulun. The recommendation for the citation had been made by Colonel Flag.

Sadly, I wondered if Black Jack had received the same.

Since his interview back in Pearl, the Padre had not heard a word from his government and, like me, had only the hospital clothes we had been given. So after my payday I gave him a chunk of my loot and we called a cab and drove to the closest PX. There, we caused quite a commotion as we shopped, dressed only in our bathrobes and slippers. When we finished, we had purchased replacements for some of the items lost to the Japs. New clothes, new shoes, new kits, and shiny new Captain's bars make for a new man. By the time we returned to our little two-room cottage, we felt on top of the world, knowing that our darkest days were behind us...and we thanked God for it.

Having no idea how long we would be stuck at Palm Cove, we planned to make the best of it by doing next to nothing. With a white, sandy beach out front and a chow hall full of good food, our accommodations beat the hell out of any transit barracks back at Pearl, and we were determined to enjoy every minute.

As the days slipped into weeks, and with our bodies continuing to mend, we wrote letters, read, walked, and devoured three and sometimes four meals a day. Soon, I was running again, a few miles each morning and then a few more, into a small village, each afternoon. Here I would pick up some beer or a bottle of rum for Cocktail Hour. Many an evening we spent drinking and watching the sun go down, talking about the guys we'd known back in camp and their watery grave. It continued to be a sobering subject, no matter how many drinks we consumed.

By my twenty-fifth birthday, May 31st, I weighed in at just over 160 pounds, and Jasper was at 152. For the most part, our various diseases were under control, except for the malaria, which kept flaring up. We had been told that we would suffer with this problem for the rest of our lives, although medication would help. The night sweats and chills had become as common as our evening cocktails.

On the afternoon of my birthday, while jogging back from town, I looked up to find Dr. Lovejoy running towards me. As he neared me, he blurted, out of breath, "I've been looking…all over for you…There's some brass…waiting to see you…in your cottage. Why didn't you tell me they were coming…? We could have made preparations."

Not breaking stride, I ran past him, answering, "Didn't know they were coming…sir."

As I approached our little bungalow, I noticed a parked Navy staff car with a four-star flag. Milling around this car and our cottage was a small group of nurses and orderlies. Nearing the front door, I looked down at myself. Dressed only in a sweaty t-shirt, shorts and canvas shoes, I wasn't very presentable…but what the hell.

Bursting through the doorway, I found Jasper standing in front of two men who were seated on our rattan sofa with theirs backs to me. Standing alongside the Padre was a Navy Commander with aides piping on his uniform, and a pug-faced seaman holding a C6 camera.

As the two men from the sofa stood up and turned my way, I was floored. Standing before me, dressed in a summer-white uniform with six rows of colorful ribbons, was Admiral King. He looked older than I remembered, with his eyes set deep with dark worry rings. Next to him, dressed in a khaki uniform with a gold bar on his collar, was Riku Togo. Gone was his scrawny body, replaced both with flesh and a face full of confidence.

I didn't know what to do first -- hug Riku or salute the Admiral. Bringing my sweaty body to attention, I made myself do the proper thing.

As the Admiral returned my salute and extended his hand for a shake, he said, "Damn nice seeing you again, Dutch. You gave us quite a scare."

Taking his hand and looking him straight in the eye, I answered, "Nice to see you, Admiral…and this fine-looking Lieutenant standing next you." Then, reaching towards Riku, I shook his hand and pulled him close for a sweaty hug, telling him, "You are a sight for sore eyes. Never thought I'd see you again."

Pulling back from my embrace, Riku replied, "You look great. I thought we'd lost you."

"We'll have plenty of time for gabbing later. What's in the sack, Dutch?" Admiral King interrupted, nodding towards the bag I was holding.

"A bottle of rum…sir," I answered.

"Good. Why don't we have a drink while you get yourself cleaned up for the ceremony?"

"The ceremony, sir?" I handed the bag to Jasper.

"That's why we're here. You get cleaned up and I'll explain."

After a quick shower and shave, I donned one of my new uniforms and we all moved outside, retiring to the shade of a nearby palm tree. Here, with Jasper and a small group of personnel from the hospital watching, Riku and I faced Admiral King as he started the ceremony. The proclamation he read was full of praise and appreciation for actions taken on Tulun Islands, 14 February 1944. The words he used, such as gallant, bravery and fearless, were embarrassing, and I felt my face getting flushed. Glancing over at the onlookers, I hoped it didn't show. The upshot was that the Marine Corp had awarded the Legion of Merit to all raiders involved in this 'superbly planned and executed raid.' Further, because of the 'heroic actions' of my photographic crew in securing 'Top Secret Japanese Documents' during the raid, the Navy had awarded us the Navy Cross. And finally, for my one year in Jap prison camps, I was given the POW medal. As the Admiral finished with the proclamation, he stepped forward, taking the medals from his aide. As the camera worked, he pinned them on Riku and me, after which he moved back a few steps and came to attention, saluting us both. Then, with cheers and applause from the crowd, the three of us shook hands and had more pictures taken. Later, I learned that the raid on Tulun had been a costly endeavor, with eleven Legion of Merits being awarded posthumously. In many ways, this recognition seemed hollow, in light of all that Marine blood.

As we finished up with the pictures, I overheard Admiral King whisper to his aide, "I've given them the honey. Now it's time for the vinegar."

Turning to the crowd, he excused everyone, announcing that he wanted to talk to us privately. Once we were back inside, Admiral King asked for another rum and coke. As Jasper set about mixing drinks, I took the rattan chair facing King and Riku in our cramped little living room.

As we waited, I said, "Admiral, those specials orders you gave me saved our bacon many times…and they saved our lives on Tulun. I want to thank you for them."

In the warm window light King cocked his head to one side while looking me straight in the eye, "You and your crew did a great job in the Pacific, and we heard back only glowing reports. I'm sorry about Sergeant Malone. I know how hard that loss must be." Then, flashing a grin, he changed the subject, "You've got thirty-day 'survivor's leave' coming, and another thirty days for your year in hell. After that, you can have your old position back at OWI, if that's what you want."

His talk of the future caught me off-guard, and I wasn't sure how to respond. Returning to OWI wasn't an option I had even considered.

"Thank you, sir. I'd like to think about it." Turning to Riku, I continued, "When did you get your commission, Lieutenant?"

Beaming with pride, he answered, "Right after Tulun. Colonel Flag promoted me and hired me as an interpreter."

"How is he? Where is he? Was the information we found really useful?"

Smiles crossed their faces as Admiral King asserted, "He's fine and has just moved his little shop to the Marianas Islands. That information about the I-400 submarines was invaluable. The Japs were building up a whole fleet of them. Each one of those monster boats carried three planes and had a range of almost 8000 miles. Their plan to destroy the Panama Canal was as real as sin. Thanks to your information, we've sunk half of these boats, and what remains is bottled up in homeland ports, getting daily raids from our B29's. Without the Tulun raid and your intelligence, we could have lost the Canal, which would have set back the war effort by years."

Hearing this news, part of me was happy and proud...but another part wasn't. Even if our lucky find had helped the war effort, it had been a costly operation.

"I told Sergeant Malone about the Nip documents just before they cut off his head, Admiral. Until then, he had no idea what had been in the briefcase. After I told him, he smiled at me and said he was proud to have made a difference. Then the bastards slaughtered him."

Silence gripped the little room while I unfastened the top buttons of my shirt and reached for my chain. Unsnapping Jack's battered dog tag, I handed it to King while saying, "This might not be the time or the place, but here's Gunnery Sergeant Malone's tag. I've been waiting to give it to someone who would care. He was a very good man." I swallowed hard. "A very good Marine."

Reaching across, King gently closed his fist around the tag. "He made a big difference. I promise I'll see to it."

Then, not wanting to get choked up again, I changed the subject. "How did you know we were here, Admiral?"

"I first got the report that you were alive when you were on Guam. I called your Uncle Roy right away. He about passed out on the phone. Then your disturbing pictures and debriefing report came across my desk. That's when I started planning this little ceremony. But when I got to Pearl and found out that you had been transferred to Palm Cove, I was confused. This was the last place I thought I'd find you."

Just then, Jasper stepped between us, passing out drinks. As he did, I answered with a grin, "It's was just a Navy snafu, sir. We're okay."

Taking his drink Admiral King replied with a smile, "The Navy doesn't make mistakes, Captain. We make 'clerical errors.' I talked to Dr. Lovejoy when we arrived, and he confirmed that you guys are physical and mentally okay." Raising his glass, he concluded, "Here's to victory, boys."

As I sipped the warm drink from my plastic cup, it tasted bold and sweet.

Then, as if reading my mind, Jasper remarked, "If we had known you were coming, Admiral, we would have gotten some ice."

"Don't worry about it, Padre. This brings back old memories."

Turning my gaze to Riku, I asked, "So, where are you stationed, Lieutenant?"

Riku glanced over to Admiral King to get a nod of approval before he answered, "I've volunteered for a new unit commanded by Colonel Flag. It's called the Pathfinders. We're forming up teams on Saipan for the invasion and/or surrender of Japan."

"What's your mission?" I asked.

Riku gave me a blank stare for a second, and then King spoke up. "That's another reason why we're here. I have more news. From the international Red Cross, we learned that the hell ship you were on, the Nissho Maru, somehow made it to Japan, and what was left of the 14th Regiment was taken to some POW camp near Kobe. There are hundreds of these POW camps and tens of thousands of prisoners scattered all across the Nip home islands. That's part of the Pathfinders' mission -- to locate and liberate."

His words struck me like a rock. If the Regiment had made it...so had Colonel Hisachi and Sergeant Yoshio. That just couldn't be. I had buried them in my mind, but now, like ghosts, they were rising again.

I glanced over at Jasper, who seemed frozen in place by the news. The glass he was holding was halfway to his open mouth, not moving. His head was cocked and his eyes wide, as he hung on every word.

"I don't see how that's possible," I finally replied. "The gash in the hull was over twenty feet across, and the sea was rushing in when we jumped. Are you sure of the intelligence, Admiral?"

"Yes. One of the Red Cross Agents was on the docks when the ship limped into Kobe Harbor. He interviewed a few of the men before the Nips put a stop to it. They told him that the skipper of the Nissho pumped seawater into the opposite bilge, lifting the damaged side up and out of the sea. Then the Japs passed down welding torches to the Aussies, who cut away the damage and welded iron plates over the hole. It took all night, but the pumps held and the ship trimmed out the next morning and continued on to Japan. They reported one Nip destroyer sunk and four Aussies and one American lost in the battle. War-time tactics and heads-up seamanship saved the hell ship."

"Do you know the name of the camp my mates were sent to?" the Padre blurted.

The Admiral pivoted his head towards Jasper. "No. We think it's a camp close to a mountain town by the name of Yashiro. If that's true, they would be slave labor in one of the copper or tin mines in the area. But that's only a guess."

Gazing down at my half-consumed drink, I swirled the glass, my mind racing. There could be no future for me without payment for Black Jack's death and the wharf massacre. Finally, looking up, I found the Admiral and Riku silently staring across at me. "So, can I volunteer for the Pathfinders, Admiral?"

"Me, too," Jasper added without hesitation.

Taking a swig from his drink, King answered, "You guys have done your bit. For you, the war could be over. This is going to be a dangerous mission. If the Japs don't surrender and we have to invade, these teams will be dropped behind enemy lines to do recon and send back troop information. If Japan does surrender, these teams will be the first to set foot on homeland Japan to photograph and report on the docks and piers, so that the Navy can get in. Then and only then will the teams be released to locate and liberate POW camps. Might be something you want to think about, before volunteering."

I glanced over to Jasper. He nodded towards me.

I answered, "We've thought about it, Admiral, and we want to sign up. We understand the Nips. We talk their language and know their tactics. We can be a big help, sir."

Finishing his drink, King stood. "I was hoping you'd feel this way, Dutch. I'll get the paperwork started and clear the mission for the Padre with the Australians."

Getting to my feet, I reached out and shook the Admirals hand. "I promise, you won't regret it, Admiral. We won't let you down, sir." Turning to Riku, who had also risen, I shook his hand. "It'll be nice working with you again, Lieutenant."

His face came alive with a smile so big, it showed his yellow teeth. "It will be like old times, Dutch."

As Admiral King reached the front door, he stopped and turned back to me, looking stern. "For this operation only, Captain, I'm promoting you to the temporary rank of Lieutenant Colonel. One way or the other, Japan is going to be crawling with American brass, and you're going to need the rank to get anything done. I'd promote you to full bird but you're too damn young. But I remind you -- our mission is reconnaissance, not revenge. Do you understand Colonel?"

Bracing myself, I saluted. "Aye, aye, sir!"

Returning my salute, he turned and walked toward the door. "And put some more weight on. You guys still look skinny to me."

Ten days and five pounds later, we received our orders to report to the Pathfinders on the island of Saipan. Just before we departed, Jasper's back pay caught up with him and we made another trip to the Navy PX in Pearl. There we purchased clothing and other personal needs for our new assignment, and I acquired a set of silver oak leaves. Wearing the new symbols of my elevated rank proved to be uncomfortable, with officers much senior to my age now having to salute me. Thanks to my Rabbi, I was sure that I was the youngest Lt. Colonel in the USMC, a fact that made me very nervous.

Also, while in Waikiki, I found a Leica III camera outfit at one of the local pawn shops. From the serial number on the camera, I knew it had been built in 1942 and must had found its way to Hawaii as spoils from the European war. It was a great find at a great price, as the proprietor had no idea of its worth and was only asking for its redemption value of one hundred and fifty-two dollars. Walking out of the shop, I knew Black Jack would be pleased with my purchase.

Saipan

Our transportation to the Marianas was aboard a C-47 cargo plane. These twin-engine workhorses, which had wings that would slightly flap on take-offs and landings, were nicknamed Gooney Birds. Our aircraft and eight others were being transferred to Saipan, after seeing duty in Europe. With the Nazis defeated, hundreds of thousands of men and tons of material were on their way to reinforce the allied positions in the Pacific. Gossip had it that the invasion of homeland Japan would make Normandy look like a practice drill. It was rumored that over three million men would be needed to secure the Nips' home islands, with another half million in reserve.

The scope of this invasion boggled my mind. From experience, I knew that if this was true, the waters around Japan would run red with American blood -- a prospect not lost on the crew on my plane, who had won the European war only to now be facing the Land of the Rising Sun. Their dream was home and civilian life, not more war. And who could blame them, after what they had been through? America was war-weary, and we all prayed that the Japs would surrender before we had to invade.

Our nine-plane squadron carried a cargo of dismantled Waco CG-4A gliders that had seen service in Italy. These gliders and their crews were assigned to the Pathfinders as part of the build-up for our mission. The flight over was long and bumpy, with stops for fuel at Midway and Wake. Twenty-two hours out of Hawaii, with the sun hot and the humidity unbearable, we finally touched down on Saipan. Stepping off the plane, I glanced towards the baking sun and quietly said to myself, "Welcome back to the tropics. What the hell I have done?!"

The main airfield on Saipan was gigantic, with dozens of B-29 squadrons making daily bombing raids on Japan. When these bombers filled the air, the skies darkened as if they were swarms of locusts. At times, the Army Air Corp had over a thousand planes on missions, dropping ton after ton of high explosives on the Nips' home islands. Together, they constituted the largest and most deadly air armada in the history of warfare.

Late that morning, when I set foot on the tarmac, I was right in the middle of the biggest and busiest airport on earth. Saipan was one of those places and times that will never be forgotten.

As we stepped off the plane, Jasper and I were picked up by Lieutenant Togo in a jeep. He drove us across the airfield and down miles and miles of hangars, warehouses and Quonset huts to our headquarters. When we reported in, we were assigned quarters and told that Colonel Flag wished to have dinner with us that evening in his hut.

After a couple of drinks at the O-club, Jasper and I retired for a long overdue nap. Then, at 1800, Riku returned with the jeep and drove us to the Colonel's tin Quonset hut. Here, for the first time since Tulun, I was reunited with Colonel Flag, who was surprisingly warm and friendly. After some light-hearted kidding about my new silver oak leaves, he showed us into his sparsely furnished quarters.

Time hadn't changed him much. He looked a little thinner, a little tanner, and his handshake seemed a little firmer.

While the junior man, Lieutenant Togo, mixed the cocktails, I introduced the Padre. During the first round of drinks, we made small talk about Admiral King, Australia, and the defeat of Nazi Germany. With the second drink in hand, the Colonel started talking about the conditions of the Pacific Theater. Our losses on Iwo Jima and Okinawa had been overwhelming, and estimates out of Washington predicted we could face over a million causalities in the battle for Japan -- and that figure didn't count the millions of fanatical Japanese soldiers and civilians that would be wounded or killed. He explained that all Japanese civilians were being trained to battle the American 'devils' on the beaches with bamboo spears, sticks or stones, whatever weapons they could find. These civilian kamikazes were being told to stain the sands red with American blood.

Colonel Flag painted a bleak picture for invasion and, worst of all, thought the war could last for another two or three years. Then, after the total defeat of Japan, there might be another ten or twenty years of occupation. This depressing war seemed to have no end or reason...a stark reminder that war is the biggest depository of evil.

Over a spam and pineapple dinner served by the Colonel's orderly, Flag outlined the mission and organization of the Pathfinders. There were eighteen four-man mobile teams being trained on Saipan, with six teams each made up of personnel from the Army, Navy and Marines Corp. Each mobile team consisted of a team leader with the rank of Major or above, an interpreter, a photographer, and a driver/rifleman for security. The Navy teams were to be dropped in, and would then concentrate their efforts on Japan's major port facilities in and around Tokyo. The Army teams would focus on Japan's major airfields and command-and-control operations in and around Tokyo. The Marine teams would be on the docks, piers and warehouses of secondary harbors in and around the southwestern approaches to mainland Japan. The overall objective of each team was to find, photograph and secure, if possible, airfields or seaports that could be used by either an invading or an occupying army. Each of these mobile teams was to be supported by a small communications and security group that would also be dropped in to set up fixed areas of operations, establishing radio contact back with headquarters.

If we went in with an invasion force, which the Colonel thought most likely, we would be attached to larger airborne groups for protection, but our independent mission would remain the same. If Japan surrendered, we would go in alone, as the vanguards of an occupation force. Finding ports of entry was Job One. Then, and only then, could we search out and liberate POW camps.

"If we invade, it won't be until September or October," the Colonel snorted while lighting up a cigar. "We'll need that much time to get enough troops and equipment over here from Europe."

"The C-47 we flew in on had a dismantled Waco glider aboard. Is that how we are going to be dropped in, sir?" I asked.

"That's the plan," Flag answered through a haze of blue smoke, "Unless your target is hot or in the mountains. In that case, you'll parachute in. We like the Wacos because they can land almost anywhere, and each Gooney Bird can tow two gliders carrying a jeep for transportation and a packed BT3 utility trailer for supplies. After all, you'll have to carry in everything you'll need. There are no supply depots on the ground."

"Do we know what condition the seaports and airports are in, sir?" Riku asked.

Getting up from the table, the Colonel went to a hutch and removed a bottle of brandy. "Pretty bleak. Our bombers have destroyed their harbors and pockmarked their airfields. We've sunk most of their Navy and decimated their air force." Returning, he poured himself a healthy shot of brandy in a water glass, then passed the bottle my way. "But there's still a lot of sting in this Jap bee. These suicidal bastards still have three million men in their army, and they'll fight to the death when we invade. And if Japan says it's going to surrender, how the hell will we know it's the truth? We just can't trust our little yellow brothers, so the only good Jap is a dead Jap." Raising his drink towards Riku, he concluded, "Sorry about that, Lieutenant Togo."

An uneasy silence filled the room as I poured myself a drink and passed the bottle across the table.

"So much for current events," the Colonel asserted, and cleared his throat, "What I would like to hear is what happened on Tulun. That is, if you don't mind talking about it, Dutch."

Suddenly, all the penetrating eyes at the table seemed to focus on me. Flag and Riku wanted the full story, with all its bloody details, and I realized that I had never told Jasper much about the raid. But if I was going to tell my story, it would be without tears or emotion. Lt. Colonels don't weep.

Reaching into my breast pocket, I pulled out a stack of prints. "Okay, and I brought some photos so you can all see how Black Jack died. But they tell only half the story."

An hour later, with the brandy bottle near empty, and with sad faces all around, I finished my tale, clear-eyed.

For the longest moment there was anguished silence. Then, staring down at the remains of his drink, Flag remarked, "So that's why you volunteered for the Pathfinders. You want to kill that Jap Colonel and his Sergeant. Guess I can't blame you." Then, looking sternly up and across at me, he continued, "I'll do what I can to get your team assigned close to Kobe, but our job is recon not retribution. Do you understand that, Colonel?"

"Yes, sir. You're the second person to tell me that, sir. I understand. But don't ask me to forgive or forget."

The next morning, we met our assigned driver/rifleman, a twenty-five-year-old Sergeant by the name of Glen Bryan. He had spent the last three years as a guerilla fighter in the jungles of the Philippines. He knew Jap tactics and spoke their language but, most importantly, he was a small-arms expert and wore an Expert Rifleman's Badge. For years, he had been on the receiving end of supplies sent in by Colonel Flag and, after being liberated on Samar, he turned down a chance to return to America and volunteered for the Pathfinders. Glen, with his cropped blonde hair, was a battle-wise killer of a mud Marine who hated the Nips as much as I did. His cold blue eyes, square jaw and chest full of courage fit right in, and I liked him right away.

On that same morning, we were also introduced to our support group, which consisted of four Army pilots for the C-47 and the two Waco gliders, two Navy radio operators and a six-man Marine security team. This group would land in the C-47, if possible, and take up a secured, fixed position so we could fly out our film and reports. Our mobile and support team was designated Trailhead Thirteen.

We spent the next few weeks getting supplied and securing the equipment we would need for our mission. This included planning out what we would need to pack in the utility trailer. If we went in as part of an invasion force, we would carry mostly arms and ammunition. If we went in as liberators, we would carry mostly food and medical supplies. In either event, we would go in personally armed to the teeth, with our jeep equipped with a Browning machine gun on a swivel pod. We would also take as much drinking water, food and gas as we could carry. Our new camera equipment consisted of a C-6 outfit and a new Bell and Howell 16mm film camera. Immediately, I started training Jasper to use the Speed Graphic, while Riku would shoot motion pictures and I would use my Leica. With three of us shooting, the photo interpreters back at headquarters wouldn't miss much.

Also at this time, we started training flights in the Waco gliders. I found these flights both frightening and exhilarating. These tapered boxcar-type planes were made of nothing more than wood, canvas and aluminum tubing, with no motor or defenses. The front of the glider had a large fabric bubble, with plastic windows. This area served as a cockpit that could swing up and open to load men and equipment. The eighty-four-foot wing span above the fuselage gave the plane lift as it was towed by long cables connected to a Gooney Bird. The CG-4A was an ugly plane that could take off and land on a dime.

At first, I assumed that riding in a glider would be a quiet way to die, but during my first flight I found the noise inside, from the flapping of the canvas, almost deafening. And the idea of a fully loaded jeep roped to the floorboards just behind the pilot seats was spooky. If the glider came in too fast or at too steep of an angle and crashed, that jeep would shoot through the cockpit like a bullet. Being a glider pilot took a lot of nerve, a lot of luck, and a lot of talent. Maybe the engraved 'G' on their flight wings stood for 'Guts'!

In mid-July, inside a hot hangar bigger than most motion-picture sound stages, Colonel Flag called together all the teams and announced that the Pathfinders were doubling in size to thirty-six teams. All the groups that had completed training and outfitting on Saipan were being moved to Okinawa, to make room for the new trainees. Transfer of men and equipment was to begin immediately, with the teams being fully operational from our new location within seventy-two hours.

Then, from the podium, he made a shocking announcement. "When you arrive on Okinawa, you will concentrate your future preparations on a mission that is a prelude to occupation. That is all."

As the Colonel stepped down and walked across the hanger floor, a hush gripped the assembled men, since we had been training for a mission of combat reconnaissance, being part of a large invasion force. We speculated that this green light to an occupation mission meant that the war was nearly over.

Okinawa

Our accommodations on a small secondary airstrip on Okinawa were crude, but in our slow-flying C-47's we were just six hours from Tokyo. The Pathfinders, with all of our planes and crews, shared this small field with a squadron of P-51 fighters that were flying escort missions with B-29's over Japan. It was planned that these same fighters would escort the Pathfinders to our assigned drop areas, if and when the war ended. Okinawa was war ravaged, but what few areas we saw that had somehow missed the destruction were quite beautiful. The countryside, architecture and people gave us a snap-shot of what to expect on mainland Japan. Here we settled in, continuing our training and making preparations for our mission.

Then, on the morning of August sixth, the whole world changed with the news that a B-29, the Enola Gay, had dropped a single bomb, called the Little Boy, on the Japanese city of Hiroshima. This first-ever Atomic Bomb had wiped this city and most of its residents off the map in a split second, propelling America into world leadership.

With this news, the Pathfinders were put on full alert and told that Japan's surrender was expected within hours. By 0945 that same morning, Colonel Flag briefed all the teams and assigned drop areas and specific targets. True to his word, my group was given the Kobe area of docks, piers and warehouses. Each team was provided with maps and current aerial photographs of their targets. Our pictures included detailed blowups of all the surrounding airfields, as well as close-ups of the waterfront.

Based on these images and other intelligence, it was recommended that we land at a small airfield just east of Kobe. This isolated field had missed most of the bombings and looked to still have an active runway. On the other hand, the docks and warehouses ten miles west had not been so lucky and appeared to be in shambles. Each of these facilities would have to be investigated and photographed from the ground, in preparation for the occupation force. Finding safe harbors for our troops and supplies was critical, to support our secondary mission of liberating the POW camps.

From a raised platform in our ready room, Colonel Flag ended the briefing by saying, "If the Nips surrender, you men will be the first foreign invaders ever to set foot on mainland Japan. How her people will react to your presence is not known. Go in prepared for peace but ready for war. You are the vanguards to a large supporting force and, while you wait for us, you are the law. After you have completed your primary mission, you will be released to search out the camps. Deal with any problems as your team leader orders. They are the judge and jury. Stand by your planes. That is all."

That evening, waiting in our team tent next to the tarmac, discussing the day's events, Jasper asked, "What was all that stuff about judge and jury?"

Sergeant Bryan, with a bottle of beer in hand, grinned while answering, "Means there's no rules for engagement. We can deal with the Japs in any way the Colonel here sees fit."

At the sergeant's comment, Riku quickly turned towards me, with his gaze on fire. "I hope we're not going in with vengeance. The Japanese people have been through enough. Our mission should be liberation for all of Japan's citizens."

Clearing my throat while looking directly at him, I countered, "I'm not worried about her citizens, I'm worried about her army. How does a soldier go from kamikaze warrior one day to peaceful citizen the next? I know this bushido crap, it has mulled and maimed long enough and I don't see Japan's Army stopping just because the Emperor says to surrender."

"I think you're wrong, Dutch. If it's the Emperor who says to stop, they will stop. That's also part of bushido."

"I hope you're right, Lieutenant. I'm tired of war."

Three days later, Nagasaki fell to the second Atomic Bomb, called the Fat Man. Nearly half the city was destroyed, and over fifty thousand people were dead or injured by another split-second of terror…but still no proclamation came from Emperor Hirohito. A few days after that, the Soviet Union declared war against Japan. Then, finally, at noon on August 15, 1945, the Emperor announced to the people of Japan, via radio, that he and his government had accepted the terms of the Potsdam Declaration, and that all hostilities would end at midnight. Japan had surrendered. It was V-J Day!

Within hours of the surrender, our operational orders were issued. At sunrise on 16 August 1945, the first eighteen teams of the Pathfinders were to be on Japanese soil. At sunrise of the seventeenth, the second waves of eighteen teams were to deploy. Our groups were to stage their departure from Okinawa, with the longest flights to Tokyo going first. These C-47's and gliders, escorted by ten P-51 fighters, were to start departing at 0100. The

Marine teams, flying the shortest routes, supported by four P-51 fighters, were to depart, starting at 0230. The plan called for all Pathfinders to be on the ground by 0700.

Sleeping, the night before our mission, was out of the question. Most of the men went to church, then spent the night checking and double-checking their gear. Call it mission jitters or a reality check. Most of us weren't sure of the surrender or our mission. Just after midnight, with all the runway lights glowing, the Marine groups started milling around the flight line, watching the Navy and Army teams depart. First, the flight line crews would push the CG-4A's out to the runway, while other crews coiled long tow cables in front of them. Then the C-47's would taxi out in front of the gliders and have the cables hooked to their tail section. Next, with the other end of the tether line attached to the gliders, the Gooney Birds revved up their twin 1,200-hp Pratt & Whitney engines to maximum power and released their brakes. As the C-47 lumbered down the runway, picking up speed, the coiled tow line would get ever shorter, until it was dragging both of the Waco's. With the Gooney Bird's engines roaring and spitting long strains of red and yellow flames from the exhaust, these gliders would follow down the runway picking up speed. Just before the C-47 lifted off, the two gliders behind would become airborne. Finally, in a heartbeat, all three planes would be in the air, slowly climbing and turning towards their destination.

The noisy show of flight and flame was a colorful and exciting spectacle to watch. By 0145, all twenty-four gliders had successfully pulled off the tarmac, towed by twelve C-47's heading north for an unknown destiny. Fifteen minutes later, all ten of the P-51 escorts were airborne and on their way to catch up with the first teams.

After the fighters departed, our gliders were pushed out onto the tarmac and prepared for take-off. As I impatiently waited with my crew next to our Waco, Colonel Flag drove up in a jeep and waved me over.

"Here's the latest information we have on the POW camps in your area. We think you'll find two camps in the Yashiro area and another in a small town by the name of Kasai, some twenty miles west. After you have secured each camp, radio your position and

I'll get an airdrop in with food and supplies. Make sure we don't kill any of these poor bastards with the air drop! After what they've been through, this would be a hell of a time to die. There are two hospital ships making their way towards Japan as we speak. With any luck, they should be on station within the next two or three days. Get the worst cases to the hospital ships, anyway you can, and get the walking wounded and other POW's down to the closest serviceable dock so we evacuate them on troop ships. Any questions?"

"Yes, sir. What about the guards and camp commandants?"

"If they resist, shoot 'em, no questions asked. If you don't, and they have committed war crimes on Japanese soil, lock them up locally. If their crimes were committed elsewhere in the Pacific, ship them back to Guam, where they will stand trial."

"Will I need written orders to get all this done?"

Chewing on an unlit cigar, Flag grinned at me, "That's why you're wearing that silver oak leaf. Write your own damn orders. In the next few months, Japan is going to be a chaotic cesspool of American brass. Don't let the Army and Navy push you around. Get your mission done any way you can. Improvise. I understand you're good at that. See you soon."

"Aye, aye, sir."

In the blue glow of the runway lights Colonel Flag reached down for the gear shift and glanced back, flashing a smile, "And, Dutch, don't get yourself killed. The war's over...we think!"

CHAPTER THIRTEEN

We were three hours out, flying at eight-thousand feet heading north-northeast. The ebony morning was crystal clear, with only starlight marking our progress. I was riding in the co-pilot's seat, with Riku sitting in a jump seat next to the roped-down jeep. Our pilot was doing his best to keep our glider just a little below the prop wash from the C-47 that towed us. Close to our left and just behind us was the second Waco, with Jasper, Sergeant Bryan and our Bantam utility trailer. Our three-plane group, Trailhead Thirteen, was third in the line of six Marine teams. Buzzing around these groups were the four P-51 fighters flying escort. It was cold inside our dark, noisy glider, with the only interior illumination that of a single lamp reflecting on the control panel. Both the pilot and I had headsets on so we could listen to the chatter between the Gooney Birds. Our intercom communication was provided by a long, thin wire wrapped around the tether cable between the gliders and tow-planes. Once we broke off from the tow line, all radio contact would be lost.

"Trailhead Eleven changing course to 272 degrees and dropping down to five-thousand feet," the pilot of the lead C-47 announced over our headsets.

Just before we started following this same maneuver, our pilot pointed out through the window to the right and nodded at me. Twisting my head, I could see the first blush of daylight painting the eastern horizon. Watching the red and amber new day, I thought, *hopefully, the first day of world peace.*

A few minutes after our turn and change in altitude, our pilot removed one of his headset cups and shouted in my direction, "Can you see Mt. Fuji, up north?" Then, doing the same with my headset, he repeated his question.

Looking in that direction I replied, "No...just haze or smoke. How long before we get to the LZ?"

He held his wristwatch up to the faint light from the window. "Less than an hour...We caught a tail wind. We're a little early."

With light reflecting off the eastern sky behind us, we could finally look down and see the dim outline of the Japanese home islands. On our left was Shikoku, the smallest of the four main islands. Looming in front of us and to the right was Honshu, the largest and most populated island. All of the Marine targets were on the southern approaches of this island.

Ten minutes later, our radio crackled. "Trailhead Eleven and Twelve turning for target...Good luck, Pathfinders."

These two teams had assignments some hundred and fifty miles north of our position. As they turned to leave, so did two of our fighters. Moments later, we heard Trailhead Fifteen and Sixteen turn west for their targets around Okayama. As they turned, the last two fighters followed them.

Removing the cup from my ear again, I shouted towards the pilot, "What happened to our fighter escort?"

Doing the same, he replied, "Those teams have the furthest to go, so they get the escorts...but they can be back in a flash if we need them." Then, pointing forward, he continued, "Kobe is just ahead of us...We should be okay."

Looking down and in front of our tow plane, I could see the small dark dot that was our target. It looked a long way off, and we were still flying over open water.

Moments later, our C-47 radioed, "Two meatballs coming up at eight o'clock. Prepare for evasive action."

Shaking my head in disbelief, I found them in the haze, climbing almost straight up for us. We were sitting ducks, with no escort and no way to defend ourselves. But the war was over...wasn't it?

Removing his entire headset, our pilot turned, shouting, "If those meatballs make a pass, they'll go for the C-47 first. If that happens, I'll disconnect and go into a steep dive, so be prepared."

"Dive to where?" I shouted back. "We're over water. If we land in the drink, we'll sink like a rock with this jeep aboard."

In the metallic early-morning light, he nodded towards the door next to Riku. "You guys stand by the door and jump, just before we hit the water...It's your only chance."

"And when the jeep comes shooting through the cockpit on impact, what are you going do?"

With a toothy smile, he cocked his head to one side and replied, "Duck!"

Shaking my head back at him, all I could say was, "You glider pilots are nuts!"

Zoom...zoom. The two meatballs arched over our tow cable, just in front us, missing it by inches. Twisting, our keen eyes watched as they flew out to our right about a mile and then started turning back towards us.

"That was damn close," I shouted, "but they didn't fire a shot."

"If they're Kamikazes, they're setting up for attack now! Stand by for release," our pilot yelled.

Three heartbeats later, from out of nowhere came two of our P-51 fighters. They just appeared on our right and from below, positioning themselves between our planes and the meatballs. They were so close, I could almost reach out and touch them. Looking over, I gave a thumbs-up to the trailing escort. He returned the sign and then peeled off, chasing the meatballs out of the skies.

"That was too close for comfort. The war's over," Riku shouted from behind.

With our target in front of us, we started our descent to two thousand feet while Trailhead Fourteen turned right for their target, Osaka. As we approached Kobe, we had a good view of the city. It was nestled on the coastline, with rolling hills and high mountains just behind. Turning west over the smoky city, we could look down and see that the harbor was littered with sunken and half-sunken ships of all sizes. And the waterfront looked to be in shambles, with smoldering buildings lining the docks.

A few minutes more and we were west of the city.

"Our airfield is dead ahead," the pilot from the C-47 finally announced. "The main runway is pock-marked with bomb craters but the taxiway looks serviceable. There's a grassy strip between the two that looks okay for the gliders. Stand by for release count."

Looking just ahead of the Gooney Bird, I could see what he was talking about. The airfield had a single damaged landing strip and taxiway running east and west. Next to these strips were a few hangers and outbuildings. Other than that, the airfield was surrounded by open, grassy fields. As the C-47 flew over the western edge of the airfield, they started the three count. On

"Zero," our pilot released the tether cable and immediately dropped the nose of the Waco.

Swish...we were on our own.

Watching the ground coming towards me, I thought we were at too steep an angle and going too fast. With my knuckles white, I reminded myself of how much we weighed. Damn, we were going in fast...

Then, just a few hundred yards off the ground, our pilot pulled back on the wheel, raising the gliders nose. With this maneuver, the plane flared out with its wings taking over, slowing our descent for a gentle but abrupt touchdown. A few hundred yards more of rolling across the grass and we finally came to a stop.

Breathing a deep sigh of relief, I turned to our pilot. "I hope this is the last time I ever have to ride in one of these flying coffins. That was an...interesting landing."

Grinning back at me, he replied, "Welcome to Japan. Please watch your step while deplaning!"

Kobe

By the time the second glider came to a stop, some fifty yards behind us, Riku and I were outside our Waco, moving towards the nose bubble. After our pilot released the levers inside, we pulled and pushed the fabric dome, opening up the interior for jeep removal. While Riku jumped into the vehicle and started the motor, the pilot and I quickly slid out the ramp planks; then he drove out of the plane.

After circling the airfield, the C-47 was on final approach for touchdown on the taxiway as we jumped into the jeep and drove over to the second glider. There we helped remove the trailer, and hitched it to the jeep.

Standing in the early morning sun, watching the Gooney Bird complete its landing and turn back towards us, Sergeant Bryan asked, "Do you want the flag, sir?"

Looking around the deserted field, I answered, "Yes, with weapons and helmets. Let's drive over to the tow-plane. I want to talk to the guys."

As we stopped next to the Gooney Bird, I called for the men to gather around the jeep, and told the security team to search the hangars and outbuildings. If they were clear, we should then set up camp on the grassy strip next to the Wacos. That way, they could see anyone approaching from hundreds of yards away.

My final order was for them not to go looking for trouble. Then I reminded them that we would be back before dark. Finally, after checking the jeep's radio with the communications boys, we drove away.

Driving between two old hangars, we came to the open gate of the fenced-in airfield. Turning right on a gravel road, we headed towards Kobe. With Sergeant Bryan driving, Jasper riding shotgun, and Riku and I in the rear, we bounced down the country road with the sun in our eyes. The Padre, with his gold cross attached to his collar, looked out of place in a steel helmet, with a carbine across his lap. I knew he didn't like being armed but, with our reception in doubt and our mission on the line, he knew it was necessary.

On the other hand, Bryan looked every bit the part of the conquering invader, wearing a pair of .45 pistols in shoulder holsters and an M1 Thompson in a boot next to the wheel. If we got into a fire fight, I knew I could count on the Sergeant. Across from me, sitting just next to the large, flapping American flag we'd attached to the jeep, was Lieutenant Togo. In my mind, he symbolized what I prayed we would find: a future for Japan. He had a love for the Japanese people and wanted in the worst way to make a difference. But I knew if the chips were down, that he would stand by me and his America.

While my confidence in our mission was still in question, I had no qualms about my team. I only wished Black Jack could have been with us.

Soon the gravel road gave way to a hard-paved street, as we drove through residential areas on the outskirts of the city. For the most part, these neighborhoods looked normal, with no signs of war damage. But one thing was strange: other than a few lone dogs barking our passing, the streets were totally deserted. It was as if space invaders had landed and abducted all of the people.

Finally, the street crossed a wide boulevard that our map indicated was the main thoroughfare through Kobe. Turning left, we approached the city. It was then that the landscape started changing. The small buildings lining the way all seem to have fire scars and broken windows. As the buildings got taller, the damage got worse. Soon, we were driving past entire blocks that had been destroyed, with smoldering rubble filling the vacant spaces. Most of the side streets were blocked with fallen buildings and debris.

The avenue we traveled had been cleared; we could see neatly stacked piles of debris on the sidewalks. Downtown Kobe was a sooty black ghost town with tall skeletons standing where buildings once stood. The sight and smell of this damage reminded me of the fiery inferno it must have been during the bombings. If there was a picture of hell, downtown Kobe surely resembled it. A few times, we did see people, but they always scurried away into the shadows as we approached. Their actions surprised me...but then, what had I expected? A victory parade down this war-shattered boulevard?

My plan was to start our survey on the edge of the waterfront, a few miles east of the city. Our map and aerial photos showed a large industrial complex with a dry dock that was labeled Terminal Seven. From this position, we would work back up the six-mile waterfront to Terminal One. In all, we would cover eleven docks and piers, along with all of the surrounding warehouses. Each of these facilities, and the harbor, needed to be thoroughly investigated and photographed. The Navy wanted ships in this port within the next seventy-two hours, and we needed to tell them where safe portage could be found.

After getting lost a few times in the rubble blocked streets, we finally snaked our way around and came to what looked like our first target, the industrial complex...although it was hard to tell, as the only thing still standing was a large brick smokestack that towered five stories over the twisted and bent steel that had been the shipyard. Everything was gone or destroyed, with most of the charred wooden dock lying in the waters of the harbor.

With a clipboard in hand for my written narrative, we retrieved our cameras and began our survey. Half an hour later, we moved down the waterfront, looking for Terminal Six.

As we drove down the line of docks and piers, we were surprised by the massive destruction our lenses captured. At some terminals, we found the piers still standing but the bones of rusty, half-sunk ships moored in the slips, like a graveyard. At other locations, the docks had crumbled, or the channel leading to the pier was blocked with sunken debris. Nowhere could we find a serviceable portage. Kobe's waterfront was just a long black line of deserted devastation.

By 15:00, we had reached our final target, Terminal One. This complex looked different, as it had been constructed from steel-reinforced concrete. Dismounting the jeep, we stood looking out towards the harbor, hoping we had finally found a safe moorage. A long concrete pier with a dock on either side flared out from the waterfront into the water some two-hundred fifty feet. Between the two docks was a long, narrow warehouse made of brick, with a tin roof. This roof had a few rips and tears, and was charred black in places, but still looked as if it might be water-tight. Just to the right of the terminal, running parallel to the waterfront, was another long transit dock made from cement blocks. Turning our attention to the murky harbor channel leading to Terminal One, the water looked deep and appeared to be clear of obstacles.

Standing by our jeep, planning out the survey in the hot afternoon sun, we were just grabbing our gear when Sergeant Bryan shouted, "Rifles across the way -- in the shadows next to that burned-out building!"

Instantly, we ducked behind our jeep on the water side, while Bryan jumped into its rear, swinging the .30 caliber machine gun around.

Click – Click!

I heard him slide a round into the chamber. Looking across the road, alongside what remained of a waterfront building, I could see the outline of three men in the dark shadows. It took a few blinks before my eyes adjusted to the dimness; when they did, I could see that each man held a rifle.

"Permission to fire?" the sergeant shouted.

With tension in the air, there was a long pause…then Riku replied, "Hold your fire. They're not pointing those rifles at us."

Then, suddenly, Riku stood up from behind the jeep, shouting in Japanese while he waved his hands toward the shadows. Jumping to my feet, I grabbed my Thomson from the rear seat and released the safety, holding it at ready.

"What the hell are you doing, Lieutenant?" Sergeant Bryan demanded, peering down the barrel of the Browning.

Slowly walking around the jeep, Riku answered, "Let's see what these guys want. The war's over." With his hands still in the air, Riku strolled towards the shadows, all the while calling to them in Japanese.

"Son of bitch! What do you say, Colonel?" Bryan asked, with his finger on the trigger.

"Give the Lieutenant a chance. Don't shoot unless they fire."

As the Lieutenant walked across the road towards the three men, they slowly moved out of the shadows and into the sunlight. They were a strange-looking bunch, dressed in baggy civilian clothes but all wearing some type of military cap. The rifles they loosely carried were all pointing down or away from us. Riku finally met face to face with them, and they talked awhile. Soon he turned and walked back towards the jeep, grinning.

"Stand down," he shouted. "They're no threat." Returning to the trailer, he rolled back the tarp and started rummaging inside.

"What's up?" I asked.

"They're World War One vets, and they want to trade their weapons for food. I'm going to give them a bag of rice."

Relieved, I relaxed and slipped my safety on again. "Not the rice. We're going to need it for the camps. Trade them some K rations...one meal for each rifle."

Looking back at me, with sweat rolling down the side of his face, Riku pleaded, "They're old men and starving, sir...and it took a lot of guts for them to come out and see us."

"Okay...two meals per weapon. But no more! We'll need this food for our guys."

Riku knew that I was right. He nodded in reluctant agreement and retrieved six meals.

The rifles Riku brought back were old and rusty, and we threw them in the harbor. But the old soldiers seemed happy with the deal; they kept bowing in our direction. Fearing that more people would appear, I stationed Sergeant Bryan with the jeep while we started our survey.

An hour later, we had finished our work. Because of its concrete construction, Terminal One with its adjoining dock looked serviceable. While there was some superficial damage to the warehouse, the piers seemed structurally sound and could service two or three ships while the rest of the harbor was being cleared. Terminal One would be Kobe's insertion point.

Returning to the jeep, we found Bryan sitting on the hood, smoking a cigarette, with his Thompson on his lap. Shaking his head, he eyed us putting away our gear. "Glad you're back. We've got more locals across the street, this time even some women. They've been there awhile, watching."

"Can I go see what they have, Colonel?" Lieutenant Togo asked.

Looking across the street at the group of eight or nine people, I replied, "Okay, but we can't afford to feed the city. One meal per person. And get back here right away. I want to get back to base."

As Riku walked away with a handful of K rations, I instructed Sergeant Bryan to take down the American flag, as it seemed to be a magnet for people looking for help. But then, our flag always had been that symbol.

Just as he was doing so, a lone bike rider approached us from behind. Coming to a stop next to the jeep, an odd-looking Nip, dressed in a clean white shirt and baggy trousers with a stove-pipe straw hat, said in broken English, "Me doctor, need medicine. You help?"

Rolling up the flag, Bryan turned to me with sour face, "Don't do it, sir. We'll need all we have. Let the Japs feel the sting of defeat."

Jasper, standing next to me, pouring water over his hot dirty face, looked my way his eyes intent. "I've seen your grit, Dutch. Now show me your goodness. Help the guy out."

What do you say? What do you do? They were both right. My mind raced back to all the brutality the Japanese had visited on us, all the death and destruction. Helping civilians out was not something I had thought about…but now I had to.

Moving to the trailer, I pulled out one of our small medical kits.

With Sergeant Bryan shaking his head, I handed it to my former slant-eyed enemy. "This is the best I can do, for now. More is on the way."

Bowing, not looking at me, he took it and peddled away in a cloud of dust.

Re-securing the tarp over the trailer, I whistled and waved towards Riku, telling him to return. As Sergeant Bryan started the motor, Jasper and I got into the jeep and waited. After bowing to the group a few times, Lieutenant Togo finally turned and ran our way, carrying a canvas bag. As he jumped into the rear seat, we took off, bouncing down the road.

On the way back to camp, Riku shouted over the Willie's engine, "Want to see what I traded for?"

When I nodded back to him, he reached into the bag without saying another word and began pulling out the items inside. First out was an old rusty revolver, followed by a kid's wooden toy gun, and finally three old knives, one of which was quite handsome, with ivory handles.

"That's just swell," I shouted back.

Then, with a big smile on his face, he raised one finger into the air, as if to say 'wait a minute.' Rummaging inside the bag again, he pulled out a brown bottle, twisting the label my way so that I could read it.

Looking across I could see it was a bottle of 'Chivas Regal.' Grinning from ear to ear, Riku handed it to me, yelling, "Thought we might drink to Jack tonight. What do say, Dutch? Just like old times!"

Now it was my turn to grin from ear to ear. What a hell of a good idea!

As we drove through the gate at camp, we noticed a large group of civilians milling around in the shade between the two old hangars. As we approached, they scattered from our path, giving us the road. As we passed the shabby group, they all lowered their heads, not saying a word or making eye contact. Most of the people were old men and women, with a few children hiding behind the adults. As we turned onto the tarmac, we could see that the Waco gliders had been positioned on the taxiway and were attached again to the C-47, waiting for departure. These planes were to fly back tonight, carrying our film and reports. They would return tomorrow, with more men and equipment. Next to the planes, on the grassy area between the runway and taxiway, my team had assembled four large army tents. Pulling to a stop outside one of the tents, we were joined by the sergeant of the security team.

"Any problems?" I inquired.

"No sir. The field is deserted. Inside the hangers, we found only two old biplanes. All of the other out-buildings are empty."

"What about all those people over by the hangers?"

"They've been there most of the day, sir. We think they want food."

"I don't like it. Take a couple men and herd them back out the gate and close it, then station a guard on it. Shoot over their heads if you have to, but I want them off the airfield."

Upon hearing my order, both Riku and the Padre turned my way, with looks of contempt.

"These people are starving, Dutch. We can't just shove them out the front door," Jasper pleaded.

"The hell you say," I answered back. "We can't feed all those people, and we don't need a food riot tonight."

"Please give them something, Colonel," Riku inserted.

Shaking my head ruefully, I turned back to the Sergeant. "Okay...give them each a K-ration. And Lieutenant Togo will go with your men and tell them that more is on the way. But I want them off the field within the hour."

"Aye, aye, sir!"

After giving our film and my written narrative to the flight crew of the Gooney Bird, I went inside the radio tent to make contact with headquarters. Over the noise of the C-47 warming up, and with the help of our radio operator, I was soon talking to Colonel Flag.

"Go ahead, Trailhead Thirteen," Flag's static-filled voice roared over the speaker.

"Mission accomplished," I answered back, keying the microphone. "Terminal One and adjacent transit dock look serviceable, and the harbor channel leading to the facilities seems clear of wreckage. All other docks and piers are out of service. Over."

"Any ground problems? Over."

"The town is in shambles and the civilians starving. No resistance yet, although we will need more men, food and supplies to determine whether the area is secure. Over."

"Reinforcements are coming tomorrow. Have the bird and gliders departed with your film and report? Over."

"Yes, sir, they are taking off as we speak. Are we released for Phase Two? And how are the other teams doing? Over."

"Some minor problems around Tokyo, so keep your guard up. Stand by for Phase Two until after we have viewed your film and report. We will contact you at 0700 with disposition. Over and out."

Just as the Colonel signed off, the twin Pratt & Whitney engines of the C-47 thundered overhead, shaking the tent. Walking outside, I looked up into the warm evening light and watched the three-plane group turn south, heading for Okinawa. *First day of occupation*, I thought, *and no one died. What a bonus!*

Liberation

After a meal of K-rations and a few Chivas toasts to Black Jack, my crew and I sprawled out on cots and slept for almost ten hours. Early the next morning, we received our orders to proceed with Phase Two of Operation Trailhead.

With the jeep and trailer packed, and the flag flying, we drove out through the front gate just as the C-47 and the two gliders returned, making their final approach with more supplies and men. According to plan, aboard these planes would be a Navy dive-and-demolition team that would survey and destroy any obstacles underwater in and around our selected harbor insertion. With any luck, we would have American ships in Kobe harbor within forty-eight hours. These ships would unload massive amounts of men and materials, and then provide transportation home for our liberated prisoners. Those POWs not well enough for the long ride home would be transported to the hospital ships. All the Navy had to do, now, was find the tens of thousands of allied prisoners hidden away in hundreds of remote camps in Japan, Korea and Formosa. It was a daunting task, and speed was of the essence.

Our first target for liberation was a camp located a few miles outside of the mountain town of Yashiro. G2 and our photo interpolators believed the Nips were running a tin or copper mining operation up there, using the Padre's old regiment and others as slave laborers. From the tattered 1938 road map I had been given before the mission, the town appeared to be no more than sixty miles northeast of Kobe. At that distance, we hoped to arrive by mid-morning.

Just a few miles outside of camp, though, we found that neither the roads nor my map were cooperating. The paved roads we traveled were unmarked, and there seemed to be more of them than there should be. Then there were the unexpected obstacles we had to navigate around: downed trees and power poles, landslides and damaged bridges. It took us three hours to travel just twenty-five miles. At one point, we came to a major river that, from the map, looked to be our half way point, but the bridge across the deep gorge had been bombed out of existence. All that remained was blackened, bent steel and mounds of cement rubble.

Bringing the jeep to a screeching halt at the edge of the precipice, Sergeant Bryan turned to me. "So, sir, now what?"

Dismounting, I walked to the edge, peering down the ravine. I searched for some sign of another place to cross, but saw none.

Returning to the jeep, Riku raised his head from one of his deep mind searches and stated, "Just a half a mile up this river, there is a railroad bridge we might be able to use."

There was a long moment of silence. Then the Sergeant asked, "How do you know that, Lieutenant?"

"Back on Okinawa, I saw an old tourist brochure for Yashiro. It had a map that showed the rail connection from Kobe. And, knowing my Japanese ancestors, it was probably drawn to scale."

That look of disbelief that I had had seen many times before raced across the Sergeant's face "Yeaah...sure, sir. You remember the scale and details of a map you saw weeks if not months ago."

Jumping back into my rear seat with a smile, I said firmly, "Actually, Sergeant, he can. He has an amazing photographic memory. Riding with the Lieutenant is like riding with the Auto Club. Let's go!"

Sure enough, just about a half mile up river, we found the bridge. After driving over a farmer's field, we steered the jeep onto the rail-bed, straddling the tracks. As we moved across the open span with our tires thumping, I shouted to Riku, "What kind of town is Yashiro?"

"It's a ski resort in the winter, and a place where the rich and powerful come in the summer for the mineral waters. It's a small village, high up in the mountains."

Nodding back to him, I thought, *how interesting! Even Imperial Japan has their share of haves and have-nots.*

Just across the gorge, we found and joined the main road again. The two-lane paved road we traveled snaked in and around beautiful mountain streams, with tall trees on both sides, always getting higher. In many ways, the journey looked very much like the countryside of British Columbia. The day we had spent in Kobe had been hot and humid, but these mountain elevations brought us relief, with moderate temperatures. As we traveled, we passed through a few small hamlets, but they all seemed deserted.

An hour after crossing the river, we came to Yashiro. Just before entering the town, we stopped and checked our weapons, then proceeded at a slow speed. The town itself was picturesque, with the architecture of a Swiss village. The buildings were all constructed on the mountain side of the road, with wide boardwalks in front of the wood-framed buildings. At the center of town, we found a pair of three-story, western-style hotels with other buildings attached. Everywhere we looked, however, the doors were closed, the blinds pulled and the street vacant. Where had all the people gone?

Just behind Yashiro's buildings, we could look up to the mountain top and see the groomed, cleared area used as the winter ski slope. Nestled in the tree line around this cleared area were other chalet-like structures.

The quiet little village seemed spooky. We crept through it, looking for any signs of life, but we saw none. Just on the other side of Yashiro, we stopped next to a high, beautiful waterfall to refill our canteens and talk of the town. We were all surprised that we hadn't seen anyone, but Riku guessed that the residents were all hiding from the 'western devils.' "These people have been told for years that the American soldiers would rape and kill the civilian population. They're scared of us."

Getting back into our jeep, we continued toward our objective. Soon, the paved road gave way to a dusty dirt road that curved its way ever higher around the mountain. About two miles outside of town, we came to an open barbed-wire gate with a sign that said, in Japanese: 'Restricted Area – No Entry.' Driving through it, we noticed that we were now at the timber line and the landscape had changed to rocks and scrub brush. After half a mile more, we arrived at the camp.

Stopping a few hundred yards from the main gate, I took out my binoculars and scanned the area. The main barbed-wired gate was closed, with a movable timber barrier in front. Just inside, to the right of the gate, was a tall deserted guard tower. Outside, on the left, was a small sentry shack. On a small rise behind this tiny house were three barrack-type buildings and a small wood-framed cottage. This area looked to be housing for the guards, but I could see no activity.

Just on the other side of the wire was an open area with three long log poles sticking up to the sky. Behind these poles were neat little rows of shanties that I figured had to be the housing for the POW's.

At the far side of these hovels were two large, tall, wooden derricks, with heavy equipment scattered about and mounds of rock rubble. These had to be the mines. The camp had the bleakness of a moonscape, with colorless boulders and brown dying scrub brush. And, just like on the moon, nowhere in the warm noonday sun could I see any signs of life.

Moving forward, we stopped again by the guard house. While Riku and the Padre moved the log barrier, I walked to the gate, only to find it chained closed with a padlock. Taking out my side arm, I shot three rounds into the rusty lock -- which promptly blew apart.

The sounds of my shots echoed off the mountain and swirled around the camp. If anyone was home, they knew we were here.

Slowly driving through the gate, we came to a stop by the three log poles and dismounted, bringing our weapons to the ready. Then, cupping one hand around my mouth, I shouted at the top of my voice, "Hello! Anyone here? We are U.S. Marines!"

Then we waited.

Slowly, ever so slowly, we started seeing movement, first in the shadows of the shacks, then through darkened doorways. Figures started stumbling towards us, some using sticks as crutches, others dragging one foot in the dust, while still others were helped by buddies who could walk. Like black ants leaving the hill, they moved into the sunlight, coming our way.

What we saw made our mouths drop and our eyes blink. These were men with dirty faces and open sores, dressed in rags for clothes, with bones protruding from their skinny emaciated bodies. As they hobbled towards us, they stared at us from their deep-socketed eyes as if they couldn't believe what they were seeing.

The first man to reach us came up to the Padre, dropped to his knees, placed his dirty hands on Jasper's pant leg, and began to weep. Soon, we were surrounded by these walking skeletons.

Dumbfounded, I was unable to speak.

Finally the Padre broke the silence, shouting, "God bless you all! We are here to help."

"Blimey," came a shout from a man in the crowd. "Is that you, Padre?"

Turning, I watched the man push through to the front row. If I hadn't heard his voice, I would have never recognized him as Major Dunn. He was nothing more than a hunched-over, walking scarecrow, with rags hanging from his skinny limbs.

Jasper knew instantly who he was, and stepped forward to gently embrace his frail commanding officer.

Finding my voice I asked, "Remember me, Major?"

Turning his head away from Jasper's hug, he looked at me through tears for a long moment, and then replied, "Yes, I do. We thought you guys were all dead."

"Are you in charge, sir?" I asked.

"I guess so. The American Major who was in command died, a few weeks ago. But there's not much to be in charge of."

"Is Doc Ross here?" the Padre asked.

"Yes, but he's helping a kid who's about to meet his maker. We die like flies around here. Do you have any water?"

Fumbling for our canteens, we handed them out to the crowd. "There's plenty more in the trailer," I shouted. "And we also have rice, beans, K-rations, candy bars and cigarettes. We'll see that you all get what you need. You men are officially liberated!"

Loud, long cries of joy erupted from the crowd as Sergeant Bryan mingled with the guys, passing out chocolate bars and smokes.

Turning back to Major Dunn, I quietly asked, "Where are the guards?"

"They disappeared, two days ago. Just walked away. There are still a few living over in their old barracks, but they don't come in here anymore. Is the war over? Where is the relief column?"

"The column will be here in a few days. Yes, the war's over. The Nips surrendered at noon on August fifteenth."

"And what is today's date? Is it still August?" Dunn asked with a confused, distant look.

As the Padre explained dates and events to the Major, I moved to help Riku remove the tarp from the trailer. He hadn't said a word, and his face was as white as a sheet. As we folded the canvas, he looked around the grounds. "If I hadn't seen this with my own eyes, I would never have believed the Japanese could do this. My god, Dutch, look at these poor bastards."

Just then, from the crowd, I heard, "Lieutenant Clarke, did you bring me any medicine?"

Turning, I found Captain Ross squeezing through the onlookers. His gray hair had turned snow white, and he walked with a limp. His eyes looked almost black, deep-set in his skull. Reaching out, I gingerly grabbed him, giving him a hug. Releasing him, with both of my hands still resting on his skinny shoulders, I looked into his sunken eyes and replied, "How could I forget you, Doc? We have medical kits, complete with the type of medicines the Navy doctors thought you would need most."

He stared at me for the longest time, and then said, "Good. I guess I should be calling you 'Colonel.' Did you bring any blankets? It gets real cold up here at night, and our guys are freezing."

With his body looking like a hat rack, the Doc's mind still seemed sharp as a tack, and I knew that he was probably the real person in charge. Taking him over to the trailer to show him the kits, I explained that I would order blankets for the planned air drop that would happen the next morning. Then I asked, "How many men are here?"

"As of last night's count," he replied with sad eyes, "we have sixty-one still living from the old regiment, one-hundred and forty-two U.S. Army from the Philippines, and another twenty-one American flyboys shot down over Japan. The total is two-hundred-twenty-two souls...but I'm the only doctor still alive, and I lose two or three a night to hunger, exposure or disease. We really need those blankets."

"Okay, after we get the trailer unloaded and the men fed, I'll take my guys back to the town we drove through and appropriate some blankets from the hotels we saw."

Satisfied, he nodded his head in agreement, then started helping Riku and I unload the trailer.

Soon, other weak hands joined in. As we slowly worked, I asked about the tall logs dug into the rock.

The Doc explained that, with the ground so hard, the Nips couldn't dig deep enough holes for the bakkin kou, the penalty boxes, so they used poles instead. Here, prisoners would be tied for days, exposed to the elements for the slightest infraction of the rules.

For me, his story brought back murky visions of my time in the box back at Camp Ireland. "Sounds like the work of Sergeant Yoshio and Colonel Hisachi. Were they here at this camp?" I asked.

"Yes," one of the other men said with a frown on his face. "But they ran off like rats, just before most of the other guards."

Just the thought that the Colonel and Sergeant were still alive twisted my guts with anger. But with the war over, I knew somehow, that justice would soon catch up with them.

After a near riot, with pushing and shoving prisoners vying for a meal of K-rations being tossed about like loaves of bread, I took the Doc and Major Dunn aside and told them that they had to reestablish discipline in the camp. We needed the able-bodied men to start cooking rice and beans for the evening meal, and then they had to control the amount of food intake for each man, or they might eat themselves to death. It was a dirty job, because everyone was so hungry, but it had to be done.

Overhearing my conversation, an Army Sergeant scowled. "I don't take no orders from Aussies!"

Turning to him while pointing to my collar, I scowled back. "Yes, you do, Sergeant. This silver oak leaf says so. If you don't, you'll be last in every chow line, and the last to leave this hell hole. Got it?"

The Sergeant looked at me for a long, mutinous minute, then shouted, "Yes, sir!" With that, he turned and walked away.

Two-hundred and twenty-two surly men was the last thing we needed. Walking to the jeep, I turned the radio on and reported back to base. I told them how many POWs we had found and exactly where the target for the next day's airlift should be. Then I went into great detail about all of the detours that would have to be taken to get the relief column up to the POW camp. In closing, I stressed the need for blankets, more doctors, and more medical supplies, because Captain Ross was overwhelmed, with many of the men on the brink of dying. After confirmation that my message had been relayed back to Colonel Flag, we loaded up the jeep and headed back towards Yashiro. The Padre had asked to stay behind to help, so only Riku and Bryan accompanied me on that return trip.

Approaching town, I told my guys that we would start by asking, first, for the blankets we needed. However, if they weren't forthcoming, we would take what we needed. My goal was to load the trailer with fifty blankets before we headed back to camp. If there weren't enough in the hotels, we would go house to house, to find more. Between bonfires and blankets, I hoped that every man in camp would stay warm tonight.

Driving into town, we saw a few people on the boardwalk, but they all scrambled away as we approached. Stopping in front of the first hotel, we got out of the jeep slowly, checking the alleys and rooftops for any trouble. Once we were confident that all was clear, we moved to the hotel's massive wooden front door and tried to open it.

It was locked.

Sergeant Bryan, using the butt of his Thompson, started banging on it.

Moments passed, and no one answered. Just as we were about to use our side arms to blow away the lock, we heard shouting coming from down the wooden walk. Turning, I found a small Oriental man quickly moving our way, shouting while he waved one hand in the air. As he got closer, I could understand his clumsy English. "American soldiers! American soldiers! Me surrender!"

As he approached, I did a double take. It was Toby, the Korean boy who had served as Colonel Hisachi's orderly. Dressed in black baggy trousers and a white shirt, and carrying an earthen jug, he stopped a few feet away from us, babbling, "No shoot! No shoot! I surrender!" Still waving one hand in the air, he fixed his gaze on Sergeant Bryan. Then he turned to look at Riku, and I could tell that his heart sank when he saw a Japanese person wearing an American uniform.

I cleared my throat. "Toby, do you remember me?"

A shocked look raced across his face: how could I know his name? He turned to me with an inquisitive look. Then, suddenly, a grin appeared. "Yes! Lieutenant Dutch."

"Where is everybody?"

"They scared, stay inside. Guards from camp come here, drink too much...cause trouble because lose war. People hide."

"Where are all those guards now?"

"They take over houses, all over mountain. Drink too much...very bad."

"Is Colonel Hisachi here?"

Scowling, Toby replied "Yes. He send me for more sake. But I see your jeep and escape." Setting down the jug, he pulled up one of his sleeves, showing us black and blue bruises on his arm. "He and Sergeant Yoshio took over house just behind town. They very drunk, very bad."

"Will you take us to him?"

He thought about it for a moment. Then the young man's face slowly took on a smiling glow as he said, "Yes. Yes!"

As I hurried Toby towards the jeep, Riku whispered, "Who is this guy?"

"The Colonel's orderly. You know, Hisachi, the camp commandant. The prick who killed Black Jack."

As we drove behind the town, Toby told us in his pidgin English that, when he left, Yoshio had been passed out in a rear bedroom, with Hisachi sprawled out, half-drunk, in a chair overlooking the garden.

Parking under some shade trees a few hundred yards from the house, we got out and followed Toby down a dirt path through some underbrush to just outside a small courtyard wall. Here I stopped the guys and told them to check their weapons. I knew that making a surprise visit to two drunken Nips, with the mountains full of other guards, wasn't too smart, but I was focused on vengeance.

Peering over the short wall, I could see the house. It was a small wood-framed, U-shaped chalet with shoji doors in the center that opened onto a courtyard. In the shadows just inside those open double doors, I could see a man slumped in a chair, holding a bottle at the end of one dangling arm. He seemed to be asleep.

With the scent of flowers in the air, and a wind chime rustling in the soft breeze, we quietly moved through an iron gate into the garden. Using hand signals, I directed Sergeant Bryan to sneak down one side of the yard while we did the same on the opposite side.

With me in the lead, we crept along the wall until we reach the opened doors. Standing erect on the outside of one of the shoji panels, I slowly moved my head so that I could see into the room.

Colonel Hisachi was alone and looked to be out like a light.

With that copper taste in my mouth, and my finger on the Thompson's trigger, I slid though the doorway in one fast, fluid motion. Three steps later, I had the barrel pointing six inches in front of his slumbering face. By the time I was in position, Riku and Toby had joined me from behind, and Bryan was in the room on the opposite side.

Towering over Hisachi, I looked down at him. He looked remarkably neat, in his brown riding britches and tan uniform, but his heavy breathing reeked of booze. Glancing at his belt, I noticed that his holster was empty. I looked to the small table on his left and saw the butt of his Nambu pistol under a folded Nip newspaper. Without taking my eyes off the Colonel, I quietly reached down with my right hand, slid the gun out from under the paper, and handed it off to the men behind me.

Then, using the barrel of my Thompson, I poked hard at Hisachi's sleeping body and shouted, "Wake up, Colonel! Judgment day is here."

Startled, the Colonel opened his eyes, dropping the bottle and quickly reached for his pistol on the table. As he rummaged under the empty paper, he blinked rapidly, trying to understand. Then, very slowly, he withdrew his hand, with a small rueful grin.

"I know you," he said, peering up at me intently. "You're my San Francisco friend. Where did you come from?"

"From your worst nightmares...you miserable bastard. I'm here to avenge all the men you've killed."

Blinking again, shaking his head, he looked around the room as if searching for reality. Was this a bad dream or were we real?

"I only followed orders," he stated. "You have no right to accuse me. The guilty criminals are in Tokyo, not here. The war is over. We demand to be allowed to go home."

He and I stared at each other for a long, silent moment. Then I slowly placed my M1 on the newspaper on top of the table. With my right hand, I reached up to my belt and pulled out my K-Bar knife. With my other hand, I searched my knee pocket for a picture of Black Jack's execution.

"Here," I said, holding the knife and the image in front of his distorted face. "Here's your death warrant, you bastard. Who in Tokyo ordered this?"

As he focused his bloodshot eyes on the picture, his face turned to stone.

"How did you get that?" was all he could ask.

"I have more...including the Wharf Massacre. All those women and children are here, today, demanding justice. I'm going to slit your throat and watch your life bleed out. Then -- and only then -- will those people rest in peace."

My words brought the room to silence as fear sped across Hisachi face. My blood was boiling, my heart racing with primal fury. As he watched my twitching knife, he knew he was about to draw his last breath.

"Dutch..." somebody said, behind me.

I ignored them.

"Dutch...this isn't the right thing to do," Riku finally blurted out, "Leave him to the tribunals.'

Turning my fuming face towards Riku, I answered back, "Screw the right thing. He dies, right here, right now."

"Justice is not revenge," Riku replied. "Justice is right. This is wrong."

"Kill him!" Sergeant Bryan snorted.

"Yeah, kill him!" retorted Toby.

I turned back to Hisachi and saw that he was weeping, his whole body shaking. Panic filled his face, and his lips quivered. "I had nothing to do with the wharf incident. That was all Yoshio's idea. I will testify against him. Please -- let me live."

I glared down at him. "No. The verdict is in. You die."

But what I said and what I felt were two different things. Looking into his pathetic, frightened face, I wasn't sure I could do it in cold blood. Deep down, I knew Riku was right: Colonel Hisachi was best left to the hangman.

But I had promised Black Jack revenge, and now was my opportunity. If only Hisachi would go for my weapon on the table, I'd have the excuse I needed...

But his eyes were closed; he was too scared to watch.

From behind me Riku stammered, "Dutch...please. If you kill him, you're no better than they are."

The handle of my knife felt like it weighed a hundred pounds. Then I heard the wind chimes sing as a stiff breeze rolled through the garden doors and up my spine. In that instant, I felt Black Jack's spirit touch my soul. As he flashed through my mind, I heard him whisper, 'Not this way, pal...Use what I taught you.'

Frozen in place for a few more heartbeats, I finally understood Jack's message. Slowly, I relaxed the hand holding the blade. "You're not worth my efforts," I told Hisachi. "Our pictures will convict you."

Bang! Bang, bang!

Bullets whizzed past my head, and I heard Toby cry out and crumple to the floor. The other two shots ran wild through the room and into the garden. I looked up from Hisachi to see a moving shadow on the other side of the rice-paper door.

Brrrrrt...Brrrrrrrrrrt!

Sergeant Bryan's Thompson spat to life, tearing holes in the far door and wall.

But the shadow had turned and was running.

435

Reaching for my weapon, I shouted to Riku, "Take care of the kid and watch the Colonel," and bolted towards the door. By the time I got across the room, Sergeant Bryan had already crashed through the closed door, three steps ahead of me.

As I entered the next room, I caught a glimpse of a large man who had just jumped out a window and was running towards the forest. The Sergeant had his Thompson to his shoulder.

Brrrrrrrrrt!

He let out a long burst of machinegun fire. The bullets echoed off the mountain.

Some fifty feet ahead of us, the figure on the path froze in his tracks. He stood erect as the back of his uniform turned crimson, then fell to the ground, face down.

Sergeant Bryan and I bolted through the window and rushed towards the man, with our weapons ready. When we reached him, I kicked away the pistol he had dropped. The Sergeant's burst had riddled his back to a raw, bloody mess, and he showed no signs of life. Using my foot, I rolled him over.

It was Sergeant Yoshio, with dead, open eyes.

As I stood there, looking down on his mangled carcass, a grin must have raced across my face, because Bryan asked, "Did you know him, sir?"

"Yeah," I answered, not taking my eyes off his limp body. "He was one miserable bastard that deserved killing."

"Well, if he had any friends up here, they certainly heard the ruckus."

"Sergeant Yoshio's only friend was Hisachi, and I'm not sure he liked him very much."

"What would you like to do, sir?"

"Check his pockets for any information. Then drag his body around to the jeep. We'll put him in the trailer and take him back to camp."

Bryan nodded his approval and dropped to one knee to begin searching. I turned and walked slowly back to the house, pleased yet disturbed with the kill.

Back inside, I found Riku dressing an arm wound on Toby. He had the kid on the floor, propped up against a wall on one side of the open double doors. Across from them on the other side was

Colonel Hisachi, seated Indian-style on a mat. He wore a white headband that had a red rising sun in the center and Japanese symbols all around. In both hands, he held a long dagger with the blade end pointed towards his belly. He didn't look up as I returned.

"How's the kid?" I asked.

"He's okay. The bullet grazed his arm but it missed the bone. Did you get the sniper?"

"Yeah. It was Sergeant Yoshio. Bryan's dragging his body to the jeep so we can take it back to camp. He'll need some help."

"Sure. I'm almost done here."

"What's the Colonel doing there?" I nodded toward Hisachi.

"He's looking for his bushido, but I don't think he's found it. He moved there a bit ago, trying to work up the courage to kill himself."

Watching Riku patching up Toby, I was surprised how cold that comment was, as if he was talking about the weather.

"I don't get you, Lieutenant," I said. "A few minutes ago, you were begging me for his life and now, like a cool breeze, you could care less if one of your people kills himself."

Finishing with Toby, Riku stood and looked at me. "He's not one of my people. After seeing his camp, I know that he's the problem, not the solution. If he kills himself, his blood won't be on my hands or yours, and the world will probably be a better place. But it doesn't really matter -- I don't think he has the guts to do it."

Moving to Hisachi, I knelt next to him, facing the garden, and said, "Sergeant Yoshio is dead and it's time to go. Give me the knife and we'll take you back."

All the time I had been in the room, his gaze had been fixed on the blade. Now, that gaze shifted slowly to me.

"Please," he whispered, "help me. I can't face the shame of a trial. Help me."

Watching his pleading eyes, I answered, "No. That would be too easy."

Sobbing, he shook his head. "I can't do it," he groaned, and dropped the knife. With a face filled with shame, he let his body slump against the wall.

The room filled with the sound of his heavy breathing.

Bang! Bang!

The sounds startled me. Twisting around, I saw Toby holding the Colonel's smoking pistol in his outstretched hands. The expression on the boy's face was one of fear mixed with satisfaction.

Turning back, I found Hisachi with blood oozing from his chest as he looked directly across the room to Toby. Struggling for a breath, he asked softly, "Why?"

"You pig!" Toby shouted back. "You took what I didn't want to give."

With disbelief in his eyes and a bloody hand over his wounds, my enemy looked up at me. Then, with a last gasp, his head drooped to his chest.

Colonel Hisachi was dead.

By the time I stood, Riku was at Toby's side, removing the pistol from his shaking hands. We were all silent for a moment, dazed, replaying the events.

Standing over Hisachi's slouching body, I finally reached down and removed his headband. "What's this all about, Lieutenant?"

"It's like an autograph book. All of his family and friends signed it before he went off to war. Its more bushido crap. You're supposed to wear it when you kill yourself."

Glaring down on the Colonel's body, I wondered why I didn't feel joy. Why had his death touched me? Folding the headband, I put it in my pocket. "How sad, war truly is the final destination for evil."

"Yeah, it sure is." He hesitated. "What about the kid, Dutch?"

Forcing my mind back to reality I answered, "Given the circumstance, Hisachi's death is of no concern. We'll take the boy back to camp. He's been through enough. Somehow, we'll see he gets home."

We took both bodies back with us and sprawled them out on the boardwalk in front of the hotels. And as we were doing it, a strange thing happened: the town seemed to come alive. At first, a trickle of people opened their blinds and peered out their windows. Then doors were unlocked, and small groups ventured out to see the Colonel's and Sergeant's corpses. The locals were a curious bunch, still frightened of us but relieved that their town was no longer under the grip of the unruly guards.

The hotel's proprietors hesitated at first to give us the blankets we needed, but after some animated conversations with Riku they relented. As we worked at filling the trailer, other guards appeared, dropping their weapons off next to the bodies. Then, in small groups, they marched off, headed farther down the mountain. The war was over for these soldiers, and they wanted to go home. Watching these men as they marched out of town was the first time I felt confident in our mission, with hope for the future. An hour later, with fifty blankets and some warm coats loaded in the trailer, we spread out the tarp, put the two bodies on top, and drove out of the town.

When we arrived back at camp, we laid the corpses out next to the poles in the afternoon sun, for all to see. As the prisoners gathered, looking down at the remains, many had smiles on their faces. Others kicked and spit on the bodies. Soon, even the remaining guards ventured into the compound to satisfy their curiosity. Some of these soldiers looked down on the Colonel and Sergeant with faces full of anger, and then pissed on the corpses. No one laughed, but no one cried. It was a damn sad thing to watch. Later, after a strong protest from the Padre about my care of the corpses, I had a detail of the guards bury the bodies in some soft ground just outside the front gate. Here, only Jasper stood and said a few words; no one else seemed to care. With their past evils buried, we all looked to the future, trying to forget.

With the aid of bonfires, blankets and warm coats, the night passed with no deaths. The next morning brought three C-47's roaring over, filling the sky with parachute-loads of supplies. They even dropped in two Navy doctors to assist Doc Ross. With these supplies and help, I knew the men would make it until the relief column came.

With our mission accomplished, I called my crew together to say our good-byes and move on to the next camp. Time was of the essence, and other prisoners needed liberation. As we milled around the jeep, shaking hands, I overheard the Padre say to Major

Dunn that he wished he could stay with his old regiment but that he didn't have any orders. Taking Jasper aside, I asked if that was really what he wanted to do. He said yes, but that the only orders he had from his government attached him to Admiral King's staff.

With a somber look, I reached into the jeep for my clipboard and hand-wrote him a new set of orders, directing him to return with what remained of the Fourteenth Royal Engineers. Then, with a mail-call grin, I signed my name to the bottom and beamed. "Guess that's why the Admiral made me a Colonel. Take these orders and go home with your flock. You've earned it!"

Glancing at the paper I handed him, he stepped forward and gave me a bear hug. As he pulled away with weepy eyes, he said, "You have no idea how much this means to me. We have been through so much together! You counseled me in my darkest hour... you made me laugh when I was sad...you nursed me in my poorest health...and you've helped save my friends, my regiment. Now we must part. You're a good man, Dutch Clarke. May you live the rest of your life in peace; I'll miss you...Gods speed."

EPILOGUE

With seagulls swooping down on the green foamy wake of the troopship *Lady Blue*, we departed Pearl Harbor and set course for San Francisco. It was May of 1946, and I had just filed my final report, photos and relinquished my temporary rank from my Japan assignments with Admiral King's headquarters. At his command center, I had wanted to say my good-byes to the Admiral but was told that he was flying to Japan just as I was flying towards Hawaii. We had crossed paths somewhere over the vast Pacific.

My orders were to proceed to the mainland for thirty days of leave and then report to Camp Pendleton for some type of a mustering-out ceremony. This was something I did not look forward to, as the war and my military career was over and I had to get on with my life. But my orders had been signed by Admiral King himself, and I knew they were not just suggestions. He had been my Rabbi, and a good one at that, and had even offered me a promotion to Major if I signed up for another hitch, but I'd turned him down. During the last four years I had seen enough and done enough; civilian life was now calling. With that in mind, I guessed a short ceremony at Camp Pendleton wouldn't kill me.

Having enough combat points, I could have taken a C-54 passenger plane to the mainland, but I'd elected to take the troopship instead. Aboard the *Lady Blue*, I hoped to get my mind right for the life that lay before me. With almost two thousand men aboard the ship, all heading stateside to be mustered out, there seemed little need for military courtesy. Officers mingled with the enlisted, telling jokes and shaking hands. Lieutenants called their superiors by their first names, and salutes were hard to find. In some ways, it was as if the last four years had never happened.

During these bright, warm days, most of the guys were drawn forward to the bow of the ship. There they talked, in the sun of their tomorrows and the future. For some reason, I and a handful of others were drawn to the stern of the ship, where we stood mostly quiet. Standing by the rail, we watched the tropics slowly slip by, and with it went our past. If we talked, it was always about yesterday, never about tomorrow. Almost four years ago, I had started this journey, looking for answers. Now, all I had was more questions: Why had I lived? Would Black Jack's shroud always cast a shadow on me? What could I have done? What should I have done? Why had God let so much blood stain the sands?

And, of course, there was Colonel Hisachi and the men like him. Many had found justice but many more had not, simply slipping into history. American was war weary and tired of revenge. Now there were even those in the press who said we shouldn't have used 'the bomb,' that Japan would have surrendered without it…but at what cost? More civilians had been killed in the fire bombings of Tokyo than with both atomic bombs, and still they had not surrendered. Our air power had destroyed Japan's landscape and brought her industries to their knees. And still they did not surrender. It was only after Japan's Emperor found his 'will' to stop the fighting that the war ended -- something he could have done months before we used our atomic bombs, but he hadn't. But still, with all these facts, the media second-guessed the war's outcome and blamed America for using the bomb.

I guess this is the price we pay for a free press; I was only disappointed that the media had lost their honesty and objectivity. My camera lens had caught the destruction and defeat of Japan, over the past nine months, and it hadn't been a pretty sight. The Japanese people were struggling to put food on their tables, heat in their homes, and hope in their future. They had been defeated in every way, but Lieutenant Togo, who had stayed behind to work with the fledging new government, believed they would rise again as an economic power.

I had my doubts. Deep inside, I still harbored a hatred for all things Japanese. I disdained its culture and felt little pity for its people. But then, my assignments had been to photograph most of the POW camps on the mainland, and I had seen their brutality first-hand. This hatred inside of me gnawed at my guts, and I prayed I would lose it once I reached home.

The Navy never did release any of the images Black Jack and I had taken at New Ireland, although later I heard that some of the pictures were used at war crime trials as examples of the conditions within POW camps. Maybe America really wasn't ready for this vivid truth. The set of images I retained had months before been filed away in my duffel bag and more or less forgotten. Such reminders were not healthy. Other than that, the steel pin in my hip, occasional sweats from my malaria, and nightmares of men dying, I hadn't changed much....

Who was I kidding? I worried about what Laura would see in my heart, and what future there would be for me. I had changed. Everything had changed.

We docked in San Francisco on the morning of May 20th, and I was in the first group of officers released to the gangway. With my sea-bag high on my shoulder and the sun on my brow, I raced down the plank, searching the sea of faces for Laura.

As if by magic, just to my right, I caught a glimpse of her, shouting and waving. It was as if she glowed, with the sun streaking through her hair, and her face bright with the biggest smile I had ever seen. Reaching the dock, I let my bag slip off my shoulder and leaped through the first three rows of onlookers to reach her. In one fluid motion, we came together in an embrace rich with tears and kisses.

Her first words to me came in a whisper. "You've been gone so long..."

Looking into her beautiful, moist eyes, I whispered back, "Did I lose you?"

"Oh, Dutch, you can't lose me. I'm attached to you like your shadow. I love you!"

With her words, all my apprehension seemed to melt away. Her look, her voice, her scent had lived in my imagination through so many dark years, and now it had all come true. She was my love, my soul mate, my future. Holding her face in my hands, looking into her big blue eyes, I nodded yes and kissed her sweet, wet, red lips again.

Home I was...and home I would stay, next to Laura and Theodore, until heartbreak separated us, many years later. But that tender love story has yet to be told.

Laura and I spent the next three weeks touring the Golden Gate city, savoring Fisherman's Wharf and exploring Chinatown. Compliments of Uncle Roy, we had a suite at the Mark Hopkins Hotel, where we dined and drank at the Top of the Mark. We even took a few twirls around the dance floor, but after stumbling on Laura's feet more times than I could count, I always gave up in frustration.

Against a backdrop of striking sunrises and the spectacular sunsets, we rekindled our love and answered our passions. We seemed to start just where we had left off, as if the last four years were but a distant memory. Laura's inner beauty proved to be as dazzling as her physical beauty; she could fill any room with head turns and happiness. The respect, the love and, most of all, the compassion she showed me were unlike any that I had received at other times in my life. Before long, we got back into step with everyday reality. It was then that I resolved to erase the ugliness and hate of the previous years, and to look to the future, which held the promise of so much love and adventure. I thanked the Lord for all my blessings.

In the middle of June, Laura boarded a train north to reunite with Theodore and her parents, who were looking after him. There she would make plans for our upcoming wedding. That same evening, I boarded a train south to take care of some business and that mustering-out ceremony.

Riding the rails in a drab, malodorous compartment, I watched the countryside slip by, and marveled at how bountiful and peaceful the landscape looked. Gone were all the signs of war. Relaxing on my bench seat, I asked the porter for a bottle of Flagstaff, and removed the pouch of tobacco that I had purchased at the station. It had been years since I had rolled my own cigarette, and it took a couple tries before I was satisfied with my efforts.

As the porter placed the brew in front of me, I lit my smoke and paid my tab. Tipping his hat and smiling, he told me the train would be in to the Hollywood station on time. Then he continued, "Use to be our trains were full of soldiers like you, Captain, but we don't see so many anymore. I'm glad the war's over, but I miss all those young men. They had so much youth and promise! Call me, if you need anything more."

After he departed, I turned my attention to the darkening landscape, took a swig of beer, and thought about the porter's words. How true they were... So where had all that 'youth and promise' gone? As my mind wandered off, ghostly images reflected back on the inky window pane. They moved...they laughed...they cried....

My pal, Kurt Benson, from boot camp made it through the war, minus three fingers he lost on Okinawa. But this handicap didn't slow him down, as he soon became one of the most productive commercial fishermen in Ketchikan. A few years after returning home, he married a local girl and eventually had five kids. We stayed close, lifetime friends, and I always looked him up when we came to visit Laura's folks. On those trips, he would take me out on one of his boats where, over a bottle of scotch, we would catch up on fishing and friendship.

My other pal from boot camp, Jim Wilson, the comedian, returned to Seattle without a scratch. There he married and had two children. Over the years, he became a successful and prosperous insurance man. We got together a few times, after the war, and enjoyed each other's stories of furloughs gone by. It was during those times that I found out he'd never lost that sense of humor -- or his nickname. He was a joy to be around, but in the end we became more of Christmas-card pals.

Of course we had lost Hank Marks and Dick Nelson on the sands of distant islands. I told myself a thousand times to look up their parents, but I never did. It would have been the right thing to do...but I guess their memory was etched too deeply in my mind with images of things I wanted to forget. But each of these two men had spilled their blood for my future, and I regretted my inaction.

The *USS Argonaut* never did make it back to Pearl. The Navy speculated she went down with all hands, off of Bougainville, while trying to sink a mule using her last Mark 16MS in rough seas. The Argonaut's name was officially stricken from the Naval Vessel Register at the end of February 1943. She had been a good boat, with a great crew of ninety officers and men who would be missed and honored by family and friends for years to come. Our mission aboard her helped save the 16MS program, but at a terrible cost. I would never look at a submarine again without thinking of the men of the *USS Argonaut*.

Commander Jacobson of the PT squadron RON3 fared much better. He and his men 'yachted' their way through the Pacific wreaking death and destruction on the enemy until war's end. Right after our departure from Wagina Island, his squadron helped rescue the crew from the famous PT 109. Years later, he became the Undersecretary of the Navy in the Kennedy Administration -- the perfect position for a yachtsman from Nantucket.

Lennie Ford jumped out of his Marine uniform just as the last bombs fell on Japan. His job was done and he landed on both feet as the vice president of publicity for Paramount Studios. With the war over and the heroes coming home, he knew just what the public wanted: movies to help them forget all those dark, bleak yesterdays. Of course, his 'secret weapon,' Margaret Meede, joined him as his personal assistant. For a number of years, they helped guide the studio and all those new silver-screen idols to the top of the entertainment business. In 1950, they left Tinsel Town and moved to Burbank, where Lennie became President of Operations for a fledgling television network by the name of NBC. Soon after, he convinced the Board of Directors that Maggie would make a great program director. She was the first woman ever to achieve such heights, and it proved to be one of the best decisions the board ever made. She led the way to prime-time variety shows and late-night television. Lennie loved to tell all who would listen that Maggie was so valuable to the network that two of the feathers on the NBC peacock belonged to her. These two people, I'm proud to say, remained dear lifelong friends.

Carole Lane was not so lucky. She missed out on playing the female lead in George Cukor's film, 'Leathernecks,' and after months of unsuccessfully trying out for other films, she went on tour with the USO. The show traveled to both Europe and the Pacific, entertaining the troops. I understand, from those who saw the show, that she did a great job and always brought the audience to tears at the end of her performance with that story about her brother dying in the skies over London. Once an actor, always an actor! Upon war's end, she came home and made a film about her travels entraining the troops; its title was 'Three Women in a Jeep.' It did reasonably well at the box office, although, it proved to be her last movie. Tragically, Carole Lane died from an overdose of drugs in 1947, after a failed love affair. The news of her death saddened me as, each time I boarded a train, I would think about that special night we had spent together. I guess a man never forgets his first encounter.

Riku Togo returned to the states in 1948, after marrying a beautiful and petite Japanese gal from Kyoto. Tucked inside his briefcase was an exclusive contract to be the sole US importer for an upstart company by the name of Sony. Their first product was the transistor radio, which flooded the American market for years to come. Needless to say, he and his family prospered for many years. In the end, he proved me wrong: Japan, with his help, did become an economic giant, and Riku Togo, using his sharp mind and instincts, became a very rich and powerful American industrialist. Black Jack, Riku and I had bonded together like glue when we first started out; even after Jack's demise, that bond remained. We stayed in touch over the years, and even saw each other occasionally. He had been my conscience on those first dark days of occupation, and I slept better for the rest of my life because I had listened to his advice.

Jasper Young, the Padre, returned to Australia with what was left of his decimated, beloved 14th regiment. Upon leaving the service, and after a few months of R&R, he and his team of men returned to the islands of the South Pacific, looking for the remains of fallen warriors. They searched the jungle battle fields and the deserted POW camps on behalf of governments and families looking for closure to those horrific years. Years later, after returning thousands of body bags home, Jasper rejoined the service, where he was promoted to Brigadier and put in charge of all Australian military chaplains. I never did see Jasper again but, in one of his infrequent letters, he told me that his team had searched the graveyard at Camp Ireland but found no remains. Apparently the Nips had removed and burned all the evidence of their brutality, just before the war's end. He went on to apologize for not finding Black Jack's body or any signs of the Wharf Massacre. "What was left was merely charred buildings, with no bodies. But I knew they were still there, as I could feel their spirits and touch their souls. May God have mercy on all those who died in these hell-holes." The Padre had been my spiritual leader during my darkest days, and I was gratified by his many efforts on behalf of our fallen heroes. God bless Jasper Young.

Then there was that Marine photographer I had met on the train, Captain Thayer Soule. He did return to Virginia, where he trained hundreds of combat photographers and artists. Because of his efforts, and those of men like him, today we have a visual record of the triumphs and tragedies of the War -- dramatic images of people, events and places that are etched into our minds, never to be forgotten. But this, too, came at a price. During the war, combat photographers suffered fatalities four times greater than that of a typical soldier.

With the swaying and rhythm of the rails, my window flowed with ghostly faces all through the night. There were so many not to forget, so many lives touching lives with a lifetime of memories.

Early the next morning, I checked into the Hollywood Roosevelt Hotel and called Maggie on the telephone. The week before, from San Francisco, I had sent her a telegram, letting her know that I would be in town over the weekend, and asking if I could pick up my car. Finally hearing her excited, friendly voice on the phone brought back a flood of wonderful memories about my days working with her. Within half an hour, I had taken a cab to her residence, nestled in the Hollywood hills. Upon my arrival, I found her waiting on the front porch of her yellow stucco and white-trimmed bungalow. She rushed my way as I came up her sidewalk, and threw her arms around me, giving hugs with smiles and tears.

"Oh Dutch, just look at you," she finally said with moist eyes. "A full captain with ribbons on your chest, and still standing tall. Damn...I thought we had lost you!"

With the early morning sun washing her face, I marveled at how good the years had been to her. That white streak in her hair looked a little bigger now, and a few wrinkles had crept in around her eyes, but Maggie was still one trim, stunning lady. And her perfume -- oh, how I remembered that perfume!

Taking my hand, she led me though her house to the veranda, where she had set up a coffee service. There we sat and talked for hours. Our conversation started out mostly about the old days at the office, and what had happened to different people, as well as what films and events they had staged, after we'd gone. Then she told me about Lennie's new job, and how she was helping him with all the new breed of movie stars.

Finally, I asked about my car. At my question, her expression turned on a dime from bright to serious. She explained that, after she and John Craft had brought it back from San Diego, they had put it up on blocks in her garage. Then, a week ago, after my telegram, John had put the wheels back on and charged the battery.

"It runs real good," she continued, expressionless. "He even had it washed and waxed." Then her eyes got glassy, and she looked away. "But..."

"But what?" I prompted, when she didn't continue.

"I didn't know what to do with it... The Navy sent me Jack's duffel bag, in early 1944. It came with your old bag. I've kept them in my garage for all these years. I think Corporal Riku packed them up when you didn't return from your mission. Anyhow, I had Mr. Craft put them in the trunk of your car. I hope that's alright. I just didn't know who to give Jack's stuff to. But I don't want to open up any old memories for you, either. You know, about...Jack's death."

Looking into her hazel eyes, I could see that she was about to cry, "That's okay, Maggie. I think I've come to grips with his death. Don't you worry about it. I'll take care of the bag."

Slowly getting up from her chair, she gazed down on me and replied, "But there's more. I'll be right back."

Turning, she went into the house, and then returned with a fat brown envelope and a bottle of brandy.

Taking her seat again, she slowly poured a shot of the brandy for each of us into our coffee cups. Then, taking the envelope, she handed it across to me. "This is for you. There's $10,855 in it. Jack named me as his executor and you as his beneficiary, in his will. Ten thousand dollars is his GI insurance, and the balance is his back pay and benefits. I typed out an accounting and put it inside the envelope. It's all there."

Looking into the envelope, I saw the wad of cash inside. Her news caught me off guard. I stammered for words...and anger came out, instead. "I don't want his damn money, and I don't want his sea-bag. I don't deserve either one." Suddenly, I was weeping. "Maggie, I couldn't even save my best friend's life! If it weren't for me, he'd still be alive."

Maggie stared back at me in shocked silence. Then, pouring another shot of brandy into my cup, she said, "I'll bet you did the same for him, in your will. In some ways, you two were as different as night and day, yet in others the same as water and ice. What you had with Jack was special. You two were brothers. He went off to fight alongside of you...and didn't come home. I don't want to know the details of his death, but I'm sure you did the best you could for him. And I'm also sure that anger and sorrow won't bring him back. Did he have any family?"

She was right; I had named him on my insurance, since Laura and Uncle Roy were well taken care of in my will. With my hands still shaking, I took a sip from my cup. "A bum of a father, who's more than likely dead by now. The last Jack knew his father lived on skid row in LA. Other than that, there's no one."

Reaching across the table, Maggie grabbed my hand and gripped it hard. "Well then, you will have to keep it. He wanted you to have it. It was important to him. I'm so sorry your homecoming is full of sorrow...I didn't want this for you."

Forcing a smile, I replied, "But it's not. Not really." And I proceeded to change the subject and tell her about my engagement to Laura.

At the news, her face glowed. "Oh, Dutch! I'm so glad you have found that special someone, that person you will spend the rest of your life with. We'll celebrate tonight! Lennie and I will take you out on the town and, if it's alright with Laura, I'll give you that dance lesson, like I promised."

I praised the Lord for bringing me home to such friends. "Trust me, her toes won't mind. I need all the help I can get, when it comes to dancing."

That afternoon, back at my hotel, I took Jack's bag and carefully unpacked it onto my bed. For the most part, it held underclothes, uniforms and toiletries. Deep inside, however, I did find a few personal items: the record albums I had given him for Christmas in 1943, a few books, and a photographic paper box that contained a handful of his favorite pictures. Leafing through those images, I was surprised by how many of them there were of me and him together. And then I found the pictures of his girlfriend in the white towel, stepping out of the shower. A small grin raced across my face at the memory of that near-disaster.

Digging a little deeper, I found more images of this same gal, taken just before we departed on our first assignment. What was her name? I couldn't remember, as I had only met her once, at my New Year's Eve party. All I could recall was that I'd liked her.

At the bottom of the bag, I found a wooden cigar box which held papers and letters. On top were some V-mails from Maggie, and even a note from Lennie. Underneath was a stack of six more open envelopes...and two unopened letters. All of this mail was from the same person, Miss Monica Jackson...

That was her name! Checking the return addresses, I noticed that she had moved away from Hollywood in June of 1943, relocating to South Los Angeles. The two unopened pieces of V-mail were postmarked December 1943 and had arrived after our raid on Tulun. Holding the letters, I was surprised by how many there were, and I wondered whether I should read them. I knew Jack and Monica had been an item before our deployment, but was it right to read my dead pal's letters? He had been so silent about her...but then, he never did talk much about his personal life. Finally, sitting down next to the window, I took the first letter in hand and, feeling like a voyeur, read it.

Monica's beautiful handwriting came alive on the paper as she talked about her job, her life and how much she missed Jack. Her words were positive, her outlook bright and full of hope. She thought about him every night, his touch, his passion, his scent. She loved and longed for Jack Malone, and would wait for him until he came home.

Putting down the first letter, I blushed, then took the next and continued my escape into Jack's most private life.

In the letter postmarked June of '43, she said she was moving back home to Watts, to be with her mother. There she would change jobs and continue to wait for Jack...

After reading the six opened letters, I decided I had snooped enough and would not open the final two V-mails. Jack and Monica's secrets were safe with me, and I knew that, if anyone deserved Black Jack's money and memories, it was her. Maybe it would help bring some closure and comfort.

Early that evening, I met up with Lennie in the bar at the Brown Derby. Over two martinis, we talked of war and winning. He hadn't changed much from my days at OWI. He had lost some weight and, while his dark eyes looked tired, the salt-and-pepper goatee he sported made him look very distinguished. Also gone was his Hollywood uniform of riding britches and ascots, replaced with an expensive three-piece suit and short, trimmed hair that made him look every bit the studio executive.

An hour later, when Maggie arrived, we went into the dining room, where Lennie introduced me around the room like a returning prodigal son. I shook hands with Clark Gable and Spencer Tracy, and even got a kiss on my cheek from Marlene Dietrich, who said she remembered me from the USO show, so many years before. They all treated me like royalty, and I had a wonderful Hollywood welcome-home party.

At ten o'clock, Lennie excused himself to attend another bash, so Maggie and I slipped out to the Roosevelt Hotel for more drinks and dancing. By early the next morning, when the band finally stopped playing, Maggie had me gliding around the floor, flowing with the music. Laura's toes would never suffer again and, because of Maggie's patience and persistence, I would love dancing for the rest of my life.

The next morning, I loaded up the car for the drive to Camp Pendleton. Before departing, however, I was determined to look up Monica and give her Black Jack's money. Driving to South Los Angles, I found the Watts area, a middle-class neighborhood of modest wood-frame homes. With the help of some directions from a local gas station, I soon found the correct street and numbers from Monica's return address.

Stopping my car, I stared out at the small home for a number of minutes, not really sure what I would say to her. Finally, mustering up my courage, I slowly walked up the rose-lined walkway and rang the doorbell. When the door opened, I was confronted by a gray-haired black lady, peering out at me.

"Yes, Captain? May I help you?"

Disappointed that it wasn't Monica, I stammered, "Ah, I'm…I'm looking for a Miss Jackson. Might she be at home?"

Gazing back at me with a sudden scowl, she shook her head no. "There's no more Miss Jackson here. She married, a few years back, and moved away."

"Could I get her new address? I really need to look her up. We had a mutual friend who died in the war, and I have some letters to return to her."

The woman hesitated. "I'm her mother. You could give them to me. Who would this friend be?"

"Jack Malone. He was my best friend. I also have some money for her."

"I remember that boy. He was nice to Monica and me. She took his death real hard. I'll give you her new address if you'll promise to be gentle with her. She loved Jack very much. Maybe your visit and a little money will help her find some good from his memory. But stay clear of her husband, Axel. He's a lazy, good-for-nothing nigger with a short fuse."

Nodding, I said, "I promise that my visit will help her in many ways. Jack loved her very much."

By the time I stepped off of her mother's front porch, I had Monica's address, along with driving directions to her apartment. Mrs. Jackson said it was a ramshackle place, built during the war for the shipyard workers, and not a fit place to live.

As I pulled up in front of the large, three-story apartment house, I could see that she was right. The building was typical of the temporary housing built by the government in the early forties for the war effort. It had already seen its better days and was in dire need of paint and maintenance.

Inside the main lobby, I climbed three flights of stairs and looked for directions to the right number. After walking down a dark and dingy corridor, stepping over toys and junk littering the hallway, I came to Apartment 323. As I raised my hand to knock, I heard a commotion coming from the other side of the door. With screaming and yelling ringing in my ears, I knocked loudly on the door jam.

Quickly, the ruckus fell silent, and the door was soon opened halfway, revealing a big, burly, jet-black man, wearing a dirty white t-shirt. He was one mean and ugly-looking guy, with so much kinky hair that it curled around his shirt sleeves and stood up on the back of his neck. He reminded me of Fatso from the *USS Argonaut*, just in a different color.

"What the hell do you want, honkie? We ain't buyin' no war bonds," he growled at me.

His breath reeked of booze, and he had one hand on the inside of the door, ready to slam it.

"You must be Axel. I've heard about you. I would like to see Monica. I have something for her."

He stared at me for the longest moment with his blood-shot brown eyes. Then he turned his head into the room and shouted, "Girl, there's some honkie soldier boy out in the hall who says he has something for you. Get your ass over here!" Turning his head back to me, he continued, "I'll be watching you, so keep your hands off my wife."

Just then, the door opened all the way, and I found Monica gazing out at me through one bruised and swollen eye. The sight of her pretty battered face, shocked me.

"Hello, Monica. Do you remember me? I'm Dutch, Jack Malone's friend."

At the sound of Jack's name, her face lit up like a neon sign. "Yes! We spent New Year's together, before you guys shipped out."

Under an old, baggy dress and a dirty apron, she still had a trim body. As she talked, she stepped in front of Axel and used her body to gently shove him from the doorway. "I wondered if you had made it home. How did you know where to find me?"

"I went by your mother's house, and she told me. Can we talk for a moment? I have something for you."

"Sure," she replied. Turning her head towards Axel, she said, "I'll be in the hall talking to Dutch, with the door open." Then she slipped out into the hallway, pulling the door almost shut behind herself.

I could see Axel's fuming face through the crack as he peered out on us.

"Are you okay?" I whispered.

Taking a long moment, she shook her head 'no' and stared into my eyes, then replied, "Yes...I think so. The Navy never told me how Jack died. Did he suffer?"

"No. I was with him at the end, and it was fast." Reaching into my pocket, I pulled out the two unopened letters and handed them to her. "Yesterday, when I was clearing out some of his things, I came across these letters. They must have arrived after we'd been captured. I wanted you to have them. And there are other personal things you might like to have -- his sea-bag, his books and some photos."

Her one good eye rolled in its socket as she motioned her head towards the partly closed door. "I want them, but not now. Axel would have a fit. Could you send them to my mother's place?"

"Sure...but there's more."

Just then, the door behind her cracked open a little farther, and a young child slipped through it into the hall, babbling, "Mommy! Mommy!"

Reaching down, Monica picked up the toddler and settled him on her hip. As she did, I couldn't take my eyes off the little guy. His skin was a light brown, and the delicate features of his face looked so familiar....

Watching my reaction, Monica finally said, "Dutch, I'd like you to meet Jack, Jr. Axel and I married for all the wrong reasons. He is just the stepfather."

With that news, a grin washed across my face. All I could say was, "I'll be damned! Black Jack lives on."

"I never told him I was pregnant until in the last letter, after Jack, Jr. was born. He had too many other worries, and what the hell could he have done about it?"

She looked so gloomy, holding Jack's son, gazing at me through her mangled eye, that I wanted to reach out and hold her, then pound the hell out of Axel.

But I didn't.

"Well, he can do something about it now," I finally replied, reaching into my other pocket. Handing her the fat envelope, I continued, "Here. I know Black Jack wanted you to have it."

With the thumb of her free hand, she flipped open the envelope. When she saw the chunk of cash inside, her one good eye got as big as a saucer.

"You don't know how much I need this..." she murmured. "It will change our lives. But I can't take it now, because Axel will just blow it on booze and the ponies. Will you give it to my mother?"

"Sure. I'll take it over now, on my way out of town. Jack Malone was the brother I never had, and now that I've found his son, I'd like to be part of his life -- if you'll allow it."

From the other side of the door, Axel's angry voice rang out. "What the hell is taking so long? Open that goddamn door!"

Handing the envelope back to me, she kissed me on the cheek and whispered, "Trust me, you will be. Junior and I will soon be moving back with Mom. You can contact us there."

Leaning down, I kissed Jack Jr. on the top of his head. "Will you be alright, here?" I asked Monica anxiously.

"Yes. I'm a survivor...but you better go, before there's trouble."

Before Axel could throw open the door, I winked at Monica and her son, then turned and walked away, content that Jack Malone was back in my life.

As ordered, I reported to the main administration building at Camp Pendleton on Monday morning at 1000 hours. When I got there, I was told that the mustering out ceremony would be held on the adjacent parade grounds at 1100 hours.

As I walked over to that area with some other Marines, we talked about how the camp had changed since our days of basic training. Most of the barracks buildings were now boarded up, and gone were the endless lines of recruits. With the war over and men flowing out instead of in, the new USMC was but a shadow of the old. But the memories of the old ran deep, and the sight of it all brought back a rush of those long, hot days and short, warm nights.

As we walked and talked, I looked down at the program I had been handed, and was surprised to see that the speaker for our ceremony would be none other than Admiral James King. The thought of seeing and saying goodbye to my Rabbi lifted my spirits. His name reminded me that we had all traveled many long, dark paths since completing training.

When we arrived at the grounds, we found a large, raised platform with a podium had been set up in front of a sea of wooden chairs. On each side of these chairs were grandstands for family, friends and civilians. The physical setup was very much like a typical commencement ceremony.

As I mingled with other officers and soldiers, looking for a friendly face, I was approached by a Bird Colonel and told that I would be sitting up on the raised platform. Looking up at the stage, I could see chairs on each side of the podium, half of which had folded American flags on them. My spot was to be at the very end, next to the last flag. I asked the Colonel why I was to be on the platform but he said he didn't know.

With the sun now hot in the sky, and sweat beginning to run down my face, I made my way through the crowd to the platform and waited for further instructions.

At 1100 hours, an officer approached the podium and blew a whistle. Instantly, the mingling men in front found seats, and a hush fell over the grounds. Next, the officer at the podium invited the six of us who were to sit on the stage to take our places. As we filed up the stairs, I noticed that four out of the six were civilians.

Just as we found our chairs, the Marine band started playing the hymn from the bleachers. As music filled the air, a color guard marched down the center aisle, followed by a ten-man honor guard in dress-blue uniforms, carrying white-painted M1 carbines. These men took up their position to one side of the stage, next to a large flag pole flying Old Glory.

As the hymn continued, I looked across the sea of faces in the audience; There had to be well over five hundred officers and men, all dressed in their khaki class A uniforms, with another five hundred or more family and friends in grandstands. Most of these spectators were waving small American flags on short wooden sticks. The sights and sounds brought a lump to my throat.

With the final notes of the music, a Brigadier General approached the podium, telling the audience to take their seats. Then he made a few short, welcoming remarks and introduced Admiral King. As the Admiral, who was sitting in the front row, stood to walk up the stairs to the platform, the audience and spectators rose, giving him a standing ovation. Finally, from the podium, with the sun bright on his face, he raised his hands, asking for quiet. Then, in a firm voice, using no written notes, he began to speak.

"We are here this morning to say farewell to some of the officers and men who have served their country in its hour of need. Many of you came to us as boys and will leave here today as men. Over these years, you have seen the immorality of man, climbed the mountains, and crawled through the sands, all in the cause of freedom. A half-decade ago, America was caught sleeping while the world burned. We must resolve, today, never to allow this to happen again. Any nation that stands divided invites defeat, while any nation with resolve and unity breeds peace. But our road to peace has been long, and many have not traveled it all the way home. This morning, we will also pay tribute to the thousands who paid the ultimate price, as symbolized by the six flagged empty chairs on the deck behind me. To receive our recognition, each of these fallen heroes is today represented by a family member or friend."

Glancing over to the Admiral, I watched as he reached slowly under the podium. Taking out one typewritten sheet for each Marine brother, he read from the papers.

The first three heroes had been part of the group that had raised the flag on Iwo Jima but were later killed in action. This historic event had been immortalized by the famous photograph taken by Joe Rosenthal. For each fallen Marine, the Admiral read with passion a short summary of their heroic actions and the circumstances of their death, then announced the types of medals being awarded posthumously. As he completed each story, a family member or friend stood and took the folded flag from the empty seat to the podium, where Admiral King pinned the ribbons on it. He then offered a few short, whispered words to each recipient, after which they returned to their seat.

After the boys from Iwo came the story of a brave young Second Lieutenant who saved most of his pinned-down platoon by single-handedly charging a Nip pillbox on Okinawa.

Next came the gripping story of a Corporal who survived the Bataan Death March and almost three years of imprisonment, only to be killed in a Jap prison camp in the Philippines on the very day of liberation. His story reminded me forcibly of the cruelty and depravity of the Japanese Empire.

"Our final tribute is to Gunnery Sergeant Jack Malone, who is represented here today by his commanding officer and friend, Captain Dutch Clarke. Jack Malone had many special talents, as he was proficient with both a carbine and a camera. His photographic skills helped save a vital Navy torpedo program while he worked in combat conditions on both submarines and PT boats. Then, in February of 1944, his crew and a team of Marine Raiders made a reconnaissance mission on a small Pacific island by the name of Tulun. There, Gunny Malone found and photographed in detail a new type of German-and-Japanese-made radar system, and then destroyed it. On this same mission he and his crew found detailed Jap plans for a bombing raid on the Panama Canal, from aircraft that flew from the decks of new top-secret submarine. Recognizing the value of these plans, he and Captain Clarke insured their recovery and delivery to the US Navy. While doing so, both men were captured and tortured to the limits of human endurance. Because of their actions, a potentially devastating attack on our vital link between the Atlantic and the Pacific was aborted. These two men showed unusual cunning, honor, commitment and sacrifice, during and after the raid on Tulun. Unfortunately, Sergeant Malone was murdered by a Japanese officer while in a POW camp on New Ireland. For Gunnery Sergeant Jack Malone's actions, the United States Marine Corp is awarding him the Navy Cross for valor, the Legion Merit for the raid on Tulun, the Purple Heart for wounds suffered at the hands of the Japanese, and the POW medal for his imprisonment."

Turning towards me with a somber look, the Admiral concluded, "Captain Clarke."

I stood and walked to the podium with the folded flag, where I placed it in the Admiral's hands. Taking the flag he slowly pinned the four ribbons on it. Then, handing it back to me, he whispered, "I promised you back in Hawaii, before the war's end, that I would give Jack the recognition he deserved. I know his death has been hard on you, and I pray that this flag and these ribbons will in some small way help you with your friend's death. God bless you both."

Coming to attention, I gave Admiral King a sharp salute, which he returned. As I turned and walked back to my seat, the Admiral asked the audience to stand. Then a lone bugler began playing Taps. As he did, seven of the honor guard stepped forward, pointed their weapons to the sky, and fired their first volley.

Ka-boom!

The shots rumbled off the grandstands and across the grounds. As they prepared for the second volley, two other members of the guard reached the flag pole and began slowly lowering the flag to half-staff.

Ka-boom!

The sounds of the second shots mixed with the melancholy notes from the bugle put a lump in my throat. With tears racing down my cheeks, I watched the Stars and Stripes slowly descend the pole.

Ka-boom!

The third volley of the twenty-one-gun salute echoed across the field. Glancing down at the medals attached to the folded flag, I knew that someday I would give them to Jack, Jr. Then I would tell him to always cherish his freedom. While it may not seem that valuable when you have it, you realize that it's pure gold when you lose it.

Because of men like his father, America was very rich.

APPENDIX - OVERVIEW

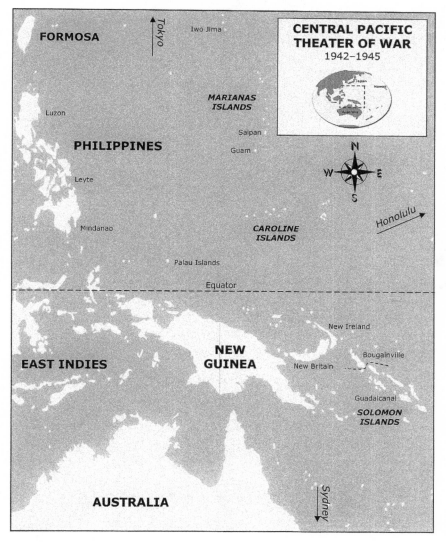

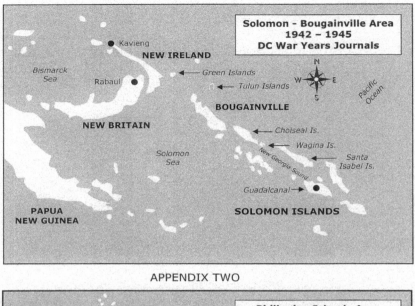

APPENDIX TWO

APPENDIX THREE

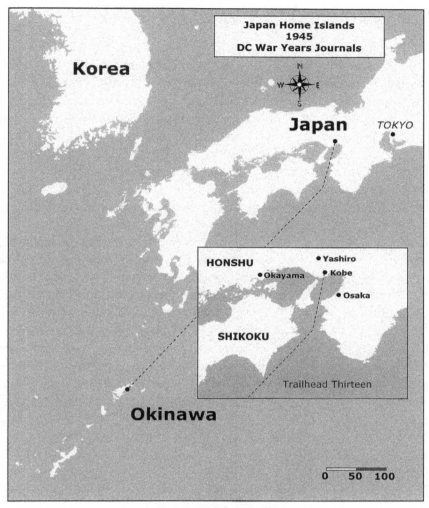

APPENDIX FOUR

ACKNOWLEDGMENTS

To Bernard (Bernie) Olsen, my mentor, my friend, who spent his war years as a young Ensign on a Navy hospital ship and then, many years later, retired as a full Captain from the Naval Reserve. Bernie was a family man of peace, with kitchen-table wisdom and a determination to keep America strong. To Murray Wallace McBride (one of four McBride brothers to serve: Jerry in the Air Corp, killed in action; Jack in the Navy, and Jim in the Navy), my father-in-law, my friend, my business partner. Private McBride trekked across Europe as an Army replacement after the Battle of the Bulge. He was a young Montana boy who got seasick just looking at water and had to join the fight after weeks aboard a troopship. Murray saw some of the first enemy jets and was fired upon by boys in German uniforms who had only wooden bullets for ammunition. Later, being one of the few soldiers that didn't drink, he was put in charge of some captured German wineries. To Lt Colonel Richard Powers (Ret.), my friend and cameraman who, as a young Lieutenant, fought his way up the boot of Italy and served his country through Korea and beyond. His stories were as gripping as any book ever written. To Vern Vasey, a young Seabee, who saw action on Tinian and Saipan, and had stacks of fascinating pictures and hours of riveting stories. To Doctor Arnold Neely who performed dentistry in the jungles and surgery in the foxholes. And finally to my father, Dudley, and grandfather, Harry, who stayed at home working at the naval air stations at both Warrenton and Tongue Point, Oregon. Like Rosie the Riveter, these men gave of their sweat and toil to keep the war effort moving. All of these fine men are gone now, but their deeds, sacrifices and valor will not be forgotten.

These very special men were not extraordinary. They were just guys who answered their country's call and later cast a large shadow on my path of life. These were men who went to war, not for abstract reasons, but for the reasons of family, friends and freedom. I only hope and pray that future generations will find that same grit, spirit and devotion.

Writing this book has been a three-year adventure, with the help of many people who contributed ideas, encouragement and direction. My son-in-law and friend, Rob Waibel, read some of the story, early on, and helped me better understand my style of writing. Each chapter, as I completed it, was edited by Judith Myers. She was a wealth of ideas, inspiration and corrections. In one way or the other, she improved most of the text in my story without ever changing its spirit. Judith Myers is truly a professional editor. After she was done, I was fortunate to have John and Molly Wirch do the proofing. John is an expert historian about World War II, with a deep knowledge about the weapons used. He and I spent wonderful hours talking events, places and the tools of war. His charming wife Molly took the manuscript, asking questions about events while making grammar and typing corrections. How lucky I am to have them as friends. Map artist Scott MacNeill helped me with the illustrations and did a wonderful job. But, through it all, my main anchor and source of support was my wife of forty-two years, Tess. Almost every morning, we would spend time talking about the book's character development, grammar and vocabulary use. She reviewed and corrected every page before sending it off for professional editing, always with a smile, patience and words of encouragement. Thanks above all, and always, to my loving wife. Words have never been enough; she is my Rock of Gibraltar!

Having said all that, it's my name on the title page, and I'm responsible and accountable for every word.

Story Notes

STORY NOTES

Dutch Clarke's
War End Medals and Citations

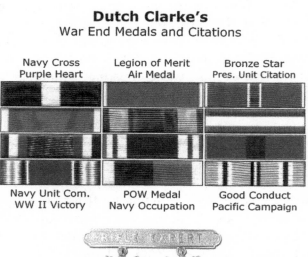

Navy Cross Purple Heart	Legion of Merit Air Medal	Bronze Star Pres. Unit Citation

Navy Unit Com. WW II Victory	POW Medal Navy Occupation	Good Conduct Pacific Campaign

Expert Rifleman Badge

STORY NOTES

The United States Office of War Information (OWI) was a government agency created during World War II to consolidate existing information services and deliver propaganda both at home and abroad.

OWI established the Voice of America (VOA) in 1942. OWI's 'Bureau of Motion Pictures' (BMP) was established in collaboration with Hollywood film studios to advance American war aims. OWI realized that the best way to reach American audiences was to present war films in conjunction with feature films. OWI also helped with publicity in promoting the many different war bond campaigns.

The Speed Graphic camera, or C6 camera, was the most famous press camera during WWII. The first Speed Graphic cameras were produced in 1912, production of later versions continued until 1973.

The 1942-1954 Pulitzer Prizes for photography were all taken with Speed Graphic cameras, including AP photographer Joe Rosenthal's image of Marines raising the American flag on Iwo Jima in 1945.

When the author first joined the US Air Force in 1960, he worked almost exclusively with the C6 cameras.

The book character, Carole Lane was loosely fashioned after American film star Carole Landis. Ms. Landis was a contract-player for Twentieth Century-Fox in the 1940s and died a tragic death in 1947. The police ruled her drug overdose a suicide. While her family believed that film star Rex Harrison, nicknamed 'Sexy Rexy,' had a hand in her death. A fascinating Hollywood story!

The '*Staff Car*' as depicted in the book, was in fact the author's first car. In 1958, at age 16, his father gave Brian a 1939 Chrysler Royal Coup. The author wishes he still had that car today!

STORY NOTES

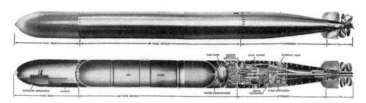

The Mark 14 torpedo was the United States Navy's standard submarine-launched anti-ship torpedo of World War II.

This weapon was plagued with many problems which crippled its performance early in the war, and was supplemented by the Mark 18 electric torpedo in the last two years of the war. Nonetheless, the Mark 14 played a major role in the devastating blow that the US Navy submarines dealt to the Japanese naval and merchant marine forces during the Pacific War. By the end of World War II, the Mark 14 torpedo was a reliable weapon which remained in service for almost 40 years in the US Navy.

The I-400 class submarine was the brainchild of Admiral Yamamoto, the architect of Pearl Harbor. He conceived the idea of taking the war to the United States mainland by making aerial attacks against cities along the US western and eastern seaboards using submarine-launched naval aircraft. Yamamoto's proposal called for a fleet of 18 large submarines, capable of making three round-trips to the west coast of the United States, without refueling or one round-trip to any point on the globe.

Following Yamamoto's death when his plane was shot down in April 1943, the number of aircraft-carrying submarines to be built was reduced from eighteen to nine, then five and finally only three. None of these submarines saw action and they all fell into American hands at the end of the war.

STORY NOTES

Author Bio

Brian D. Ratty, a retired media executive and graduate of Brooks Institute of Photography, also holds an honorary Master of Science degree. He and his wife, Tess, live on the north Oregon Coast, where he writes and photographs that rugged and majestic region. Over the past thirty years, he has traveled the vast wilderness of the Pacific Coast in search of images and stories that reflect the spirit and splendor of those spectacular lands. Brian is an award-winning historical fiction novelist, and has written numerous magazine articles about the Pacific Northwest.

Why I write

I write what I like to read, historical fiction rich with bold characters and powerful storylines. I shy away from gratuitous violence and descriptive sex; instead my stories portray adventure with vivid descriptions and believable plots. My goal is to whisk the reader away to another frame of mind... the results being a suspenseful and brisk read. **Readers Wanted!**

For more information on Brian's books, short stories, articles and recipes:
www. Dutchclarke.com

STORY NOTES

Other Books by Brian Ratty

Book Length: 376 Pages
Action – Adventure
Audience: Young Adults & up
ISBN 978-1-4490-1451-1
Soft Cover: $19.95
Hard Cover: $24.95
eBook: $3.99

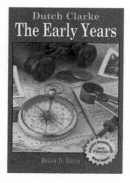

Book Length: 324 Pages
Historical Fiction
Audience: Young Adults & up
ISBN 978-1-4634-0615-8
Soft Cover: $19.95
Hard Cover: $24.95
eBook: $4.99

Book Length: 478 Pages
Historical Fiction
Audience: Young Adults & up
ISBN 13: 978-0615940779
Soft Cover: $19.95
eBook: $5.99

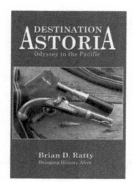

www.dutchclarke.com